Praise for *Co*

"*Sacrifice* is not for the timid or weak of heart, it is a full frontal assault on your senses. It is a dark, brutal, bloody, and terribly frightening book. Everson went deep into some dark abyss to bring this book to the light of day… I highly recommend *Sacrifice*."   —*Famous Monsters of Filmland*

"This book is a non-stop thrill ride, and I had a hard time putting it down once I started it. *Sacrifice* is a thrilling and shocking piece of genre fiction that deserves to be on every horror fan's shelf."   —*Fatally Yours*

"John Everson manages in *Sacrifice* to dispense buckets of blood, provide edgy perversity, and walk the tenuous tightrope of horror and sex without falling: it's rather an amazing feat."
—*Hellnotes*

"John Everson is bringing a whole new nightmare to the world of horror."   —*The Horror Review*

"Everson is in full form. The action is quick, brutal, and visceral. In many ways, *Sacrifice* is like that "slasher flick" we know we shouldn't enjoy but do anyway."   —*Shroud Magazine*

"Perhaps a bit like an adult version of the classic cult film *Carnival of Souls*, Everson has truly made his mark on the genre and is taking no prisoners; *Sacrifice* is hardcore horror that passes its predecessor by bounds. The squeamish need not apply."
—*The Horror Fiction Review*

"If you like your horror with healthy doses of blood and sex, this is the book for you."   —*Fear Zone*

"*Sacrifice* is a Screaming Orgasm followed by a shot of Jack Daniels. This is a novel that begs to be finished in one night, and likely will be."   —*Horror World*

COVENANT

"*Covenant*—now available as a mass-market paperback—won Everson a Bram Stoker Award back in 2004, and after reading it, you'll agree that this tight, gripping story was definitely worthy of the distinction."
—*Rue Morgue*

"I've waited four long years to read *Covenant* and it was well worth it. Everson has taken a classic genre plot and given it his own spin. This is how horror is done RIGHT."
—*The Horror Fiction Review*

"Equal parts dark mystery and supernatural horror, *Covenant* is a white-knuckle reading experience that will keep you guessing and gasping."
—*Creature Feature*

"You might even begin to wonder with writing this good, if Everson agreed to his own covenant in order to create this devilishly dark and terrifying tale."
—*Pagan Pulse Magazine*

"Truly entertaining no-frills horror, which is a damned good thing."
—*Horror World*

"Everson allows the storylines to unfurl, carefully layering each of the individual character's arcs as he crosses genres ending up with a nice blend of mystery and horror."
—*Dark Scribe Magazine*

"John Everson has written a powerful tale as readers wonder whether it is a coincidence, the supernatural, or a serial killer behind the suicides."
—*Midwest Book Review*

"Everson sets up his story well, fleshes out Joe Kiernan as a character readers can root for, and truly sets him against a pitiless, horrible evil."
—*Shroud*

Demon Ride

Cindy pulled away from the opening to flatten her back against the wall. It felt as if her eyes were going to fall out of her head. She didn't know what she was seeing in the other room, but it was anything but normal. It was as if a bunch of murderers had been possessed.

Something cold touched her in the back of the neck, and the chill shot down to the base of her spine like a shock. She gasped.

Someone spoke to her then in a voice like wind through wooden chimes. It was faint but airy. *"That's exactly what has happened,"* the voice said.

"Huh?" Cindy said, partly out loud. As she did, she prayed nobody in the next room heard her.

"They won't pay any attention," the voice said. Suddenly it was louder, and the ice grew solid down her back.

"Who is speaking?" she whispered. "Where are you?" Part of her still expected someone to walk out from around the corner of the hallway to where she could see. But part of her knew better. That part of her was petrified. And rightly so.

"I am Delivida," the wind-voice said. *"And I am as close to you as close can be."*

Cindy tried to push away from the wall… or to raise her arm… and found that she couldn't. She was locked in place.

"I've been waiting a long time for this," Delivida said.

Suddenly Cindy's leg lifted of its own accord. It was as if a puppeteer was above her, pulling the strings.

Or the reins.

"Let's go for a ride," the demon suggested.

Also by John Everson

NOVELS:

Covenant

Sacrifice

The 13th

Siren

The Pumpkin Man

NightWhere

Violet Eyes

The Family Tree

NOVELETTES:

Failure

Violet Lagoon

Field of Flesh (a NightWhere story)

SHORT FICTION COLLECTIONS:

Cage of Bones & Other Deadly Obsessions

Vigilantes of Love

Needles & Sins

Sacrificing Virgins

For more information visit:

www.JohnEverson.com

REDEMPTION

JOHN EVERSON

REDEMPTION

BOOKS

NAPERVILLE, ILLINOIS

~2017~

The characters and events portrayed in this book are fictitious. Any similarity to real persons, living or dead, is coincidental and not intended by the author. This is a work of fiction.

Copyright © 2017 by John Everson

All rights reserved. No part of this book may be reproduced or stored in a retrieval system or transmitted in any form or by any means, electronic, mechanical photocopying, recording, or otherwise, without express written permission of the publisher.

Published by
Dark Arts Books
Naperville, Illinois
www.darkartsbooks.com

Printed in the United States of America.

ISBN 13: 978-1541310254
ISBN 10: 154131025X

For Geri,
My Redemption.

Acknowledgments

THIS NOVEL BEGAN ON A fateful night in August 2010 in Santa Fe, New Mexico. Ironically, it ended in the same place, almost exactly six years later. I wrote the first paragraphs of *Redemption* while sitting at one of my favorite places in the world – the bar of the Cowgirl BBQ in Santa Fe. I've gone on an annual business trip to Santa Fe in August for many years, and on that particular night in 2010, I learned that my publisher at the time, Leisure Books, was canceling its mass market paperback line just a couple weeks after they'd released my fourth novel, *Siren*.

When that news hit, I ordered another beer, closed my laptop and stopped writing. It was a "dream is over" moment for me. It would be weeks before I wrote another word of fiction after that night. When I did, I didn't return to *Redemption*, because I assumed that wherever my next book landed, it wouldn't be with the publisher that had released *Covenant* and *Sacrifice*, the first two in the series. And nobody else was going to want the third in a series if they didn't publish the first two.

So I moved on to other projects, and eventually penned three more unrelated novels for my editor, Don D'Auria, when he moved from Leisure to Samhain Publishing. And then last year, when the horror line there began to close down, I decided, "what the hell?" Publisher or no publisher, I was going to write the book I'd wanted to write since 2007, when the original hardcover edition of *Sacrifice* was released. So while Samhain fell apart in 2015-2016, that's what I did. I wrote *Redemption*.

As with all of my novels, this book was written in a wide variety of places. I travel a lot for my dayjob and tend to get a lot of writing done while I'm on the road, and this was a most unusual year for me in that regard. I travelled farther afield than ever. Hence, bits of *Redemption* were written in Irish bars and brewpubs in Tokyo, Seoul, Amsterdam, Barcelona and Ghent, Belgium. Closer to home, some of these chapters took shape in Los Angeles, Seattle and my Naperville, Illinois hometown hangout, Crosstown Pub. (If you ever go there, get the Devil's Sweat grilled chicken wings. And a large glass of ice water!)

The final draft of the book took shape in August 2016 in Santa Fe, where a good chunk of the novel takes place. Speaking of which, if you ever visit Santa Fe, don't go looking for the Birchmir Mission; I took some geographical liberty there. The Cowgirl BBQ is certainly real, but other aspects of Santa Fe in this novel have been fictionalized.

Redemption is an important novel to me, because it finally ties up threads that I've long wanted to twine. The story originated in the mid-1990s, when I began to write *Covenant*. Then the sequel, *Sacrifice*, was written in the early to mid-2000s. So it's appropriate, I guess, that the end of the trilogy was written in the mid-2010s. Each novel really began almost a decade apart from its predecessor. Not, perhaps, the best planning for a trilogy, but that's how it happened. I hope fans of the first two novels will enjoy how it all pans out here in the pages to come.

A few thank you's are in order...

The life of a fiction writer can frequently seem lonely, thankless and a huge waste of time that could perhaps be better spent playing pinball and watching old Eurotrash movies. There have been a lot of people who have kept me going back to the keyboard over the years, encouraging me when it all seemed pointless. My lights through the dark. My wife, Geri, has given me strength. My friends, Bill Gagliani, Dave Benton, Brian Pinkerton and Mort Castle have graced me with their energy, advice and support. Shane Ryan Staley of Delirium Books published the first two novels, and then Don D'Auria picked them up and gave them a broader life in mass market paperback editions. Without either of them, this novel would probably not exist.

This third book in the series also owes a lot to fans – the people who have asked me at conventions and via e-mail for years to finish the story.

A lot of people "kicked in" and said "hell, yes, I want to know what happens." So I have to give a huge thanks to the *Redemption* Kickstarter supporters. If I could, I'd queue up some big, dramatic music and *Star Wars* scroll these names following a headline that reads Thanks, You Rock:

Anthony Beals, Josslyn L. Bond, Chad Bowden, Chris Brogden, Chris Brook, Anita Nicole Brown, Alan Caldwell, H Casper, Matthew Cheek, Stephen Clark, Lon Czarnecki, Joshua Daughtry, John Eberhardt, Tim Feely, Brian Floyd, Michael Fowler, Lynn Frost, Chand Svare Ghei, Stephen Glover, Fred Godsmark, Lionel Ray Green, Leah and Joe Guillemette, Sarah Ham, Michael John Haines, Violet Paige Hall, Sheila Halterman, Joe Hempel, Pakorn Jaruspanavasan, Albert Jones, Kim Kelly, Brian Kirk, Chris Kosarich, Paul Legerski, Shane Lindemoen, Serra Maximovich, Bob McQueen, J.H. Moncrieff, Lynn Neering, Robert Nelson, Peg Phillips, Maria Rose Randazzo, Magnus Reithaug, Tanya Semmons, Mike Sickler, Jim Simmons, Daniel White, Scott Wichman, and Christian Wood.

This one's for you.

Prologue

"*Alex, wake up.*"

She heard the words but...

"*Alex.*" There was urgency in the dark voice. It spoke again. "*We don't want to be here.*"

She heard Malachai's voice vaguely in the distance. But she couldn't seem to open her eyes. Everything was grey; all she wanted was to sleep. She stopped struggling to see, and allowed herself to drift again. She felt warm. Comfortable. Mentally, she rolled over and sighed. Alex decided to ignore the voice.

"*If you ever want to see Joe Kieran again, open your eyes.*"

The voice sounded serious, but still... she drowsed.

"*Wake up, bitch, we've got to move!*"

The voice was like a thunderclap behind her eyes, and Alex jolted awake.

"What?" she exclaimed, and suddenly the grey was gone.

In its place was a fog of red.

The floor was hard, some kind of rough limestone. The room itself was huge; she couldn't see the wall on one side. There were no windows, but an evil light seemed to glow from the air itself. There was no source. Next to her, lying on the ground, was a tangled mess of dark hair and naked, bloody limbs. A patrician nose jutted from the midst of the hair, and a long arm extended towards Alex; its black-painted fingernails clutched as if they were reaching for her.

It was the crazy chick. The "Sunday Slasher," according to the newspapers. The one who had tried to kill her, and nearly succeeded.

Ariana.

Alex resisted the urge to punch that pointy face while she had the easy opportunity. She ought to straddle the bitch, put her hands around that lily-white neck and squeeze the life out of her. And then she remembered that she couldn't punch or strangle Ariana.

She couldn't move her arms.

Or legs.

She'd been paralyzed by Ariana's boyfriend. She could still see him coming after her with a pipe. She remembered the flash of pain and the helplessness after. She tested the endgame of the memory and struggled to lift any and all of her limbs.

Nothing happened. Alex lay unmoving on the cold stone floor. She remained broken.

"Where are we?" she whispered.

"Welcome to Hell," Malachai's voice answered in her head. *"And I do not suggest that we stay awhile."*

Alex tried again to sit up, but nothing happened. "Well it's going to be hard to leave," she whispered. "If you remember, I can't move."

"You can, with my help," Malachai whispered.

"What do I have to do?" she asked, dreading the answer.

"Get me out of here."

"I could say the same."

"Ask for my help," he said. *"I can move your limbs for you."*

Alex thought about that for a moment. What did she give Malachai, if she gave him control of her body? He was a demon, after all. A demon who had nearly gotten her and Joe killed. She took in the veins in the rock on the ceiling, and the red haze that floated through the air. And tried again to move her legs or arms. Or head.

Nothing happened.

Malachai was her only hope, like it or not. She had resigned herself to that realization once before, in the labyrinth of caves just outside of Terrel. His strength had raised her limbs before. It was a bitter pill, but easier to swallow this time. Necessity bred acceptance.

"Help me, Malachai," she finally whispered. The words barely slipped through her lips, and suddenly she felt her head lift, and her arms bend, on their own. She flexed her fingers to take control of herself.

"*We need to move,*" the low, ancient voice said in the depths of her head. He sounded worried. It was an unexpected emotion from a demon.

"I don't know where we are," she said. "And where are we going to go?"

"*Out of sight. It doesn't matter where, but we can't stay here. They'll have felt us come through.*"

Alex willed herself to sit up, and her body followed. Malachai was somehow a part of her. The world swam around her for a moment. When her head stopped threatening to slide off, Alex took a deep breath.

"What do we do?" she asked.

"*Get up, get out of this room, and hide.*"

"Why are you so scared?" Alex asked. "Aren't you a frikkin' demon?"

"*There's a reason I left here and made covenants to stay on your world,*" Malachai said. "*You don't want to find out that reason.*"

"So what do we do?" she asked.

"*Hide.*" Malachai advised a second time.

Alex looked at Ariana, still lying unconscious on the stone floor. "And what about her?"

"*What do you care?*" Malachai said.

"What will they do to her if they find her?"

Malachai didn't answer, but instead, a picture suddenly flashed before her eyes. A naked woman, arching her back, mouth wide open, seemingly in orgasm, yet, covered in blood. A stake between her legs, a fountain of blood jetting from a hole in her middle…

Alex was vindictive sometimes. But not that cruel. Besides, she was alone in hell. The demon-caller might prove useful somehow. This was her scene, after all.

She nudged the unconscious woman with her foot.

Ariana stirred, moaning softly before opening her eyes.

"Wake up, bitch," Alex said, echoing Malachai's words of seconds before.

"We've gotta move."

Chapter 1

THE DREAM WAS OVER. Again. Joe Kieran leaned against the rough wood rail of the long bar at the Cowgirl BBQ and tilted back the last dregs of a local Santa Fe brown ale. He thought it tasted a bit flat, but he drank it fast anyway.

A girl with a warm, high-cheekboned face, a tight "Tramps & Thieves" tank top and a black, silver-studded cowboy hat refilled it almost as soon as he set the glass back on the bar. She was clearly of American Indian descent, like many he'd met out here. They'd gotten to be on a first-name basis these past couple days.

Her name was Cindy, and that hurt him every time he said it. That name conjured so many memories for him. But the Cindy he had loved was dead and buried, back in Terrel.

He'd driven just about as far from Terrel as he could this past week. From east coast nearly to west. And the hills of New Mexico promised there were still miles more that he could get lost in. He liked it here, with the vagabond, foreign-accented carpet salesmen and vapid, well-heeled tourists snapping up turquoise jewelry from vendors set up on the sidewalks to sell trinkets for twice what the junk was worth. The tourists spent money like water and were clueless of the real shit going on around them as they planned on their nightly excursions to watch the sun set at the outdoor opera pavilion on the edge of town. He saw why they flocked here though. It was a beautiful place, an oasis with good food and culture and scenery.

Despite all that, Joe thought after another night or so, he'd be moving on. He felt the call of the isolation promised in those hills. Maybe he'd head north.

Maybe to Taos.

Joe Kieran wanted to lose himself in the countryside. The concept sounded simple, but the execution seemed to always be just outside of his grasp. As it apparently was now. Above the backbeat of the band outside on the patio doling out a funky retro '70s disco classic, he heard someone say a word that always made him look up.

"Demons."

Joe had some experience with demons. He'd spent the last few weeks trying to forget it. He'd lost both of his girlfriends to demons, back in Terrel.

So when someone said "demons," Joe paid attention.

Demons connected him to Alex.

And every day that passed, he prayed that she was still alive… somewhere. In that place beyond where he could see. Honestly, he still was trying to find her. He kept looking for the chinks in the armor. Listening and seeking out stories about the places where the walls between worlds grew thin.

The places where he might somehow find a way to bring her back again to the world in which she belonged.

"The demons sometimes come through the cracks in the walls," the man at the other end of the bar was saying. He was a thin guy, with shaggy blonde hair and sunken eyes that seemed to jut when he spoke. A small audience gathered around his barstool. Joe tuned in hard to the conversation. A short, dark-haired guy wearing an untucked, pinstriped blue shirt was nodding at every word. The thin man was adamant. He looked convincing.

"There are cracks in the walls…" he said. "That's how they get through. They can slip right through the cracks. And if they do…"

Joe's head cocked, straining to listen.

The waitress interrupted the conversation on the other end of the bar, picking up glasses and dropping a green slip of paper. Apparently the bill. "I think you've had enough tonight, Arnie," he heard her say. "I don't need you scaring off the customers."

The man shook his head and a mass of ragged curls colored

the air. "I'm sure 'nuf just telling him what happens out there at the Birchmir," he insisted.

The brunette only smiled and tapped the green check. "You know the rules," she said.

The thin man complained but he dropped money on the bill, and slipped off his bar stool, missing a step as he went. Joe thought he was going to topple, but he recovered, and stiff-walked out of the front door of the bar onto the patio without looking back. Joe hoped he didn't stagger into the band – they played right next to the exit to the sidewalk.

"What's up with the Birchmir?" he asked, when Cindy came back to his half of the bar.

She rolled her eyes and the glitter of her eyeliner flashed in the low yellow bar light. "He comes in here every week and talks about how ghosts come out of the walls in the old Birchmir Mission, just outside of town. Give him a beer and he'll give you a ghost."

Joe smiled, but there wasn't really a lot of smile in it. This sounded like a lead.

"I would love to talk to him sometime."

Cindy smirked. "Good luck with that. If his breath doesn't kill you, his stories will."

She disappeared to help a newcomer at the bar. Joe considered. Was there anything worth checking out in the blather of the drunk?

It was impossible to tell. Part of him wanted to investigate. Part of him wanted to drown the other part in a heavy slosh of bourbon.

Truth be told, Joe wanted to get lost. That seemed to be a cyclical desire for him. He had left Chicago when his investigative reporting for the *Chicago Tribune* ended up getting his girlfriend indicted. How close to the bone should you really have to go for your day job? Well, that story had been too close for him. He'd packed up and driven to the tiny southeast coastal town of Terrel, gotten a job at the half-assed newspaper there, and within a few months, had found out that the litany of dead bodies that annually plagued the cliff outside of Terrel had occurred because the damn town literally had a deal with a demon to protect it from *other* demons – the Curburide.

Joe himself had ultimately made a deal with "the devil" that inhabited the cliff (a creature that called itself Malachai) and saved a pretty blonde named Cindy from being sacrificed to the invisible – but still deadly – demon's hungers. And then he'd hit the road to try to get lost again, only to find himself back in Terrel less than a month later, this time trying to save Alex, a teenage hitchhiker he'd picked up on the way to Denver who, strangely enough, could actually talk to the dead. And once again Cindy was at the center of it; she'd managed to get herself tied up on a sacrificial altar, thanks to her loser brother.

That time around, he hadn't managed to save Cindy, or Alex. The former got herself sacrificed to the succubic Curburide demons by an ex- almost-nun named Ariana. The latter – poor, broken Alex – used Malachai to help her drag Ariana and the flood of Curburide demons back through a rift between the Earth and the hellish world of the dark demons. Alex had closed the door that Ariana had opened... but in the process, she ended up on the wrong side of it.

For the third time in his life, Joe had felt the urge to run. After he left the cave beneath the cliff where Cindy's body lay, slaughtered and bloody, he hadn't had to think a bit.

He had packed the few things he really cherished and a couple hours later, driven out of town. He'd stayed in many places since then, but never stayed long.

The hills of Santa Fe weren't far enough. The Pacific Ocean wouldn't be far enough. Because the memories of Alex's blood-spattered face disappearing above his head into a swirling blackened hole in, what... the freakin' air... haunted him every night. Hell, every morning too.

He missed her smart-assed comments and her fake black hair.

He missed Cindy too; he'd tried to leave Terrel to get out of her life and instead he'd simply ended up back in it just long enough to see her die.

What he didn't expect? He missed Malachai, a devil he couldn't trust. Because the devil you know....

Joe tipped back a shot of bourbon and Santa Fe Cindy came back to his place at the bar with a smile and a tip of her narrow cowgirl hat and slid the empty glass off the bar. "Another round?" she said sweetly.

Joe shook his head. "What are you doing tonight?" he asked. His voice only slurred a little bit.

Cindy tipped her cowboy hat back an inch and looked at the clientele that still held on to the edge of the bar. A man in a half-buttoned, faded orange Hawaiian shirt and long white hair curled wildly to his chest gestured and laughed at a slumping brunette leaning on his shoulder. A guy who looked as if Viet Nam were only last week – plus 40 years of wrinkles – nodded in conversation with a skinhead covered in boneyard tattoos and piercings beside them. And a Chicano in a dew rag held court with a group of other Mexicans on the far side of the bar.

Cindy sized up her options fast.

"I'm driving you home?" she suggested. "I don't think you should drive, and I caught a ride here tonight."

Joe paid his tab, and handed her his car keys.

Chapter 2

"You fuckin' bitch!" Ariana flipped a stray lock of kinked black hair out of her eyes. Which were on fire.

Alex could see her thinking of those last minutes, when she'd tried to finish a sacrificial ceremony to fully open the door to Earth, so the Curburide demons could come through. But instead of being a savior, she'd woken up on the other side, in the world of the Curburide. Nobody here was going to thank her for opening any trans-world doors, or anything else. Just the opposite…the game had changed completely.

"What the hell were you thinking, dragging us through the doorway like that?" Ariana demanded.

Alex smiled, though the side of her grin trembled. "I got you out of Terrel, didn't I?"

"Who said I wanted to get *out* of Terrel?" Ariana hissed. "I had created the cycle of Sacrifice. I had given the Curburide the last offering. I was ready to take my crown as their mortal queen…"

"Queen of the demons?" Alex laughed. "What, did you think they were going to flock around you and feed you grapes? They would have eaten you alive, you stupid dipshit. They were using you."

"Of course they were using me. And I was using them. That's how the worlds go 'round."

"Yeah, well, they don't need you anymore," Alex pointed out. Literally, pointed out. She gestured behind them. The doorway out of the tiny room they'd ducked into just a few minutes before was beginning to glow a dull red where the air slipped through the cracks. Something was behind them. And it was coming after them. Something hungry.

"Where the hell are we?" Alex asked, as she watched the red glow build, illuminating the outline of a door.

Ariana laughed. "Pretty much where you never, ever wanted to be," she said. "You've dragged us up into the world of the Curburide."

"So you should be happy," Alex said. "Didn't you kill all those people so that you could be with them?"

Ariana shook her head. "I killed to give them something they wanted so that they would reward me. Coming here, is not going to help that. They don't need my help to be here. So I'm not going to have a fuckin' chance in hell of…" she stopped and looked around, as if confused for a second. "Speaking of hell… where's Jeremy?"

Alex remembered Ariana's former partner rolling off the dais to lie bloody and unmoving on the cave floor towards the end of the sacrificial ceremony that had landed them here. It seemed like just seconds ago. "Jeremy… won't be joining us."

"Well, someone apparently is," Ariana said, pointing toward the door. The seams were growing an ever-brighter red. "We need to be somewhere else."

"Come on," Alex said, grabbing Ariana by the arm. "There's a hallway over here."

Ariana had no choice but to follow. No matter what she thought, she had to realize that they needed to *not* be where they were. Alex pulled her down the narrow passageway through the dark. There were noises coming from behind them. Soft, wet sounds. The corridor wrapped on and on; the dark was total. Both women held the wall for support, but they kept walking.

"We're just going to get lost in here," Ariana whispered.

"Better lost than eaten," Alex said.

"*You have no idea,*" Malachai answered, somewhere inside her head.

"Which way should we go?" she asked him. "Help us out here."

He didn't answer.

Typical. A demon was never there when you needed it.

The air grew colder, damper. It stank of earth and age. The spongy sound continued to pace them from behind.

"It's cold," Ariana said, hugging her naked chest.

"You should have kept some clothes on," Alex said.

"You have to be naked to perform the Sacrifice of the Twenty-One Cuts," Ariana hissed.

"Yeah, well, see what that got ya."

"You little…" Ariana suddenly gasped as her foot caught on something soft and round. She lost her balance and fell forward, one hand grabbing at Alex as she went down.

"Watch where you're going!" a voice called from near her feet.

Alex turned and squinted at the ground. The faint glint of someone's eyes met her own. Ariana had tripped over a human head that protruded from the soggy ground. Its chin barely raised above the black of the earth. There was almost no hair on his scalp, but Alex could see a glimmer of hope in the man's wide eyes. They were blue… and bloodshot.

"Who are you?" she asked.

"Help me out of here and I'll tell you," the voice answered.

Just then, a faint red light glinted off the side of the wall behind them. There were voices now too. An angry buzz that was quickly and steadily growing.

"Curburide coming," the head said. "They're not going to like finding humans out of the filth. How did you escape?"

"Hurry," Alex said, and pulled Ariana back to her feet. "Ignore it. C'mon."

They staggered a step away, and the voice behind called. "Tell me how you escaped?" he cried. "You're not just going to leave a poor soul here, are you?"

"I left my shovel at home," Ariana said.

"Use your hands," he begged. "It won't take but a minute if both of you help."

"We have to go," Alex warned. "Now!"

"I'll tell them where you went," he threatened. "I'll tell them you were here."

Ariana shook her head. "I don't think so." She turned and raised her foot before delivering a kick right into the shadowed face of the buried man. The air snapped with the impact, and the head tilted to one side. It didn't speak again.

"Jesus," Alex complained.

Ariana shrugged. "I don't like threats."

"Well, I hope you've got a lot of muscle in that leg, because I think there are a whole lotta threats coming this way."

"Shut up and walk," Ariana answered.

"Bitch," Alex whispered under her breath.

"Damn right."

"I can smell them," a voice said from just a few yards away. Alex now saw dozens of dark round shapes on the ground all around them and realized there were many heads in the earth that had noticed them. Others struggled to turn in their direction. The whites of their eyes gave them away. She pushed Ariana in the back and they both began to run as the murmur of voices grew louder around them.

The corridor widened, and the earth began to suck at their feet. They slipped and fell as the incline grew steeper; the earth itself grew wetter, stickier. The air tasted thick, rank. It smelled like a swamp, and a locker room. And a toilet. Alex's foot connected with something hard, and she looked behind just as the object complained.

"Asshole," the ground called. Another head.

"I see light ahead," Ariana said.

And sure enough, the murky black turned to grey just a few yards away as they rounded a corner. The ceiling suddenly disappeared, and Alex skidded to a stop next to Ariana under the open sky. If sky was what it was. The air above grew hazy and faintly ocher. Clouds of mist hung like sulphur in the air, and the black, oily earth ahead led into a yellowed sea. The beach was littered with what looked to be large eggs... but Alex knew better.

They were heads.

Dozens, maybe hundreds of people buried in the muck to their necks. They stuck up from the slimy earth every few feet and led right out into the water, which lapped at the lips of those farthest away from the tunnel they'd just left.

There was a faint rumble overhead, and suddenly the sky let loose with a gentle rain. As it reached them, Alex realized it was warm. And stank.

"Oh my God," she spat, as the realization hit her.

Ariana nodded, shrugged, and used the yellow spray to rinse the dried blood from her naked chest. She'd cut herself intentionally in the ceremony in Terrel that had brought them here. As the caked blood from the wound rinsed away, it slowly revealed the long red cut of her sacrificial mark. A wound that stretched from throat to crotch. She didn't seem to mind that she was bathing in demon piss. "We're standing in the Curburide's toilet," she announced offhandedly.

"Ugh!" Alex screamed.

"Come on in, the water's warm," a head taunted from down the beach.

Ariana backhanded Alex. "Shut up, it's just piss. It's antibacterial. Let's go."

Ariana began to run down the black beach. A building jutted out from the rocks a few hundred yards away. It looked to be their only chance to hide from whoever, or whatever, was coming. Alex followed, at the same moment understanding exactly what the sticky muck beneath her feet probably really was.... but also knowing that the creatures following behind them should be exiting the tunnel any moment.

Ignoring the stink and the warm rain that ran down her cheeks like dirty tears, she followed. Ariana ran hard, the bare muscles of her thighs and ass rippling in the dreary light as Alex struggled to keep up. She could see the occasional fuzz of pubic hair between the other woman's thighs as Ariana ran, spreading her legs wide and occasionally leaping over a head protruding from the shitty earth. The other woman was definitely in shape, she had to give her that.

"*Like what you see?*" Malachai asked. "*Maybe you could get to be closer friends.*"

"Shut up," she said under her breath.

"*If you ever wanted to get a little kinky, this is the place to let loose,*" he said.

"Stop it."

"*Of course, this is also the place to be buried in shit and pissed on, three hundred and sixty-five days a year for eternity.*"

Alex ignored him, and followed Ariana's ass up the stone steps to the small building. It seemed to grow out of a small hill, and she guessed that its hallways disappeared deep underground; there was no actual "back" to the structure visible.

Behind them, she heard someone yell, and another voice answer.

"They saw us," she breathed, as they dove into the doorway. There was no door, just an entry arch.

The room beyond was small. All its walls were covered in cages – tall, silver cages, with bars made of knives. Instead of round steel, each bar was a sharp blade, and threatened both the captor and the captive.

Alex walked closer to the wall and saw that the floors were the same. There was no surface within the cages that didn't offer injury.

"I don't think this is the kind of zoo you want to be stuck in," Ariana said from behind her. "Come on."

Together they ran past the cages and into a dark hall. There were entryways along the hall, all of them shut with heavy wooden doors. They passed them, trying to find an end. The light grew fainter and fainter.

"I don't know if we should keep going," Alex gasped after awhile. "I can't see in front of me anymore."

"I don't think you want to be seen by what's behind." Ariana warned. "I can hear them; they followed us in here, into this building. We need to find another way out."

"How about this one," a deep voice said from her left. Ariana yelped in surprise.

A large, rough hand suddenly clasped Alex by the shoulder and yanked her into one of the hall doorways.

The door slammed shut behind them.

Chapter 3

CINDY DIDN'T WEAR her cowboy hat to bed, but she proved she knew how to ride like a cowgirl just the same.

Maybe it was the beer, but Joe soon found it difficult to keep up with her. When they finished, or at least, took a break, he was dripping with sweat.

"Wow," he gasped. "I must be out of shape, I can't catch my breath!" He stretched out on his back, pulling the soft white sheets around him, as she lay on her stomach next to him, hands on her chin, elbows to the bed. She watched him breathing with a faint smile. She looked like a proud cat guarding her prey.

"Too much for you?" she asked.

He shook his head "no" quickly, but then slowed his denial and shook it the other way. "Maybe," he said.

"When did you get into town?" she asked softly.

"Tuesday," he said, drawing in a deep breath.

She nodded. "Altitude. You're not used to it yet. We're at more than seven thousand feet here."

"That must be it," he breathed. Inside, he desperately hoped that was the reason.

She poked him in the side. "That or you're out of shape!" Cindy laughed and then rolled off the bed to disappear into the tiny bathroom. Joe stared around the room. She lived in a small apartment just off Guadalupe Street, the main drag through old town. He'd been a little unsteady as she'd led him up the wooden outside stairs to the third floor. Once inside, she'd offered him a glass of ice water in the galley kitchen before pulling him past the front room couch and into her bedroom.

They never sat down.

"I don't want you falling asleep on me," she'd explained.

And then she'd introduced him to her mattress and the night had gotten much more interesting.

Now as he lay there, staring at the southwestern Kokopelli art on her walls and out the small window that revealed the thousands of stars up in the desert sky, he realized he didn't know anything about her beyond her name. And the fact that she worked at the Cowgirl. And had… a unique way of twisting her hips when he pushed against them with his own.

"So why are you in town?" she asked when she returned. "Business? Pleasure?"

"Just wandering, really," Joe said, pulling back the sheets so she could slip back in next to him.

"Great place to wander," she said. "Be careful you don't get lost out in the hills."

"Are there a lot of stories about ghosts and stuff out here?" he asked.

"You mean like old Arnie was bullshitting about at the bar?" she asked. Cindy shrugged, exposing the delicate hollow of her breastbone. "I dunno. I've lived up here for seven years now, and I've never seen anything but strangers, lost souls and the quiet of the desert. There are always stories, I guess, and some old Indian traditions and folklore. But Santa Fe isn't a ghost town, if that's what you mean."

Joe shook his head. "I used to be a newspaper reporter, and I've seen my share of weird, so I'm always curious. What's the story with the Birchmir, that place the drunk guy mentioned?"

"Oh, it's just an old, abandoned mission chapel out west of town. Used to be an Indian settlement, and then in the 1600s they converted it. But with all the other churches and stuff around town, it was abandoned a long time ago. Maybe a hundred years ago, I don't know."

"And it's supposed to be haunted?"

"It's been abused is what it's been. Kids hold drug parties and black masses and God knows what else there. I think it's just an empty, lost place."

"Sounds like a lot of spots out here in the desert," he said. "Empty and alone."

Cindy slipped her hand across his chest, and pressed herself closer. "The desert, yes," she said. "And a lot of people. But not here."

"No," he agreed, as her lips explored his shoulder and neck. "It's not lonely here."

Chapter 4

SHE ALMOST FELT the lights behind her before she saw them. And then the twin arcs flashed across the yellow pedestrian crossing sign ahead of her, and the crunch of gravel said the car was slowing down and edging onto the shoulder behind where she walked.

Cheyenne pulled her bag tighter, but didn't pick up her pace. She wasn't going to outrun a car, and it was better not to show fear, if someone was thinking of messing with her. Never let them see you sweat – the words were from a bullshit deodorant commercial, but they were also her personal mantra. And she thought her ability to project cool detachment had allowed her to walk past many an explosive situation. Definitely an important skill when you had to walk just about everywhere. And the desert had pockets of rattlers lying in wait all over the place. Despite whatever you saw on the Discovery Channel, the poisonous serpents out here were more often of the human variety than snakes, she thought.

Did she have her pepper spray in the bag, she wondered. She couldn't remember if she'd transferred it to this purse yesterday or not.

The car slid next to her, rolling along slowly, pacing her. It was a 1990s Ford, silver. There was a dent just above the front wheel well.

Cheyenne didn't stop walking.

The passenger's window rolled down. A man's voice called from inside.

"Hey there," he said. "Do you need a lift somewhere?"

Cheyenne shook her head. "Nah, thanks. Just walking home."

"So you live around here?" he asked. "Not much out this way."

"Nope, pretty much just snakes and scorpions," she agreed.

"Problem is, you can't see them in the dark," he said.

"And they don't want to be seen," she said. "It all works out."

Cheyenne kept walking, struggling not to glance back in the direction of the pacing car. If she ignored him, he might get bored and drive away.

The car inched forward, not letting her get away. "My name's Darin," he said, leaning out the window.

She didn't answer.

"What's your name?" he prodded.

Cheyenne shrugged, and refused to look in the direction of the car. She still had another half mile to go before she would turn down the small road that led to her tiny adobe brick hut. It was not even visible from the road. But it was too far to make a run for right now. She needed to just keep on walking. Calmly. Steadily…

"Fine," the man said after a moment. "I was just trying to help out is all." And with that, he gunned the engine, and kicked up a spray of gravel. It ricocheted off her shins.

"Asshole," she said under her breath.

The red taillights disappeared down the road and into the dark of the night after a few seconds.

Cheyenne dug her hand into her purse to answer the question she should have known the answer to without doubt. Her hand slipped past mascara and tissues and gum… and finally closed around the small canister of pepper spray.

She breathed a sigh of relief. Hopefully she wouldn't need it, but knowing it was there…

Up ahead, a pair of headlights moved in her direction. She tightened her fingers on the pepper spray. Usually when she walked home at two in the morning, she never saw a soul. There was something very cathartic about walking along the desert roads in the middle of the night. You could taste the wind. Free of cares. Free of people. That was not the feeling of this night.

The car drew closer. One headlight looked dimmer than the other, yellowish.

The car was silver. And it was slowing down as it approached her.

"Oh shit," she said under her breath.

"Just heading back to town," Darin announced. "Sure I can't give you a lift somewhere?"

Cheyenne shook her head and kept walking. *"Just go away,"* she said in her head. *"Go away. Go away. Go away!"*

Something pinched her arm.

Cheyenne's skin felt suddenly icy cold.

She looked down and saw a small blue-finned dart protruding from her biceps. Darin grinned at her from where he leaned out of the driver's seat window. He looked like a nice guy – short dark hair, a square jaw, bright cheerful eyes. But his hand was resting a small gun on the edge of the window frame as the tires still slowly crunched the gravel. Creeping along next to her.

Pacing her.

"It really isn't safe out here at night," he said. His voice sounded weirdly far away. Under water.

And then Cheyenne's legs stopped lifting, and she toppled forward, gouging her cheek on the orange gravel of the roadside. She heard a car door slam nearby. And then two hands were scooping her off the ground.

"I wouldn't recommend sleeping out here," Darin said. "Snakes and scorpions and such, you know. Like we talked about. But don't worry, I've got just the place for you."

Chapter 5

MORNING IN THE DESERT came early. And bright. Joe woke with the rays of the sun already warm on his face. The bed next to him was empty, but he heard the shower running in the other room. Now was the awkward time. Was she regretting last night? Did he? Too soon to tell. But he did know that he just wanted to be out of here, and back in his own space (even if that was a hotel room) before he thought too hard about the question.

He searched the floor until he found his jeans wadded up in the corner and then pulled them on. Part of him wanted to just grab his stuff and leave; save them both that morning-after stumbling. But that would be rude and he would probably see her again at the Cowgirl, like it or not. Because he definitely intended on returning there, as long as he was staying in town. Plus, the water had stopped in the bathroom, so his chance for an unseen exit was already probably past.

Sure enough, the bathroom door opened a moment later and Cindy stepped out, a big fluffy pink towel cinched around her chest as she tousled her hair with another smaller one.

"Mornin' stranger," she said with a smile.

"Back atcha," he said.

She crossed the room and rubbed one hand on his bare shoulder. "How did you sleep?"

"Like a baby," he said. "Your bed is comfy!"

"It is," she agreed. "But it's more comfy if there's someone to share it with. Hope you didn't mind."

He laughed. "Hardly!"

She scrunched the towel across her head once more and

then pulled it free, letting long kinky black locks fall across her shoulders. She leaned in to kiss him. A soft, warm, gentle press on his lips. Her breath was sweet. The cold tips of her wet hair tickled his shoulder and he shivered.

"Do you drink coffee?" she asked, standing up and walking back to the bath to ditch her hair towel. To his surprise, she also slipped off her body towel, dropping it inside on the sink.

"Um, yeah, I do," he said, admiring the sun glow across the rich almond skin of her back and butt as she returned to pull a pair of underwear from a dresser drawer. She was not shy; she put one foot up on the bed and faced him as she pulled the white silk panties up over her foot before stepping down and slipping her other foot in as well. Her breasts jiggled as she pulled the panties up and then turned to the dresser to find a matching bra.

"Well, I don't have any in the house," she apologized. "But I can run up to Dunkin' – there's a store just a few blocks down the street. If you want to shower, I can grab that and some donuts?"

"Actually..." he began.

"You're not running out on me, are you?"

"...Well, no... but I would like to go back to my hotel, use my toothbrush, get a clean pair of clothes, you know."

She faked a lip pout and stared at him with two big brown eyes.

"Will I see you later?"

"Sure," he promised. "Are you working tonight?"

She nodded. "Start at five."

"Well, I'd offer you dinner but..."

"Come eat at the bar," she said. "We can talk some then. I want to see if I like you or not." She winked.

"Deal," Joe said, and pulled on his shirt. "I think there's a pretty good chance that I like you, but we'll see."

"Fair enough," she said. "What are you going to do today?"

"I think I'll head out to that Birchmir Mission," Joe said.

"I'm curious about those kinds of places."

She shrugged. "Take a bottle of water. It gets hot out there."

"It got pretty hot in here, last night," he said.

She laughed and shrugged, but he could tell she was pleased with the compliment.

"Next time I'll keep some bottles by the bed."

"There's going to be a next time?" he asked.

She shrugged. "We'll see. Depends on if I decide I like you or not."

"Five, huh?"

She nodded. "You can tell me all about the ghosts."

Joe was far more worried about meeting thieves than ghosts. After going "home" to freshen up, he picked up a burger and a big jug of tea and headed up the Old Santa Fe Trail out of town. Santa Fe's omnipresent adobe-centric clusters of low, squat businesses gave way to small one-story homes and then all buildings quickly faded in the rear view mirror. In minutes he was driving through the desert, just a strip of asphalt between the long rolling plains and hills on either side. The light brown earth was dotted with sagebrush and the occasional cactus. The road wound uphill slowly, but the real hills were a few miles to his left. Those rose suddenly to the sky, great pillars of rock and scrub trees. The clouds cast shadows over the ravines and run-off trails that led down from the tops. At this altitude, he assumed those tops were snowcapped in the winter months. But right now, it was summer, and the amount of green poking up from the desert and the hills was surprising. Part of him had expected it all to look like a big plain of cactus and sand.

His phone talked, alerting him to a turnoff ahead. With Google Maps, there were no secret places anymore; you could plug in just about any address and in seconds the calming feminine robot would talk you through how to get there. It was an amazing world, he sometimes thought. But while the digital world pushed belief in the invisible farther and farther from center stage, he knew that there *was* another world out there. Forgotten maybe. Hidden, surely. But a dangerous world still existed that was looking for a way into our own. A world most people didn't acknowledge at all.

Joe wondered if he asked his phone robot for directions to find the Curburide, what she would say. "Not in this world," maybe.

"In five hundred feet, turn left," his phone prodded. The road was unmarked, just a dusty curve of asphalt that dropped off with a bump from the main road and appeared rarely travelled. "In one mile, your destination will be on the right," the phone informed him.

And the phone was right.

A minute or so later, Joe saw the three-story, red adobe structure rising above the barren plain. He pulled down a rutted trail that wound around a small copse of trees. A dry creek bed crossed the property and no doubt fed the trees (when it had water in it) from the mountain runoff. It was nothing but brown gravel now, however.

He pulled up in front of the rambling old mission and parked the car. A cross was carved into the wall above the heavy wooden front doors. On the left side rose a small turret. Joe assumed that you could get to the rooms in the tower from within the building, but there were also steps carved in the wall on the outside. A lookout tower – a remnant from another, troubled time. To the right of the large arched doors, the building was simply a large adobe square, with the second level inset slightly from the walls of the first.

It was quiet here. Profoundly still. You could literally hear the air move faintly through the sagebrush and occasional scrubby trees. And that was all.

No cars. No radios. No electric hums.

It gave him the chills.

This was the end of the earth.

He was anxious – and a little nervous – to see what lurked inside those walls.

The big wooden front door did not budge when he pulled on the heavy copper handle. He walked around the old mission, looking for another access point. He could try to pick the lock on the main door, but if there was an easier way…

There was another door in the back, facing the long sloping drop-off valley of desert sagebrush beyond. That was fastened with a chain and a big clasp lock. If it was newer than the front door lock, it might be easier to jimmy.

But then on the side of the building, he saw something that made him grin. "That'll do nicely," he murmured. One of the windows had been broken, and the wire mesh that was supposed to protect it had been peeled away. Obviously, he wasn't the only one who had tried to visit the mission without a key.

Joe peered inside, but there wasn't much to see. A couple empty walls painted beige, with the lighter discolorations of rectangular things once hung but now long gone. An old chest remained against one wall.

Near a doorway.

"Here goes nothin'," Joe said, and hoisted himself up onto the sill. The glass had long been cleaned away, and he flipped one leg over and was inside in a moment. He flashed on his days working the police beat at the newspaper and the words "breaking and entering" ran through his head.

He shrugged it off. It was an abandoned building in the middle of nowhere – who was going to care if he took a walk through?

The interior of the building was filled with long shadows. There were some narrow windows, but not many; old adobe buildings were meant to hold in the cool during the heat of the sun, and windows only let the sun's heat bake in. It was cooler inside, and the faint hint of sage or incense, scented the air. He walked down a short hallway towards the front of the building, and quickly found the main chapel that the structure had been built around. It was a large room with a stepped altar on the opposite side from the tall wooden entry doors. Half of the pews had long since been removed; holes in the wooden floor betrayed where they had once been. But that hadn't stopped people from congregating. There were beer bottles, paper bags and other refuse lying in the corners and along the wall. A blackened spot in the middle of the room said that some squatters had built a fire here at some point. And spray-painted graffiti colored the otherwise bare walls. *Worship Him!* proclaimed one red scrawl. Next to it was a star drawn inside a circle. It looked Satanic. Somehow Joe didn't think that "him" related to the Christian God in this instance.

A pedestal still remained on the altar; maybe the only thing left from when this room was actively used for masses decades ago. It was stained with something dark. Joe walked up the two steps to look closer.

Something had puddled on the tile in front of the altar. The drip marks trailed down from the top of the altar, where, on top of that large oblong stone, the source of the drip had dried. Joe licked his forefinger and drew it across the dark smudge. The fingertip came back dusky red.

"Hmmm," Joe mused. "Could have been wine, I suppose. But somehow I doubt it."

He didn't lick the finger clean. Instead, he considered what might have been sacrificed there, and shook the image away. Sure, it could have been a goat. Or a chicken.

But he still had vivid memories of a girl named Cindy laid out on a stone dais in a cave near the ocean, blood leaking from cuts all over her body and a knife raised above her, primed to loose more. Sacrificing animals was for pretenders. If this place really had been used as the seat of a demonic ritual… he had just wet his finger with human blood.

A chill ran up his spine.

Who had died here? And when? And had the sacrifice opened a crack in the edge of the world? Had Curburide demons slithered through the hole in the world and floated in the air here, soaking up the blood and lust and pain? Looking for a way to stick around?

He pivoted and stared all around the room. A decaying, forgotten, dirty space. Empty now. But had it been a doorway? Was it still used?

Standing here in this silent space was not going to give him the answers. Joe walked across the room to a dark hallway on the opposite side from where he had come in. He crossed its length, noting a handful of empty rooms, and finding a staircase at the end. Presumably, this led to the lookout tower. Joe shrugged and stepped up the first of the stone stairs. Only one way to find out.

It grew darker as the steps corkscrewed around the center twice. He was holding on to the wall to guide himself by the time he finally arrived at a door. The knob turned easily on this one and he was instantly blinded by the noon sun and a blast of warmer air. He stood on the top of the lookout turret. There was barely enough room for four people to stand together, but from here he could see for miles in every direction; his eye traced the road back to the Old Santa Fe Trail on one side, and down the hill towards the Rio Grande Valley on the other. The floor was stained with spots of something dark; a coating of desert dust obscured, but didn't hide it completely.

A plume of smoke rolled off the road. Whatever kicked it up was headed in this direction. Joe's stomach sank. He didn't need a run-in over breaking and entering. And it was too late to get down and out to the car. Whoever it was had already left the road and was pulling up to the front of the building. But then…

Joe watched and crooked an eyebrow. A beat-up, old silver car pulled up next to his own Hyundai. It slowed, circled his car in a careful gravel-crunching creak, and then accelerated back out and down the road the way it had come in. Could be someone had come down the wrong road and was just turning around. Or it could be that his being there had scared somebody off.

He didn't stick around to offer a second chance.

"Talk to me about the Birchmir," Joe said, pushing a fresh beer across the copper clad bar in front of Arnie. An offering. It was after 9 p.m. at the Cowgirl BBQ, and Arnie was already talking loose and loud. He was well into his fourth or fifth beer of the night, and Joe figured that was the best time to get the story. Whatever story this crazy drunken bastard had to tell, anyway.

"You lookin' to lose your soul?" Arnie asked. At the same time, he reached for the new pint, pulling it possessively closer. He was an opportunist *and* a storyteller.

"No," Joe said. "But I heard what you said the other night, and I'm curious."

"Curiosity killed the moron," Arnie said. He took a deep pull on the pint. "But some just ain't afraid to die. So what the hell, I'll tell ya."

Arnie screwed up his face until the fine wrinkles looked like fissures. He looked like Robert Plant – if Robert Plant was eighty-five years old.

"The Birchmir is a cursed, hateful place," he said. "Best to leave it fade to dust out in the desert. Give it your attention, and it will only come back to life. And trust me, that is *not* a life you want to see."

"You talked about demons coming through the walls. Tell me about that? How can they do that; what brings them through?"

Arnie shook his head. "You know it's an old Spanish mission, right?"

Joe nodded.

"Well, as a mission, it was a holy place. That's like an electric light in the darkest night to a demon. It calls them like the moths to a backyard porchlight in August. They swarm. But usually, the very thing that calls them stops them from coming through. That was the way it was with the Birchmir when the Church owned it. The 'holy' kept them at bay. But once the friars walked away… well… there were others who wanted to twist that holiness that used to hold the devils away and subvert it. They didn't want to keep the demons away. On the contrary; they wanted to let them come through."

"But why?" Joe asked. "That seems a bit... self-destructive."

Arnie shrugged. "Some people're never satisfied. Think they're going to get power from demons. They never get nothing but death, but you just try 'n *tell* people that. It's like telling people to stop drinkin', else it's gonna kill ya. They don't listen."

Arnie stopped and raised the free beer to his lips. "That kind of talk ain't going to stop me. I believe it's going to make me feel better, not kill me." He wiped his lips and grinned. "See what I'm sayin'?"

"So, what did they actually do?" Joe asked.

Arnie's eyes grew wide. "What didn't they do! All manner of unholy, wicked things. They stole consecrated hosts – the body of Christ! – and pissed on them right there on the altar where the mass used to be said. They held blood orgies; they let men perform dances on the altar dressed as women, and women strapped on devices to bend them over and act like, well, you know. Obscenity. Blasphemy. Filth."

Arnie stopped and took a drink of his beer, which now was nearly gone.

"Who knows what other things they did. But they broke into that place of lost mysteries, and blasphemed and committed one atrocity after the other, all in the name of the devil. In the end, they were sacrificing animals and people on the altar where the body of Christ had once been consecrated. And in the end, they brought the devils through. I've seen 'em. They come right out through the cracks in the walls some nights when it gets cold and dark out there and you're feeling all alone. They can feel a new soul in the middle of that lost Church, and it pulls them right through."

"And then what?" Joe asked. "What do they do when they come through?"

"They ride people."

Joe's eyebrow creased. "That must look pretty strange."

Arnie shook his head. His eyes rolled in disgust. "You can't see them pop outta nothin' and start walking around, fer chrissakes. They're demons. When I say ride, I mean, they take over some poor soul and twist him or her to be their slave."

"But you said you'd seen them."

Arnie suddenly looked cross. "You calling me a liar?"

"I'm just trying to understand," Joe said. "You're standing there in the old mission, and these nuts do a pornographic ceremony, and… you see demons come out of the walls? Or people just start acting funny because you think they're possessed?"

Arnie stared at him hard for a moment. Then he put the pint to his lips and drew a long sip. When he finished swallowing, he composed himself and spoke slowly, deliberately.

"I followed these people for a long time," he said. "I wanted to know what they did in the old chapel, and so I got myself accepted by them. I went, and I watched their ceremony. It made me sick. But I tried to pretend that I enjoyed their sicko shit. And I am telling you. When that night reached its peak, I saw them come. I heard them come. The room shivered; I felt like we were in a small earthquake or something. And when I stared hard at the walls… I could see them. Just barely. I could see the wall through them, but if I stared hard, I could see them pushing their way through, hungry. Cruel faces. Long fingers reaching out. They were almost invisible, but not quite. And then they would touch one of the people at the altar, calling them, and… disappear."

"Where?" Joe asked.

"Inside the people, what do you think? That's what I'm telling you, they rode them."

"And what happened when they went inside someone?"

Arnie's eyes looked ready to pop out. "The obscene," he hissed. "I can't begin to tell you. If you want to know, you will have to go see for yourself."

Joe leaned closer, suddenly intrigued. "You mean, they are still doing it there?"

Arnie nodded. He took a slug of the last dregs of the pint, tilted it high, and then slammed it back to the bar empty. As if daring Joe to fill it again.

"Yeah, they are still doing it. The ones who're still alive. They love to be ridden. They're all perverts. And idiots."

A new voice interrupted the conversation. "Arnie, you know you're not supposed to get on the soapbox here."

It was Cindy. She slipped her fingers around Joe's wrist and squeezed. "And I told you, don't get him going!" She said the last in a whisper, but it was a fierce one.

Joe nodded. He didn't want to piss her off. And he could see that Arnie was getting agitated. But he still needed a little more.

Cindy squeezed his wrist once, and then went down the bar to help another customer. An older guy, in black slacks and an expensive striped polo. Even after just a few days in Santa Fe, Joe mentally looked at the man and internally said, "tourist."

As if *he* wasn't one himself!

While Cindy was occupied, he looked back at Arnie and said, "Tell me how *I* can see the demons."

Chapter 6

SIX FINGERS CURLED around Alex's neck and shoved her hard against a rock wall. At least, she supposed there were six fingers because that's how many that there were on the hand that pinned Ariana to the wall across from her. The realization chilled her when she absentmindedly counted the fingers around Ariana's neck… and then counted them again to be sure.

They were long, dark, gnarled. The demon itself – well, at least Alex assumed it was a demon – leered at her with teeth that seemed too large for its heavy jaw. They glistened in the dim room.

"Were you looking for something?" it asked. The voice was a low growl; like a chain dragged across an iron bucket.

Ariana answered, from the opposite wall.

"We were looking for *you*," she said. Her voice was artificially sultry. Alex wanted to barf. The woman was smooth as plastic, and just as real.

The demon didn't buy it.

"Yeah, and I was looking for dinner. Thanks for coming when I called."

He leaned in and bared dark teeth. It looked as if he were going to chew out Ariana's neck.

But then she dropped the act.

"Wait!" she demanded. Her voice was cold. Hard.

The demon stopped. It raised an eyebrow. Or, at least, the ridge where a human eyebrow would be. This creature didn't seem to have any hair. It resembled a human close enough, but obviously differed too. Its eyes were longer, as if someone had grabbed it by the corners and pulled. It wore no clothes, and its chest and belly were scarred with the dark lines of past wounds. Its sex looked heavy, and dangerous. Alex thought there might be spines at its end. She didn't lust to become the object of its "affections." It might be a tryst she wouldn't survive.

"I can help you," Ariana said.

Alex raised an eyebrow. She couldn't wait to hear where this was going.

"*No place good,*" Malachai whispered in her head.

The demon laughed. "I wasn't looking for any help," he said. "I'm perfectly capable of ripping the two of you limb from limb by myself. And I don't think you'd want to help me with that anyway. What are you going to do to *help* me?"

"I can help you open the door between worlds," Ariana said quietly.

The demon paused. It looked at her more closely. Considered.

"And why would I believe that?" it asked.

"We're here, aren't we?" Ariana said. "How do you think that happened?"

"How do I know you are the one who found your way through? There are many of us who have reached through the walls between worlds and brought back a toy. I'd guess that you are the toys of someone else. Someone who will probably be looking for you. Them, perhaps?"

The demon gestured back in the direction they'd come from. There was noise at the entrance of the hall.

Voices. Feet.

"If you don't get us to someplace safe quickly, I won't be able to prove anything to you," Ariana warned. "You know they will torture and play with us until we are dead."

The demon nodded. "As will I."

"If you don't get us out of here in about ten seconds, you'll never know what you had."

The hand tightened around Alex's neck until she choked.

"If you are not serious, I will make sure that your death is far slower and more painful than you would have received at the hands and feet of the mob," the demon said.

It yanked them from the wall, and pushed them in front of its legs, already in motion, forcing them to a staggering run. After they rounded a corner, it stopped, and slipped one arm around each of their waists.

Alex felt her feet lift the ground and her head tilt forward. And then the demon was carrying them, and they were flying through the dark. Twisting through silent corridors and vaulting up winding stairwells. The air grew warmer, and smelled of something heavy and bitter.

The sounds of the other demons disappeared behind them, and eventually, their captor slowed his pace. Alex's feet touched the ground but she wasn't free. The demon's long fingers crushed around her arm, and dragged her into an alcove in the black rock of the corridor. She was pushed ahead, and Ariana's bare skin suddenly plastered itself against hers. The demon held both of them with one arm, as it opened the door ahead.

"Welcome home," it growled, pushing them into the dark room beyond.

A flame guttered into existence on the wall ahead and suddenly Alex could actually see the room. The fire flickered and grew on its sconce. There was nothing else on that wall, but there was a collection of trophies displayed on the far one. A human skull decorated the center, but around it was a mélange of bones and other skulls; she saw what looked to be a ram's head, with curled horns hanging from the wall, but most of the bones were from creatures that Alex couldn't identify.

She didn't have time to try; the demon hustled them through the room and opened another door. Without warning, a heavy hand shoved her in the back and Alex fell forward. Her feet left the ground and she landed on her shoulder, rolling down a short ramp to crack her head against the ground at the bottom. Ariana's hip smashed into her face. She cried out from shock and pain. From above, the demon laughed.

"Make yourselves comfortable. When I come back... we'll have much to talk about."

With that, the door at the top of the incline closed, and Alex and Ariana were left in absolute darkness.

Chapter 7

DARIN DELNICK was not an evil guy. At least not by the definitions he'd read. He'd looked the word "evil" up. Many times.

Darin thought a lot about the nature of evil, and his own small place in the universe. Living in the midst of the desert, there was ample time for self-reflection. Evil was usually defined as an immoral act; but Darin considered himself amoral, not immoral. People who thought that life should or could be defined by Ten Commandments were foolish. The universe was so much more than a stage divided by a line of right and wrong, black and white.

When a lion took down a gazelle in the wild, was that evil? No. It was self-preservation. Did the lion enjoy the kill? Darin was sure that it did. There was satisfaction in a hunt that ended with prey. There was a feeling of accomplishment, as well as a hunger assuaged. Did that enjoyment of killing make the lion evil? No!

Like the lion, Darin did what he felt he needed to do to survive. As it turned out, his knowledge of the universe was probably a bit broader than most people's… so his definition of survival was also, perhaps, a bit different.

For Darin, survival meant making his way in the universe, not simply in the United States of indentured corporate slavery. And Darin knew that the universe held more devious and deadly creatures than corporate executives. He also knew that it offered more rewards… to those who could prove themselves.

Darin intended to do just that. He had spent years researching the work of those who had gone before him. Those believers in something more than simply a universe of good and evil. Those who had left something behind.

There were many dead ends, and many theories that held as much truth as a bad dream. But there were also those who had found some piece of the truth. He stood in his front room, and fingered the old leather volumes he had collected over the past decade.

Books bound in animal skin.

Books bound in human skin.

Books that had never been produced in more than a handful of hand-written copies. He had sought and stolen and brought a library of secret knowledge here, to the desert. They said you could find anything on the 'net, but they were wrong. There were some buckets of knowledge that were not only not "public," but were only transferred to a couple people per generation. Knowledge that was guarded. Knowledge that was dangerous.

Darin had always believed that the universe had more going on than a bunch of humans raping a planet and then taking the spiritual elevator up or down after they'd wound their way around the corkscrew of their mortal coil. He'd read plenty of foolish theories – really alternative religion fodder – when he'd researched the occult via the library, Amazon.com and some unsavory mail order catalogues. But all that had been like, a prequel to the real story.

He read dozens of silly spells and foolish theories about spiritual creatures still bound to the archaic, simplistic notions of heaven or hell. Most people in the last one hundred years who really believed in the existence of ethereal creatures still categorized them as demons or angels. They remained locked in a concept that had been simplistic a thousand years ago.

But Darin continued to explore the myths and beliefs of many cultures. And in the end, he had stumbled on the true beginning of his path when he had found an old, hand-bound book very close to home.

A book covered in dust and sand, hidden beneath the floorboards of one of the sleeping rooms of the old mission. It was called *The Book of the Curburide*. He pulled it off the shelf, and smiled as he leafed through the first yellowed pages of Chapter One. The author was anonymous, but the text held more knowledge of the true universe than virtually any other he'd come across.

The rewards of a successful Calling are riches and hedonistic fulfillment beyond any man's wildest dreams. But the path to union with the Curburide is long. He who chooses this path must be committed to the Calling in both heart and soul; there is no turning back. To waver on the path means not only death, but eternal damnation. Once the Calling has begun, and first blood spilled, the caller belongs to the demons called Curburide. If the Calling is successfully completed, they will also belong to the Caller – a mutual symbiotic bond is forged. But if the Curburide detect weakness, doubt or insincerity in the Caller before that bond is complete, beware…

He had studied the book for months. And he had prepared his Calling carefully. He would *not* be taken and slaughtered during the first moments of the ritual, as the Curburide demons came through to our realm, drawn by his ritual but not yet bound by any allegiance to him.

Since reading the book, he had found more references to the Curburide in the backwaters of other occult texts. He knew the names of some of the demons who had touched our world over the centuries. He would start with them; they would want to return. And he would pledge to help them.

With certain conditions.

Darin set the bags he was holding down for a minute and took out a keychain from his pocket to release the padlock from the old wooden door. Then he flipped on the light switch and a bulb sprang to life below. He'd rigged the switch to pull from a large battery, since the electricity had been turned off to the site years ago. It was a lot easier than lighting candles every time he had to go to the basement.

Darin descended the steps slowly, lost in thought as he considered his plans. In his studies, he had come across all sorts of rituals for demon calling. Most involved human sacrifice. Some revolved around torture – there was a documented Curburide calling that involved the sacrifice of victims in five different geographic locations – a sort of murderous map.

There was the Ritual of the Twenty-One Cuts, where the victim was slowly sliced in various portions of the anatomy until the final cut pierced the heart. And there was The Ritual of the Thirteenth, which involved impregnating thirteen women, sacrificing twelve of them and leaving the progeny of the thirteenth to serve as the flesh-bound portal for a demon to incorporate itself into in this world. That ritual offered the demon a foothold of near-permanence in our realm, though it also consigned the creature to several years of helplessness while its host human body grew.

Darin planned to use a different ritual. The book described the Star of Death ceremony that placed five victims in a circle, their feet to the center. When the circle was completed and their blood flowed and connected all the way around in a crimson moat, the life energy that pooled at the center would be so strong that it would allow a door between worlds to be opened.

Darin turned the corner at the base of the stairs and opened a door to a small, dark room. There he set one of the small lunch bags he'd been carrying down at the feet of a woman who lay sleeping there, head on a burlap sack bunched into a pillow. A chain secured her by the wrist to a heavy bolt he'd installed in the stone wall. He left the door open as he stepped back out into the hall so the light could get in and then repeated the action in another room, where another woman lay sleeping.

The woman in the fourth room was not sleeping. When he opened the door, she sat with her back to the wall. Her face was streaked with sweat; dark hair was plastered to her neck. Her hands gripped the chain, stretching it tight across the edge of a stone shelf that jutted from one wall. When she saw Darrin, she dropped the chain, but he had already seen what she was doing. The chain was bright silver in one spot, the edge of the rock she'd been rubbing it against was white compared to the rest of the shelf's yellowish caste.

She was trying to file down the chain while he was gone. She thought with enough filing, she could eventually weaken and break the chain to escape.

Darin smiled. Let her try. She wasn't going to be in here long enough for it to matter. All she was going to be able to do was blister her hands and dull the edge of the rock.

He dropped the bag at her feet and didn't say a word.

"Wake up," he called to the sleeping women across the hall. "I am only going to leave your doors open for a few minutes, so if you want to be able to see what your lunch is, now's the time, while I bring you some water."

From one of the rooms, the sound of weeping began. From another, the crumple of a paper bag opening.

"Let me go," the woman said from behind him. The voice was cold. Demanding. Not afraid at all. Good. She'd bring a powerful energy to the sacrifice. Darin had not read anything to suggest it, but he theorized that a powerful life force was more useful in such a ritual than the docile, beaten soul of sheep.

"Soon," he promised.

"What do you want from me?" she asked.

Darin turned around and looked at her. Her eyes were bright in the shadowy room. Her face was flushed. He could see her chest rising and falling. Her T-shirt stuck to the curves of her chest, showing every breath. She didn't look away, demanding an answer.

"I want everything you have to give," he answered. Then he walked away from her, to gather the deep steel cups he'd bought at the secondhand shop on Guadalupe Street. He filled them with water twice a day; he needed to make sure his sacrifices stayed well-hydrated. Because ultimately, he needed them to bleed.

Strong and steady.

Tonight he would go out and find himself the fifth woman.

The final feet to walk the circle around his dark star.

And then things would really start to get interesting.

Chapter 8

CHEYENNE OPENED THE BAG and quickly downed the peanut butter and jelly sandwich within. Then she ate the apple, and drank every drop of the water the asshole had left her.

The first time he'd brought food, she'd considered not touching it. Maybe it was drugged, or poisoned... but... he already had her chained up. What would be the point?

She needed all of her strength if she had any hope of getting out of this. She still didn't know what *this* was, but she didn't expect that letting her walk away alive at the end of it all was part of the asshole's plan.

Cheyenne picked up the chain with her free hand, and shifted her butt over until she sat next to the rock ledge again. People had dug their way out of prisons with a spoon. She didn't have a spoon, but she had friction.

You worked with what you had.

Chapter 9

JOE HAD DONE stakeouts before. It wasn't just cops who hung back and kept an eye out. A good reporter knew when to hole up, sit tight, and just… wait.

The tough part about staking out the old mission was that there was no place to hide. There were no buildings for miles, and the road traversed a straight, flat area that basically was the bottom of a valley. No big hunks of rock or other buildings to ditch the car behind. And he'd seen the way the car had circled his own when he'd parked there last. He couldn't leave the Hyundai on the side of the road without attracting attention, and he sure couldn't walk from town out to the mission. It'd take him a couple hours or more on foot.

But there were always ways. He didn't have to use his car to get here.

Joe pulled the rented motor scooter down the slight hill behind the mission, and laid it down near some small jutting rocks. Then he gathered a few blooms of sagebrush and laid them on top. It wasn't a perfect camouflage, but nobody should be staring down the hillside behind the mission anyway.

He was more concerned about keeping himself invisible. After dark, it would be easy, but in the meantime…

He'd worn a sand-colored shirt and light jeans, and planned to lie down near the bike behind the mission for the next hour or so until it was dark. After that, he might move up and hang closer to the building itself; it would be easier to stay out of sight then.

Was this exercise completely stupid?

He hoped not.

Arnie had been adamant that there still was a group that used this place to call demons. And he'd been equally insistent that there would be activity this weekend. It was a celestial "event" weekend – the sort that always brought out occultists, Satanists, druids, witches, call them what you would. The people who believed in the thin spots between worlds always felt that events like lunar equinoxes and solstices and comets crossing low over the earth's atmosphere were important; they claimed that these astronomical things made for astrological ripples.

And on Saturday night, actually at dawn, there would be a selenelion – a total eclipse of the moon at the moment of the sun's rising. For a brief moment, the earth would be directly between the sun and moon – the three celestial bodies forming an exact 180-degree line in space.

Joe had heard the weather man talking about this cosmic alignment as a rare event on the radio this morning. He was actually pretty excited to see it himself; usually when they talked about equinoxes and shooting stars and whatnot, the sky seemed to always be filled with dark clouds where he was. But here, in the high desert, the sky was almost always clear at night. He should have a great view; if he could stay awake all night to see it. Assuming he wasn't inside the old mission in the midst of stopping some crazy ritual at the time.

But first things first – he needed somebody to show up.

That didn't take long.

The sun was just setting when an old silver Ford pulled up to the front of the Birchmir. A dark-haired man got out, reached into the back of the car and then walked to the front of the mission carrying a bunch of brown paper bags. He disappeared inside and Joe considered whether to follow. Not yet, he thought. Something told him that the man wasn't staying. Joe shifted his weight from one side to the other in the dirt, and settled in to bide his time. He pulled out his phone and clicked the button.

8:13 p.m. It would be full dark soon.

He waited.

The breeze slipped over his back and the brush around him moved faintly. It felt good after a warm day, but in a couple more hours it would feel chilly out here. The temperatures would drop from the 80s during the day to the 50s at night. He'd brought a jacket for just that reason, though it had been too hot to wear when he'd set out. It was tied around his waist, and he'd be putting it on if he had to stay out here too much longer.

The stillness of the landscape in front of him was suddenly broken again by the quick steps of the man. The guy looked to be average height, maybe a little overweight. Thinning dark hair. Really nondescript, Joe thought, as the guy pulled the car door open and slipped inside. In a minute, all that remained to tell of his visit was a faint cloud of dust in the air.

Well, that and whatever he'd left inside. The guy hadn't returned with the bags he'd taken inside, Joe had noted. He waited for a minute, and then scanned the road in both directions. There appeared to be nobody for miles.

Joe pushed himself off the ground and brushed the dust off his jeans as he began to walk towards the mission.

He was curious to find out what was in those bags.

Chapter 10

IF YOU WANTED something done right, you had to do it yourself. That had been Cheyenne's credo since she was thirteen. She had cheated sometimes in school, to get by easily – until she'd realized that she could actually score better without trying too hard than she did when cribbing off the girl next to her. That was just the first of many realizations that it was better to depend on yourself than someone else. She'd given up on her mother before she left junior high. If she waited for mom to pick her up at a friend's house, or after school, she'd wait on the curb for hours. So she made her own arrangements to get home. And sometimes she just didn't bother going home until it was night. By then her mom was a bit angry, if she managed to remember that she had a daughter who was MIA. But half the time she was too busy chatting up her boyfriend or getting stoned to realize Cheyenne was even gone.

So she learned how to take care of herself early. And completely. Guys learned pretty quick not to fuck with her. Unless she wanted them to. She was called everything from headstrong to haughty, but she didn't care.

Cheyenne made her own way the way she wanted.

Which was why she was really pissed right now that her wrist was shackled to a stone wall. Wasn't anybody who was going to come bail her out; she couldn't sit back and cry hoping for some knight in shining armor to come to her rescue.

That seemed to be the answer of a couple other girls here. She'd called out to them a few times. It was hard to hear through the doors, but the standing hope among the others seemed to be that a boyfriend or husband or the police would turn up. And voila, the hideous day would be saved.

Bullshit, Cheyenne said to that. *Maniac's going to slaughter us one by one.* She didn't say that out loud. No need to freak anyone out down the hall any more than they already were. But that was God's truth, she was sure as shit it was.

And Cheyenne didn't intend to be hanging around when the asshole turned up with his machete. Or switchblade. Or pistol. Or rifle. Or whatever he was going to use to finally do them in. He wasn't just going to leave them down here to grow old on peanut butter sandwiches, that was for sure.

She rubbed the chain across the edge of a rock ledge for a couple hours after he left. She heard occasional cries and screams of frustration from down the hall and shook her head. Idiots. They were wasting time and energy instead of trying to get themselves out of here.

That said.

She ran her fingers over the metal in the chain link she'd been filing. She'd worn the metal down a bit, for sure. But at this rate, it would take days to break the link.

Something told her she didn't have days.

Cheyenne stopped grinding the chain and stood up. Her shoulders ached and her stomach was already growling. A sandwich and an apple wasn't enough to support this much of a workout!

She yanked a couple times on the chain, to no avail. The eyehook that held the chain was mounted on a circle of metal held fast to the rock by four screws; and the rock wasn't going to give.

But…

Cheyenne traced her fingers around the metal cup he'd left her filled with water. And then she stood and felt at the four screws that bolted the eyehook into the rock wall. Which held the chain.

Sometimes you had to be imaginative when you needed a tool. Right now, she could use a hacksaw. But a screwdriver would work too. Of course, she didn't actually *have* a screwdriver. Not per se. But you made do with what you had.

Cheyenne drank all of the water; she had been going to ration it to last awhile, but she needed the cup and couldn't waste the water.

Then she stepped up on the rock ledge and strained to reach the screws at the base of the chain. She pushed the edge of the cup into the slot in the one at the bottom and pushed. Righty tight-y, lefty loose-y, her grandpa had always said. She used that silly rhyme now to be sure she was trying to budge it the right way.

She put both of her hands on the cup, clattering the chain against the wall. She used the handle as her lever, and pushed. Something moved, and she grinned. This was going to be easier than she thought.

And then just as quickly, she frowned as she touched the cup.

The screw hadn't moved, the edge of her cup had bent. The one side was creased together.

Shit.

Cheyenne stepped back down to the floor. The edge of the cup had creased in the direction she'd been trying to turn. A wave of defeat hit her then, and she could feel her arms shaking. She was exhausted. She'd wasted hours trying to file down the chain and now her idea of unscrewing the chain holder from the wall was just as futile.

She sat down on the stone ledge and felt her eyes well. So much for all her DIY bravado. She might as well be whining and crying with the other women in this dungeon. She wasn't getting out under her own steam, that much was clear.

That the kind of weak-ass baby bitch you are? A voice taunted in her head. *I thought you were better than that.*

"There's wishful thinking, and there's reality," she murmured.

There's excuses and rationalization, the voice fired back.

Cheyenne took a deep breath. "Just what am I supposed to do?"

Try until you can't try anymore. You lose then? Then you did your best. You ain't done your best yet.

Cheyenne took another breath, and then stood up on the ledge again. She pressed the creased part of the cup into the groove this time; maybe with the reinforcement – two edges of the cup working as one – she'd have better luck. She pressed the cup down with one hand, and pressed gently on the handle with the other.

Sweat broke out on her forehead, and her arms shivered as she stretched them above her head.

Something moved, a little to the left.

Cheyenne looked up and grinned.

Darin stepped down the basement stairs again, for the second time today. The hours seemed to pass faster and faster, it seemed. He dropped a dinner sack into Emilie's room, and then Maria's. They weren't going to get excited about the menu; he'd brought the same thing he'd brought earlier today for brunch – PB&J with an apple. Simple and fast. Not much of a last meal, but, he wasn't particularly empathetic in that way.

He needed to get in and out of here quick; he had things to get ready before tonight. He tossed a bag in Jenevieve's cell, and then opened Cheyenne's. As he did, something clattered to the floor. It apparently had been wedged into the crack of the door.

The crushed remains of the water tin.

He looked at it and then shook his head at the chained woman. She sat on a small rock ledge in the corner. Her eyes didn't leave him. But she didn't say anything.

"You're going to be thirsty later," he said, kicking the ruined cup to land at her feet. He tossed the bag after it. "Better eat quick; I'm leaving the lights on down here for five minutes, that's it." he warned.

Then he left to fill the water cups of the other women. He wasn't replacing Cheyenne's cup. She just made her inevitable outcome harder on herself, that was all.

Cheyenne got up as soon as Darin left. She had worked on the cup this afternoon until the tin handle had finally come free. Now she prayed that she'd bent it to the right size; she was only going to have a couple minutes to make this work.

She could just barely reach the doorway with the chain fully extended. But it was enough. She pulled the end-over-end bent tin handle and stuffed it into the hole in the wall where the lock would slip through. If the handle did its job, the lock would turn but the bolt wouldn't really slide into place; it would be repelled by the metal stuck in the channel. And then, as soon as Darin left, so would she. Leave, that is.

She had toyed with the idea of just trying to run for it, but she didn't want to go hand-to-hand with Darin. Better to leave without him knowing. Then she could bring the police back to help the other women and catch their kidnapper. And if the lock trick didn't work, she could still always make a break for it the next time he came.

Hopefully it wouldn't come to that.

She pressed the metal into the hole, and then went back to her place in the corner, quickly undoing the lunch bag and taking a couple bites from the sandwich. When Darin came back a minute later, he saw that she wasn't finished eating, but that didn't slow him.

"Sorry to leave you with dinner in the dark but, lights out!"

And with that he pushed the door closed. Cheyenne heard the key click in the lock and held her breath.

Please let this work! She prayed.

It took everything in her not to jump to the door and yank on it instantly.

Instead, she stayed sitting, and began to count to one hundred. It shouldn't take him longer than that to have gone up the stairs and be on his way outside. If he got up the stairs, she was betting given his obvious haste tonight that he wasn't going to come back downstairs for anything.

...96, 97, 98, 99...

Cheyenne stood up in the dark and carefully stepped up on the ledge. She felt carefully up the wall, and located the eyebolt holding the chain, and the screws in its circular base. She had managed to get all of them out earlier, and only screwed them back in halfway, so she could remove them easily with her fingers. The bottom one came back out like a charm, and then she quickly removed the top and the right side. She slipped the screws in her pocket, just in case.

The left screw stuck after two turns.

"Are you fucking kidding me?" she hissed in the dark. She pressed her thumb and forefinger around it and tried to turn it, but her fingers only slipped around the cool metal.

"God damn it."

Cheyenne climbed down and felt around on the floor until she found the cup. Thankfully, the asshole had left it; she hadn't thought she'd need it again.

She stood back on the ledge and found the screw head again in the dark, and then traced the groove in its head with her finger. After a couple false starts, she had pressed the edge of the cup into the groove and twisted.

The screw turned around twice and clattered to the floor. The bolt and her chain fell forward out of the wall, almost cracking her in the teeth before she got a grip on it.

Cheyenne stepped down, left the eyebolt and its anchor on the ledge, and walked over to the door. It was pitch black, no light came through the cracks. But she found the knob easily. She'd paced this room a lot in the past twenty-four hours. She knew exactly how many steps there were to the door.

Moment of truth.

She put her hands on the doorknob and twisted and pulled at the same time.

The door moved a hair... and then caught.

"Fuck!" Cheyenne swore out loud.

"What's the matter?" a woman's voice called from somewhere down the hall. Cheyenne ignored it. She pressed one foot on the short span of wall to the left of the door, and then grabbed the knob again. She'd felt movement. She just needed to drag the bolt over the lip. It couldn't be far into the hole, she'd stuffed it good.

She took a deep breath, steeled her leg, and pulled.

The door moved a centimeter. And caught.

"No, no, no!" she spat. Then she grabbed the door knob and yanked again and again with all her might, yelling "no" with every pull.

The door suddenly gave, and Cheyenne and her chain fell backwards with a clatter to the floor.

The wind was knocked out of her, and she gasped like a fish out of water, trying to catch her breath.

"What's going on?" that voice came again from down the hall.

"Big escape plan in progress," Cheyenne answered, but her voice was too soft to be heard outside the room.

She felt around and found the ledge, and then picked up her "anchor" before walking through the doorway into the hall. It was like walking through ink. She moved her feet a couple inches at a time, and kept her hand outstretched, hoping to connect with the far wall with her fingers, rather than her face.

"This was not how I planned to spend my weekend," she thought to herself.

Her fingers finally hit a cold stone surface, and then she used that to guide herself down the passageway. Somewhere, there was a stairway up…

Chapter 11

"If you can really open the door back to our world, now would be a really good time to do it," Alex suggested.

Ariana didn't respond.

The demon had been gone for a while, but Ariana had not spoken a word since they'd landed down here. Alex had crawled around the dark space, and found a few discarded odds and ends there, but nothing of use. And no exit but the chute up. The door at the top was solidly locked. She'd inched her way up twice and tried, to no avail.

"Why did you say you could open the door?" Alex prodded. "When he comes back, he's going to ask you to prove it, and then what? Because you can't, can you? At least, not here."

"We're still alive at the moment, right?" Ariana's voice finally answered. "I had to give him some reason to get us away from the mob. If I hadn't; we wouldn't be talking about this."

"So you postponed our deaths by an hour with a lie."

"I bought us time. Does it matter how?"

"Well, I was kinda hoping you were telling the truth," Alex said. "I'd like to get out of here."

Ariana didn't answer. Alex turned her attention inward.

"Malachai?" she asked silently.

"Whatever she says, don't trust her," came the response.

"Well, duh!" Alex said. "Tell me something I don't already know. This is your world. What should we do?"

"I don't know," Malachai answered. *"At the moment, you're probably in the safest place you possibly could be here. As soon as you're spotted outside of these walls, they will capture and torture you."*

"So we should stay in a hole or die?"

"*Oh, they won't kill you. Humans don't die easily here, not unless you're skinned too often or sent to the Cauldron. You're far more valuable alive. The Curburide feed on pain, sexual energy and fear. Preferably all three combined.*"

"So if they catch us they're going to plant us in the ground like all those heads we saw?"

"*Possibly. But not likely. You're two young, attractive women. They will want to use that, not bury it.*"

"Use it how?"

"*Think about it,*" Malachai said.

Alex didn't like the image that came to mind. "Is there anything you can do to help?

There was a long silence. And then Malachai answered. "*If it comes to that, I can stop you from feeling what they do to you. If I'm still here.*"

"What do you mean *if* you're still here?"

"*Because I came over inside you, I've been able to remain that way. Hidden. You're my Trojan Horse. But if they find out I'm helping you, they will pull me out. If that happens… you'll be on your own.*"

"They wouldn't listen to you? You're one of them!"

"*If they pull me out of you while we're on this side of the doorway between worlds, you will never see or hear me again.*"

Alex felt the chill in that statement. She realized that Malachai was more of a prisoner right now than she was. And if he was discovered… well, then she was really doomed. She couldn't move without him.

"But you're a demon yourself. You're one of them." Alex said. "What did you do?"

"*We have our own politics, just as you do. Let's just say… my staying in your world for so long was akin to someone fleeing to Canada instead of serving in your army.*"

"So you're a demonic draft dodger?"

Alex heard a low chuckle in the back of her skull.

"*Does that make you think less of me?*" he asked.

It was Alex's turn to snort. *How do you think less of a demon?*

"*Careful,*" he warned.

Without warning, her arm suddenly moved of its own accord and her palm slapped across her mouth.

She got the message.

"What the hell are you doing?" Ariana asked.

Alex was glad that Ariana couldn't see her in the dark. But she'd barely thought that, when she suddenly found herself blinded and blinking. The door above had opened. Six fingers suddenly grasped her arm, and yanked her up and out of the pit.

Alex fell to the ground on her hip, as the fingers dropped her and bent to repeat the process on Ariana.

Alex sat up as Ariana rolled to her feet. She stood in a crouch at the end of the hallway. There was a closed door behind her.

"There is a hoard out there looking for you," the demon said. "You've got five minutes to give me a reason not to take you out and hand you over to them. It could be worth a lot to me to be the one to have found you."

"I told you before," Ariana said, still crouched, as if ready to spring and fight the demon hand to hand. She was naked, weaponless, and half its size. It would be a short match. "I can help you open a door between worlds."

"Hmmm," the thing nodded. "That could be reason enough to keep you, if it were true. So show me."

"What is your name?" Ariana asked. Her voice was sweet, as if ready to offer him the world.

"You can call me Elotan," the demon answered.

"Elotan," Ariana said. "I opened a door from my world to yours because I wanted to help you. I wanted the Curburide to come to our world and show people what the universe was really all about."

Elotan laughed. "You wanted to show your people how it felt to have their skin peeled while they moaned in orgasm?"

Ariana nodded. "People are so stupid. They have no idea about the highs and lows of pain and pleasure. They hide from it. They pretend that it offends them, but then, once they get behind closed doors they abuse their wives and husbands. I wanted to let you come and show them all. I wanted to see them all ridden by the Curburide."

"And you?" Elotan said. "What about you?"

"I want to be one of you."

"Do you?" he asked. His voice was icy. Dangerous. Without breaking his gaze on Ariana, Elotan reached out and grabbed Alex by the arm. He dragged her across the ground and shoved her back down the chute to the pit. The door slammed as she hit the bottom. Ariana didn't follow.

From upstairs, Alex heard a shriek. It did not sound like a cry of pleasure. Then she heard Ariana scream, "No, please." The demon's voice boomed something unintelligible, and then another door slammed. She still heard Ariana's voice, but it grew faint.

For a few minutes, she didn't hear anything. But then the hitching, impassioned cry of a woman enthralled in the rhythm of sex broke the silence.

Alex squirmed at the thought of what was happening upstairs. She didn't want to know.

Ariana screamed.

Then moaned again.

The walls couldn't hold back the conflicting sounds of pain and pleasure, though they seemed far away. Alex was glad that she didn't have to watch whatever Elotan was doing to Ariana, as much as she despised the woman.

"Time to practice what you preach," she said to the darkness around her.

Chapter 12

THE DEMON GRABBED Ariana by the hair and yanked her to her knees. She looked up at his dark skin and felt her stomach shrink. She knew this position, and knew where this was going. Already the thick rod of his sex was standing taller from where it hung between his naked thighs.

"I don't know why you're here or how you got here," he said. "But I'm not going pass up a once-in-a-lifetime opportunity."

He pulled her face close, until the barbed head of his cock was pushing against her lips. "Make me feel good, and I won't kill you. Yet," he said.

"I don't know if I can," Ariana whispered. His girth was wide; more than a mouthful. And the spines! A crown of thorns surrounded the head of his penis. The barbs were retracted, pointed back towards his groin now, but she had a suspicion they wouldn't remain in that position when he was fully aroused.

"Take it," the demon commanded.

Ariana thought back to the very first time she had read from *The Book of the Curburide*. To the very first man she had killed, in a hotel room in San Francisco. She had teased men with blowjobs and sex in order to slice their necks and release their blood so that she could see the demons. The Curburide. The masters of sex and pain. She had craved to learn their secrets, and to watch them work their torture on humanity. She had yearned to be rewarded as their queen, the wicked woman who had been brave enough to open their passage between worlds.

Now she was here, in their world. Not a queen. Just a naked woman on her knees.

Ariana let the bullet-shaped weapon press past her lips. It was hot against her tongue. Smooth. The demon looked gnarled and scarred by a thousand fights, but his sex was unblemished, a powerful tube of skin that slid easily into her mouth even as she was forced to open wider to accept his thickness. It was still growing inside her, as she tasted the tip and put a hand on the demon's hip to steady herself. She slipped the other around the base of him, and marveled at the silky smooth feel of his bare skin. She'd thought from the look of him that he'd be rough, a gravel and sandpaper monster. But he felt like silken steel.

For a moment she relaxed and let his evil cock slip deeper into her throat. She teased it with her tongue and traced the strange spiny ridges that grew out from its bullet head. He tasted… strange. She couldn't describe it. Not foul at all. She'd expected a gross bathroom taste. She'd expected taking a demon in her mouth would be like licking a toilet. But it wasn't that at all.

He tasted like spice. Not sweet, but faintly exotic. It was slight at first, but as he moved within her mouth the flavor grew richer, heated. Ginger and bitter chocolate. She pulled him inside her farther, no longer fearful of the reward, but craving it.

The demon moaned and pressed a heavy hand to the back of her head. "Not yet," he said. "Not here."

And with that, he yanked her hair and pulled her away from him. As he did, the barbs on his cock resisted, and suddenly the spice in her mouth scalded. Fingers of fire dug into the top of her palate and raked cuts in her tongue. Ariana couldn't help but scream.

As she did, her mouth opened wider and the demon shoved her away. He released her hair, and Ariana fell backward to the ground. She pressed a hand to her lips. Her palm came back warm and red.

Elotan laughed. "Get used to it," he said. "You and I are going to spend a lot of nights together."

Ariana's mouth was on fire; she could feel her tongue

swelling. "But I can't," she mumbled. She spat a wad of blood and saliva on the ground.

Elotan grabbed her hair again and opened the door behind her. Then he dragged her into a small room. Flames flickered from holes in the walls, illuminating paintings of strange scenes. Frames made of long, white bones constrained visions of dark skins twined and bent in bizarre ways on beds of blood and broken skulls. Humans were there in the mix, sometimes shared by two or three demons. One painting showed four men serving as the living furniture of a parlor; they bent in unnatural angles, as dark creatures stood around in groups of two or three, seemingly enjoying a cocktail party atop the human furniture.

Ariana couldn't see more, as Elotan roughly tossed her to the bed. She hit her head on the frame and yelped, and the demon slapped her thigh. "Welcome to your new throne, my queen."

She looked at the creature above her and quailed. This was what she had spent years searching for. But she had imagined it would be different. That the demons would be beholden to her as they came through the door she had opened. As she gave them their desires.

Now, in this situation, she was not going to be thanked, but instead, enslaved and abused.

Elotan's hands ran across her midriff and sides, tracing the lines of her ribs and feeling the ridges of her pelvis. His fingers prodded and stretched her like she was meat at the butcher's. The demon smiled and nodded.

"I've waited for you for a long, long time," he said. "They talk about what it is like to take a human woman."

Ariana reached up to put her hands on the demon's chest; his skin was crossed with knots and scars, yet still felt silk-smooth. "You've been hurt," she said, tracing a long line beneath his left breast.

Elotan chuckled. "Hurt is the heat of life." He reached between her thighs and shoved her legs apart. "And I'm going to make you feel fire."

"Please," Ariana said. She herself wasn't sure even as she said the word what exactly she was asking for. To let her go? Or to take her?

Elotan pressed against her and she felt herself stretch, unnaturally wide. But that slick skin helped her accommodate the demon easily, and then his whole body engulfed her. The demon moaned as he entered, and she saw his lips part in an evil joy. She felt a heat spark inside her, and she slipped her arms around the demon's back. She hated him and wanted him at the same time. Deep inside, she knew that as much as she'd longed to be the queen and hold the whip and laugh, she'd longed to be taken.

By someone who could truly own her.

By a demon.

Her fingers slid down his long back to hold the smooth steel of his ass as he pressed deep inside her. That monstrous weapon was pushing against her inside in places nobody had ever been. Places dangerously close to ripping. "Yes," she found herself whispering.

The demon's own breathing increased, and he laughed at her acquiescence. Elotan bit down on her shoulder and then whispered in her ear. "That was foreplay," he said.

And then he pulled himself most of the way out of her, and Ariana felt as if a molten fork had just raked the core of her vagina. She let out an ear-shattering scream and tried to push him away, but Elotan only laughed and shoved that silken razor barb inside her again. Deep inside. And then pulled back, rough and fast.

Ariana moaned and screamed with every devilish thrust.

Chapter 13

ONCE INSIDE THE old mission, Joe snapped on the flashlight. He moved quickly through the chapel; nothing had changed there. He paused at the stairwell leading to the lookout, but decided not to go up; he didn't know how much time he had. He knew what was up there. Nothing really. But the man had brought bags inside; where had he gone?

Joe walked down the back hall and peered into a couple empty rooms. The flash flared, reflecting painfully off the small windows inside. There was a kitchen area at the end of the hall, and what probably had once been a dining or banquet room next to it. He found a padlocked door next to the kitchen. Joe raised an eyebrow at that. Nothing else inside was locked. He canvassed another hallway that led to a couple more empty rooms before returning to the padlocked door. Lock picking was not one of his skills, nor had he come equipped with a toolkit. He fingered the lock and pulled on it a couple times, testing. It wasn't heavy, but it wasn't budging either. Joe walked back to the kitchen. He opened a couple drawers, but there was nothing inside.

For a moment, he was stumped. What could he use to try to pick a lock? Then he opened a pantry, and nodded. There was a pile of construction debris inside. Old piping and strips of wood. He picked up a thin strip of wood and shrugged. It was worth a try.

He took the strip to the door and shimmed it through the spot where the clasp passed across the door jam. The wood dipped in there, and the metal wasn't snug against it. Then he pulled on the wood strip. Poor man's crowbar.

The clasp moved a bit, but then his makeshift crowbar snapped. Joe slipped another segment behind the lock and continued rocking it. The metal clasp bent outwards before his crowbar snapped again.

He went and got a thicker hunk of board. He wasn't worried about someone finding that their hidey hole had been compromised. Whoever had installed the lock probably wasn't supposed to be here anymore than he was.

The new piece of wood didn't want to slide in the small gap at first, but he forced it in. Holding the flash in the crook of his arm, he wiggled the piece back and forth. After a minute, he saw one of the holding screws of the clasp pulling out of the old wood. He rocked it harder and the other screw moved. He slipped in another piece of wood then, wedging it, and gave it a hard pull.

The clasp popped out of the wood with a snap. Joe grinned, and tossed the makeshift crowbar aside. Holding the flashlight in front of him, he opened the door and peered inside. His eyes registered a stretch of stairs that led down before he saw something flash in front of him. Something came out of the dark at his head.

He tried to dodge, but it caught him above the ear and instead of taking a step forward, he fell backwards into the hallway. His eyes fireworked white pain and he crab-crawled backwards to protect himself from whatever he'd let out of the basement.

But he didn't escape.

Before he could recover, a naked woman knelt astride him. She lifted a chain and some hunk of metal over her head. She clearly intended to brain him.

"Whoa!" he yelled and threw himself to the side in a roll. Her legs didn't let him escape. Joe still gripped the flashlight and brought it up to shine on her face. "Wait!" he yelled again.

The woman paused. She still held the hunk of metal over her head, ready to bring it down on him, but she looked confused. "Who are you?" she said.

"My name is Joe," he said, and quickly added. "I'm not here to hurt you."

"Then what *are* you here for?" she said. Her voice shook. He could see her body shaking.

"I was looking for demons," he said without thinking.

The woman frowned. "You're not helping him?"

"Who's *him*?" Joe asked. "The guy with the lunch bags?"

"You know him!"

"I saw him come inside with a bunch of bags, and leave a few minutes later without them."

"That's him," she said. "That was our dinner."

"Who's *our*?" Joe asked.

"I'm not the only one he had in a cage down there. He's been kidnapping women and chaining them up in the rooms downstairs."

"Sacrifices," Joe murmured.

"What?" The woman's eyes went wide.

"The guy who chained you up was probably collecting women to sacrifice. In a ritual to invoke demons," Joe said.

"There you go about demons again."

"I've seen it before," Joe answered. "A long way away from here."

She clenched the metal rod that held the chain in her hand tighter. "So you know him."

Joe shook his head quickly. "No, I've never met him."

"Then why are you here?"

"I need to talk to the demons if he actually manages to call them. I heard in town that there's a group that meets here and sometimes, they do ceremonies to open the door between worlds."

"Do you know how fucking crazy that sounds?" she asked. Before he could answer, she added, "So you were going to watch him kill me?" Her voice was bitter and her fingers gripped the chain tighter. Her eyes narrowed.

Joe hesitated. He hadn't really thought about the fact that there might be victims in whatever ceremony was going to happen here. Not all demon invocations involved human sacrifices. Though, certainly those involving the Curburide seemed to call for it.

"No," he said. "I didn't want to see anyone hurt. But I need to talk to one. I'm trying to reach a friend."

"Ever hear of the telephone?"

Joe snorted. "My friend is in the world of the demons now."

"Your friend is dead?" she said. "Hold a séance!"

"I don't think she's dead," Joe answered. "I can't believe that. But I saw her and the bitch who opened the door between worlds disappear into the void, right in front of my eyes."

"Then what do you need a demon to…"

The woman's question was interrupted by a noise. A creaking door opening on the other side of the mission.

"Shhhh," Joe put a finger to his lips. Then he whispered. "We need to move. Now!"

She hesitated a moment, and then the sound of voices reached them. A new threat. Joe put his hand on her thigh and pressed her to let him up. She looked at him, hard. Her eyes were dark and deadly; her mouth pursed in a line of distrust. Then she lifted her leg and he rolled over to his hands and knees, and used one hand on the hallway wall to help him stand. With the other, he covered the light of the flash, dimming its reach.

Joe grabbed and slowly closed the basement door. They didn't need to telegraph the evidence that something was awry. Once it was closed, he pressed the screws in the latch back into the holes he'd ripped in the wood. They slid back, far enough that it might not be immediately obvious that the latch was no longer keeping anyone locked in tight downstairs.

He tapped the screws with his finger, and nodded when they didn't immediately slip back out. Then he motioned for her to follow.

Joe led the way down the hall back towards the chapel. Ahead of them, somebody laughed. Footsteps echoed. They heard the sounds of people dropping bags and other things. The sounds of people setting up for the night.

He hugged the wall as they reached the end. Joe peered into the chapel from his vantage at the left side of the altar. There were a half dozen of them. Four men, and two women. They were doing something at the altar, just out of his range of vision. But they walked back and forth from the few remaining pews to the front, grabbing things from their bags. Two of the men were American Indian. They were younger, late teens or early twenties. The other men were white and a little older. One of them was thin; a runner's physique. Jutting chin, beak nose, pointed elbows. The other was his opposite; the flesh hung over his wide belt, dragging the striped shirt off his waist in rolls. One of the women was also Indian; brown-skinned and black hair. Smooth perfect complexion. Maybe twenty or twenty-five, Joe thought. The other was an older woman. Older than all of them. She had lines on her face, and her greying hair kinked long and uncombed across her shoulders. One of the men called her by name. Sienna. The fat man asked her a question that Joe couldn't hear. But he did hear the answer.

"Put it in the kitchen for now," the old woman said.

Joe's eyes widened, as he watched the fat guy go back to a pew and pick up a bag.

Joe turned and grabbed the hand of the woman who'd almost brained him and squeezed. Then he pulled her back the way they'd come. Instead of returning to the dungeon, he yanked her into the stairwell that led up to the lookout turret.

They were barely up five stairs when Joe heard the steps of the man pass them in the hall. He didn't stop, but instead wound all the way around and up to the top.

When they stepped out into the small room at the top, Joe took off his jacket.

"Here, put this on," he offered. Her nakedness had been painfully obvious to him, and aside from needing to curb his prurient interest, he could see the goosebumps standing out on her arms from the night air.

"We should be safe for now up here," he said. "I don't

think they'd need to come up here for what they're doing."

She didn't take the jacket immediately, but he continued holding it out.

"Look," he said. "I think we're going to be up here awhile. So you can freeze your butt off or you can trust me."

Her lips pursed for a moment, and then she leaned over and dropped the chain and its anchor to the ground. One clasp still connected it to her right wrist. She accepted the jacket from Joe then, and quickly slipped her left arm into it. Then she pushed her right through, dragging the chain with it. Once she zipped it all the way up, leaving no cleavage, she looked at Joe again, and hugged her arms tight to her chest.

"What's your name?" he asked.

"Cheyenne," she said. "I'm a waitress at the El Gordo Americana restaurant. I was walking home from work the other night when this asshole pulled over and forced me into his car. I've got a brother and a mother but I've never been married or had a kid so I'm not ready to die yet."

She said it all in a rush and Joe couldn't help but smile. "I think we can work on that."

Cheyenne shot him a look of distrust. "I don't need your help to have a kid or get married," she said. She pulled his jacket tighter to cover the naked delta of her thighs.

Joe grinned again, wider this time. "Thanks for the clarification, but don't worry about it. I came here to try to rescue a woman, but you weren't the one I was aiming for."

"So I'm not good enough, is that what you're saying?" Cheyenne looked at him with wide eyes.

Joe didn't take the bait. "So which is it?" he said staring right back at her. "You want me to help you have a kid or not?"

Cheyenne smiled and slipped down to sit on the ground. Relaxing a little. "I like you, Joe. But… *not*. It never seems to work out with guys who rescue me from being chained up in basements."

Joe could see the goosebumps on her legs. A jacket in

the evening breeze was not enough. He sat down and slid close to her. She flinched as his arm slid around her shoulders.

"I'm not making a move on you," he explained. "But we're going to be here awhile so we should keep warm," he said.

"Is that what they call it these days?"

Joe snorted. "It's going to be a long night, isn't it?"

"Not as long as the one I spent chained to a basement wall," she said.

"Always good to have a frame of reference."

Chapter 14

Alex closed her eyes in the dark.

"Malachai," she called silently.

"*Present.*"

"Can you help me get out of here?" She could almost feel him shake his invisible head.

"There's nothing I can do," he said. "*If I use any of my power, he will feel it instantly. And I'd probably lose my hold on your body. You'd be paralyzed, and I'd be exposed and discovered. There's nothing I can do. We're both safest here for now.*"

"Safe for now," Alex said. She could hear the frequent moans of Ariana from somewhere above. "When he's done with her, it will be my turn next."

Malachai didn't answer immediately. When he did, his voice was flat. "*When it does, I can help,*" he promised.

"I'd rather if you did something now," she said. "Get us out of here."

He didn't answer.

Alex wasn't going to get any help from that quarter. She took a deep breath, and reached out farther with her mind. In the way a ghost had once taught her, back when she was just a lost teen in Nebraska.

"Gertrude?" she called. "Gertrude, can you hear me?"

Malachai was suddenly back in her head like a cold wind. "*Stop that!*" he yelled inside her mind. "*You'll get us discovered.*"

"You can't help, and I'm not just going to sit here waiting for my turn to be tortured."

"*They can hear you! All they have to do is listen.*"

"Gertrude, Matthew, Sarah?" Alex called. The ghosts of her friends. Or rather, her friends, the ghosts. The friends who had set her free from her father's prison.

"They won't answer you anyway," Malachai whispered. "Not after the way you used the power they gave you."

"You mean the way *you* used it," Alex said. She remembered the way Malachai had encouraged her to use the power not only to escape, but to sacrifice the people who had locked her up in the first place. Her parents.

"*I just helped you release the anger, and do what you'd always wanted to.*"

Alex shook her head violently in the dark. "I hated them," she said. "But I would never have used an axe. That was you."

"*Believe what you want about that, but your friends will not come. I don't know if they even can reach here.*"

Alex willed her inner voice to be strong and called again. And again.

"*Alex,*" a male whisper finally came.

She recognized his voice instantly and smiled. "Matthew!"

"*You really fucked up this time, huh?*" He did not sound happy to see her. Or to be called.

"I didn't really choose to be here," she said. "But I could sure use some help getting out."

"*Looks that way,*" he said. "*I don't know if that's going to happen.*"

"Please Matthew," she begged. In her mind, she was kneeling. "I'd do anything to pay you back. Ask Gertrude and Sarah and…"

"*Gertrude won't come. I can tell you that. Not after the last time,*" Matthew said. "*And I can barely reach you, where you're at. I have no power really there.*"

"But if you could bring help, all of you together…"

"*After what you did with the power we brought you last time, I don't think…*"

"I just need to undo the lock on the door," Alex said. "Just a simple latch. Please."

"You know I always liked you," Matthew said. "I'll see what I can do. But I can't promise anything. I might not be able to come back."

"Hurry," Alex pleaded.

"You are going to bring them all down on us," Malachai said.

"Well, you are going to let us sit here and rot until we're killed. I'll take the chance."

"You already have."

Malachai shut up then. The darkness was suddenly heavy. Close.

Alex felt the fear finally set in. She'd managed to avoid it for the most part since she'd woken up here because she had had no alternatives. She'd had to get up, run, stay alive. Now, she was just alone in a dark pit. She had time to think. And she knew that a demon would be back for her soon. He would use her and abuse her with glee. That's what he lived for.

She was just meat to be prepared and eaten. Her stomach growled at the thought of eating.

Alex realized that she was hungry. Like, starving-to-death hungry. It gave her a momentary respite to think about something that was different than "I'm about to be killed." But it only lasted a moment.

As the silence stretched, Alex closed her eyes and channeled all of her energy into calling to Matthew. If it was hard for him to "see" her here, she worried he might not find his way back. If he even wanted to find his way. Matthew had been a street punk in real life. The kind of kid that did what he wanted *when* he wanted. She'd always thought that the main reason he took pity on her and helped when her parents had locked her up and whipped her was because he was such a free spirit. Nobody held him down.

"Matthew, please," she urged.

As Alex called to him, the darkness in her mind began to change. She had opened her inner eye in calling. It was the dangerous process that Gertrude, her ghostly friend since childhood, had helped teach her how to control. For a living person to open themselves to the realm of the dead was dangerous. Most couldn't manage it even if they tried. But for Alex... If she didn't shield her inner voice, she would be like a bright light to moths. The dead, or demons, would zero in. They'd smother her with their need. Or kill her intentionally.

She had learned to target her "inner" voice, but that didn't hide it completely. And now that she was open, the landscape that she saw changed. It wasn't just blackness around her. The edges of her inner vision bled darkroom red. She could see shadows on the horizon. Things moving. And each time she'd called Matthew, she saw them stop.

Malachai was right. She had to be careful. But she also had to get out of here.

Matthew's voice interrupted her fear.

"*I found some help,*" he announced. "*But then you're on your own. If they see us here, they won't let us leave.*"

"Thank you," Alex said. "I'm sorry to drag you into this."

Matthew laughed. "*I came because I wanted to. But, you better straighten it out, kid. You only get so many tries. Trust me on this. I know.*"

Alex nodded. "I got it."

"*Get yourself in place,*" Matthew said. "*All we can do is lend you power. And I don't know for how long.*"

Alex put her fingers on the edge of the chute and looked up to where she knew the door was. Overlaid on the blackness of the room, she saw distant heads turning. Eyes looking towards her. Shapes moving. She pushed herself up the ramp until her fingers touched the door frame.

"I'm ready."

Chapter 15

THERE WAS BLOOD in her mouth. And blood on her thighs. And blood beneath her.

Everything was bloody.

And wet.

And hot.

Ariana was burning from the inside out.

He had pulled out and left her crying in agony as he pushed off the bed. Ariana didn't know how badly she was hurt. Wherever her skin was broken burned like fire. So hot, that she had screamed at first when he'd scratched her, until the bastard had clubbed her across the face. That had hurt almost as much as having his barbed flesh decide it was done inside her and rip its way fully back out, trailing slivers of her inner skin with it.

Elotan stood now above the bed. He was grinning. Or leering. His lip curled in a foul humor. He had just beaten her and shredded her from inside out. And that made him smile? *Demon*, she reminded herself.

"I'm so glad you came to visit," he said. His voice dripped with mockery. "I always wanted to come visit you, but it just wasn't my turn. It might never have been my turn. But now, you're here."

"I opened the door," Ariana said. "I spent years trying to let you in."

Elotan bent over the bed and laughed. "No," he said. "You let *them* in. I would never have gotten to go through."

"Why?" Ariana said. She felt like her voice was a drunken mumble. Her mouth felt numb and swollen and ruined.

"Because it's not my turn." Elotan said. "The entryways are guarded. The ones who can go through are chosen.

They have waited in line or paid their way."

"But you're a demon," Ariana said. Her voice slurred.

"And there are billions of us," Elotan said. "Everyone can't go through at once. The worlds would collapse. There are ranks and rules."

"So, you're no different than us," Ariana said.

A heavy hand slapped her across the face.

"Tell me I'm wrong," Ariana said.

The hand didn't hit her again.

"I have you here now," he said. "I don't need to leave."

"I thought you wanted me to open a door for you?"

Elotan shrugged. "Eventually, perhaps," he said. "But there's no hurry now."

Ariana shook her head. "I won't last long," she said. "Not if it's like this."

Elotan laughed. "What did you think a demon would do to you? Put wreaths of flowers around your neck? Maybe shower you with chocolates?"

Ariana ignored him. "I can help you get through to the other side." She said. "I can offer you a million women that will be yours. But you need to take me back with you."

Elotan stared at her without speaking. Then he began to nod. "There are places that are soft, where doors open sometimes. But those are guarded. We can't open them. We can only wait until someone like you does it from the other side. If you can open a door from here that we can both go through, I want to hear more."

"I did it from the other side. I think it would work from here too," she said.

"And what did you need to open the door?" the demon asked.

"A sacrifice," she said. "A human sacrifice."

"And where are you going to…" he stopped as soon as he started speaking and a wicked grin spread across his face.

"I like you," Elotan said. His hand began to work at his crotch, and then he climbed back onto the bed, to tower over.

His brutal but silken hands trailed across her breasts, and fingered the bloody place between her legs. "I like you a lot."

The fire lanced through her middle in a hideous mix of scorching pain and mind-shattering pleasure. The demon grabbed her by the neck and bent to kiss her with a black tongue. It was barbed like his sex and he was not gentle as he pushed it into the ruin of her mouth.

Ariana screamed, though the sound was muffled by his silken lips.

Meanwhile, he continued to thrust to rip deeper inside her. Something in the very core of her burst, and her body felt the burning of complete, consuming release.

Chapter 16

THE CEREMONY HAD BEGUN. Joe and Cheyenne had moved into the stairwell in an attempt to stay slightly warmer as the chill of the desert night set in; he periodically stole down to the bottom of the steps to try to listen and follow what was going on in the chapel.

The group really did nothing at first; it was like a weird potluck for the first couple of hours. The guys had made several trips out to the cars and brought back bowls and pots and plates and a cooler of drinks. They had used the abandoned altar as a table, while they talked and laughed and ate. Someone had turned on a portable stereo that blared a pop radio station in the corner. For a long time, there had been nothing indicating that this was a gathering of demon callers. It was more like a frat party.

Then Joe had heard the music change. "Stay here," he'd cautioned Cheyenne, and moved carefully down the stairs.

The atmosphere in the chapel had changed radically in the past half an hour. The air now was flavored in the bitter smoke of incense. And the music now played low and somber. A steady, throbbing beat echoed throughout the corridor, and voices chanted something low and guttural in another language. Or perhaps they were simply voices being played backwards. The syllables were so strange and jerky, Joe couldn't be sure.

He slipped as close to the doorframe as he could without being seen.

The dinner party was definitely over. He could smell the acrid, leafy telltale smoke of pot in the air. Some of the front pews had been moved to sit against the walls. On the floor, someone had drawn a large circle in white. Within it, two triangles intersected to form a star.

The skinny guy stood in the center of the circle. He was shirtless now, and the younger woman was busy painting a symbol on his chest with a brush. She dipped the brush in a small pint-sized bottle filled with something red. As Joe watched, a star emerged on the hairless chest of the man.

When it was finished, she handed him the brush and jar, and stripped off her top and bra. He touched the brush to the hollow of her throat, and then to the pit of her bellybutton. Then to her nipples, now fully erect. Once those points were painted, he connected them with long arcs of red, until her chest was a four-pointed oval.

Neither of them spoke, but when he finished, they bent to the center of the circle on the floor. Joe thought they actually might have kissed the ground. Then they stood, and walked towards the altar. At the edge of the circle, they stopped, and the older woman stepped forward and handed them a lit black candle. The couple held the candle together, and used its flame to light a thick, foot-tall candle that was positioned there on a stand made of latticed bones. Joe realized that there were also similar candles, still unlit, set on bone stands at three other points around the circle. Spaced out to illustrate the four directions, like a compass: north, south, east, west.

The fat guy and the other girl now walked to the center of the circle, with their own jar and paint. She stood waiting, as her partner unbuttoned his blue- and red-striped shirt and then tossed it to one of the pews. Then they repeated the ritual, with the white guy earning the star and him painting the wide shadows of her nipples and then her throat and belly before encircling them. They went to stand on the opposite side of the circle on the floor from the others.

The old woman and the last Indian man took the center and repeated the ritual a third time. Joe raised his eyes as the older woman stripped off her top. No shame there. Her grey hair hung over bony shoulders and her breasts lay wrinkled and low, pointing to the puckering stretchmarks of her belly. The man was first painted with the red star, and he then painted her with the oval. When they finished, instead of walking together, they separated to the two opposite points of the floor symbol. Now there were people at all four corners. The older woman stood at an apex of the star within the circle, and she began to speak.

"We stand at the circle of the lamb and dissect it with the power of the beast. We have eaten of the flesh but are starving for your spirit. We paint ourselves in the blood of the dead and open ourselves to the living force that waits beyond…"

Joe felt a hand on his shoulder and jumped. He turned and it was Cheyenne. She raised her eyebrows in askance. Joe stepped back away from the doorway before speaking.

"I thought you were going to stay up there," he whispered.

"Yeah, but then I find you down here staring at naked old women. What's a girl to think?"

She rolled her eyes. "What the fuck's going on?"

"They've started some kind of ceremony to call the demons."

"How long will it take?" she asked.

He shrugged. "They're all different."

"Well, someone just pulled up in a car outside," she said. "I think it might be Darin."

Joe raised an eyebrow. "This may be about to get interesting."

Cheyenne's hand tightened on his arm. "He'll discover I'm gone, and they might search the place."

"Maybe," Joe whispered. "But I'd bet they'll just try to do their rituals faster. They don't get a selenelion very often."

"Once in a blue moon?"

Joe stifled a laugh. "Exactly."

In the other room, the old woman's voice had raised. Joe put a finger to his lips and crept back to the doorway. She was speaking something in another tongue.

Low and guttural.

It sounded like *"Erbo nachtu alian chi vu sel vistiu gru."*

She repeated it again and again, and then said in English, "We are but flesh for you to savor. We open ourselves to your will. We open ourselves to your pleasure. We open ourselves to you."

They stepped as one to the center of the star within the circle, and put arms around each other's backs, forming a tight circle of flesh in the middle. The old woman held up a jar of the red liquid they had all painted on each other and poured it to the floor in their midst. Then she began chanting something.

"Urgan tel sin oru vey," she said softly at first. She said it a third and fourth time, her voice slowly raising, and then the group began to join her. Soon the mission chapel echoed with those strange, nonsense words.

The group joined hands and lifted them to the air, the chant growing louder. And then...

"Stop!" a voice commanded.

The chanting abruptly halted, and the man with the lunch bags walked down one of the aisles to stand in the midst of the group.

"That's him," Cheyenne whispered. Joe nodded. He recognized the man.

"How dare you interrupt our calling?" the old woman hissed. "You left us. You're not welcome here any longer."

Darin shook his head. "This is a special night," he said. "This place is a special place. We are here because this mission has made the walls between worlds thin. And when the earth stands between the moon and sun, the walls will be at their weakest. We can't waste this night on a simple riding ceremony. I've prepared a ritual that will open the door wide – and not just until dawn."

He paused and looked at each of the participants in the circle before he finished his thought.

"Tonight, we *will* open the door to the Curburide. But this time, it will remain open. Forever."

Chapter 17

"It must be tonight," Elotan demanded. Ariana stirred at the sound of his voice. After he had finished with her, she had somehow fallen asleep, despite the hideous fire that burned her mouth and sex. Perhaps she had not fallen asleep, but into a coma. She felt glued to the bed by her own blood. When she tried to move, her arms and legs felt stuck.

But Elotan didn't let her lie in it any longer. He dragged Ariana out of the bed by her hair.

Ariana gasped at the pain in her scalp. And as she did, she realized that the fire in her mouth was gone. When she opened it to answer him, she found her tongue was sore and tasted foul. But she could speak.

"What do you need to prepare?" he asked.

She took a breath and considered. The rituals she had performed on earth might not apply here. But if you boiled it all down...

"It is really all about energy and focus more than anything," she said. "The candles and blood and other things that we use; I think they are really just a way of keeping the caller focused."

"So what do you need?" Elotan asked again. He shook her as he spoke.

"Candles. Something to draw on the floor. I could use chalk."

"Sulphur?"

"Even better. I will need a knife, obviously. Rope or something to keep our sacrifice immobile."

Ariana thought a moment. She was drawing a blank. What else did she really need besides will, ritual, a sacrifice and a knife?

"You said that there are places where the walls between worlds are thinner. Do you know of any that we could go to?"

Elotan pulled her by the hair, demanding that she follow. He took her back to the door to the holding pit.

"I have a place," he said. Then he opened the door.

The demon gripped her by the neck and pushed her forward, ready to drop her into the sunken room. But then he stopped.

Ariana quickly saw why.

The small room below was empty.

"What?" Elotan yelled. "How?" He bent and confirmed that Alex was gone. The hand on her neck suddenly squeezed, and Ariana toppled forward, thrown through the door. She landed hard, scraping her knee and banging the back of her head on the wall.

Above her Elotan let out a howl of fury, as the door slammed shut, leaving her alone in darkness.

Alex crept slowly down a hallway. The light was yellow and dim. Every doorway seemed hazy, decked in shadow.

"*This is suicide,*" Malachai whispered in her head.

She ignored him. She was on her own here.

"*We can't help you any more than this,*" Matthew had said, after she channeled the power that he and his three friends had granted to pop the lock mechanism on the demon's cage door. "*If they catch us here, they will kill us.*"

"But you're dead," she reminded.

"*They will suck the energy from our souls. There is no return from that; we would cease to exist.*"

"Thank you," she said. "I mean it. Thank you for helping me again."

"*I don't know if we helped you or not,*" Matthew said. "*But you gotta figure it out. Us? We gotta go. Now.*" And with that, his energy, his presence, suddenly disappeared. Alex closed her eyes and for a moment, she could see a long horizon of dark blue mountains and crimson ponds in the distance. She could also see figures turning, beginning to move in her direction. Light shivered and slivered around their forms as if they were not real, but some kind of cinematic special effect. She understood that these were demons, somewhere nearby, picking up on her energy, or Matthew's. And honing in.

She shook away the image, and opened her eyes, moving quickly to the door. If they had "seen" her, they'd be visiting Elotan's house. And she didn't intend to be there when they did. She hoped Matthew found his way out of this horrible place before they set their sights on him.

Alex didn't know where she was going to go, but she wasn't going to just lie there in a pit waiting to be tortured. So she walked. There had to be someplace that she could find here where she could hide, and plan what to do next. There was a dirty light down at the end of the corridor, and she moved towards it, quickly at first, to get away from the demon's door, and then slower as she realized that demons could be lurking in the doorways and halls that she passed.

The important thing was that she walked. And walked. Alex realized that the corridor only kept shifting. She had walked around bends and turns and yet still, the light ahead seemed constant.

That made no sense.

The light should have dimmed and been lost if she'd turned. Yet it was always there, far down the hall. It was as if with every step, the dirty light ahead of her grew one step farther away.

"*Where do you think you're going to go?*" Malachai asked.

"Out into the Curburide city," Alex said. "What do you care?"

"*Things work differently here,*" Malachai said. "*There are no streets in the way you imagine. And there are no maps. You will need to think about where you want to go or you will go nowhere.*"

Alex's legs faltered and stopped. What did he mean? She was in another world, but space was still space... or was it?

She focused on the light ahead that refused to grow closer and considered Malachai's direction. Then she thought about getting to the street outside. Thought hard. Pictured herself getting there. She began to walk again, never taking her eyes from the light. After a moment, she grinned. The light was now noticeably closer.

"Now *that's* magic," she whispered.

In just a few more steps, she was there.

The corridor simply… ended. She walked through the arch and stood in front of a massive building. There were other blocky grey structures to the left and right. It looked as if she were on a city street, only there were no signs or cars. Or movement.

Alex shrugged and began to walk. She couldn't exactly get lost here; she didn't know where she was to begin with. She didn't belong anywhere. As she passed the building she'd exited, she could see that its walls stretched around a city block; they weren't straight, but curved; they jogged and disappeared into a maze of other structures. She couldn't tell where it ended. Just as she couldn't see where this street led. There were buildings that followed, one after the other until it all grew hazy and dim in the distance.

"Where am I?" Alex whispered, partly to herself.

"*Where do you want to be?*" Malachai answered.

"Are you saying I'm just making all this up?" she asked.

"*The Curburide are real,*" he said. "*How you see them… that's not.*"

"Over there," a voice called.

Alex looked to the source. A block or so away, a dark-skinned demon was pointing at her. A handful of others stood behind him in the street. At the voice, their heads shifted as one to catch her in their sights. Alex did the only thing she could think of.

She ran.

Chapter 18

"No Arnie tonight, huh?" Dexie said. It was 1:15 a.m. and they were closing up the bar at the Cowgirl.

Cindy shook her head and then high-fived the other waitress. "There's something to be said for a quiet night."

"Yeah, I'll tell you what you can say – no tips," Dexie said, throwing the hand towel at Cindy.

She caught it, and wiped down her side of the bar before tossing it to the bin. "Well, yeah, there's that. Seemed like nobody was around tonight. I think the band decided to use this as a practice instead of a performance. Did you hear them trying to figure out that Coldplay song?"

Dexie nodded. "Where's the harm? It's not like anyone was on the patio. I think everyone went to bed early so they can get up and see that eclipse in the morning."

"Maybe."

Cindy pulled her purse from under the bar.

"Hopefully tomorrow night will be better, she said, and waved at Dexie and then at Trev as she walked out of the bar and down the bricked outside front patio to the gate. Dexie had just reminded her that she hadn't seen Joe Kieran all night. And why. The early morning breeze caught her and she shivered as she unlocked the car door.

He'd told her he was going to hang out near the old mission and see if anyone turned up to say a Black Mass or whatever demonlovers did on the night of an eclipse. She'd told him he was nuts, but he wasn't having it. He was a reporter, he'd said. This was what he did.

She hadn't bothered to point out that he wasn't working and so there was nobody to write the story for. Even though she barely knew him, she already could tell it wouldn't have made a difference.

Cindy looked up at the moon, currently shining white, bright and full in a cloudless sky. The sky was full of stars, silent and watchful. She hoped they were watching over Joe Kieran right now. She had only known him a couple days, but she liked the guy.

As she started up the car, she thought about swinging past the mission, just to see if she could spot him and make sure he was okay.

"That's idiotic," she told herself. "If you could see him that easily, so could they."

"Stay unseen," she whispered, and pulled out onto Guadalupe Street.

Chapter 19

CHEYENNE HUGGED Joe's back as she peered into the chapel over his shoulder. She pressed close to him not so much to see as to get warm. The jacket was great, but she could feel goosebumps on her thighs. And the jacket wasn't really long enough to stay down over her butt. She kept pulling it, trying not to expose herself, but it kept sliding back up. So standing behind Joe she was not only keeping warm, but avoiding giving him more of a free show than he'd already had.

This was the most fucked up situation she'd ever heard of. It wasn't enough that she'd been kidnapped and locked naked in a basement. Oh no. She had to be kidnapped by some asshole who was somehow in league with a group of Satanists. And then she had to be rescued by a guy who wanted to horn in on their ceremony to talk to spirits? What the fuck?

She wanted to bolt away from the whole deal. Let this guy stand here and watch a bunch of half-naked idiots chanting nonsense if he wanted to. Only trouble was… the only way out was through the pentagram, or whatever that was they were all standing around in the chapel. She was stuck. All she could do was try to stay warm and stay out of sight until the devil worshippers decided to leave. Which apparently was not going to be soon.

Asshole had just shown up and was talking to them about some special thing he wanted to pull tonight. He held one finger up in the air, and disappeared out the front door of the chapel for a minute. When he came back, he had a woman with him.

She was blonde and thin. And her eyes looked like they

were going to pop out of her head. There was duct tape across her mouth and her hands were tied behind her back. Darin was holding her by her hair.

"What makes you think you can keep the door open this way?" the old woman asked him.

"I have the book," he answered. *The Book of the Curburide.* Believe it or not, it was hidden right here, in the chapel by someone. So its power has probably been invoked here before. Maybe that's part of the reason this place has always been a soft spot; a doorway. With the book, and the power of this group, and the sacrifice of the star, we can do more than just offer the Curburide an hour with us. We can take them home."

The old woman shook her head. "How do you know the book is real? There are a million of these kinds of spell books published by posers and fakes."

"It's authentic," he promised. "I wouldn't have planned all this if I wasn't sure."

Darin pushed the woman at the thin guy. "Here Mike, keep a hold of her." The woman looked ready to run, but Darin grabbed her by the elbow. "Don't let go," he cautioned Mike. Then he looked at the Indian guy.

"Telly, come with me."

Joe suddenly pushed away from the wall and grabbed Cheyenne by the arm. They moved quickly back down the hall and halfway up the dark stairs until they were out of sight of the main floor.

"He's going to get the other women," Joe whispered in her ear.

A pang of fear stabbed Cheyenne in the heart.

This was where the shit was going to hit the fan.

Chapter 20

THE STREET BECAME a blur. Grey buildings, sulphur sky. She could smell something burning in the air; it was rich like incense, but flavored with something more bitter. Like clove cigarettes.

Alex ran. In her mind she tried to see. She had always been able to open her inner eye to see the dead. Could she see the Curburide? She turned a corner and stopped, leaning over with her hands on her knees to catch her breath. For a moment, Alex closed her eyes and forced her inner eye to see.

The world was a blue shadow there. Things moved all around her. Clouds? Smoke snakes? Demons? She struggled to see farther into the shadows, and then she saw the lights. Hundreds of pinpoints.

Thousands maybe.

They glowed like stars on the horizon, surrounding her in every direction. But they weren't stars. They shifted and moved, impatient light, looking for something to shine upon. Some of them moved and turned, and she could see the hazy air their light cut through. She realized that all around her, the bright stars were turning away from whatever they were looking at, and trying to focus on her. The beams of light grew closer and closer to her.

"*Close yourself!*" Malachai demanded.

At his voice, Alex abruptly opened her eyes, and the blue shadows faded away. She was on a grey street corner. The horizon was a smoky shade of fire, deep orange and grey mixed and churned. She needed to get off the street. Standing in the open in a world of creatures that fed on her kind was not a good recipe for survival.

She walked, scanning the doorways on either side of the street for some place that looked promising. She didn't know what she was looking for until she saw the stairs leading down. A dark basement entrance to a building that speared up dozens of levels into the brackish moody sky. A place to hole up, if nobody was around.

Alex descended the stairs and found an ornate wooden door at the bottom. It was carved in channels and filigree, the kind of entry you might find on an old mansion or museum. But this door was streaked with mold and pitted with rot. Down here below the street, it was being eaten away by weather and time. She put her hand on the stained bronze of the knob and tried to turn it.

The door opened.

Alex's heart jumped. She actually hadn't expected the door to budge.

She stepped inside, and gently pushed it shut behind her. She stood in a small foyer. Wooden buckets and boxes lay about on the floor, while the walls were covered in long metal tools. She wasn't sure what most of them were for; the handles extended into long twisted blades or wires. One split into two metal rods that appeared to be connected to a mouth. The pulleys ended in a long narrow jawbone pocked with yellowed, pointed teeth. There were gaps where some of the teeth had gone missing, and the spring between the metal rods was rusted.

Alex reached out to touch the handle of the thing, wondering what you did with a jaw on a handle.

Snap!

She jumped back as the teeth clacked shut.

Okay, then. She still couldn't divine the purpose, but she would be careful not to put her hand anyplace near *that* thing.

Alex moved on. The foyer opened into a long narrow room. Some kind of sitting area. There were a couple of easy chairs and tables. The light was very dim but she could see there were piles of stuff everywhere. When she bent to look at what anything was, the objects changed from indistinct shapes of grey to sharper, defined things. But even with definition, the things were no more comprehensible than the shadowed blobs. Bone lattices connected by pulleys and wires. Electronics on tables connected with spaghetti wires to bloated sacks fleshy and sickly pink.

In one wall, there was an opening meant to be a fireplace, though that wasn't its current use. A mantel above it held a row of jars and candles and strangely twined things that draped over the side like misshapen socks hung out to dry. Inside the hole where the fire should be, Alex saw a tower of broken faces. Eye sockets and teeth. A pile of skulls in all shapes and sizes. There could be no fire there; the bones filled the space completely. On one of the chairs nearby, a full human skeleton sat, one arm perched on a small table beside the chair. It looked like a sentinel, waiting for her. Ready to speak with a bony larynx at any moment.

Alex shivered. The room was ghoulish. She moved past it, and found a bigger room beyond. This place was draped in veils. They hung from the ceiling and the walls. Some were dark chocolate, others pale and milk white and others the color of dirty sand. She saw designs painted on some; dragon's heads and geometric symbols. The Greek alphabet. Spiders. Skulls.

A long couch dominated the center of the room. The air was musty here, heavy with age. There was no obvious light source, but still, Alex could dimly see. She walked towards the back of the couch and stopped when she reached it, putting one hand on the back as she looked about. Her fingers touched what seemed to be velvet on the rounded top of the couch back. It felt good to the touch, and she stroked it absently, while looking at the ballooning veils and tapestries that hung everywhere. They were almost suffocating, there were so many. It felt as if they would all fall from their hooks and cover her if she moved the wrong way.

What was this place?

Fingers covered her own and squeezed.

Alex jumped back, but the hand did not let go. She looked down and saw aged fingers, covered in a dusky grey wrinkled skin, veins showing through like buried worms.

"This is my home," a voice whispered, answering her silent question.

Alex yanked her arm back, but the fingers did not release her. "Wait," the voice whispered. "I don't get many visitors here."

The hand gripped her like a vise, and a woman slowly rose from the hidden depths of the couch. Alex tried to pull back, but it was no use. The demonic woman was ancient. Her face was lined like water-stained parchment, all ripples and valleys and divots. She had deep-set eyes, black or brown, Alex couldn't tell. They were dark pits in a hideously lined countenance that still managed to shine with an inner light.

"Tell me how you came to be here," she said.

From the grip on her wrist, Alex knew that it wasn't a request.

"I was brought here," she said. Lame response.

"By who?" the demon asked. Its voice was soft, but it masked a danger that Alex couldn't identify. She could feel it though. She was in terrible danger here. This creature might appear old and feeble, but if Malachai had taught her anything, it was that nothing in the world of the Curburide was really as it seemed.

"A woman who wanted to meet you," Alex said.

"Meet me? I don't think so. I would have heard such a calling," the demon said. Her lips looked like scars.

"Not you, in particular," Alex corrected. "But demons. She wanted to meet all of you."

"And what did she hope would come of that?" the ancient thing asked. It reached out another thin, but solid hand and gripped Alex by the forearm. "Your kind doesn't fare well here," it said. "Although we always enjoy having you."

"I'll just go then," Alex said. She tried to back up again.

The old woman shook her head. "It's not safe for you

out there. As soon as you step outside my door, they'll be on you." The grey curls of the woman shook. "You were looking for someplace to hide out, I know." She smiled, those pale worm lips stretching like salmon yarn. "I wouldn't mind some company, and you could use some food, I'll bet."

As she suggested it, Alex's stomach growled again. It had been a lot of hours, maybe even a day, since she had eaten.

The old woman levered herself off the couch, somehow always keeping one claw hooked around Alex's wrist.

"Come," she demanded, and pulled her towards another door. This one led into a kitchen. But while Alex recognized the basic implements of a kitchen – sink, cabinets, a table – she wasn't sure of the meaning of some of the things that hung from the walls. Like the other rooms, there were many things made of a strange hybrid of bone and metal. Alex wasn't sure what such implements were to be used for. But before she could think too hard about it, the demon pressed her into a chair.

"What is your name, child?" the old woman asked.

"Alex," she answered.

"Strange name for a pretty girl," the demon said. She reached out a long, thin finger and traced the line of Alex's jaw. "A very pretty, brave girl walking down these streets alone."

"It's a nickname," Alex said. "But I like it."

"My name is Helone. I don't like my name much at all. But it's mine. So I suffer through eternity with it."

The old woman turned and reached into one of the cupboards. "I think this will do well for you," she said. When she turned around, she held a bowl full of chopped up... well, it looked like cornflakes. Alex wasn't completely sure.

It didn't matter. She didn't suppose she could exist here forever without some kind of sustenance. So she would try it.

Helone sat down across from her at the small table. She pushed a small pitcher towards Alex. "I can't offer you fresh milk, but this might be a bit like honey for you. It will give you strength."

Alex accepted the handle, and poured it over the cereal. Or whatever it was. The "honey" came out thick and golden black. It smelled like lilac that had begun to die. Sweet, yet vaguely, naggingly charnel.

The gurgling in her stomach helped her ignore the questionable scent, and she spooned the darkened flakes into her mouth, praying that the taste would not make her puke.

"This is... pretty good," she said after the first bite. Her mouth came alive with a blast of citrus and smoky honey and something bitter but well-balanced. It cut through the sweetness and fought the citrus. She could almost taste the flavors fighting with themselves, each piece struggling for dominance.

"What is it?" she asked.

Helone shook her head. "Best you don't know."

Alex stopped with one spoon halfway to her mouth.

The demon smiled. "You need your strength. Take it."

Alex hesitated. And then she thought of lying in the bottom of Elotan's pit, starving.

It might make her sick, but she was going to eat now, while she had the opportunity.

Helone nodded. "You take the opportunities where you can find them," she said.

Alex's chest tightened. It was as if the demon had listened to her thoughts like she was speaking them out loud. Maybe for the demon she had; maybe hearing thoughts was that easy. She thought of shuttering her mind; Gertrude had shown her how to do that a year or more ago, so that she could stop the spirits from hearing her. From responding to her every thought and whim. It got tiresome – and dangerous – to have your every feeling answered.

When her father had understood the ability she had, that hadn't been good. She'd needed to learn how to hide it.

"I don't know how you came to my door," Helone said. "But I'm glad you did. You might be a strong girl, but you would not have survived out there for very long. We are a hungry breed, the Curburide."

"So I've heard," Alex said. She gestured at her bowl. "Are you just fattening me for the kill?"

Helone's dark eyes widened. She looked shocked and hurt. Alex didn't buy it, but she didn't knock it either. She wasn't sure what the game was here, but she didn't trust the old woman. For starters, because she wasn't a woman, regardless of her shape and wrinkles.

"I'm as much a woman as you," the demon whispered, answering Alex's thoughts. *Damnit.* She'd tried to shield herself as well as she knew how.

"But you're Curburide," Alex protested. She aimed to keep the demon answering her public voice as she buried the private.

"And I live here alone," the woman said. "I don't roam with the packs like some wild dog. And..." she paused and looked hard at Alex. "I'm feeding you, not sucking on your bones, aren't I?"

"Thank you," Alex said. "I can't argue with you there."

She shoveled in a couple more bites of the cereal. She desperately wanted to ask what it really was, but part of her knew that she wouldn't really want to know. And there was something else she really wanted to ask.

"Do you know how I can go home?" she asked.

Helone's eyes flashed. "Perhaps the same way you came?"

"I didn't open the door that brought us here," Alex said.

The demon nodded. "That is a problem, then. Let me think on it awhile. In the meantime, you will be safe here."

"But they are looking for me."

Helone nodded. "I'm sure they are. I'm sure the whole city is searching for you right now." She levered herself upright from the chair. Alex could see how bony she was. The skin seemed to hang off her arms in wattles of parchment. Flesh that no longer was supported by substance.

"They can look all they want out there," Helone said. "As long as you are in here, they can't see you. I made sure of that a long time ago. I don't like to be spied on. And my doors are locked tight."

"But I walked right in," Alex pointed out.

Helone nodded. "So you did. But you're not Curburide."

Alex felt herself tremble as the import of that set in. This house was built to let in humans, but not Curburide, who actually lived in this world?

"I choose my company carefully," Helone said. She lifted the empty bowl from in front of Alex and held out a gnarled hand. "Come, you need to rest."

Alex took the old woman's hand, and let herself be led down a hallway near the great room where she'd found Helone. There were a handful of unmarked doors, and Helone pushed one open and let go of Alex's hand.

"You can stay here for as long as you like."

"I'd like to leave tomorrow," Alex said. "I want to go home."

Helone nodded. "I will see what I can come up with. But in the meantime, stay here and stay safe, heh?"

Alex nodded, and stepped into the room. There was a large bed, and a narrow chest of drawers nearby. There were pictures on the wall, but she couldn't quite make them out. The edges of the room seemed faint, as if she'd stepped into a drawing that hadn't quite been finished. A painting not quite ready to be framed.

At the moment, she didn't care. The insanity of the past twenty-four hours overtook her and she laid down on the bed.

"Sleep well," Helone's voice came from far away. Alex was so tired didn't even hear the door close. But she stirred awake for a second and saw that she was alone in the room.

"From one prison to the next," she said.

The sound of an old woman's faraway laughter opened her dreams.

Chapter 21

THERE WERE SCREAMS in the hallway below. Joe felt Cheyenne stiffen next to him. He understood. If it hadn't been for him stumbling on the door to the basement, those screams would have been hers right now.

"Let go of me!" a woman yelled. "I mean it!"

Joe stifled a smile. It wasn't funny, but the girl had no leverage here. She was a prisoner and a couple guys were hustling her through a hallway to where a whole other group of people were waiting to receive her. A stern "I mean it" wasn't going to make anyone suddenly take their hands off her. Sucked to say, but she was pretty much doomed.

A moment later, Joe heard the footsteps pass the doorway to the stairs again, presumably to get the other girls.

Sure enough, that's exactly what they did. In a couple more minutes the hallway resounded with a new struggle. After they passed, Joe put a finger to his lips, made sure that Cheyenne saw him, and then climbed softly back down the stairs.

He peered around the corner there for several minutes, careful to make sure that nobody was still out and about in the hall or basement. Then he slipped around the corner and moved towards the entry to the chapel. There were angered voices coming from there.

"Somebody *let* her out!" Darin yelled. "She couldn't have punched out that door lock on her own."

"What about the wall chains?" someone asked.

"Fuck the wall chains," Darin said. "We need to find her; this ceremony depends on five sacrifices."

One of the women said something. Joe couldn't make it out, but it really set Darin off.

"Are you kidding me? We've been coming here to this abandoned rock heap for the past two years and you've been getting your jollies out by letting the demons play with your pussy all night long before they have to slip back through the door they came in from. And now you're telling me that when we have the opportunity to let them come and be with us all the time, you'd stand on a morality you haven't practiced since you were a kid?"

Joe peered around the corner. Mike and Telly each held a woman by the wrist. Two more lay on the floor in front of them. Joe assumed they were unconscious. He saw why in a moment.

"All right," Darin said. "I can't force anyone to do this. I've got it all set up. It's exactly what we've talked about for years. But whoever doesn't want to be part of it, now's the time. Please leave and let the rest of us do what we came here to do."

Nobody said anything. And then, the woman who had apparently been arguing with him about going through with the ceremony walked to one of the pews and picked up a purse. She looked at the older woman and said, "I'll stop by tomorrow for my other things, okay?"

Sienna nodded, and the woman walked towards the exit.

Darin watched for a moment, and then shook his head. He didn't say a word. But he raised his hand. He was holding something. Joe realized he was aiming.

There was a soft *pfft* and the woman froze. She reached around with one arm to feel the opposite shoulder blade, as if looking for an itch. Joe saw the tranquilizer dart just as the girl registered what it was. She turned around and looked at Darin. Her face was a mask of disbelief and horror.

"You wouldn't," she said.

Darin shrugged.

The woman toppled over and lay unmoving, on the ground.

"I need five." Darin said. "And if you're not one of us, well, then you're one of them."

Darin walked across the chapel and dragged the limp woman back to the circle they'd drawn on the floor. He laid her in the middle of it and pulled a ball of twine from his pocket. Then he pulled her arms above her head and used it to bind her wrists together. He cut the rope with a pocketknife and then bound her ankles. When he was finished, he directed the other men.

"I need them placed along the centers of each arm of the star, feet to the center."

Telly laid his captive down and Darin quickly tied her wrists and ankles and then repeated the same action with the woman Mike held.

Then they dragged the two unconscious girls into position and repeated the action.

"They'll wake up in thirty to forty minutes," Darin said. "I only used enough to keep this simple. We need to have them awake before we start."

"Why?" Telly asked. "What difference does it make?"

"Because it's their fear and pain mixed with our calling that opens the door," Darin said. "Without that, we're just cutting meat. We might as well have brought a side of beef."

One of the girls on the floor that hadn't been tranquilized spoke. Joe was surprised to hear her voice; both women had been strangely quiet through this whole thing. He supposed they'd already screamed themselves out while waiting, chained up downstairs.

"Why are you doing this?" she asked. "We didn't do anything to you."

"No," Darin agreed. "But you're going to do something *for* me. Something amazing."

Chapter 22

ALEX WOKE IN A FOG. She couldn't believe she'd not only slept, but slept *soundly* in a demon's house. But she had. The bed was insanely comfortable; the sheets silky smooth and warm. She'd fallen asleep almost instantly.

But now she stirred, and everything around her seemed dim. Grey. Unfinished. For the first moments when she had opened her eyes, she couldn't remember where she was. And then it had all come back, and she forced her drowsy eyes open wider, taking in the room with more intent.

The place grew sharper as her eyes focused. It was still dark, but she could make out the small table next to her bed, and the chest of drawers across the room. She could also see the pictures on the wall, which she hadn't really paid attention to the night before. There were five of them around the room and each looked to be a photo taken out of a fairy tale. In one, a young girl in a blue dress sat eating a bowl of something at a table. Behind her, a dark-skinned woman stood; a demon. Her hands hovered just above the child's shoulders, six fingers long and curled, as if she were giving the girl a backrub from six inches away. The demon smiled, but not in a happy way. She looked… hungry.

In another picture, a boy child lay in a huge four-poster bed, with a silk top and pillows piled two deep. He was curled in a ball, sucking his thumb, with eyes wide, staring at the edge of the bed as if waiting any moment for something to appear.

The reason was obvious to the viewer; a demon lay on the floor beneath the bed, head and hands just visible at the opening. The demon's arms were spread, as if it were embracing the child from three feet away.

She recognized the story behind the third painting instantly. Two children stood inside a cottage room, each holding lollipops and smiling at each other. The room was made all of candy; the doorframes were chocolate bars, the sink spout, a hook of peppermint. The table looked like gingerbread and the floors were poured peanut brittle. A demon was once again in the center of it all, an old crone with a jutting chin and a warty nose. She pried a gumdrop off the window sill with one hand, while offering a candy cane to the children with the other. Alex noticed again, that she had six fingers, and that the nails on each were long and black. Sharp and dangerous.

"You're awake at last!"

Helone's voice startled her. The demon stood in the doorway. Alex could barely believe she stood; she looked emaciated beyond life, the skin shrunken to clutch her very bones. But her face at least looked to have a little more animation in it than yesterday. When Alex had first found her on the couch, the demon's face had looked like death, sunken and pale. Now the creature looked more alive; its eyes beamed with energy.

"I'm just happy to have company again," Helone said, answering her thoughts. Alex quailed. She had to remember to shutter her mind here. The Curburide could hear her thinking easily, if she wasn't careful.

"Thank you for taking me in," Alex said. Silently she added, "And not eating me."

"Not all Curburide are the same," Helone said. "Anymore than all humans."

"Well, thanks. And good morning!" Alex said.

The demon's lips parted, revealing a row of thin, yellowed teeth. Alex realized the old woman was smiling as she shook her head.

"Oh no, child," Helone said. "It's not morning yet. You slept through the afternoon. It's past time for dinner."

"Oh!" Alex said. "Everything's so dark, I thought it was night."

Helone shook her head. "When your castle has no windows, it can be whenever you want it to be. But right now, outside these walls, it is evening. A very special evening, in fact."

Alex sat up in the bed, and swung her feet over the side. "What's the occasion?"

"The planets are aligned," Helone said. "This is a night when the walls between worlds are thin. For a little time, we can enter your world, and enjoy the pleasures of your flesh."

Alex felt her heart leap. If the Curburide could get to Earth tonight, perhaps, so could she.

"How do they get there?" she asked. "I mean, how do the Curburide get through the walls?"

Helone smiled, thinly. "I know what you're thinking, but I don't think tonight is the time for you. There are places we know, where doors sometimes open on nights like this. But they must be opened by humans, and they only stay open a little while. So on nights like tonight, the Curburide gather, and watch the places where we know the walls are thin."

Helone held out her hand, to help Alex off the bed. "You would never get near any of the doorways tonight," she said. "You'd be eaten alive before you even got close."

Alex's heart sank as fast as it had leapt. "Then, how will I ever get through, if all the doors are watched every time they might be opened?"

Helone didn't answer immediately, but instead led Alex out of the room, through the dark, and back into the kitchen. The table was set with blue china, and something steamed from a bowl set in the center.

"Don't fret about going home right now," Helone said. "I've made you a nice dinner to help get your strength up."

"But," Alex began.

Helone pressed a bony finger to her lips. "You're human. I think you might be able to open a door home from one of the thin places when we don't have every Curburide in the world standing around watching them. But you'll need to be strong."

Alex considered that, as Helone pulled out a chair for her and pressed her into it.

"Sit," the demon commanded. "Eat."

Chapter 23

ARIANA WOKE IN THE DARK. She lay curled and stiff on a cold hard floor. Her bladder was achingly, painfully full. She stretched and remembered.

It wasn't just her bladder that was in pain. It was *everything* inside her from the delta of her inner thighs to her belly button. She'd been screwed and shredded inside at the same time. She reached a hand down to explore. How bad was it? Could she walk? Was she hemorrhaging?

Her fingers traced plenty of rough trails along her inner thighs. Dried blood. But she encountered nothing wet. That didn't mean she wasn't mortally injured from inner perforations, but it was a good sign, she thought.

She pressed gently on the outer bits of her sex and winced. It might not be bleeding now, but it sure had been. She pushed up from the ground to get to her knees and opened her mouth to gasp from the shooting pains inside. But the action only opened a new cauldron of hurt. As soon as the moan left her mouth it doubled in volume to become a cry of unexpected pain. Her mouth.

Her mouth was still raw and bloody. she felt it warm with new blood as she opened it.

"Oh, fuck me," she whispered.

As if on cue, the door above her opened. Elotan.

"Thanks for the invitation," the demon said, and a hand reached down and grabbed her by the hair, hauling her up the chute again. She cried out at both the new pain and the old wounds, and the demon laughed in a low, dangerous rumble. He held her out in front of him, and traced a long, dark fingernail down from the sore, bite-marked tip of her right nipple to her belly button.

"I've been looking for your friend for hours," he growled. "Unfortunately, I'm not the only one. There are many others here who felt the two of you come through the door. I had to stop finally, because everyone is getting ready for tonight. There are too many eyes open right now. I don't think she was caught yet; word would have spread. Unless she was grabbed by someone like me."

"What do you mean?" Ariana asked. She could barely understand her own words. They came out in a slur.

"Let's just say, I don't play well with others," the demon said.

The look in his eyes suggested that she not ask any further questions about that.

"However," he continued, still pawing her. "I find that I do play very well with you."

He slipped a silken steel arm around her waist and lifted her easily from the ground, like he was picking up a sack. Then he moved towards the bedroom.

"No," Ariana cried out. "I can't, not again."

Elotan tossed her easily on the bed. "Oh darling," he said, climbing in after her. "You absolutely can. We've only just begun."

His barbed tongue stifled her scream.

Chapter 24

CINDY KNEW it was stupid. She barely knew this guy. She'd talked to him a few nights at the Cowgirl and then taken him home. So what was she doing? She'd known him less than a week and now she was chasing after him? Following him?

It was two in the frikkin' morning. What kind of stalker behavior was that?

She argued all this in her head as she continued to drive steadily down the Old Santa Fe Trail towards the Birchmir Mission. The wheels hummed steady, soothingly on the open road and Cindy yawned.

A big one.

The moon was bright tonight; she wondered what it would be like in a couple hours when the big eclipse happened. It sounded like it would be cool to see, if she could stay awake.

Speaking of which, she hoped Joe hadn't fallen asleep out in the desert behind the old mission. You never knew what might come wandering the plains after dark.

Cindy shook her head. "You stupid bar bitch, when are you going to learn?" she said out loud in the car. "Drinkers get drunk and drifters drift. You might take one of them home once in awhile, but not to keep. You sure don't take either of them home to mama."

She flipped her right turn signal on and eased onto the road that led a quarter mile into the sagebrush to the old mission.

She could see a bunch of cars parked outside of its doors as she approached. So Arnie had been right about that. Whether they were partiers or Satan worshippers she didn't know, but there absolutely was a group of people who definitely didn't belong here at this abandoned place in the middle of the night. This was not supposed to be an "active" public property.

There didn't appear to be anyone outside. She killed the headlights just the same, and slowed the car to a crawl. She didn't really have a plan; she certainly wasn't going to try to crash the party and go inside.

Cindy let the car roll up the last few yards of the drive and put it in park near where the rest of the vehicles were parked. She got out, and closed the door slowly. Quietly.

Her eyes scanned the front of the building and then looked out into the desert, where she knew he had planned to hole up and watch.

"Stakeout," he'd said. Reminded her of *Magnum, P.I.* or something. She snorted. Joe didn't really look like the P.I. type to her. Whatever that was.

She couldn't see the motorbike he'd rented, anywhere. Probably around back, somewhere. Maybe that's where he still was.

Or maybe not.

Eventually, he would need to leave the dirt and follow the devil worshippers inside if he was going to see anything. Had he already done that? Had they discovered he was spying on them? Cindy ran one hand nervously over the hood of her car and shook her head.

"Where are you now, Joe?" she murmured.

Chapter 25

"WE HAVE TO DO something," Cheyenne whispered in Joe's ear. Her hand squeezed his arm to punctuate her demand. In front of them, five women lay like the spokes of a wheel inside the circle of white that had been drawn on the chapel floor. Their bodies gave substance to each triangle that formed the points of the star within the circle. Three of them remained unconscious. All were naked and tied.

Darin had pulled the demon callers off to one side to talk. They all sat or stood around him on one of the remaining wooden pews.

Joe stepped backwards, urging Cheyenne to do the same. He nodded towards the stairway to the turret, and then quickly moved across the hall and up the stairs. He didn't stop climbing until they reached the fresh breeze of the night. Cheyenne followed him to the wall. The ground below looked like a parking lot, with a half dozen cars pulled up alongside each other.

He spotted Darin's beat-up silver Ford right away. The rest of the landscape was empty of any evidence that humans might be nearby. They were alone in the "outback" with a group of devil worshippers, no weapon, and in Cheyenne's case, no clothes.

"I can't take down seven people with my fists," Joe finally said, turning toward Cheyenne. "I don't want to see anyone hurt any more than you do," he said. She cut him off.

"They're not going to be hurt, he's going to slaughter them," she said. "We're really just going to sit there in the doorway and watch?" Her voice began to rise above a whisper, and Joe put a finger to his lips. Cheyenne rolled her eyes and hissed. "Seriously?"

"What would you like me to do?" Joe asked. "Are you a black belt in karate or something?"

"You think I can't help?" she asked. Cheyenne put her hands on her hips in anger, forgetting for a moment that she wasn't wearing pants. The sight was a little comical, even in the tenseness of the moment, and Joe couldn't stifle a faint smile.

"Oh no, I'm just a stupid girl who got herself caught and needed the big boy to come help me, right?" Cheyenne opened her eyes wide and stared hard at Joe, daring him to answer her. "Never mind that I managed to get my chain out of the wall and my ass out of a locked cell without your big boy help."

Joe put up a hand. "Look," he said. "You want to run through the center of the chapel and get picked off by your friend's tranquilizer darts, be my guest, but I'm not…"

"No," she said. "Of course you're not. You came out here to see some blood sacrifice and talk to the demons who show up to lick up the pain. Of course you're not going to do anything to stop this."

"You're not being…" Joe began, and then stopped. Cheyenne shook her head and walked the two steps to the other side of the adobe tower and slid to the ground with her back against the short wall. She pulled her knees up so he couldn't see what he shouldn't see, and hung her head down so that he couldn't see her face anymore either.

He let her be for the moment. She had him dead to rights on the last part. He had come out here, knowing if it was really the scene that Arnie had said it was, that someone was probably going to die. He hadn't honestly processed it in his head that way, but it was true. He knew how the game worked. He knew what Ariana had done in her ritual sacrifices to let the Curburide come.

People died.

He had not come out here with any intention of stopping it. He wanted to use it for his own purposes. Sure, they were arguably "noble" purposes, but was the death of five women downstairs worth the life of a single teenaged girl who might or might not still be alive in a realm ruled by demons?

When you thought of it like that, well, Joe Kieran sucked.

He shook his head. What could he say?

Joe looked over the turret at the empty landscape beyond. The beauty of the night sky slipped like a rich blanket beyond the shadows of the hills to the west. Dots of black darkened the hills where bushes and small shrubs and sagebrush somehow clung to life on the arid soil. Life was tenacious, and precious. He felt a chill as he thought of how easy it would be to die out there, wandering around in the hills for days. Even if you weren't killed by the summer sun, what would you eat? Could you find your way to a small creek that actually had not dried up for the season? Or could you wander for miles in the right direction and find the Rio Grande? It always ran.

He would die if he was lost out there. The thought chilled him.

Joe didn't want to die.

He didn't have any right to let anyone else die either, not if he could do something about it.

But if he broke up what was happening downstairs, he might never see Alex again.

Back to Argument Ground Zero.

Joe closed his eyes and thought of her hair, crazy and red, before she'd dyed it to disguise her identity as they drove across Colorado. He remembered the lilt of her laugh and the infectiousness of her smile.

He was dying to see her again.

But he couldn't let five women downstairs die *for* her. He took a deep breath and swallowed hard, pushing Alex's grin from his mind. Not here. Not today.

"We can't take down six people on our own," Joe said. Cheyenne didn't look up from her knees.

"But we can try to get help from people who can."

She looked up then and met his gaze.

"Don't do it for me," she said.

"I'm not," he said. "*We* will do it for them."

She nodded. "So what's your plan?"

Joe grinned. "You're the industrious one. I was hoping you'd handle that part."

Cheyenne rolled her eyes. "Figures."

"Hey, you said you didn't want me playing big shot hero. So I'm leaving that part to you. You can have all the credit."

"Uh-huh." She pushed herself back up to her feet and walked over to where he stood. Looking past his shoulder, she said, "I don't suppose we can climb down from here."

Joe shook his head. "Our only way out is through that room. We will have to go right out the front doors."

"Do you have a car out there?" she asked.

He shook his head. "Motorbike. Out back. Down the hill out of sight."

"Some rescuer you are. You expect me to double you on a motorbike? Seriously?"

"Would you rather walk?"

Cheyenne raised an eyebrow. "Good point."

"You still want to do this?"

Cheyenne gave him a glare. "I'm not going to sit here and watch these freaks kill five women and not do anything. I still can't believe you'd consider it."

Joe felt his heart contract at that. He hadn't really planned to watch a murder. Or multiple murders. He wasn't *that* cold. It hurt to think someone would think that about him. But then he considered the past women in his life. They probably would all have had similar things to say. His past relationships had not ended well. Joe shrugged. Maybe there was a reason he was a reporter who had no home and no newspaper.

"I didn't come out here to watch people be killed," he said. "I just want you to know that. I did come out here to try to save a really cool girl by capitalizing on the stupid shit these people are doing downstairs. But I didn't come out here to watch murder. I mean that."

He shook his head and started talking again, before she could interrupt. "Now. As for what we can do? Not a lot. I don't think we can knock out all six of them and untie the girls and all run away. But you and I can try to make a dash for it out the front door, down the hill, get my bike going, and head down the road a mile or two until we can find a phone and call the police."

"You're not going to do any Quentin Tarantino roundabouts and take a couple of them out while we go by?"

Joe shrugged. "I'll leave that to you."

"Figures."

"You're not wearing jeans, it will be easier for you."

She slapped him across the back of the head. "I'm having second thoughts about letting you rescue me."

"Too late," he said.

"We're not out of here yet."

"Point taken. And the longer we stay up here…"

Cheyenne nodded. "So, I'll follow you?"

Joe nodded. "Here's the plan. It's really simple. Run fast. Cuz I will."

When they reached the entryway to the chapel, the ceremony looked ready to begin. Darin stood at the center of the circle, while Sienna stood at the top point of the star. Mike and Telly stood at the east/west points of the circle, while the Indian girl stood at the bottom. All of them held knives.

"They may not have guns, but they are armed," Joe said. "Are you sure you can run outside without shoes?"

Cheyenne nodded. She'd do what she had to do.

"Then," Joe began, and looked quickly back at the room. "No time like the present!"

Joe took a breath, let it out, and then looked at Cheyenne. Her eyes met his and didn't blink. She was waiting for him to make the move.

He ran.

"Hey, stop!" a voice called out, but Joe didn't slow. He crossed the open area between the altar and the handful of broken pews in the back half of the chapel, and kept going, not looking back to see what the demon callers were doing. He could sense Cheyenne right behind him. They were committed now. He just needed to get out of this building. Joe hit the front door of the chapel and slammed it open with his hands and his weight as behind him someone yelled, "Wait, hey!"

Cheyenne darted past him as soon as he cracked the door and he rolled his body off of it and outside as soon as she did. It closed instantly behind them.

"This way," he called, and dashed as fast as he could to the side of the hill where the bike was concealed.

"Hurry!" Cheyenne said.

Joe ran down hill in the dark, catching his foot on a rock and stumbling, but refusing to tumble. For a moment he panicked, thinking that he should have seen the bike already. If they overran it…

But then he saw the glint of its chrome in the moonlight, nestled under his quick camouflage. Joe darted towards it, and almost lost his balance again as he skidded to a stop in the loose earth next to it. He pulled it upright as Cheyenne caught up to him. Joe threw one leg over the bike and she joined him, putting both hands around his waist.

"You call this a bike?" she complained.

"You're welcome to hitchhike," he said, fumbling with the keys from his pants pocket. And then he had the key in the ignition, the engine coughed to life and they were slaloming up the hill.

"I think we got this," he said, as they crested the hill and veered onto the asphalt circle in front of the mission.

"He's out here!" Cheyenne screamed in his ear.

Joe stole a glance to the side and saw Darin standing outside the double doors of the old building. The old woman stood by him as Mike, Telly and the younger woman ran towards the bike.

"I got this," Joe promised, and kicked one foot hard on the gas as soon as they reached the pavement.

"He's got the gun," Cheyenne warned.

The bike caught the traction and shot forward, at the same time as something cold shot Joe in the neck.

"Oh shit," he said, hoping against hope that the prick wasn't from the prick he thought it was.

But it was.

He felt the ice slipping through his veins and his head grew instantly heavy. Behind him Cheyenne's arms gripped him tighter.

He was about to ask if she could drive when Cheyenne announced, "He shot me with a dart."

They had just reached the turn onto the main road. If Joe kept going, they would topple the bike on the middle of the asphalt in the next minute, and both of them would be out cold, lying in the middle of the road.

"Shit," Joe said, and took his foot off the accelerator.

Chapter 26

"Is this hell?" Alex asked.

She spooned a dark-looking stew into her mouth, and intentionally refrained from asking what the chunky bits were. She needed sustenance, and it didn't taste bad. She'd decided that the fact that it didn't taste vile was all she needed to know right now about what the demon was feeding her.

Helone laughed. It was a slow, aged laugh, and lasted many seconds until the demon shook her head and leveled her eyes at Alex.

"Is your world heaven?" Helone asked.

"Hardly," Alex said, thinking of the torture her parents had put her through. They had been hardcore religious nuts, and her father, in particular, had never been able to stomach the fact that she could see and talk to the dead. He'd spanked her for the talent, grounded her, threatened her and then finally tied her up for flogging in their basement. He would have killed her to "save her soul" ultimately, if she hadn't turned the tables. No, Earth was hardly heaven.

Helone nodded. "This may seem hellish to you, and your world seems like nirvana to us. But for those who live there, no. They are neither heaven nor hell. They're just home."

"Why do the Curburide want to leave here so badly then?" Alex asked.

Helone nodded at the bowl in front of Alex. "That's easy," she said. "Your world is like a candy store. Millions and billions of people, all of them just waiting to be picked."

"So I'm just food to you," Alex said. "You're just fattening me up right now, like in the Hansel and Gretel fairy tale in that painting in my room." The food in front of her suddenly seemed less palatable.

Helone arched one eyebrow. "I'm not going to cut you up and cook you," she said. "We are not like that."

"Then what are you like?" Alex asked. "Demons don't have a very good reputation in our world, although there always seem to be idiots who want to contact them."

"We can help those that interest us," Helone said. "In your world, we have power that your people desire. And you have energy that we need. Our power wouldn't exist without it. That's what we feed on."

"What do you mean?"

"We gain strength from the energy of your emotions. The more primal the emotion, the better."

"So when demons manage to find a door and come to Earth, you rape and kill… to eat?"

Helone nodded. "That's the easiest way to release your energy. You're most open to the Curburide when you're in the midst of passion – whether from fear, pain or sexual intercourse."

"You play with your food," Alex said.

The demoness shrugged.

"My mother always told me not to do that," Alex said.

Helone laughed. "*Your* food is dead. There's no point in playing with it."

"Are you feeding off me now?" Alex asked.

"Look at my hand," Helone said. She extended it across the table.

The skin was wrinkled and thin. But the demon's fingers looked fuller than earlier, when Helone had first clutched the back of the couch and sat up.

"You can see the difference already."

Alex nodded. "So you don't have to kill to feed from us."

"No, but we have to be able to be around you for a long period. And most of the time when we have access to your world, it is only for moments or a couple hours."

"What do you do when you can't feed on us?" Alex asked.

"We have creatures here that we feed on, and we open doorways to other places, too," Helone said. "We're not dependent on humans for food. You are a novelty. A dessert. Many Curburide will never even have the chance to taste human energy."

"But you have before?" Alex asked.

Helone nodded.

"Have you ever had other humans right here, in your house?"

Helone nodded again. But she didn't elaborate.

Alex thought of the skulls and bones she had seen when she had first entered the house. A chill traced her spine.

"Have you ever let one of them leave?"

Helone's eyes flashed. She clearly didn't want to follow this line of conversation. "There have been some."

Alex took a breath and felt her face burn, as she braved the question she had to ask. "Will you let me leave?"

The demon stood up, and walked to the kitchen sink with Alex's bowl.

"Perhaps," Helone said. "We'll have to see how things go."

"What can I do to convince you?" Alex asked softly.

"Just be yourself," Helone said. "Keep me company for a while, and we will see."

Chapter 27

JOE HEARD VOICES somewhere close. But they were voices speaking nonsense. Or at least a language that he couldn't understand. None of the syllables made sense. His eyes felt glued shut, too heavy or stuck to try to open. But when someone screamed, he broke the seal. His eyes shot open and he saw a nightmare before him.

He was back in the mission chapel, lying on the floor. The scene was blurry at first, fuzzy yellow as he struggled to focus. The air was thick with incense and his head still felt foggy from the drug. In front of him was the ritual circle. The five captive women remained there, but now they were clearly all awake. They struggled against their bonds, rolling and writhing on the floor as their captors periodically used their feet to push them back into their places within the arms of the inner star. And their captors were all as naked as they were, spread out around the circle and chanting in unison with Darin and Sienna. The two stood together at the center of the circle, with the feet of the women all pointing at them.

Joe tried to sit up and realized that he couldn't move his arms or legs easily. His wrists and ankles were tied. Just like the women in front of him. He hadn't ended up as one of the sacrifices, but he didn't have much choice but to watch the murders unfold.

Where was Cheyenne?

He turned his head away from the ritual, and saw her. She lay right next to him, wrists tied and lying still on her belly. They had removed his jacket from her so she lay naked, just like the other women. Her skin was pale; he could see the goosebumps on her shoulder. He realized he was cold himself, and it finally occurred to him that they'd stripped him as well. What the hell.

They had plans for him. He didn't know what, but he guessed he was now to be part of the proceedings, somehow, not a bystander. He was still outside the ritual circle, so he guessed that was a good thing. Maybe. At least he wasn't going to be sacrificed.

The chanting continued, over and over. It sounded tribal. It had a rhythm Joe imagined the chants of ancient druids had. Strong and guttural. But lulling too. Sienna and Darin said the first half: *"Kibu Ana Baten Sa."* And their followers responded with, *"Childis Mota Sien Ra."*

Over and over they chanted, as the women on the floor begged for mercy. "Please don't do this," one of them cried over and over. "I have kids," another said. "Don't kill their mama." They received no answer. Mike and Telly stood with their feet on either side of their victim's heads, holding the women in place with their ankles.

"Cheyenne," Joe whispered. He was only a foot or two away, so he used his feet and butt to slowly inchworm a little closer to her. When their hips touched, he tapped his feet against hers. "Cheyenne, wake up," he whispered in her ear. The chanting kept the group from hearing him. He hoped they wouldn't notice that he'd scooted closer to her.

Finally, he saw her chest rise in a deeper breath, and her head shifted. She was stirring. When she opened her eyes and they met his own, he smiled with relief. Cheyenne blinked a few times and then looked past his head to see what was going on in the center of the room.

"Some rescue," she whispered.

Joe raised an eyebrow. "You get what you pay for," he answered.

She moved her arms, testing the bindings. Joe realized that the wrist cuff and chain from her cell below ground had been removed. Replaced by a new restraint. "Too tight," she said finally.

Joe nodded after testing his own as well. There was no give in the twine. In fact, he realized his fingers felt a bit numb.

The chanting suddenly ceased, and the room was silent.

"Now we offer the blood of our hearts for the soul of the Curburide," Sienna said, raising a silver blade high in the air. The others did the same, and then brought the knives down, in a slow, careful arc until the blades met their bare chests. The smooth cleft of the Indian woman's butt was closest to him, as she faced the center of the circle, focused on Darin and Sienna.

But Joe could see Telly clearly as he moved his knife. The big man stood on the opposite side of the circle from him, and as soon as the blade touched the man's nearly hairless chest, the blood sprang up. A trail quickly ran down his sternum, and then hung at his bellybutton before finally dripping down onto the shriveled retracted head of his penis. Joe couldn't help but muse that either Telly was simply not aroused by the current proceedings, or he wasn't much to speak of in bed.

"We offer our blood to you," Sienna continued, "but not only that."

All of the captors held their knives out in front of them in unison, tips pointed towards the center of the ritual circle. And then they knelt, their knees on either side of their sacrifice's heads, and placed the blades at straight out. Joe could see that the Indian woman's blade nearly touched her intended victim's bellybutton.

"*Obi dai sra vamen ki!*" Sienna said. The group answered her with the same words.

They said it again, and again, slowly drawing their knives up from belly to breast of their sacrifices.

"No, please!" one woman screamed. One simply cried, while another called her captor names. "Get off of me you fucking asshole," she yelled. But the chanting didn't waver.

"Taste our blood with theirs," Darin said.

"A communion unholy," Sienna answered. As she did,

Telly and Mike and the Indian girl all moved from their sacrifice's heads to their feet. They crawled up and over the women then, draping their bodies atop the bound women on the floor. Darin left Sienna's side and draped himself over the body of one of the women.

"We offer our blood to you," Sienna intoned. "We offer our passion. Show them our passion my children. *Umu dos.*"

Mike and Telly and the rest answered her. "*Umu dos.*"

Sienna called the words again.

Again the group answered. The words became a call and response chant between their leader and those on the ground. It took on a sexual, erotic rhythm as the hips of the demon callers began to shift and grind atop their sacrifices. Joe could see the smooth rump of the Indian woman rising and falling in the air above the blonde she lay on top of. Her body moved slowly, serpentine. Her long, straight black hair draped over her face, obscuring her features, but when he caught a glimpse of her eyes, he could see they were slitted, her gaze distant.

The woman beneath her struggled, trying to roll one way or the other, but the Indian girl kept her pinned. She leaned her chest in to press against her captive's, and came up each time with more and more blood smeared across small slope of her breasts.

Cheyenne broke his prurient fascination with the ritualistic rutting.

"Joe," she hissed.

He turned away from the lurid scene and saw her lifting both eyebrows – in essence, pointing with her face and eyes.

"Look on the pew over there."

There was a familiar pair of jeans rumpled up, along with shoes and a shirt. "My clothes?" he asked.

"Next to them."

He raised his head slightly from the ground and saw what she was talking about. The ball of twine sat there, along with a box cutter.

The pew was just a few feet away, but getting to it would

be a trick. Even in their current orgiastic state, one of the demon callers was bound to see him get up. And with his hands tied, he wasn't going to be able to use the blade very easily or quickly regardless.

"Roll towards me on your side," Cheyenne whispered.

He did as she asked, and instantly felt cool fingers on his wrist.

"Try to watch them," she said. "It will be less obvious if you're not looking at me. Tell me if anyone starts looking at us."

He tried to arch his back so that his hips faced her while his head tilted up. He could stare straight up at the dim ceiling of the chapel, or force his gaze sidelong to see the sacrificial circle.

"Nobody's paying attention right now," he whispered. "Sienna has her eyes closed. The rest are... busy."

The intensity of the chant was slowly growing, the words accompanied by groans and gasps and as Joe spied around the circle, he could see that the men were no longer "simulating" sexual excitement. They raised their hips high above the women, and then speared themselves down. He caught a glimpse of Telly, and saw the big man no longer appeared to be hung like a boy. His shriveled sex had unfurled and he was, if not hung like a horse, certainly long enough to do the job.

He couldn't tell if violation or consummation was their aim, with them still raising their bodies high above the women before slipping their arousal back between their captives' legs.

"*Umu dos. Umu dos.*" The chant continued.

Fingers worked at his wrist.

"How's it going?" he asked after a minute.

"They aren't boy scouts," she whispered back.

"That's good, right?"

"Yes."

A few seconds later, he felt the pressure on his wrists release.

"Got it," she said.

He looked back at her and saw the white of a smile on her face.

"You have a gift for getting out of things," he whispered.

She made a wry face. "That's what all my exes say. Try to do me."

"I thought you didn't want me to..."

"Shut up and untie my hands, asshole. I'll watch the party."

Joe found the knot and began to push the loose strand of rope back through the thick of it. Cheyenne may have been a master at escape, but he had not ever been a boy scout. He sucked at knots.

"What about our feet?" he whispered. "They may not be paying much attention, but they're bound to see if I move down to untie them."

"That's what the knife is for," she hissed.

"That's going to be a little dicey," he said. "They'll definitely see me as soon as I move over there to grab it."

"One step at a time," she answered. "Stop enjoying the view and undo my wrists."

Joe started. He realized with embarrassment that he *had* actually been staring at her chest as he worked on the knot. It was worth the look. He had never been this close to a naked woman before and not been engaged in some sexual exploration with her, so, to not look at the pink nipples just inches from his face with a bit of interest... *Jesus*, he said to himself. *Focus.*

Joe threaded the rope through itself, and then again. It stuck and he squeezed the twine hard between his fingers, trying to give it some tautness. It was a lousy kind of rope for untying, as the hundreds of individual threads that made up the rope split apart easily.

The chanting behind them continued to grow in volume.

"Stop" Cheyenne whispered.

He froze, just as Sienna addressed the group.

"Yes, my children," she intoned. "Give yourselves to them. Give your seed. Give your blood. Give your soul."

"She's looking at everyone," Cheyenne warned.

"I can't roll back to my back," he said. "She'll see my hands are free."

"Just don't move."

One of the women on the floor screamed.

"Yes, that's it, my children," Sienna encouraged. "*Umu dos!*"

The circle responded with a frenzied cry and Sienna's voice raised. "*Umu dos!*"

The group answered, and now there were more cries from the bound women. If the men hadn't been forcing their way inside their captives before, they certainly were now. The cries were no longer of fear, but pain. Joe wondered about the point of the Indian woman's simulated sex; there would be no penetration or "sharing of seed" from that coupling. Ejaculate must not have been critical to the ceremony. Or maybe these idiots were just making it up as they went along.

"Your spirits are raised," Sienna called from the center of the circle. "Your vessels are wanting. Get it done."

Joe kept working on the rope, but whispered, "Seems to be the prevailing sentiment."

"You are an ass."

Joe pulled the twine and looked up to meet Cheyenne's eyes. "Yeah, well, I'm the ass that just untied your hands."

She grinned as the rope slipped off and she flexed her wrists.

"OK," she said. "You're half an ass."

"Half-assed?" Joe whispered. "Yeah, that sounds about right."

"Inch forward," she said. "Just a little at a time. If we can get closer to the bench, when I go for the knife, it will save us a second or two."

He nodded. Slowly, they each began to shift along the floor, inching their way towards the pew with the twine, and the box cutter. The rhythm and the cries behind them escalated. Joe kept an eye on the ceremony, making sure that nobody broke their salacious focus and paid attention to them. It was a low risk. The four men were deep in the throes of fucking now; their asses moved in a steady, brutal rhythm; they were not looking up. The Indian woman was much the same. She had forcibly locked lips with her captive, and now her whole body clung close to the woman on the ground. Joe saw that she had shifted so that could grind her pelvis up and down on one thigh of the woman. Her hair was a black drape that shifted and hid both of their faces.

Sienna, the high priestess of it all, stood naked in the center of the ritual circle, her sagging, wrinkled body not engaged in forced fornication, but she kept one hand moving between her thighs as she held a small book in her hand; presumably the book that described this ritual. Her voice grew stronger and faster as she led the entire group towards violent, obscene orgasm.

No, nobody was going to notice that they had gotten a foot or two closer to one of the pews. Joe inched along with Cheyenne.

"It is time," Sienna called. "Oh, Curburide hear me. Hear us. We call you now from the circle of pain. From the circle of ecstasy. We call you with blood on our hearts and seed in our loins. We call you to open the door and take us as your own. We are your children. We are your servants. We are your lovers. We are your playthings. We offer our passion to you. We offer our bodies. We offer our blood. We offer this sacrifice of sex. As we spill ourselves inside these vessels, we give their lives to you."

While she spoke, Sienna's hand moved faster, more forcefully between her wrinkled, age-spotted thighs and her steady voice broke as she screamed to the room. "Now my children, take them now! Raise your hands to the sky."

Two of the men groaned in undisguised orgasm. At the same time, Mike, Darin, Telly and the other man, as well as the Indian woman right in front of Joe, all reached out to the floor. It was like choreography. A second later they lifted their arms in the air as one. Their hips never stopped moving. The chapel suddenly echoed in screams of terror as it became clear what was about to occur. All of the demon callers held knives above their heads.

"Now," Cheyenne said.

She stopped inching and instead rolled to her hands and knees and pulled herself forward the last five feet in a second. Joe stayed on the floor, but flipped his body around so that his feet pointed at her. Cheyenne picked up the blade from the pew and fingered the trigger to extend the razor. Then she got back close to the ground, and sliced the twine that held Joe's ankles tight.

He felt the pressure on his legs abruptly ease, and then she was pressing the metal handle into his hand.

"They haven't noticed us yet," she said. "Hurry, do me." Before he could say a thing, she added in a whisper, "No comments!"

Joe scooted back until his head was at her calves. Then he held her right leg and slipped the box cutter between her ankles. She helped, putting pressure on the rope, trying to pry her legs apart. He didn't want to cut her, but he needed to be fast. Someone was going to notice what was going on any second now. The chapel echoed with terrified screams as Joe sawed back and forth on the many loops of brown rope around Cheyenne's ankles. The blade bit through the twine easily, loop by loop. And then, in a flash, he was done. Her ankles shot apart.

"With this sacrifice, we call you. We have loved for you. We have killed for you." Sienna called. The screams from the floor grew frenzied. They began loud, but quickly dulled. Their voices sounded as if they came from underwater. Screams became horrible gurgles of pain and fear.

The demon callers had brought the knives down on the necks of the women.

"The circle of blood is drawn!" Sienna said. She continued in another tongue, pronouncing a long guttural passage.

It sounded like a prayer from hell.
"C'thalna sein frunte ung torna metaok, Uma Dos!"
Joe rose to his knees. "Ready?"
Cheyenne nodded. She put her hands on the pew, ready to rise and run.
"Curburide we call you," Sienna said. "Take these feet, take this blood, take these souls."
The demon callers all now held the heads of their victims by the hair, shifting them back and forth. There were slits on both sides of each victim's neck, and blood jetted and spread in a messy but deliberate trail along the outside of the ritual circle. As they moved their sacrifices' heads back and forth, each woman's trail of blood grew closer and closer to the growing river from the next victim. Joe saw the Indian woman connect the line of blood she'd released with her finger to that of Mike's sacrifice. And then he connected his to Telly's.
"Cin Seem un nei, Curburide," Sienna called.
"Cin Seem un nei, Curburide," the group responded.
She called it again, and they repeated. Again and again. Louder and louder.
One of the gurgling cries beneath the chant turned suddenly strange.
Joe swore one of the dying women laughed.
"Yes!" Sienna cried. "I feel you. You are here, you are with us now! At last!"
"Go," Cheyenne said. She grabbed his wrist and pulled and they both stood and launched themselves down the aisle towards the front door of the chapel.
Behind them, laughter erupted. It did not sound happy, or human. It came now from several voices, and grew in volume as Sienna cried out something guttural and loud in the strange language. Her voice sounded different. Almost a dark echo of itself.
Before they reached the door, Sienna finally noticed their flight.
"Stop," she yelled. "Nobody leaves here alone!"

Chapter 28

CINDY SAT IN the parking area of the Birchmir for less than ten minutes before dozing off. She'd gotten back in the car to wait, and only rested her head against the window to bide some time, but the slow night at the Cowgirl had sapped her energy. She closed her eyes for a moment, just to "rest" them. And that was all it took.

She woke up almost two hours later, with her head painfully kinked. "Crap," she whispered, rubbing the back of her neck and looking around. There was no movement outside. But obviously from all the cars, something was still going on inside. Where was Joe? Was he even still here? She decided if he was, that he had to have taken his stakeout indoors. There was no point in sitting out here watching a quiet building all night.

None of your business. It's late. Go home! The voice in her head cautioned, but as usual, she ignored it. She'd wasted enough time just waiting here. She made sure she shut the car door quietly, and then ran across the open ground between where the cars were parked and the mission door.

Joe had said he would be watching the mission from the valley behind the structure, so she walked to the back of the building first. There were a couple small windows, which she stayed away from in case anyone was nearby inside, and then saw the broken one Joe had used to climb into the Birchmir on his first visit. Was that how he'd gotten in tonight too?

Cindy walked away from the old structure and looked out across the plain beyond. While it was the middle of the night, the moon and stars were bright enough that she could see individual plants and trees far out into the expanse. The moon was low on the horizon, getting ready for "the big event" at dawn. She scanned the hillside but didn't see any evidence that Joe was out there. If he was, he should have recognized her by now, and flagged her down.

No, the air held only that gentle quiet of just before dawn. She turned back toward the mission then, and her eye caught on a glint of something shiny on the ground near the front wall. She walked towards it until she could make out the black rubber of a tire. A motorbike. And it didn't look old and rusted and abandoned. Someone had dropped it here recently.

Internally, she nodded to herself. Yep, that had to be the one Joe had rented.

She looked at the windows of the Birchmir wondering how long he'd been inside. Had he been discovered? Was he safe?

A scream broke the slumbering silence.

And another one. And then a chorus. They came from inside the building.

Cindy quickly walked along the wall until she was standing just outside the broken window. With her ear to the opening, she listened, and now could hear the rumble of many voices. They were chanting something, as the screams multiplied.

What the hell? She'd never taken Arnie seriously, but obviously some fucked up shit went on out here. Her mind flashed on the night Joe had come home with her. He'd been so sweet in bed. Kinda funny, but kinda serious too. She could tell he had secrets and a past she was curious about.

What if he was in there and they'd discovered him? She might never get the chance to learn more about Joe.

She put her hands on the sill of the window and decided to see for herself.

Cindy felt around and confirmed that the sill was free of glass, and then she pushed up, and angled her head inside. The room was very dark, but she could make out enough to see that the floor was clear beneath the window. She just needed to slide her body across the sill and land quietly in that empty space. No sweat.

A moment later, she was in, and dusting her hands off on her pants. The chanting and screams were louder inside, and she thought they were picking up in intensity.

She tiptoed across the room and scoped the area beyond. An empty hall. The way to the right was dark. But to the left, there was a glow on the wall at the end. And the voices were definitely coming from that direction. She crept silently down the hall until she reached the end and had no choice but to turn right. The corridor moved past another couple closed doors, before opening onto the chapel. She could tell immediately that's what the big room was; her corridor opened onto a view of an altar.

Cindy hugged the wall that was closest to the interior of the chapel, and eased her way to the edge. When she was close, she pressed one cheek to the cold wall and inched forward until her right eye could see around the edge and into the seating area of the old chapel. She almost lost it, when her vision registered the scene in front of her. At first with all of the nudity, she thought it was an orgy, but then she saw the blood.

An old woman stood naked in the center of an occult symbol drawn on the floor. She was calling out words in a foreign tongue; she seemed to be the high priestess or something. There were white lines drawn inside the circle, but they were obscured by bodies and smears of red. Five women lay inside, spread evenly around the space, their feet all facing the wrinkled priestess. There were others there too, holding the victims down. Four men and a woman. They all held knives. Bloody knives.

The necks of all the women had been slashed, their blood spread in a smeary channel that ran all around the outside ring of the circle. A circle of sacrificial blood.

Cindy pulled her head back from the edge. *Holy shit.* This wasn't just black magic bullshit with mirrors and candles and goats or something. These fuckers were actually *killing* people! Her stomach shrank to the size of a stone. This was not good. She should not be here. Cindy pressed her back against the wall and forced herself to breathe, slow and easy. She hadn't seen Joe in the circle. At least, she didn't think so. But there had been so much blood. Where was he?

Someone inside the chapel began laughing. It barely sounded human. Her skin goose bumped when she heard it. Another laugh joined in a moment later. The screams from the women seemed to be dying down. *Probably because they're dying*, her inner voice said.

The priestess suddenly yelled something that clearly wasn't part of the ritual. "Stop," the old woman commanded. "Nobody leaves here alone!"

What the hell? Cindy thought. She pressed her face to the wall and peered around the corner again, straining to see what the woman was upset about. The five women remained on the floor. They may have all been dead by now. None of them were moving and a couple of them lay with their mouths open wide and eyes unblinking. Their captors all seemed to be still in place as well, though two of them were now standing. Seconds later, they began to run towards the chapel door.

"Let them be," the priestess said. She waved them off. "The Curburide are here. It doesn't matter what they do now, they won't get far."

As the priestess was speaking, a dark-skinned American Indian woman with waist-long black hair stood up. She'd been lying on top of one of the bloody women, and her cocoa-brown chest was now smeared with a more vibrant hue. Cindy realized it wasn't just the blood of the dead woman on the floor that coated her; the Indian girl was also bleeding herself, from a long slash down her middle.

But Cindy only noticed that for a moment. Because as the bloody woman stood, her dark eyes opened wide as if in surprise. She turned her head first left, then right, in oddly fluid motions that looked as if she were a swan, angling her head on a long stalk from side to side. The woman then held her fingers out in front of her, and flexed them slowly, and then faster. She looked as if she'd never seen her own hands before.

Then the woman opened her mouth, and laughed.

Only, it wasn't the sound of a woman laughing. It wasn't even the sound of a man.

That sound couldn't have come from her, Cindy thought. There was no humor in the laugh. It was low and nasty, like a metal grate dragged over nails. Or some kind of animal caught in a trap. The inflection mirrored laughter, but not.

Still, the woman's mouth was moving and the sound matched those motions. The horrible laugh did come from the Indian woman.

What the fuck? Cindy thought.

"Welcome," the old woman said to the laughing girl. "What is your name?"

'the fuck? Cindy thought again.

The Indian woman's eyes seemed to bug out of her head, as her teeth flashed white in a disjointed grin. The horrible laugh stopped and the strange voice said, "Gonorah." It sounded like the guttural noise of someone vomiting.

Next to her, one of the naked men stood up. He had unruly black hair and a pointy nose. Cindy thought his face looked almost birdlike. In a bird of prey kind of way. His chest was also covered with blood, and his penis hung obscenely long and garishly red. A wound of male sex.

"At last," he said, in a voice almost as wrong as the woman's. It sounded sharp, and shrill. "I have been waiting forever."

"You're here now," the old woman answered. "And you won't have to go home after just an hour or two, as they usually do."

Another voice laughed, and another naked man stood up from the floor. He came up behind the priestess and wrapped thick bearlike arms around her wrinkled, sagging belly. The grey thatch of her pubic hair brushed his hand as she shook her backside to rub against him.

"This time, the door will not close," the old woman promised.

Gonorah nodded. She raised both hands in the air and turned in a pirouette. "They are coming," she said. "More and more of us."

The black-haired guy slipped an arm around the curvy waist of the bloody Indian girl, and dragged Gonorah close to him, until her small breasts squashed against his ribs. He leaned in and stuck his tongue in her mouth. Instead of slapping him, she threw her arms around his neck and vaulted herself off the floor, to grind her pelvis on his. Now it was her forcing a pink tongue into the other's mouth.

Cindy pulled away from the opening to flatten her back against the wall. It felt as if her eyes were going to fall out of her head. She didn't know what she was seeing in the other room, but it was anything but normal. It was as if a bunch of murderers had been possessed.

Something cold touched her in the back of the neck, and the chill shot down to the base of her spine like a shock. She gasped.

Someone spoke to her then in a voice like wind through wooden chimes. It was faint but airy. *"That's exactly what has happened,"* the voice said.

"Huh?" Cindy said, partly out loud. As she did, she prayed nobody in the next room heard her.

"They won't pay any attention," the voice said. Suddenly it was louder, and the ice grew solid down her back.

"Who is speaking?" she whispered. "Where are you?" Part of her still expected someone to walk out from around the corner of the hallway to where she could see. But part of her knew better. That part of her was petrified. And rightly so.

"I am Delivida," the wind-voice said. *"And I am as close to you as close can be."*

Cindy tried to push away from the wall… or to raise her arm… and found that she couldn't. She was locked in place.

"I've been waiting a long time for this," Delivida said.

Suddenly Cindy's leg lifted of its own accord. It was as if a puppeteer was above her, pulling the strings.

Or the reins.

"*Let's go for a ride,*" the demon suggested.

Chapter 29

"Have another drink," Helone suggested, and waved Alex across the room. There was a carafe there of something ruby red that slid heavy and rich across the tongue. Alex had already sipped one glass, and her head felt light because of it. Helone had downed three.

"I don't know," Alex said, and the demon's face lit.

"You only live once," Helone answered. "You told me you didn't like to hide from life."

Alex couldn't resist a smile at that. She got up from the smooshy, cushioned chair she'd been in for most of the past three hours and walked over to the carafe with her empty glass.

They had spent most of the evening in the sitting room, Helone lounging on the couch, Alex on the chair. They had talked about all sorts of things, from daily "demon" life to what it was like growing up in Nebraska. Helone had asked her about her talent for talking to spirits, and Alex had shrugged. It was just something that had always been natural for her. Her parents had chalked it up to a child's vivid imagination at first, when she'd sat in corners playing with dolls and jacks and blocks talking animatedly to a person who wasn't there.

Only, it wasn't imagination; the spirits *were* there. Her parents couldn't hear them, but Alex had gathered a handful of ghosts who used to sit with her and play with her every day... until her father had finally decided she wasn't imaginative, but possessed.

After he'd had the house exorcised, her friends hadn't come back. But that hadn't stopped other spirits from drifting into their house in the following years. "I learned not to let him see me talking to them," Alex had told Helone.

The old demon nodded. "I've walked a similar road," she said. "I love humans, and don't want them to be hurt when they're here with me. That's why this house is built the way it is. Nobody can see me talking with you here. Nobody can come inside without my permission."

"Isn't that a normal thing for a house?" Alex had said. She pictured the deadbolts on the front door to her parents' house.

Helone had smiled. "No," she said. "The Curburide move through things like air. We abide by the structures we build, most of the time, simply for comfort. But we're not bound by those things. We go where we wish, see who we wish."

"So what's different about this place?" Alex had asked.

Helone looked around the room before answering. "With age comes privilege, and wisdom," she said. "I've lived a long time. A very long time."

"What is a long time?"

"Your kind were still squatting in caves when I first built this house," Helone had said.

Alex poured herself another glass of the ruby liquor. It was sweet, but heavy. She couldn't have drank it fast if she wanted to; it was overpowering in a gulp. It was meant for sipping. She looked at the old demon, lying sprawled and clearly comfortable on the couch.

What must it be like to live for eternity? A long night like this one was barely a blink to her. And from her stories, she rarely stirred from this place, just walked these rooms week after week, sometimes not even moving from one place for days. It seemed like it would be a prison, even if a comfortable one.

"What was it like to live in a prison with your parents?" Helone asked. Alex hadn't guarded herself enough again. The demon had heard her path of thought.

"It was bad at the end," Alex said. "I just wanted to be left alone."

"So you could do as you pleased. Talk to the spirits who you enjoyed."

Alex nodded.

"If your parents had been different, would you have minded staying in your home?"

Alex shook her head. "No, but that's not the same thing as living there forever. I would have grown older, gone away to college, moved into my own house."

"Where you would have lived for the rest of your life?"

"Maybe, but people usually move around more than that."

"When you can go wherever you want, you find it doesn't matter if you stay in the same place," Helone said.

Alex sat down in the chair and took a sip of the drink. She instantly felt a warm trail light up her esophagus, and a buzz grew in the back of her brain. She'd had beer and wine back in Nebraska with her friends – hiding out after high school in the cornfields with a cooler. But this was different. It was like drinking flowers and honey and fire.

She wondered if Helone would kill her if she surrendered and laid back and let the liquor claim her completely.

"You still don't trust me," Helone whispered.

Damnit.

"I trust you more than some," Alex said.

"More than your father? More than your mother?"

Alex nodded.

"You paid them back for what they did to you."

"It was them or me," Alex said.

Helone made a harrumphing sound. "You had help. You could have just left. You chose to take it further. Perhaps you're not so different from the Curburide that you fear."

"They would have called the police to find me and bring me back," Alex said. "My father would have had his way eventually. I had to put a stop to it once and for all."

"Hmmmm."

Helone closed her eyes, and her head settled farther back into the couch cushions. She didn't say anymore, as her breathing settled into a quiet but steady rhythm.

Why did demons need to breathe? Alex wondered, as she took another sip from the glass.

The room felt strange suddenly, as she mimicked Helone, and laid her head back on the cushions. There were shadows everywhere, from the silken scarves and sheets that draped the ceiling and the walls. And the skulls that leered from the corners of the mantel. Alex closed her eyes for a minute, to clear her head…

…Alex woke with a start. She knew instantly that she'd dozed, not just closed her eyes. But for how long? She looked around the room and nothing had changed; the lighting was still the same, the veils still hung from everywhere above her. She looked at the couch in the center of the room.

It was empty. Helone was gone. Her first thought was that maybe the demon had simply gotten up to go to the bathroom and would be right back.

And then she realized how ridiculous that might be. Did demons pee? She had no idea. They fed on energy… what would they expel as waste? Black clouds?

"I don't wanna know," Alex murmured. She pushed herself up off the couch pillow and stretched. She felt fuzzy. As if she'd awoken from a deep dream, though she couldn't remember dreaming.

She rose from the couch and yawned. Wide. As if she could sleep for a week. After the last few days, maybe she could.

The demon's mantel looked jammed with all sorts of things. What did an ancient being keep for memorabilia? Alex crossed the room to get a closer look. There were things there that she didn't understand. Odd shapes and colors that she couldn't quite get her mind around. One piece seemed to have a sort of Escher-like rainbow of interlocking colors and angles but when she stared hard at it, the shape grew… less clear. She couldn't have described it if you asked her to. In fact, just looking at it made something inside her tremble and quail. Her stomach began to feel nauseous. For a moment, Alex wondered if maybe the liquor that Helone had fed her had messed up her system, but as soon as she dragged her eyes away from the oblong-square-round object, the nausea disappeared.

There were other things on the shelf that she could look at and understand. Candleholders, carved in some kind of creamy stone (or bone?), with tall spears of wax jutting from their centers. They bordered each end of the mantel, next to triads of human skulls. No subtlety in décor there, Alex thought.

There were glass things too; a red vase with some kind of spiny black frond sticking out of it. The thing had dozens of crooked branches, which opened into smaller spines that spread out into a kind of dark web. It was intricate, if not beautiful.

There were many smaller things strewn across the mantel too. A ceramic thimble. A small wooden doll. A leather hair tie with small white and turquoise beads. A faded black and white photo of a woman. A string of pearls. As Alex looked across the mantel beyond the larger things that you could see easily from the chair, she realized that it was like a junk shop; or the top of someone's dresser. Littered with disconnected things that must have meant something to someone, but probably not to Helone. What would a demon want with a tattered book of human poems by Walt Whitman?

Alex reached out to pick up a leather bracelet. But as her fingers brushed it, she stopped. Something moved in the corner of her vision. She froze.

It wasn't Helone; the movement came from above. High off the floor. She turned her head a fraction, then another and cautiously looked up at the ceiling. One of the veils seemed to be fluttering, faintly. Though there was no vent or breeze in the room.

As she stared at it, the motion stilled. A chill ran down

her spine. Something had made that thing move. Something was here with her. She pivoted, and slowly turned, looking all around the room. It was dark, but not so dark that she couldn't make out the floor and corners and couch and walls. The room appeared empty. But what hid behind the hundreds of tapestries and veils that covered every corner of the ceiling?

Alex took a deep breath and looked back to the mantel once more. She refused to show fear to whatever had moved in the room, but she no longer felt very interested in exploring Helone's junk collection. She did still want to look at the bracelet, however. There was a design on it stitched in blue and lavender and she was curious to see what it was. She lifted it in the air to study. And as she looked at the beads, which formed a circle with a transected Y in it – the hippy peace sign – the veil in the corner suddenly rippled and moved. This time, she wasn't shy.

Alex turned towards the movement and called out, "Who's there?"

The gauzy, translucent fabric above twisted, and jutted out from the wall. It looked like a face pressing through a thin sheet. The veils and hangings around it shivered as it pushed past them. Alex took a step back, though the moving veil remained hooked to the ceiling. The face pulled back and the thing went limp again. She realized she'd been holding her breath, and let it out. What the hell was that?

Two hands suddenly pushed through the veil. They reached for her, pulling the veil tight from its anchor. The fingers were still several feet away from her, but she could see them shifting and moving behind the fabric. Struggling to reach out for her. The fingers stretched and contracted, never fully taking the shape of a hand and wrist; the veil didn't wrap tightly around the whole form, but she could see what it was nevertheless. It was like a hand trying to push through a balloon – partly visible, partly outlined.

This is what a ghost really looks like, she thought. Alex had talked to spirits all her life, but they'd always shown themselves to her in human form. They looked normal. Whatever was trying to press its way into the room through the veil was... only partly formed. And malevolent, she was sure.

Alex set the bracelet down, and back-stepped slowly towards the couch. Perhaps it was time to return to the bedroom Helone had set her up in.

The fingers kept reaching and twisting behind the fabric. Silently. It was eerie. Alex took a breath and forced herself to turn away from looking at it. She began to walk towards the doorway, but as she approached, one of the veils on the wall beside the exit billowed out. It was as if someone had just shot an air hose into the center of the thing. This veil was hazy and brown, almost chocolate-colored and had no designs painted on it. But as it expanded, Alex could make out a face clearly, and hands and arms. This one looked more fully formed. She decided she wasn't going to wait to find out what it wanted. The doorway was only three or four steps away. Alex bolted.

The hangings on the top and other side of the exit suddenly came to life, and shot out across the opening. She didn't stop. Alex dove at the doorway.

Arms wrapped around her as she did. Silken fingers grabbed her wrists and ankles and an arm shot around her middle. Her momentum pulled them from their hooks on the wall, and she felt the fabric stretch, but the ghostly arms didn't let go. Alex's motion stopped, and she found herself hanging in the doorway, staring down the hall towards the kitchen and bedroom.

A fly in a web.

"Let go of me," she demanded.

All at once, the fingers did just as she asked. She fell backwards as they did, and landed on the floor on her rump. The veils all around the door now held clearly human shapes. They blocked the exit completely. Instead of limp veils, the fabric had been completely "filled out" and two large men stood there. They folded thick arms across nearly see-through chests. One of them had a dragon tattoo on one bicep. She could see their chins and the dark pits where their eyes were. She could make out the dimples around the larger one's waist, and see the soft outline of his penis, hanging down, unaroused.

It suddenly occurred to her that this form wasn't simply pressing its shape against a veil; it was inhabiting a tapestry whose natural shape included two arms, two legs and a head. The tattoo was... really a tattoo.

She looked at the other figure, and then at the deflated billows of veils that hung all around the room.

"Oh my God," she couldn't help saying aloud.

What she had chalked off as thin tapestries and "veils" weren't veils at all. These were not oddly colored and inked silk decorations.

The room was decorated in hundreds of *human skins*!

And right now, something was re-inhabiting a couple of them. The arms were a perfect fit in the "sleeves" of the hanging. The tapestry was clearly constructed with legs as well.

Suddenly it all made sense. This room was not just Helone's sitting room. This was her trophy room. And Alex was the latest prize.

Fear gripped her heart, and panic overwhelmed her. She was *not* dying in this room! She scrambled to her feet and stared down the two figures that now blocked the door. They had been big men once. But they were skin and air now.

She launched herself at the crack of space in between them, hoping to slide through the gap before they could close on her. She met a balloon wall. The figures closed the gap and Alex didn't even get her hand punched between them.

One of them laughed faintly.

She lay there on the floor and stared up at them. They left her alone. They seemed content to stand there, arms crossed, blocking the way like some kind of ghastly bouncers. Only these bouncers were keeping her in, not kicking her out.

What did they want with her?

"It's not what they want," a voice said behind her.

Damn it, she wasn't closing her mind again. Alex forced the wall up around her mind as she turned towards the voice. A skin fluttered in the back corner of the room, near the fireplace. Alex rolled to her feet and stepped around the couch to face it.

"What do you want?" she asked. Her voice was not friendly.

"What I've always wanted," the voice said. The shivering skin was now filling out; there were stumps for arms and trunks for legs.

"Do you remember when you were just a little girl, maybe four or five?" the skin asked. Alex could now see the outline of a face pressing against the pale skin.

"A little," Alex answered.

"There was one day when you were riding your bicycle outside, and talking to someone invisible."

"I'm sure they weren't invisible to me," Alex said.

The ghost ignored her. "You weren't watching where you were going, and you hit a rock on the pavement. You fell over and scraped your shoulder and knee, and came running to the house."

Alex could see the full shape of the spirit now, from the tight bobs of the curls on its head to the short cut of its fingernails. But like silk stretched over a face, it didn't fit perfectly. There were places around the chin where the material bagged, and the eyeholes in the abandoned skin didn't seem to quite conform to the shape of the woman now inhabiting the skin. But the light of brown eyes did appear within the holes as the voice spoke.

"I was waiting for you," the lips said. "And I told you then, that those demons wouldn't protect you. They'd leave you there on the ground when you stumbled and fell. But I would be there forever. Nobody'd ever love you like I did."

"Mama?" Alex whispered. Her eyes were brimming, but now she could make out the familiar sag of her mother's cheeks and the world-weary look in her eyes.

"Yes, Alexandra," the skin said. It reached up with both arms and pulled at something on the ceiling. She realized a second later that it had detached the skin from its hook when it drifted to the ground before her.

"I will always be your mother," the ghostly thing said. "And a mother's love is forever."

Alex forgot herself and opened her arms to accept her mother's embrace. Tears streamed down her face as she touched the soft skin that her mother's spirit wore. It was not her mother's skin, she knew that. It didn't fit right. But there was solidity behind it. And right now all she wanted was to go back to her mother's arms as she had as a child. She'd been hurt badly. Worse than ever.

"It will all be all right now," the ghost whispered, petting her hair with borrowed fingers. "Mama's here."

A vision of her mother flashed before Alex's eyes. The last time she'd seen her, in the backyard of their home in Nebraska. Her mother's eyes had been open. Her mouth wide from screaming. Her face had been painted in blood. Alex felt her legs grow weak. This was too much.

"I said I'd always love you," her mother said. Her arms pulled Alex tighter. "But that was before you killed me with an axe."

"Mama, I'm sorry," Alex cried. "I'm really, really sorry. I didn't want to do it, but you and dad…"

"So you've found our lost lamb," a deep voice said nearby. Alex lifted her head from her mother's soft shoulder, and saw another skin filling with form nearby. She recognized the derision in the voice instantly.

"Dad?" she said.

"You have lost the right to call me that," the spirit said, stretching one of the arms of its newfound skin. "I renounce you. You are no longer my daughter. You are a murderess. A concubine of the devil."

Alex tried to push out of her mother's embrace and realized that the arms were no longer hugging her, but holding her prisoner.

"Mama let go," she said, struggling. "I didn't want to do it," she said. Tears streamed down her face as her voice cracked. She remembered that horrible day vividly; calling Gertrude and all the spirits who were her friends to help her. She'd been a prisoner in her own basement. Her father had stripped her naked to horsewhip her, and then dressed her in sackcloth to atone. But he had not intended to stop at that. He'd read the stories of the Old Testament too many times. She was going to be his Isaac; a sacrifice to the Lord. He would save her soul from the certain damnation that would come of talking to ghosts, and prove his allegiance to God at the same time.

"You were going to kill me," she screamed. "You were going to kill me and the only choice I had was to kill you first."

She remembered the power surging through her, as her friends shared with her their strength, and Malachai helped guide her hands. She didn't know how it had gone beyond simply escaping and turned into a bloodbath, but she had been filled with a fury that went beyond simple human rage. Beyond what any teenager could handle.

"You had many choices," her father said, stepping forward. "You could have served the Lord as your mother and I did, rather than consort with devils."

"They were not devils," Alex screamed. She beat her fists on the false shoulders of her mother, as the fleeting joy of seeing her mom turned to regret and now quickly anger. "Let go of me!" she demanded. "Gertrude and Matthew and all the rest were good people. You were both just too crazy to see that. The rest of the world knows that to worship God, you don't need to wear sackcloth and give him sacrifices."

"The rest of the world is going to hell," her father said. "But we're here now to finish our job as parents."

"We want to send you to heaven," her mother whispered.

A bolt of heat shot through Alex's belly as she realized her mother wasn't here to comfort her. She drew her leg back and then drove the knee forward, catching her mother in the crotch while pushing away with her hands.

The gambit worked. Alex stumbled backwards as the arms released her. She caught her balance on Helone's couch.

When she straightened up again, her parents stood before her, naked inside stolen skins. It was a horrible thing. She could see scars on her father's chest that she did not think were his, and the sag of her mother's small, empty breasts. She had never seen her parents this way. Despite the heat of the Nebraska summers, her father never took his shirt off. Her mother had always worn dresses.

They advanced on her slowly, and she backed away.

"Why are you doing this?" Alex cried. Her chest was on fire with a war of emotions. For a moment, she had felt a return of all the love and comfort being in her mother's arms had given her as a child. And then in an instant, all of the anger and hatred of her teens had returned. Nothing changed after death; they were still intolerant, evil people hiding beneath the mask of righteousness.

"We are your parents," her father said. "It's our job to raise you right. And part of that job means having the understanding and fortitude to know when to dole out punishment. We're here to do our job."

He rushed forward and Alex ran around the couch, putting its width between them. Her mother and father divided and moved to opposite ends. One of them was going to reach her.

"There's no place for you to go," her mother said.

"You always had to make things difficult," her father added. All at once they both came at her and Alex ran from the back of the couch to the door. But the burly men there wouldn't budge. She slammed against their silky, dead skin and met a solid wall. Her father's hand closed around her arm, and Alex lashed out, punching him hard in the face.

She yanked herself free and darted past her mother to the other side of the room again.

"We can do this all night," her father warned. "We are eternal, and sooner or later, you *will* join us."

Alex edged closer to the fireplace and shook her head. "I don't think so."

Her parents came at her from both sides of the room, but this time, she was ready. Alex grabbed the wrought iron poker for the coals of the fireplace, and stabbed at the chest of her father as he reached for her.

The skin ripped easily, but no blood came. There was none to spill. Her mother's eyes flashed angrily and she leapt forward, trying to take advantage of the moment while Alex was stabbing the tool into the skin worn by her husband. But Alex yanked the poker back and swung it like a bat to connect with her mother's head.

It snapped to the side, but instead of cracking, the skin actually molded itself around the poker, giving way to its mass for a second.

Balloons, Alex thought. *They're just like balloons. There's no blood or real body there. There's nothing really to hurt, just to deflate!*

She grinned, and held the poker in front of her like a spear. "For the last time," she screamed, "Leave. Me. Alone!" And then she lunged, stabbing the spear in and out of her father's chest and belly and groin in rapid succession. He backed off, whether in pain or surprise or just instinct, she couldn't tell, but Alex didn't slow. When he staggered off-guard, she turned the attack on her mother.

"No, pookie, please," the spirit begged, using the nickname she once had called Alex as a child. The word was like a counter stab right back at her heart. Alex cried. The tears almost blinded her. But she didn't stop. She pulled the poker back and then stabbed again, catching her mother in the right breast. The dead skin tore and hung like tissue paper across her mother's wrinkled belly. And that was right where Alex stabbed next.

"Haven't you hurt us enough?" her mother's deceivingly gentle voice asked. The words this time made her slow her attack, but by then, her father had recovered. He leapt back at her, his fingers scrabbling for her elbow even though his chest hung in ribbons. She could clearly see the wall through his middle.

She swung the poker again and caught him in the side of the head. This time though, she didn't simply use it as a bat. As soon as it connected, she yanked it backwards fast, and the hooked arm at the end of the poker dug a trench across his cheek. It tore open the skin from his ear to the side of his mouth. The result was a lopsided, strange visual when his lips tried to move as he yelled, "You've already killed us, what more can you possibly do, you wicked child? I am so ashamed that you are my daughter."

"Murderer," her mother cried, holding her hands across the holes in her chest. She hung her head in shame as her voice wailed, "I raised a murderer."

"Parent killer," her father corrected. "Murderer is too good a name for her. The only thing that could be worse than her crime would be…"

"Stop!" Alex screamed.

"I won't," he continued. "It's time you face the evil of your heart. Have you had abortions too? Are you a parent killer *and* a baby killer?" he asked, holding the skin of his cheek together with one hand so his lips could speak. "How many boys have you prostituted for?"

"Go… back… to hell!" Alex screamed. For a second, she felt a surge of power inside her, the same red flash of rage that had fed her on the day she had taken an axe to her parents in the backyard of their Nebraska home in order to save her own life and escape. That strength fed her again and she lashed out in a sudden fury, slashing the poker back and forth, carving her parents' stolen skins into ragged pale ribbons that finally gave up their false, borrowed forms and collapsed to the ground, empty of animation.

And just like that, her parents were gone again. She had never felt more grateful.

Alex sank to the ground. The shredded skins lay just a couple feet away. They didn't move. She wished with the deepest wish of her heart that they would remain that way. Tears coursed down her cheeks and her chest heaved in deep, out-of-control sobs. The last thing she had ever wanted to relive was the day she had killed her parents. For the past few weeks she had told herself over and over, almost every morning when she woke, that it had been necessary, that it had been the only way. But part of her never fully believed that.

And now she had been forced to do it all over again. Was she really as evil as the Curburide themselves? The tears came so hard she choked.

From behind her, she heard the soft sound of hands clapping.

Alex turned.

The guards had disappeared from the doorway.

Helone stood in their place.

Her skin no longer looked old and parchment thin. She looked younger. Radiant.

She was smiling.

"That was amazing," she said.

The demon traced her black lips with the tip of her tongue, and then laughed.

Chapter 30

ARIANA WOKE in the dark, the sheets soft and warm around her shoulders. Elotan's bed felt different than her own – the coverings lay thicker, heavier; almost like velvet. Her skin felt caressed by every movement. This part of the Curburide's world felt much more like heaven than hell at least. She shifted to roll on her side. As she did, she felt a twinge of pain from her mouth, and also from between her legs. The violation of the night before replayed itself full force in her head, and she moaned in disbelief as she remembered Elotan raking her insides with his demon prick.

What kind of sadistic, misogynistic joke of nature grew barbs on its fucking cock?

Ariana stretched out flat again; it hadn't hurt as much that way. She reached a hand down between her legs to see how seriously she was injured.

As the memories returned, she realized how badly she must have been hurt. She shouldn't even be alive right now. That thing, unfurled inside her, gouging back and forth? It occurred to her that this wakefulness could be a last gasp; maybe these were the last thoughts that she would be having. After what he'd done to her, she might have been bleeding to death here in his bed all night.

But as she slipped her hand down the skin of her belly and then across the rough stubble of hair below, she quickly realized that things had changed since the demon had left her.

She was tentative at first, but then her fingers slipped across the lips of her labia and even pried and tested within.

Nothing was wrong. She felt the same as she always did when she slipped two fingers in to masturbate. Slippery and swollen, but whole.

She remembered being split apart by the penis of the demon, and had seen the blood. But now... No scabs, no wounds. Her skin was soft and her sex unbleeding. She knew that Elotan had been here. Had bedded and shredded her. Had left her sobbing and bleeding in his bed.

All evidence gone.

Her skin was soft and unblemished. And while she'd felt a remnant of pain when she had shifted position on the bed, she realized that after stretching, even that was gone. She felt as if she'd awoken at home after a good night's sleep. She slipped her fingers all the way from her pelvis to her ass and all felt normal. She could feel some of the thick hairs that lay where she never got the razor, and traced them forward until her fingers were suddenly warmly sticky. She pulled them back. She was not ready to lose herself in *that* just yet. She needed to understand where she was.

And how it was that she was not dead.

"Nobody dies here," Elotan said from the doorway, answering her unspoken thought. She felt a chill as she realized he had just listened to her thoughts. So he knew what she'd been thinking as he'd ripped her insides out last night.

The demon grinned. "Yes," he said. "You have a deliciously graphic mind."

"What do you mean, nobody dies?" she asked.

"Nobody dies on earth, either," he said. "But you can't see and can't understand the transition. Here, we are reborn every night. If we are hurt during the day, the next day we wake healed."

"How unfortunate for the people you're torturing," she said in a low voice.

Elotan grinned. "Perhaps. But you must admit, how *very* fortunate for us!"

He walked towards the bed and yanked her upright to a sitting position by her hair. "I can do whatever I like to you," he said. Then he released her and she fell back to the pillow.

"And then I can do it all over again tomorrow. It makes life worth living."

"So if I stab you with a knife a hundred times?" Ariana asked.

"I will wake up tomorrow and use the same knife on you one thousand times," Elotan promised. "And I'll enjoy it greatly."

"I'll keep that in mind," Ariana said.

Elotan pulled the sheets back from her chest, and traced the circle of an areola with one dark fingernail. "Do," he said. "I'd hate to have to ruin this."

"I thought you said it would heal."

"I said you wouldn't die," Elotan said. "That doesn't mean you'll always enjoy living with what's left."

Ariana considered that. "How much can I come back from? If you cut off my arm, will it grow back?"

"Perhaps," Elotan said. "Get up."

Ariana complied. She swung her legs over the bed and was still surprised when she felt no pain at the action.

"What are we going to do today?"

Elotan laughed. "You are going to enjoy your time in a dark hole, while I go look for your friend."

"She's not a friend."

The demon looked at her and made a face. "You *were* ready to sacrifice her pretty easily," he said.

"Take me with you to look for her," Ariana asked. "Let me see your city."

Elotan shook his head. "And have you try to escape like she did? Do you think I'm a fool?"

Ariana held out her wrist. "Put a chain on my wrist. I will walk as your slave. Whatever you want. But I have spent the last few years of my life trying to let your kind into my world. I never guessed that I would end up coming to yours. Please let me see it."

"You want to see how we live, eh?"

Ariana nodded.

"I don't know if you will like what you see," Elotan said.

But at the same time, he scratched a fingernail across his chin. Thinking.

"The doors to your world will be closing again soon. After that, I will show you some of ours. You will need to be tied to me, and not just to stop you from running off. There will be Curburide who will be insanely jealous to see me parading you around. We will need to stay out of sight as much as possible."

"If they see me with you, will that help to improve your status?"

Elotan looked at her with a narrowed eye. "Don't flatter yourself."

"I know that having a human on a chain here has to be worth something," Ariana said. "I'm not an idiot."

He looked ready to slap her, but then, after a second, he nodded. "There will be some who are impressed."

The demon suddenly turned and walked out of the bedroom, and Ariana sat on the edge of the bed, wondering what she should do. Follow him? Wait?

She hadn't decided before he came back. He held a yellow veil in his hand. It was jumbled up in a ball and still the ends cascaded nearly to his ankles.

"Put this on," he said. "I can't parade a naked woman through the streets here, or there won't be enough left of you to regenerate in the morning."

Ariana smiled and wrapped the translucent silk around her shoulders, draping it across her chest and then belly. She knew that her body was still visible. Maybe even more visible; the haze of the silk only made the outlines of her nipples and bellybutton more tantalizing to the gawker.

"So what are we going to see?"

"I think I will show you what happens to humans who somehow end up here. Some of them ask for it. Some are taken. None are happy."

"Sounds like the Curburide need to take a course in hospitality," Ariana said.

Elotan slapped her across the face.

"How's that?" he asked.

Ariana felt the heat spread across her cheek.

"You get an A," she whispered.

Chapter 31

"That is amazing," Cheyenne said. They stood barefoot on the cold earth along the side of the road, staring at the moon hanging in the sky to the west. It looked as if it had been dipped in Kool-Aid. The craters and plains were all dusky red as it floated just above the edge of the horizon. Overhead, the sky was still the deep blue of night, but to the east, the sun was rising, a low blazing orb that hung in counterpoint to the bloody moon setting on the other side of the world.

"Yeah," Joe said. "So, I guess that's a selenelion."

"The moon looks spooky," Cheyenne whispered. "Like a horror movie."

"Yeah," Joe said. "Only, if this was a horror movie, one of us would probably have more clothes on. Namely me."

She poked a finger at his bellybutton, and he jumped back. "I kind of like it better this way," she said. "Why should the girl always be the one to have hard nipples and goosebumps? Why shouldn't the guy be the one to lose his clothes and show everyone his hard…"

"Okay, you can stop right there," Joe laughed. Without thinking, he slipped a protective arm around her bare shoulders, and she pressed herself tighter to him. Her whole body suddenly released a "shiver bomb." Cheyenne trembled from head to toe and he squeezed her close to still her. "At least it's not winter," he said.

"True," she agreed. He'd been worried when he first touched her shoulder that it was too much, too familiar. But she wrapped an arm around his back as well, cupping her hand on his hip. "But neither one of us are dressed for a desert dawn."

"How about a selenelion?" he said.

She snorted. "I guess. But it's almost over."

Joe looked and saw she was right. The dusky red was faded slightly, and now the edge of the giant orb was settling below the horizon. He knew that the moon was really below the horizon already; only the refraction of the earth's atmosphere allowed them to see both the moon setting and the sun rising at the same moment. He'd learned that much researching what this cosmic event was supposed to mean. At the moment of eclipse, the earth was actually perfectly aligned between the Sun and the Moon, the three celestial bodies in a 180-degree line. But for a few minutes both appeared visible, one rising, one setting, thanks to the refractive "lens" of earth's atmosphere.

The breeze tickled the hair between his legs and Joe was suddenly acutely aware of their lack of clothes. It was more than a little surreal to be standing casually naked and holding each other at the edge of the desert at the edge of dawn. Watching an eclipse together. Meanwhile, demon worshippers were sacrificing people just down the road.

"This night has not gone exactly the way I had hoped," Joe said.

"I know," Cheyenne said. "You were hoping to connect with your girlfriend, and instead you ended up with me. Sorry I messed up your plans."

Joe shook his head. "Don't be sorry. I'm not. But, I really didn't think I'd end up walking barefoot for miles on an empty road."

"I don't think we've even walked a mile yet," she said.

"Good point. My feet already hurt, though."

Cheyenne nodded. Joe couldn't help but see her breasts bob as she did. He was arm-in-arm and nude with a woman watching the dawn, and they hadn't had sex. *Well... that's a first*, he thought, just before mentally slapping himself and forcing his eyes away from her undeniably desirable body. Part of him wanted to hit on her; how often did you end up in situations like this? But part of him was also thinking of Cindy, from the Cowgirl. They weren't committed, but he *had* just started something with her. And then there was Alex. He didn't plan to start anything with her, if he found a way to bring her back from the Curburide. And yet, somehow, being with Cindy and now *thinking* of being with the beautiful woman next to him made him feel in a weird way like a total cheat.

"*One pair of legs at a time, stud,*" he said to himself. But that only made him look at the smooth skin of Cheyenne's calves and thighs. And the thin line of dark hair at the delta of those thighs that pointed the way towards. They had escaped, and now they were alone…

Blood was now surging towards his groin and he felt a stirring that could only lead to a very visible, very embarrassing moment of truth if he allowed it to continue.

"We should probably start walking again," he said, removing his arm from her shoulders. He instantly missed touching her though; her skin was so soft…

"Yeah," Cheyenne said. "I don't really want to walk into town starkers. But I definitely don't want to be doing it at noon."

"Hopefully someone will come along the road and give us a lift," he said.

"Would you stop to pick up two naked hitchhikers?" she asked.

"I'd slow down at least!"

"Pig."

Joe shrugged. "*God* created men, not me."

They started walking down the road as the light of the moon finally disappeared on the horizon. But the sky was quickly growing brighter in the east. They walked on the pavement, a few feet from the edge, trying to avoid stepping on glass or rock debris that hugged the edge of the road. Or the arms of a cactus. But it was still tough on the soles of their feet.

"Have you always lived in Santa Fe?" Joe asked.

Cheyenne shook her head. "No," she said. "I grew up

in Albuquerque. And I guess I was made in Wyoming. My parents took a road trip when they were in college and spent the night in Cheyenne. They said there was nothing else to do there, so that's how I got made."

Joe laughed. "Nice. Any brothers or sisters?"

"Yeah, I'm the oldest of four. Three girls and one brother. He never used any of our hand-me-downs, though mom sure tried to get him to."

"Are they named after state capitals too? Austin, Juneau, Madison?"

"Ha!" Cheyenne said. "Nope, just boring names. Jamie, Carol and Mike."

"You're the oldest?"

"Yep. I'm the big sister and big example. So as soon as I took a few classes at community college, I decided to ditch the rest of 'em and moved up here to start my exciting new life as a bar waitress. I have aspirations to one day become a restaurant hostess. I gotta show the kids that you really can grow up to be anything you want."

"Uh-huh," he said. "So what really happened?"

"My dad's an asshole and I got sick of listening to his bullshit about going to college and becoming a nurse or something. So one day I packed a bunch of stuff and caught one of the Roadrunner shuttles up here. And I've never gone back."

"You ever see your sisters or brother?" he asked.

Cheyenne shook her head. "They don't have any idea where I'm at. And I'm keeping it that way."

Joe raised an eyebrow. Somehow, this situation sounded like there was something more serious at the core than just a dad blowing bullshit.

"So, how long have you been up here?" he asked.

"Six years in August," she said.

"That's a long time not to talk to your family."

She snorted. "Best six years of my life. Even if I am still just waitressing!"

"Have you met anyone here?" he asked.

"You mean a boyfriend?"

"Yeah."

"Nope, I've kept myself free and single. Never know when you might have to move on, ya know. Why, are you interested now that you've had time to check out the merchandise? Earlier you said you absolutely weren't."

It was Joe's turn to laugh.

"I've moved on quite a bit myself," he said. "Speaking of which, since you've lived here more than a week, do you have any idea how long it will take us get back to town from here?"

"I don't know," she admitted. "I don't come out here much so I'm not really sure how far we've come. Maybe another hour?"

The headlights of a car suddenly popped out of the darkness from the direction of the Birchmir.

"Maybe we won't have to walk it though," she said and turned in the direction of the lights. Cheyenne put her thumb out in the universal sign for "hitchhiker" and then crooked her knee as if she was hiking up a skirt. "Do you think I'm showing enough leg to get us a ride?"

"I think you're showing enough everything," Joe said. "When they see me, they might keep going though."

Just then Joe noticed another pair of lights behind the first. And then a third. His stomach suddenly turned to ice.

"Get down," he said, and grabbed her arm.

"Why?" Cheyenne asked, but he yanked her down into the gully next to the road.

"Down," he insisted. He pulled her down to lie on the dusty hill that sloped away from the asphalt. The headlights closed the gap fast. But once they were almost upon them, the car began to slow. There were four cars now behind the first, and all of them stayed in a line, creeping along the road.

"Get lower," Joe said, and they scrambled down the slight hill to crouch in the ditch.

"I thought we wanted to catch a ride," Cheyenne whispered.

"Yeah, but not with them! Don't you think it's odd that it's barely dawn, we've not seen a car in an hour and then all of a sudden there are a handful all coming from the same direction?"

"People need to come into town to work shifts at the hotels," she said. "They start early."

"Do they all slow down and look for hitchhikers when they disappear?" Joe asked. "Those cars are from the mission."

"How do you know?"

He didn't answer her at first. Above them on the road, the cars filed by, and finally passed. Joe held his breath until the last taillight disappeared.

"I trust my gut," he said. "It's kept me alive so far."

"I think you just wanted to get down in the dirt with me," Cheyenne said.

Joe turned to look at her face. Her eyes looked up at him in a gaze that said she really wouldn't mind if he came closer and her lips were pursed in a way that begged a kiss. For a second, he thought she was actually serious, and then she couldn't hold it any longer, and broke into a laugh.

"Gotcha," she said, when she saw his face.

"Careful," Joe said. He slipped one arm across her back and then grabbed her shoulders with each hand, as if to hold her down. But Cheyenne's body suddenly rolled towards him, throwing him off guard. She flipped around and he lost his grip on her arm.

Before he knew what happened, she had straddled his waist, grabbed both his wrists and pinned them to the dirt over his head. Joe found himself face to face with her breasts. Her knees dug hard into his sides, preventing him from moving.

Cheyenne was grinning as she stared down at him. Her hair fell across one cheek, but this time it was clear she wasn't trying to be seductive.

"Don't mess with me," she warned. "I can take you down."

"I thought you said you didn't want to take me down," he said.

"You know what I mean."

Joe could feel the soft press of her inner thighs and the velvet soft skin of her sex brushing his belly. Her breasts were covered in specks of reddish dirt, and the pucker of her bellybutton below them was tantalizing. Despite what she'd just said, he felt his cock begin to stir.

"I know," he admitted. "But this is… awkward."

Cheyenne laughed and pushed off of him. Joe sat up and willed his libido to cease.

"Sorry. I used to wrestle a lot with my brother," she said.

"I was just joking," he said.

"So was I." Her face was bright with humor, but Joe wondered if that was all. Despite the situation, he was really enjoying spending time with her. She was strong and funny. Down to earth. And really sexy. He realized he needed to abort this line of thought immediately. Damn, they needed to get some clothes on!

"Now that you've lost us our ride, shall we start walking again?" Cheyenne stood up and brushed the dirt off her belly and thighs.

"I guess we gotta," Joe said, and stood up himself.

She glanced at his waist and stifled a smile. "Keep that gun in its holster, cowboy," she said, and then scrambled up the hill.

Joe felt his face flush with heat.

After a moment, he took a deep breath and joined her.

Chapter 32

"How could you?" Alex cried. She sat on the floor near Helone's couch. Tears cut hot paths down her cheeks. "I was so stupid; I thought you were different."

The demon knelt beside her and reached out to hold her arm. Alex looked down and saw that Helone's six fingers were now plump; gone was the withered, parchment-like look of her skin. She'd fed on Alex's fear and anger. And apparently fed well.

"I am different," Helone said quietly. "If I wasn't, you'd be screaming in pain and oozing blood from all parts of your body. Look at yourself. Are you whole? Healthy?"

"What you did to me was horrible," Alex said. "I think I'd rather be beaten."

"That could be arranged," Helone warned.

Alex yanked her arm away. She was still crying, but inside, her heart grew more and more angry. The demon had set her up, gained her trust and then milked her. And she'd fallen right into the trap.

"Those weren't even my parents, were they?" she asked finally.

"They were what you think of your parents," Helone said.

"So it was all fake. How did you do it?" Alex asked.

Helone shrugged. "I can do a lot of things you would not understand." She gestured to the room. "These skins are empty. They can be filled with many things. And many things far more horrible than your dead parents."

"So you can't actually bring back the ghosts of my mom and dad," Alex said.

Helone looked hard at Alex for a moment without answering. When she did, Alex felt her chest grow tight.

"I can, and maybe I will, if you give me problems."

Oddly, that struck Alex as funny, and she couldn't resist a sour smile. "So, if I don't obey you, you'll call my mom."

Helone nodded. "Come on, get up. I'm sorry that I had to do that to you, but it's over."

Alex rose, and as she did, Helone smiled and held her arms out. "I know it was painful, but look at what you've done for an old woman. I could go to the prom!"

Helone pirouetted and Alex had to admit, the dinner of her emotions had done wonders. The shriveled dark skin of the old woman now shone with the gloss of a healthy young adult; her chest was firm, the breasts defied gravity again, and her belly no longer looked aged and paunchy. It was tight and firm. Helone's black thighs were curved and muscular, and her eyes glowed with an orange fire that actually made Alex feel really nervous for the first time since she'd met Helone. Before, she'd appeared a decrepit old woman. A demon past her prime. A has-been. Now… she looked ready to eat anybody alive who got in her way. She looked truly dangerous.

"I'm glad I could help," Alex said, though the bitterness of her voice said otherwise.

Helone laughed. "There will be many who will be jealous," she said. "I think I'll go outside tomorrow. There's no point in wasting youth on the dark."

"Does that mean I can go out too?" Alex asked.

Helone shook her head. "Imagine a giant banquet table of hot fudge sundaes and cakes and cookie plates all sitting in the middle of an empty park square in the middle of your New York City. How long do you think that square would remain empty?"

"Not long?" Alex said.

"No, not long," Helone said. "If I took you out there, it would be the same thing. You'd draw Curburide like a table of sweets. And I don't feel like fending them all off. I will go out myself while you remain here safe."

"Youth wasted in the dark?" Alex said. Her sarcasm was pointed.

"Youth saved in the dark," Helone corrected. She took Alex's hand and pulled her out of the room. "Come, you've had a long night. It's time to sleep."

"I don't feel very tired right now," Alex said.

"That wasn't a suggestion," Helone answered. "It's time to go to your room. We'll talk more later."

She led Alex back down the hall and then waited until Alex stepped inside. She turned and Helone stood there, blocking the way out.

"Dream well," the demon said. And then she shut the door. Something metallic clicked.

Alex tried the handle and nodded when it didn't move.

"From one cage to another," she murmured.

Alex laid down, but she couldn't sleep. She kept seeing her mom and dad, their faces brimming with sadness, disappointed and accusing.

She kept seeing exactly what she'd run away from.

And that only led her to think of Joe, and the few weeks she'd spent with him. She'd had to kill her parents to leave with her own life, and shortly thereafter, Joe had picked her up on the side of the road. He had had other things on his mind at the time and hadn't questioned her too much about what she was running from. So she'd gotten into his car and let him drive her far from her home, still on the run really, no matter how far they went, moving from the Rocky Mountains to Phoenix to Austin and New Orleans.

He had shown her so much, in such a small amount of time. And all the while, they had been on the trail of a murderess. Because Malachai had let them know about Ariana's plan to help the Curburide overrun the world. And it had all ended up with her dragging the murderess through the doorway to hell.

Here.

Maybe it was her appropriate just reward for what she'd done to her parents. But, she wasn't dead yet.

So there was still hope.

Alex got back out of bed. She didn't have to just lay here and wait. She put her hand on the door handle again and twisted. It didn't budge. But she didn't believe it was a lock she couldn't break. She'd escaped from Elotan's dungeon, after all. Sure, she'd had help with that, but...

Alex twisted the knob again, and it didn't even creak. She wasn't going to break this lock by force. At least not that kind.

She put her mind into it, instead. She willed the doorknob to turn.

Nothing happened.

Alex closed her eyes and reached out with her inner voice to call Gertrude and Matthew and all of her spirit friends. One by one she called their names, imagining their faces here, in the room with her. That used to make them appear before her almost instantly. But the "airwaves" remained silent. The room remained empty. Did they not hear her, or did they not care anymore? Either answer was painful.

She walked away from the doorknob and looked on the dresser for a hairpin or a paperclip; something she could use on the lock. But there was nothing. This was the room of a prisoner, after all.

Alex sat back down on the bed. Momentarily defeated. Helone had used her, drained her and left her in her cage while she went out on the town. The thought made her furious. She'd started, against her will, to trust the demon and look what it had gotten her.

The anger drove her back to the door. If she could move a lock with the help of her friends, why couldn't she do it herself? Why couldn't she tap into Malachai's strength, who lay quiet, inside her. The demon hadn't said a word to her in twenty-four hours, but she knew he was there, or else she wouldn't be standing. He was her crutch.

Her power.

Alex smiled. She might not be able to do a thing alone, but she wasn't alone, was she?

"You and I are one," she whispered in her head. She assumed he heard. But she didn't wait for his answer. Instead, she closed her eyes again as she grasped the doorknob and drew on invisible strength she knew was there. And somehow, from somewhere, it came. There was a fire in her arms, faint, but palpable, as if she was suddenly a lightning rod of static.

She felt jittery, ready to unload the energy she'd unlocked somehow. It couldn't stay inside her or she'd burn up herself.

The power inside her grew stronger; she focused it on the doorknob. She'd done this sort of thing before; she knew how it felt to channel invisible fire. It was a hard feeling to describe, but it was amazing.

Sparks surged all through her body, but especially in her fingers and face. If she wanted to, she could probably have zapped a blue arc from her fingertip to the doorknob. She felt as she imagined a spotlight felt – a focal point of unstoppable light.

Alex closed her eyes and aimed that energy through her fingers to the doorknob. The power now had a place to go and eagerly surged through her arms and into her hands. "Let me out," she whispered. And as she did, the energy left her.

Something inside the doorknob clicked. She put her hand around it and turned. The knob moved easily.

The door opened.

She was free.

Alex released a breath she hadn't even known she'd held. She was out of her room, but there were more doorways to pass, and she didn't know where Helone was right now. She hadn't heard her since the demon had locked her in the bedroom. Alex hoped that Helone had gone out, flush with the health of a renewed body.

Or spirit.

Whatever her "form" was. Certainly it was refreshed and reinvigorated compared to the wrinkled, withered thing she had first found here. All thanks to Alex's pain.

The hallway was silent and she tiptoed past the kitchen and then the room of skins. It was dark and quiet there; Helone did not appear to be lounging on the couch, as was her wont.

Alex held her breath, and passed the room. She moved as silently as she could down the hall and into the room she'd first entered when she'd slipped into Helone's home. The place with a fireplace filled with a pier of skulls. The trophy room. There were bones everywhere, and now she realized that they were the bones of people like her. People who had been lured into Helone's home under the false impression that it was somehow a refuge from the hell outside.

Alex no longer believed that.

She was going to take her chances with the demons outside.

The door was locked. She'd expected that, but it still was a disappointment when she twisted the knob and found that it wouldn't budge. And there was no keyhole or deadbolt to work with either. How it was locked? She didn't know. Helone's magic, most likely. If she could overcome that once, she was sure she could again.

The foyer remained empty, as did the trophy room. Alex put both hands on the knob and once again, reached inside her, to draw on her secret well of power. The secret that had been silent ever since she'd come to Helone's. She knew he was still there though; without Malachai, she wouldn't be walking.

The familiar feeling surged, and she focused it on the doorknob, just as before.

And just as before, within a few seconds, the door lock clicked and Alex was free. She pushed the door open and stepped outside, pulling it shut slowly behind her. She took a deep breath, and for the first time really considered where she was going to go.

"*Yeah, what now?*" Malachai said inside her mind.

"Ha, so you are there," Alex said. "What's with the disappearing act?"

"*If Helone had found out I was with you, we would both be in a lot of pain right now. I gave you strength, as you asked. But I had to stay hidden.*"

"Thanks," Alex said. "But why would she be so angry? Did you do something to her?"

"*Not to her.*"

"Then what? Who is Helone anyway, and why should she care about whatever you did a hundred years ago?"

There was no reply.

"Malachai, talk to me. Whatever trouble you are in here now impacts me; I deserve to know what it is."

"*I'm a deserter.*" Malachai said, finally. "*You have your draft dodgers. They are reviled and chased down. Here, we have those who escape into your world illegally, and don't return. That's what I did. And once I was in your world, during a night when the doors were open, I used covenants with humans to gain me more and more time away from here. They provided my anchor, allowing me to stay.*

"*Without a covenant, I would have been dragged back through the doorways. That's the physical law we are bound by. We can visit your world, but without something to hold us there, we are quickly dragged back. Instead, I made new deals to protect me. I didn't want to go home… and I definitely don't want to be here now. Helone is one of those who guard the doorways. If she knew I was here again, and connected with you… it would not have gone well for either of us.*"

"I don't know how I feel about being helped by a demon who is a criminal. I always thought you were an upstanding demon," Alex said.

Suddenly her legs turned to water, and her spine evaporated. Alex fell to the steps in front of her, a helpless cripple who could not move her arms or her legs.

"Malachai stop it, come back!" she begged.

"*Be careful about what you say,*" Malachai warned.

Alex lay with her cheek on the third step. Her head hurt from the fall, and one of her ribs had caught the edge of a step.

She could feel the pain, but she couldn't move a muscle. All she could see was the wall of the stairwell a couple feet away.

"Okay," she said. "Point taken. I need you. But you need me too, at least until we get back to earth."

Nothing happened. Alex continued to lay paralyzed on the stairs. She wondered if her head was bleeding. It really hurt. And felt hot where it touched the stair.

"Malachai, do you really want to lay here and let Helone drag us back inside?"

"*She's not there,*" he said. "*If she was, we would never have gotten out. She is ancient, cunning and strong.*"

"Maybe she is just asleep."

"*Curburide do not sleep.*"

"Then where is she?"

"*Last night was a night of open doors. She is probably out checking on how things went.*"

"I thought she never left her house."

"*She is the Queen of the Doors. That's why her home is filled with the skins of those who have come through.*"

"So she would kill you if she found you," Alex said.

Suddenly the strength returned to her limbs.

"Where should we go?" Alex asked. "Can you find one of the doors?"

"*They'll be closed by now, but still guarded.*"

"Can we find one that is not guarded, so we are ready the next time it opens?"

"*We can look. But it's not likely. Curburide thirst for human suffering. They know where all of the cracks between the worlds are.*"

"Then how am I going to get home?"

Malachai didn't respond immediately. When he did, Alex felt her heart sink.

"Ariana may have had the right idea. You may need to open a door on your own, rather than waiting for one to be opened for you. But to do that, you will need to perform a blood sacrifice."

"And how am I supposed to do that?"
*"Find Ariana.
And kill her first."*

Chapter 33

THE CITY GREW brighter. That's the only way Ariana could describe it. Elotan led her through winding streets, bound to him by a leather cord. At first, the buildings had all seemed drab, run-down. Windows were boarded, foundations cracked. Sometimes the places seemed hazy, lost in the dingy yellow light. But when she focused, she could see that the sidewalks were broken and the weeds grew sickly and tall around them.

But that was changing. The doorways of the buildings looked cleaner now. Some decorated in skulls or symbols. The yards were neat and the pavement unbroken. There were lights in the windows, not cracks.

"Is it much farther?" she asked.

Elotan shook his head. He pointed at a building just a couple blocks down the street. A blue light shone from beside the door. "It's just ahead."

They crossed a street and she could finally read the sign that decorated the brick above the door. It was a simple black rectangle that stretched across the lintel. The letters were made of bleached bones. They spelled BLEEDING BAR.

As they reached the front, Ariana could see the same title repeated in red lettering on one large window to the right of the door. The steady beat of a drum pounded from within. Inside, she could see more than a dozen Curburide seated at small tables. Their eyes were focused on a small stage in the front of the room. Something was moving across it. She could see the bare legs of a dancer…

"Come on," Elotan yanked her tether as he pulled open the front door. "Time to show you off."

He pulled her inside. They stood in the entryway of what appeared to be a small cabaret. Demons lounged around small square tables as a pale human woman danced for them on a stage with a pole. *Danced* might be overstating the case, Ariana quickly realized.

The woman was staggering, and used the pole as support to hold her up while she circled it. She was dark-haired and large-breasted. The roll of her belly jiggled as she moved. But that wasn't what drew Ariana's eye. It was the blood that spilled down from the cuts that covered the front of her body. They began at her shoulder and stretched horizontally across her body like a gruesome set of window blinds. Straight red lines that bled fast and steady.

"Elotan," a large demon called from one of the tables. He sat with legs spread and an enormous erection visible between his legs. A female demon lounged beside him, her head cradled in the crook of his arm.

"Hello Portis," Elotan answered. "It's been a long time."

The demon waved at the stage. "We've been entertaining ourselves without you. This one's strong."

"How long has she been here?" Elotan asked.

Portis shrugged. "Three months? Six? When did we see you here last? It's been a long run. Ricandis went too far one night and nearly ended it, but since then… she's been amazing."

Elotan stepped over to the bartender and said a couple words. Then he ushered Ariana to an empty table. A moment later, the bartender came by with two glasses. Clear goblets filled with something ruby red.

"What is this?" Ariana asked.

"Bloodwine," Elotan said. "Distilled from the passion and anguish of that woman on stage."

Ariana gently pushed the glass back away from her. "I'll pass."

Elotan shook his head. "Taste it before you refuse. This is the wine of life. There is nothing sweeter or more bitter. It will sustain you through the hardest days. You wanted to know the Curburide, then know us."

Ariana met his gaze. Was this just another veiled torture? Would this poison her, gag her? But Elotan looked completely earnest now, if you could gauge his heart by that dark face and piercing eyes. When he smiled, it was like a starburst against a moody sky.

Elotan drank, and sighed with pleasure.

Ariana picked up the goblet, and put her lips to the glass. She was terribly thirsty, and hungry. Elotan had not fed her today.

A drop of the liquid touched her lips, and Ariana's eyes widened.

"Oh my God," she whispered.

The elixir was heaven. And hell.

Sacred and desecration combined.

She drank a full mouthful, and then had to set the glass down. Tears began to stream from her eyes and her body trembled uncontrollably. Ariana grabbed the edge of the table to anchor herself, and closed her eyes to immerse herself in the sensation. Her mouth bloomed with honey but her belly felt on fire. There was a dirty bitterness to it at the same time, impossible conflicting sensations that drove her tongue mad and sent orgasmic tingles and painful electrocutions through each of her limbs. Her thighs moistened and she stifled the urge to slip a hand between her legs. Her skin felt completely strange, as if someone else's had been draped over her body. Where the yellow silk covering touched her was like the irritating scratch of sackcloth. But when Elotan took his eyes from the stage and reached over to hold her neck, she flashed with pleasure. As his hand squeezed, she moaned.

The demon laughed. "I told you," he said. "Take it very slow. That's a glass to last all night."

When the fog finally cleared from her mind and her body stopped trembling so that Ariana could sit without clutching the table, she began to take closer stock of the demons in the room. Several were there in pairs, and some in groups. All were naked as Elotan was, and she could see that the males, like Portis, sported unashamed erections. In a couple instances, female demons idly stroked their partners, while both watched the stage. At one table in the corner, a female demon stretched back in her chair with her head against the wall. She had jet black hair that hung to the floor, and round breasts that were knobbed with small gumdrop nipples. They were clearly erect and surrounded with what looked like thorns. Their sexual organs were barbed, just like the men's. The demoness had propped her legs wide apart, heels touching opposite legs of the table, as a male lapped between her thighs. At one point, maybe after feeling her gaze on him, the demon looked up from his service, and met Ariana's gaze. His eyes shone bright and feral, and he stuck his tongue out at her. It was torn and dripped with dark blood.

Ariana looked away, and realized that one of the tables in the front row had emptied. Three male demons and one female all now joined the human woman on the stage. They circled the woman and the pole and held hands, preventing the bleeding woman from escape. She didn't even try, though the terror in her eyes was clear. She shook her head again and again as tears rolled down her bloody cheeks. "Please no, not tonight," she begged.

One of the males slipped his black arms beneath her pits and raked his nails across the gashes on her chest. The woman cried out. The other men sank to the ground and grabbed her calves. With long tongues they licked her flesh, moving steadily upwards. Meanwhile, the female demon pressed her hips to the dancer's body, shaking and rubbing herself against the captive woman. She sucked at the woman's crying mouth and then licked a long pink tongue lower, to trace the wide nipples of both breasts. When she stepped back, one of the demons on the floor had claimed the middle spot between the dancer's legs; his mouth completely covered her sex. The other male joined the female and both took turns sucking on the woman's breasts as the demon that held the woman captive bent her backwards and took her in an endless kiss.

Ariana realized she was holding her breath.

Elotan was holding his erection.

The attention of the entire room was riveted on the stage. The corner couple had stopped their own play to watch as the demons on stage kissed, caressed, and stroked the bleeding woman to an extremely audible orgasm. Her cries came in hitching, growing bleats of unbridled pleasure. But as she reached her peak, filling the room with sexual screams, she began to punctuate each wave with a word.

"No!"

Again and again the woman thrust her hips into the male's face that drove her pleasure, as her mouth cried out "No, no, no, NO!"

Ariana wondered at that, but only for a moment.

At the pinnacle of her passion, the demons changed their strategy. As the woman let out a room-shaking cry of orgasm, the demon who held her from behind bent down to kiss her once more. When he came up for air, the woman let out a wet shriek. Her body suddenly shook hard, an epileptic's seizure of spasming. The kissing demon spit something thick and red to the ground. At the same time, the demons at her breasts pulled away, their mouths slicked in red. The female demon chewed and grinned, making a show of her enjoyment for the audience before swallowing.

Ariana saw the human woman's nipples were gone. Dark blood rushed down her torso and someone in the room shouted, "More!"

The cunnilingus demon stood and spit blood and flesh to the floor and then grinned wide at the bar patrons, his white teeth flecked with red.

"Strip her," someone called. Ariana frowned at that; the woman was already naked. Strip what? But the meaning became quickly clear. The three men held her by arms and legs as the demoness stood beside her trembling body. With one finger, she slipped her long nail beneath the gash at the top of the woman's collarbone, until it slipped out on the other side and protruded from the gash a half inch lower. And then she pressed her thumb to the middle and pulled. The skin separated from the dancer's flesh like wet, well-soaked wallpaper. It clung at first, but then with a sticky, sucking resistance, lifted. When the demoness reached the other shoulder with a single solid strip of peeled skin, she ripped it off and held it up for the room to see. The thin strip dangled there, wet and glistening, and the room exploded with cheers.

"Holy shit," Ariana whispered.

Elotan slipped an arm across her shoulder. "You wanted to be the human queen of the Curburide," he said. "I don't think you could handle it. This is just a teaser."

Ariana took a sip from the goblet of bloodwine, and as the liquid pain and pleasure mixed like fireworks in her blood, she leaned into Elotan's embrace and settled in to watch as the demoness on stage pulled another strip of skin free. The screams were constant now, but noise now came from the entire room, as the demons moaned and cheered and feasted on the pain reverberating in the air.

"Yes," Ariana said, spreading her legs and indulging in the decadence of it all. She had always found a savage enjoyment in watching the men she had sacrificed writhe and die in front of her on the floor. "Yes, I think I can."

Ariana had always found most other people to be stupid sheep. Maybe that was why she'd had so little remorse after the first one she'd slaughtered. People were simply animals, and animals were meant to be slaughtered and consumed. She took another sip of the bloodwine and let her eyes roll back in her head. If this was what the demons could derive from what she saw now on the stage, then she had been right all along to try to bring them to earth.

She slipped two fingers inside herself, and arched her back at the resulting wet spasm. She was more turned on right now than she had been since the first time one of her intended victims, Jeremy, had tied her up, turned the tables and beaten her before fucking her. She'd given it all back to him on the sacrificial altar, but that unexpected violent sex had made her feel a little like this. Trapped yet unrestrained. Completely open to whatever pain and pleasure would follow. She opened her eyes from the memories and looked again at the bloody stage.

The dancer's breasts looked strange when stripped of their skin and "caps." They hung like meaty raw melons on her torso, as the demoness continued to slice the last strips of skin from the dancer's belly. Her screams had dulled now. They were more whimpers than terror. She'd given in to the pain. At a certain point, the pain was so extreme, you couldn't feel anything more. Maybe that's why the demons suddenly changed their tactics.

The male who had been attending to her sex with his mouth lay down on the stage, and the others gently laid her on top of him. Her body shook and jolted with tremors as the demon caressed her back with six dark fingers. His nails raked across her bare, creamy shoulders with tenderness, rather than violence. And then he pressed his black lips to hers, and her body stiffened. The trembling ended, and Ariana smiled. Elotan had taught her the impact of a demon's kiss. It was not as heady as bloodwine, but it did electrify your nerves and open the floodgates below.

She made an unconscious moan herself as she watched the demon's hips begin to move underneath the dancer. She knew that the dancer's pain was now being changed, transmuted by the demon's tongue and cock to pure, heavenly pleasure. She found herself jealous of the sensation, despite knowing the horrible pain that would follow when he pulled out. There was no heaven without hell.

Elotan's eyes were suddenly two inches from her own. They bored into her with a humor and curiosity. "You are not like most of them," he said.

She opened her mouth and licked her upper lip beneath his gaze. "No," she whispered. "I'm not."

The demon's mouth covered hers, and as his tongue

filled her mouth, his hand grabbed her wrist and dragged it to his lap. She knew what to do. His prick was like wood stripped of its bark in her fingers; hard and unyielding, yet smooth as silk to slip across. He did not feel wet, yet her hand glided up and down in his lap as if he were covered in a sheen of oil. She felt the wicked barbs that lay hidden around the head of his cock begin to engorge and rise from where they had lain tight to his skin.

So that's how they worked. They waited until the demon was fully aroused (and presumably inside) his mate before they extended and latched on to the inside, ensuring that the coupling could not end until he was done.

Elotan let out a throaty moan as her hand tightened and quickened. Then his arms suddenly encircled her, and raised her up from her chair. The demon flipped her around like a doll, and brought her down to sit on his knee.

"Not yet," he growled, and pulled her back in his lap until her shoulders rested on his chest. One of his arms wrapped around her belly, holding her in place, as the other slipped beneath her silk covering and explored her chest. His hand moved down between her thighs, palming the stickiness of her arousal as his other hand squeezed a nipple between thumb and forefinger. She felt the needles of his penis drawing blood where they pressed into her back. But Ariana didn't care. She opened her legs to his fingers and lolled her head back, exposing her neck to him.

On the stage, the dancer had looked up from the demon she lay upon to take another long demon cock into her mouth. Her head matched the rhythm set by the demon inside her as she worked his friend with bloody lips. Somehow the ecstasy of their touch had raised her from the haze of pain, and she appeared to not simply be being used; she was actively, anxiously participating.

And then the other male moved between her legs and pressed the large globes of her ass apart before guiding himself into her other entry. Ariana grimaced at the thought of what would happen when two demon dicks pulled out of that woman at once. Would she be left with simply one large hole between her thighs?

She was perversely fascinated to find out. The demoness on stage moved from one male to the next, coaxing and kissing as the rhythm of the four bodies grew dangerously fast. Cries of passion came from the stage and the audience. The air was thick with the scent of sex and iron and a darker spicy bitterness that Ariana could not identify, but found she craved. She inhaled it like perfume, drawing it in and holding her breath as Elotan massaged the trigger inside her.

She felt the energy rise and she now moved greedily against his hand, but then without warning, he withdrew.

"Not yet," he said again and raised her up from his chest to sit straight.

On the stage, the demon who had been getting head was now taking the demoness against the back wall. The woman's mouth was open in a perpetual O as she cried out with each thrust inside her. The moment was coming, Ariana knew, as the cries grew faster and louder. The demons both beneath and on top of the woman growled out something guttural and loud. And then suddenly their group grinding stiffened and ended in a hideous scream.

The demon behind her pushed one hand against the woman's back and ripped himself free as he stood. The stage went silent as her scream turned to a silent rictus of pain. The dancer's face was frozen, her eyes bugging out. And then the demon beneath her grabbed her by the two raw meaty shoulders and lifted her up and off of him, dropping her to the ground on her back. He got up and stood next to the other. Their drooping phalluses dripped blood on the stage, as they clasped hands and bowed to the audience. Behind them, the woman's eyes remained open, staring sightlessly at the crowd while her body shivered uncontrollably. She had clearly been pushed beyond.

One of the members of the crowd stood up and walked to the stage. He was smiling as he bent down to lift the woman up. He threw her over his shoulder like a sack and then turned to the bartender at the side of the room. "She might need a couple days after this one," he said. Then he turned to the other demons still on stage.

"Nicely done," he said. Then he nodded and walked off with her to a door at the back of the club.

Elotan's hands gripped Ariana by the waist and lifted her to her feet. He stood up beside her with a grin.

"Okay," he said, taking her by the hand and pulling her towards the stage.

"Now it's time."

Chapter 34

CHIVALRY WENT OUT the window when the car slowed down and pulled towards them on the curb. Joe didn't want to step in front of Cheyenne, he wanted to step behind her. He wasn't exactly the nudist type.

Feelings aside, he wasn't a complete coward. Joe stifled the urge to hide and stood beside her until the car pulled up in front of them and stopped. The driver was a short, squat American Indian woman. She rolled down the passenger window and leaned towards them. "You look like you need a ride somewhere," she said. Her voice was musical, high-pitched and soothing. And full of questions.

"We do," Cheyenne answered immediately. "We were robbed; could you drop us at my house? It's just a couple miles from here."

The locks on the car door snapped, and the woman nodded. "Sure."

Joe opened the back door and Cheyenne slid across the vinyl seat first. As he sat, grimacing at the cold kiss of the material on his back and butt, she was already giving the driver directions to her house.

The sun was now on the horizon and it seemed as if they'd been walking for a couple hours. Joe's feet felt swollen and hot. The rest of him though, was chilled with the quiet breeze of the desert dawn.

"So what happened to you then?" the woman asked, as the car pulled back onto the highway. Joe opened his mouth to speak, but Cheyenne took the lead again.

"Couple of muggers out near the old Birchmir Mission," she said. "Took our money, our clothes and our bike and left us there."

"That's a long walk from here," the woman said, glancing back at them in her rear view mirror.

Hope you're enjoying the view, Joe thought sourly.

"Make a right here," Cheyenne announced at a turnoff that barely even looked like a road. Just a trail of gravel and dust where some cars might have slid off the asphalt. But as they made the turn and slipped down and around a hill, Joe saw the small street sign atop a bent metal pole jutting from the midst of a sagebrush bush. The main road to Santa Fe disappeared behind them and a moment later, they were in the driveway to a one-story adobe house that overlooked a deep, brown valley. The place looked small, just a square hut really, with a door and one wide front window. There were others farther down the street, all spaced well apart.

"Can you get in?" the woman asked. "You don't have your keys."

"I keep a spare hidden," Cheyenne said. "But thanks."

They both got out and Joe bent over at the driver's window and also thanked the woman for stopping and helping them. Then they walked quickly to the front door of the house. Cheyenne held one hand across her crotch in a pointless display of modesty and waved with the other. She waited until the car pulled out of the driveway before she stepped to the left of the stoop and lifted the top half of what appeared to be an ornamental plastic rooster. When she turned back to Joe, she held a gold key in her hand.

"Always helps to have a pet cock," she said.

Joe felt himself blush and Cheyenne didn't miss it. With a raised eyebrow, she looked from his waist to his face and then clarified. "It's a male chicken," she said. "What were you thinking?"

Without waiting for an answer, she slipped the key into the lock and pushed open the pale green door. Once inside, she flipped on the lights to a small living room, and motioned at the couch. "Make yourself at home. I'll be right back."

He walked her ass disappear around the doorway that led to a small kitchen and hall. Joe sat on the edge of the couch, leaning forward to obscure his privates, a fairly silly exercise after exposing them to Cheyenne and the world for the past three hours. But inside her home, his nakedness felt more visible. This whole situation was completely ridiculous.

Something soft hit his thigh, and Joe grabbed for a pair of grey sweat shorts as they dropped to the tan carpet. A New Mexico State T-shirt followed. "You should be able to get those on," Cheyenne said. "I like to wear baggy stuff at home, so they're large."

She hadn't put anything on herself yet, and somehow Joe found that more embarrassing here inside her home than he had walking on the side of the road. Context.

"I'm going to take a shower," Cheyenne said. "Then we can call a cab and go to the police?"

Joe nodded. "Sounds right," he said.

"I'll be quick," she promised and then disappeared around the doorframe. Her hand hadn't quite left the doorframe, when her head and one shoulder popped back into view.

"Hey," she said. Her voice was softer.

Joe was already slipping one leg into her shorts. He stopped, and turned, still exposed, to face her.

"I just wanted to say thanks for getting me out of there," she said. "I'm glad I wasn't one of those girls on the floor. And I'm sorry you didn't get to help or talk to your friend."

Joe nodded. "It's okay," he said. "I never wanted anyone to die just so I could find out if Alex was still alive somewhere. I just wish I knew where she was right now. I wish I could do something to help her."

"Maybe you still can," Cheyenne said. She gave him a quick, hopeful smile, and disappeared down the hall.

Chapter 35

THE NONDESCRIPT grey buildings were subtly changing. They looked… older now. There were more cracks in the stone faces, and the spots on the bricks darkened. The architecture, too, looked older, more ornate with stone gargoyles and carved insets. Alex focused on moving forward. If she didn't, if she just studied a building, her feet moved, but she didn't get anywhere. It was like being in a bad dream where you were stuck in place without logic. Walking, while nothing moved.

"Why is that?" she asked Malachai.

"*You're not moving through a physical world, as you know it,*" he answered. His voice was a low whisper in the back of her mind. "*Everything you see here is… an approximation of what you expect it to be. Your mind is giving certain things shape and form in a way that it can understand. But that isn't necessarily the way it looks or behaves for a Curburide.*"

"So it really is all a dream?"

Malachai gave a low chuckle. "*Oh no,*" he said. "*It's very real. What you experience here is no dream. If they decided to crush your soul here instead of just torturing you, you will not only be dead, you will cease to exist.*"

"Isn't that the same thing?"

"*No,*" he said.

When he didn't elaborate, Alex asked, "What's the difference?"

"*If you don't start moving, we might both find out,*" Malachai said. His voice was no longer calm. Alex paused and focused on seeing with her inner sight. The world around her suddenly looked more like a radar overlay than a street with buildings. And she could see a handful of bright lights on the horizon. They were all coming from different directions, but they looked to be converging, right where she was.

Alex ran. She passed several buildings and saw a couple demons in the distance who appeared unaware of her, though one peered her way in apparent confusion when she passed.

"*Get out of the street,*" Malachai said.

Alex turned towards a corner building. It looked like a factory, long and squat, with hundreds of small, evenly spaced windows. She pulled on the curved handle of the front door, and it opened easily. She slipped inside.

"Now what?" she thought.

She stood in an empty hallway, but there were lights ahead. And nearby she could hear the steady oscillation of something mechanical. She moved towards the sound and as she did, heard something else. It didn't follow the steady rhythm of the machine. It grew and moaned like a wind through an old drafty eave. A whisper. A whistle. A scream. It was many sounds in one, and none of them were steady or machine.

"What is that?" Alex whispered.

"*Shhhhhhh,*" came Malachai's unhelpful response.

She turned down a hallway and saw three demons walking away from her; they'd just come from another side corridor. Alex waited until they had turned into another hall before she continued walking.

"Where should I go?" Alex whispered in her head to Malachai. This time she got no response at all. Okay. He was petrified of being discovered right now. She was on her own. Part of her was wishing she'd never left Helone's. At least that demon had spoken to her and been friendly to an extent. Maybe it was all to juice her up for the "squeeze," but it was better than being caught and thrown in a hole to wait for the execution. She wondered how Ariana was faring there. The vindictive part of her hoped that Elotan was being brutal.

Be careful what you wish for, her conscience warned. *Cuz karma's a bitch and you're tromping through her backyard!*

Alex walked down a long corridor with no doors or windows. It was all simply grey. Dingy floors, dingy walls, dingy ceiling. The material had no seams or cracks, however. And no easy escape route, she noted, once she'd walked for a few minutes. Alex stepped up her pace and focused hard on the pale light that shone from the end of the hall. After another minute of walking, she finally reached the exit. She turned a corner and found herself in a wide open football stadium of a room. Here, everything was different.

Overhead, the ceiling was a lattice of windows to a smoky, piss-yellow sky. Beneath that ominous light, Alex saw what looked to be a factory, only this wasn't a place making widgets, this was a factory of pain.

There were rows of wooden racks from one side of the huge room to the other; she counted fourteen. Each rack stood a few feet apart, and a tangle of thin pink tubes hung from what looked like a grapevine trellis built across the top of each row.

The tubes snaked to connect to the arms and legs of the pale figures bound to each of the racks that she could see down the long rows.

"What the hell?" she whispered to herself. Hell, indeed.

There appeared to be no demons in the room at the moment, and Alex tiptoed into the huge chamber. The noise that she had heard down the hallways earlier came from here. The oscillation of pumps colored the air, and the moans of anguish broke the rhythm every few seconds. The voices came from all around the stadium-size room. All of these people were alive… and clearly in pain.

Alex had no idea what the tubes were doing to them, but it couldn't be good. She crept along the side wall and came up behind one of the racks. They didn't really appear to be made of wood, she saw, now that she was closer. They were tan in color, and lightly veined, but there was a trace of pink amid the lines. And purple. Almost as if the structures themselves were made of flesh. Living torture beds. And the tubes that came from the ceiling lattice, they separated when they reached the bodies into a hundred thinner arms, each one attached to the victim on the bed.

At first glance, Alex had thought the victims were human, but now that she stood next to one, she realized she wasn't sure. The rack was at an angle, so the creature appeared to be both reclining and half-standing with its head lying three or four feet higher than its toes. It was naked and had the basic features of a man, two arms, two legs. But its skin was like marble. White and pasty, mottled in grey. She could see the ribs beneath its flesh, and the scars of many wounds across its thighs and belly. It was the eyes that really made her wonder though. They were large, yet saturnine. They opened as she stood next to the upright bed, and widened as they took in her presence. The eyes made the creature look alien.

There were tubes connected to its forehead and cheeks, shoulders and neck, chest and groin and thighs. There was even one attached to the end of its tubelike penis; the effect was to make the thing look endless, as its thick stalk tapered into a pink flesh tube that stretched up and away from the bed.

The thing's belly was strangely clear of the tubes, however. And covered in marbled scars.

"Who are you?" the man whispered. His words sounded like the hiss of sandpaper.

"My name is Alex," she answered. She kept her voice low so that nobody in the other beds would hear. From somewhere down the line, she heard a scream.

"How... are... you... free?" he asked. Each word seemed to come slowly. With a painful effort.

"I escaped," she whispered.

The man's eyes widened even more than before. "If... they find... you here... they will eat... you alive."

"Who are you?" Alex whispered. "And what is this place?"

Another scream erupted from somewhere down the row of racks.

"I... am Meldut. This... is... the winery," he answered.

"Are you... were you... human?" she asked.

Meldut made a sound that might have been laughter. "I am... Sildren," he said. "You would... call us... The Hunted."

"The Hunted?" she asked. "What do you mean?"

"Curburide can't... survive... by... feeding only on... humankind," Meldut said. "Not enough... doors."

A new scream. Closer this time. Alex looked down the line of tubed prisoners and saw the reason. Something was moving down the line of racks on the top of the "grapevine" trellis that all the fleshtubes extended from. It looked almost like a small mining cart, only it was high in the air. When she spotted it, the thing was withdrawing a tube from the bed it hovered over.

"So where do you come from?" she asked, now keeping an eye on the travelling cart. It was moving closer to them.

"The Sildren... share this place."

"So you are demons too," Alex said.

"We are... the Hunted," Meldut said again. "You are... hunted now, too."

"I need to find a way home," she said. "They can't hunt me there. I'm looking for a door."

"Not here," Meldut said. "This is... the winery."

"Winery?" Alex asked.

"Bloodwine," Meldut said. "It comes from... Sildren."

Alex looked down the row of bodies and grimaced. This wasn't simply a torture chamber, but a milking factory. Somehow that made it even worse. She had a vision of a dairy farm where all the cows were tubed and tortured, while outside a mob of boisterous people stood around drinking glasses of milk and laughing. She shook the image away.

"Where do I go to find a door?" she asked.

"Look for the... star."

"What star?" Alex said. "You can never see the stars here... the sky is nothing but cloud."

Meldut shook his head faintly. "The star symbol. It is marked on... buildings where there is... a door. There are many... here... nearby."

Alex looked at the tangled mess of tubes that led from Meldut's pale flesh and up into the air. Now and then, one of the fleshy things pulsed. Meldut was being milked.

"How long have you been here?" she whispered.

"Too long," Meldut said. "Longer than you have... lived."

Alex toyed with the idea of trying to rescue Meldut. She couldn't free the factory of victims, but she could help the one who helped her. Maybe.

"Could you take me to a door? I could pull these things off of you," she offered. Her voice, however, betrayed her doubts about that. The end points of the tubes looked to be perfectly merged with Meldut's flesh, as if they literally had grown out from him. There were no seams. Even if she could pull them off... would he simply bleed to death from all the holes in his flesh?

"You can't separate... the juice... from the grape," Meldut said. His eyes narrowed. "I am part... of the machine... now."

"I don't think I can find it on my own," Alex said. The impossible nature of finding a single building in a strange city weighed her down even heavier now. She had a clue, but how could she ever seek it out alone without being caught? At first she had simply focused on getting free from Elotan, and then from Helone. But now that she was free... she had no idea where to go. And it was only a matter of time before she stumbled back into the clutches of a demon. This was their world, not hers.

"Focus... and you will see," Meldut said.

A new scream. This one just a couple racks away. Alex took a breath as she looked at all the things connecting Meldut to his prison. He was a part of the machine... and the eye of the machine was coming this way.

"Go," Meldut whispered, and Alex nodded.

She backed away and struggled for something to say. Good luck? Goodbye? What do you say to someone you're abandoning to eternal suffering?

"I'm sorry," she said finally.

Alex backed away from the Sildren until she was near the outer wall of the factory room. The trolley thing now poised over Meldut's body, and she watched as a tube dropped from its center. The thing had a spherical end to it, but on that sphere, she could see a series of pointed barbs. When the sphere dropped and landed on Meldut's belly, he screamed once, and then was silent. The tube then withdrew back to the trolley, which began to roll away, turned on the aerial track to begin its work on the next row.

The Curburide lived on pain, Alex realized. So that was what they were really "milking" here.

"Jeez," she whispered. Being whipped and chained in her parents' basement while wearing sackcloth no longer seemed so bad.

Alex felt her eyes well up as she imagined the constant suffering that was present in this room. This was truly hell, for the Sildren anyway. She imagined herself lying there on a rack hour after hour, year after year, constantly being sliced and bled. This was definitely *not* where she wanted to be caught.

She began to walk down the long aisle on the outer perimeter to the far side of the milking room. The room seemed endless, as she hurried along the wall. There were moans from the figures on the racks periodically, but with all of the hundreds of bodies here, it was actually eerily quiet.

Her steps quickened with every rack she passed. She did not want to end up here. For a second, she thought of Ariana, and wondered if Elotan's torture would have been worse than this. What was he doing to her now? Alex didn't really want to find out.

She had to find her way home.

Fast.

Chapter 36

"Time for what?" Ariana asked, as Elotan dragged her by the hand towards the bloody stage.

"Your performance," he said. "I didn't bring you here to be entertained. You *are* the entertainment."

Ariana shook her head vehemently. "No, Elotan, don't do this. Keep me for your own, don't…"

The demon backhanded her across the mouth. She felt the heat rise in her cheek as her lip instantly swelled. The grip on her wrist did not loosen. "You are mine to do with as I wish," he said. "I rescued you from the mob that chased you. You exist or don't, by my whim. Don't forget that."

Ariana still tried to resist, but he thrust her forward until she had no choice but to step up or fall face-first onto the stage. Elotan growled, "Perform well and I will reward you. Make me look bad and I will punish you. And I promise that *I* can give you more than any pain you feel here tonight."

She knew in her heart that what he threatened was true. Elotan was using her to buy status… or something. If she screwed that up for him, he would be deadly.

"Don't let them kill me," she whispered.

The demon nodded, slightly, and answered in an equally quiet tone. "That would do me no good at all."

Then Elotan raised his voice so the whole bar could hear. "For your pleasure," he said. "A seductress and a killer. She was not stolen here against her will; she wanted to be here. Can you believe it? She wished she could be with the Curburide!"

The room exploded with laughter. Someone shouted, "She won't wish that after tonight!"

Elotan put a hand up.

"This is her first time, so let's be gentle, eh?"

"I'm hungry," someone said. "Can she spare a kidney?"

A ripple of low laughs again.

"You're cut off, Bimini!" Elotan warned.

"Fine, you can take home her kidneys, but we get everything else," the demon taunted.

Elotan looked towards the bartender, and nodded. "Play something so she can dance," he said.

Ariana felt more nervous now than she ever had in her entire life. She had once joined a convent and masqueraded as someone with a conscience, and managed to play it cool. She had worn a skintight catsuit and gone to clubs to pick up men she wanted to kill, no problem. She had slit men's throats and licked the blood from the knife. Or, more commonly, the razor's edge. She had delighted in causing pain to the idiots she lived among – on earth. But now, the tables were turned. She was no longer in control.

"Entertain my friends," Elotan said, and waved his hand at her. "Dance like you're dancing for me."

Ariana looked at him sharply when he said that. She had never danced for him. He had raped her on his bed, but there'd certainly been no dancing involved. The beat of the music had resolved to a slow, steady grind, and in the back of the room, someone began to clap along with the music. He wasn't the only one. Another joined, and then another.

The demons were taunting her, pushing her to perform. Meanwhile, Elotan stepped back from the stage and moved to stand by the bar. He wasn't going back to his seat, but he was no longer standing at her side as protection.

Ariana was on her own. In a roomful of demons who wanted to toy with her, to drink from her fears and lusts. She stepped back to the dancer's pole that occupied the center of the stage. There were bloody finger smears across the bar, and she really didn't want to touch them. But this was not the place to be shy. They would eat her alive if she showed fear or hesitation. In fact, those were exactly the emotions they thirsted for. She wouldn't feed them those. She refused.

But they also thirsted for the baser lusts. She could work with that. She understood those. Ariana took a breath, and willed herself to be calm. No, not calm. Sexy. She was in a see-through yellow silk wrap in front of a room full of men who didn't cover their cocks. Who wore no clothes at all. She would be able to tell really quickly if she was dancing effectively or not.

"Let's see if we can get a rise," she challenged herself. And with that, she began to walk around the pole. Slowly at first, testing the room. She let just the tips of her fingers maintain contact with the pole as she moved around it. The music seemed to grow louder, to surround her; maybe the bartender turned it up, or maybe she just was feeling it as she let herself slip into the mood. She didn't care. Ariana felt her heat rise. Blood pulsed faster through her skin as she twirled herself around the pole, letting the silk trail behind her. She flexed her thighs, testing the sensation of opening herself.

It felt good.

It felt unholy.

Ariana grinned. She lived for that.

She stepped in front of the pole and with one hand pulled the yellow silk first one way and then the other, back and forth across her breasts. It would have been more of a tease if the material wasn't already almost transparent. She didn't know the song, but the drum pounded steadily, tribal, as the bass wound around it like a serpent, throbbing, throbbing, twining…

Ariana surrendered herself to the music, and arched her chest forward, taunting the demons with her barely covered breasts before yanking at the yellow silk and releasing them completely. She didn't need any warmup help, she thought, wrapping the silk around her ass and then pulling it forward between her legs before tossing it out in front of her, beyond the stage. It settled in the lap of a demoness who sat hand in hand with a male. Ariana couldn't help but stare at the thin sinuous neck and unashamedly bare chest of the demoness;

her skin was glossy black and perfect. Her breasts were small but full; the nipples were pronounced, dark fleshy caps, and very erect. She was clearly engaged by Ariana's dance, and now held the silk to her face and inhaled before handing it over to her partner. Ariana played on that, and dropped to her knees on the stage in front of the two of them swaying back and forth to the beat as she massaged her breasts just a couple feet from their faces. Playing it.

The male's eyes were inscrutable, though the evidence in his lap was irrefutable. The demoness though – she made no effort to hide that she was enjoying the show. She drew a coal-black tongue across her open lips as Ariana shook her breasts while moving on hands and knees, crawling in the wet spatters of blood remaining on the stage to hang over the very edge.

The demoness nodded, and Ariana focused on returning the lip lick with a slow reveal of her own tongue. She drew the tip across her front teeth, and closed her eyes as she stuck it out until she could touch the tip to her top lip. Ariana could lose herself in moments like these; the feeling of sexual tension engulfed her in a dizzying blanket as her thighs clenched and her middle gyrated of its own volition. She was electrified by the rhythm of the music and the teasing black, wet tongue of the demoness.

As she swayed, eyes closed while she imagined touching the creature just beyond the stage, there was suddenly another wet feeling on her lips, and Ariana's eyes shot open to see the black pupils of the demoness staring into her own. While she'd been lost in the feeling, the woman had stood up from her chair to lean towards Ariana across the stage. The demoness's silky dark tongue was tracing the edge of her own, and Ariana suddenly felt faint. She could feel the needles of the demoness's tongue rake against the soft vulnerable flesh of her own, and each pricking movement sent shivers down her spine and across her ass. The hidden nerves between her thighs instantly ached with a yearning to be touched and prodded and plumbed like she had not ever known. Ariana felt lightheaded and sauna-hot, dizzy with the excitement and unthinkable need. She reached out to grab the shoulders of the demoness to steady herself before she fell forward off the stage. But as she touched the silky skin of the woman, a heavy hand suddenly grabbed her left nipple and squeezed. The pain was instant, sharp and unexpected.

Ariana jumped backwards on impulse, which only made the hurt worse, because the demon didn't let go. Instead, he yanked her forward by her nipple, so that she lost her balance and fell into him. A palm caught her in the face and pushed her with so much force that she toppled backwards, skidding towards the pole on her ass.

"No touching," the demon said. He sounded angry. And jealous. "Dance," he commanded.

The voices around the room echoed his demand. Ariana blinked away the sting and welling tears, and pushed herself up from the sticky stage. She had been getting into the dance, but now…

Something hit her across the temple and clattered to the stage floor nearby. She heard the sound of something rolling and grabbed the pole for support before looking down. An empty glass. Probably from bloodwine.

The natives were restless and some of them were drunk. She needed to get back in the mood, and fast.

Ariana grabbed onto the pole with both hands and swung herself around, shaking her backside at the audience as it swiveled, and then stopping when she came around to make eye contact with the patrons again. She touched the glass that had hit her head with her foot, and then slipped her toes up to the edge. With a deft motion she rolled it up onto the top of her foot where it rested for a second, and then with a calculated kick, launched it in the air towards the bar with her toes.

The barkeep reached up a hand and caught it mid-air. Someone let out a catcall. Another clapped.

She had their attention again now.

Ariana ran a fingernail across the nipple that the demon had pinched (it was still throbbing, but she kind of liked that) and then slid that finger down to the tiny cup of her bellybutton, before driving it across the thin line of hair that arrowed its way lower, to the apex of her thighs. She shimmied and thrust her pelvis forward and back several times with her hand buried there. An overtly sexual grind with a hula shake. When she brought the finger back out and held it up, it glistened with her excitement.

Ariana enjoyed being naked.

Ariana enjoyed teasing.

Ariana enjoyed pain.

So did the Curburide. Someone yelled from the middle of the tables, and she could hear the clink of bloodwine glasses as they lifted and returned to their tables. In front of her, the demoness had leaned back in her chair, spreading her legs suggestively for Ariana to see. The thick black petals of her sex looked ready; moist and swollen. Open and wanton. They were no more shy than she was. Ariana threw her head back and ground her hips against the pole. She imagined it was Elotan's own pole; his girth felt almost as wide and hard as this when he was aroused. She had feared the first time that if his spines didn't kill her, his width would.

The beat suddenly changed, and the hypnotic throb of the bass turned to a gunfire of slapping, pounding intensity. Ariana followed it, gyrating faster first to the left of the stage, and then the right. She felt her breasts rippling with the motion, jiggling for the crowd like unfettered flesh balloons. Out of control and in the moment. She was caught up in it again now, and let the feeling own her.

Ariana threw her body to the floor to roll around in a breakdancing sort of circle before she kicked her legs to the sky. She pulled her fingers from calf to thigh as if she were drawing on a pair of nylons, and then she moved to face the bar and spread herself for all to see. The noise from the crowd answered her with claps and hoots and growls. Ariana rolled to the right to rise. But as she did, she felt a wet spot beneath her shoulder. She looked down and saw there was actually a wide puddle of crimson there, bled from the last dancer.

Ariana smiled as a twisted idea struck her. The Curburide loved sex. And they also loved blood. She'd give them both.

She pressed both her hands into the still somewhat warm blood, and then stood up quickly, still shaking her hips to the pounding beat.

But her hands...

Her hands moved to their own melody. They grabbed her breasts and then slid, slow and moist downward, down, down to the place where her middle ended and her legs began. That place that every demon in the room wanted to split.

She rubbed the blood of the last dancer across her and laughed, her teeth flashing in the bar lights as she twirled and painted her skin red.

There was applause from somewhere but she didn't look for the source. Instead she looked right into the front row and caught the eyes of the demoness who was masturbating at the edge of the stage.

Ariana crooked one finger and caught the dark woman's eye. She made a hooking motion with her finger, drawing the demoness up and out of her seat.

The demoness stepped up onto the stage and met Ariana in an embrace that made Ariana's knees grow weak. The black woman pulled her tight, pressing breast to breast, hips to hips. And when Ariana looked into the depths of the creature's eyes, she saw hunger there. Raw, animal desire. Her mouth was suddenly filled with the demon's slick tongue and she answered with the press of her own back.

Together, they began to dance, bound together as one being by their arms, which explored each other's backsides. Ariana marveled at the silky smoothness of the demoness's ass; her flesh was firm, hinting at the wicked strength beneath, yet it felt as if her fingers would skate off the skin because she was so velvety smooth. Ariana grabbed the demoness's ass and pulled her body even tighter. The creature responded by digging her fingers into Ariana's back like claws.

Ariana's eyes widened and she coughed a cry of hurt. But the demoness wouldn't take her tongue back. She pressed it deeper into Ariana's throat while her claws dug trails in Ariana's back.

The demoness tilted Ariana backwards, and she went with it, throwing herself into the dip. But that was only a feint. The demoness held Ariana, almost horizontal from the ground, and then grinned, a white flash of hungry teeth just before she released her clawing hands.

Ariana fell to the stage and the demoness squatted on top of her face, smothering her in black demon sex lips already very moist from excitement. She breathed in the scent of demon arousal and felt her own sex swell. The scent was wicked and sharp; not like human spice, yet still recognizable as a scent of arousal. The demoness was horny, and wanted to use Ariana's tongue to plumb her need.

Ariana complied, sticking her tongue out to taste the other woman. Her tongue felt first hot, and then numb as the sensation of white ice crept down the back of her throat. She couldn't taste, couldn't feel, and then it all suddenly came back, a bitchslap surprise in her face and neck. An explosion of sensation that made her scream. She was howling into the dark maw of the demon's sex, and somehow, Ariana was okay with that. She closed her eyes and let the demon grind against her lips, using her to find her own pleasure as she wanted. Ariana stuck out her frozen tongue and let it do what it could. She wasn't sure what that was, because she could barely feel it. The intensity of the sensations had short circuited her nerves. But she was reminded of the explosion that had come with her first taste of bloodwine. She was lost in this moment, and she let the demoness smother her.

From somewhere far away, she could just make out the sounds of cheers and then there was something else touching her. Something that spread her thighs roughly apart. Something that thrust into the ready and open channel that led to her core. Something that hurt when it slid in, but hurt way, way more when it slipped part of the way out.

Ariana cocked her head between the strong thighs of the demoness and saw the demon who had pinched her nipple now pressed himself inside her. He kissed his mate, or girlfriend, as he used Ariana.

Ariana responded, gripping the giant thing inside her, and bucking her hips to move it, accept it, warm it. She wanted to show this demon a good fuck, and as long as she could keep her lips where they were, she thought she could just about do anything.

But that, unfortunately, was where the fun ended.

Hands grabbed at her feet, and suddenly the demon yanked himself out of her. It felt as if someone had just pulled a knot of fishing lures through her vagina. Ariana screamed out involuntarily, though her pain was muffled by the thick, slick lips of the demon's sex.

The demoness suddenly stood up from her crouch, and moved from using Ariana's mouth to kissing her boyfriend. As the two of them abandoned her and slipped into an erotic embrace, Ariana suddenly was dragged away and across the stage to where a group of male patrons stood waiting. There were a half dozen of them, and their grins widened as she drew close. Ariana knew that the fun part of the night – for her – was absolutely over.

Their erections were all in full bloom, ready to impale, with the spines that normally lay flat at their cockheads already raised up from the flesh. Ready to grip and cut inside of whatever they speared.

A hand gripped her by the hair and yanked her to her knees. She was suddenly face to face with an nine-inch tube of demon meat that had a single focused eye and a crown of deadly thorns. She knew what was expected.

"Kiss me," the owner demanded, and Ariana raised one eyebrow in irritation, though she struggled not to show it.

"Really?" she whispered, mostly to herself. But opening her mouth was a mistake, because it was instantly filled. And while it tasted like warmth and spice and the delicious thrill of sin, it also promised blood and pain far worse than any dentist's drill.

Fingernails raked across her breasts, as one of the demon's horny friends grabbed her from behind and thrust his personal weapon between her legs. And he *was* using it like a weapon. She could feel the blood already dripping down the inside of her thighs from the last invasion. As he used that lubrication to make his own path easier, Ariana closed her eyes. Her mouth was filled to bursting with a fucking porcupine dick that promised to rip her lips apart if he pulled it out and her pussy felt much the same. She could feel the heat and pain with every slight push the demon made; it was hideous and marvelous at the same time because it wasn't only pain, it was ecstasy when he moved inside her.

Then another spear of pain sliced upwards and inside, ripping open that place she had never wanted to let any man inside. She stiffened and wanted to scream, but her mouth wouldn't open any farther. For a moment, she panicked, until she forced herself to breathe through her nose.

"Just sex," she told herself over and over. She had to ignore the horrible searing pain that happened every time one of the demons pulled back. But the pushing in, almost made up for the pain. It was as if they were shooting her up with morphine when their cocks hit the farthest penetration inside her.

And then the knife-edged pain as they retreated.

"Just sex," she thought to herself, again and again. "I can do this."

Someone in the audience called out the words that made her suddenly doubt that she could.

"More holes," the demon demanded. "We need more holes."

Something speared her in the side, and her whole body jerked and clenched. A moment later, she felt a pole open the fresh wound wide as it pressed itself into her middle.

Then another stab from the other side. Barbed tongues licked at her ears as two demon men fucked the holes stabbed in the flesh of her sides while one lay beneath her and ripped her uterus out, while still another stood behind her and effectively performed a colonoscopy. And through it all, she still had a barbed dick in her mouth, shredding her tongue and the top of her palate with every movement.

Ariana felt high with the mix of pain and blood. She wanted to scream louder than she'd ever screamed in her life.

And at the same time, she felt the drug of the demon's need. Instead of trying to pull away, she gave her body up to them, moving with all of their thrusts to accept, push back, accept, swivel around. The pain became transcendent.

She moved and cried and closed her eyes as the stars rained over and through her brain.

From somewhere far away she heard clapping.

And that was right about the time she felt liquid fire pour into her mouth as well as her sides and the world went white with heat and hideous sound before it turned silent.

And black.

Chapter 37

THE TAXI DROPPED THEM off at the Santa Fe Police Department on Cerillos Road. Cheyenne paid the cabbie with some money she'd had stashed away – literally – in her mattress. ("You never know when someone's going to come looking in your cookie jar," she'd explained.)

"The town looks a little different down here," Joe observed. They stood in the parking lot of police station and he looked off towards a strip mall and a sign that read Valdes Business Park.

"How do you mean?" she asked.

"Not so much adobe," he said. "Or art galleries or the whole Old West look."

Cheyenne shrugged. "It's like any other town," she said. "Old Town and the Plaza are for tourists. And weekends."

Joe smiled and they began to walk towards the front door. "So, to sum up, 'life is a strip mall?'"

"Or a strip joint," she said. "Really depends on the day and what you need."

He didn't have an answer to that.

Cheyenne led the way inside. Joe tried to walk quieter; he wore a pair of her beach flip flops and even though they were tight and too small for him, they still slapped at the ground as they approached the front desk.

He looked down and grimaced. The Day-Glo pink didn't help either.

"What's the problem?" the on duty sergeant said. He didn't look terribly interested in the answer.

"I was kidnapped and robbed," Cheyenne said. She pointed at Joe and added, "He helped me get away, but they still have our clothes and wallets and everything."

The sergeant looked at Joe and raised a thick black eyebrow, sizing him up. Joe suddenly felt very conscious of the V-neck cut of the T-shirt he wore. Just add another line to his list of "things I never thought would happen to me" – go to the police wearing a woman's clothes.

"Hang on," the cop said, and disappeared from the desk for a minute. When he came back, he pointed at a door. "Lieutenant Mistral will take down your story," he said.

The door opened, as if on cue, and the desk clerk looked back to his magazine. A thin, young cop with short blonde hair and glasses stood in the doorway and motioned to them. They followed him into a small conference room. He offered them Dixie cups of water from a water cooler and then sat across from them at a small, well-used table. There were gouges and half-drawn letters carved into the fake paper woodgrain that covered the pressboard. *Who carved graffiti while inside a police station?* Joe mused.

"I understand you were kidnapped and robbed," Mistral said. "Why don't you start at the very beginning and tell me what happened?"

Joe nodded. "We weren't actually together at..."

Cheyenne cut him off.

"I was walking home from work and this asshole pulled up and offered me a ride. I said no thanks and he left, but then he made a U-turn, came back and shot me with a tranquilizer dart."

"And this was, when, exactly?"

Joe sat back as Cheyenne told the cop her story, up to the point when Joe opened the door to the basement and let her out.

Mistral nodded and put a hand up to stop her. He looked directly at Joe then, and asked, "And you were in the old mission, why?"

Joe opened his mouth to answer, and then closed it again to consider his words. "I was there looking for devil worshippers so I could latch on to their occult ceremony and talk to a demon," didn't sound like the right response under the florescent lights of a police station interrogation room. But, it was the truth...

"I had heard there was going to be a ceremony that night because of the eclipse," he said. "I was curious about it."

"What sort of ceremony?" Mistral said. His face was unreadable, but Joe knew what he had to be thinking.

"I heard that they were going to be trying to call spirits there that night."

"So you're a follower of the occult?"

Joe shook his head. He wasn't sure what to say, but Cheyenne solved that problem.

"He wanted to crash their party and talk to a demon so that he could save his friend who's on the other side."

Mistral's poker face slipped for a moment at that, but the mask was back when he turned to Joe.

"So you were hoping for a séance?"

"Sort of," Joe said. "But instead I found Cheyenne."

The cop wrote something on his notepad and then looked at Cheyenne. "So this guy lets you out of the basement where you've been chained up. What happened next?"

Cheyenne recounted the events of the past several hours. Mistral raised an eyebrow when she reached the point about the women's throats being cut, but otherwise, said nothing. Joe also kept quiet. He could tell the man didn't trust him.

When she finished, Mistral kept writing on his pad for several minutes. The silence grew uncomfortable. When he finished, the cop looked up at both of them.

"What I'd like to do, is take another officer out to the Birchmir and look around," Mistral said. "See if the victims you describe are still there. If we find your clothes, we'll grab them for you. What I'd like you to do, if it wouldn't be too much trouble, is to stay here until we get back. I'll likely have some questions for you once we walk around the place. Is that okay with you?"

Joe nodded.

Cheyenne shrugged. "I should be to work by six, if they haven't fired me. Speaking of which, can I use your phone?"

Mistral pointed to the door. "There's one in the hall. Just dial nine to get out." He stood up and moved towards the door himself. "There's also coffee and a snack machine just down the hall here. Make yourselves at home. I'll be back as fast as I can."

He disappeared out into the hall and closed the door behind him.

"So now we sit," Joe said. He settled back in the plastic seat of the chair, but there wasn't a comfortable way to lounge. These seats weren't made for relaxing.

"We could play a game," Cheyenne suggested.

Joe made a face. "With what?"

"How about Truth or Dare?"

He laughed. "I think I've had just about enough dares for one day."

"Perfect," she said. "Then you can choose Truth."

"I thought you had to call someone?"

"You're right," she said. "I should let work know I'm alive. Be right back."

Cheyenne disappeared out the door and Joe took a deep breath and stared hard at the white blank wall in front of him.

No cracks in that wall for demons to slip through. Joe snorted to himself. That's what his life had come to. Looking at walls to see if there were cracks that might let monsters in. A far cry from looking into conspiracies and corruption in city government for the *Chicago Tribune*. Where he'd had a pretty promising career going just a year ago.

For a short time, he and Alex had driven across the country, and stopped in hotel after hotel to find the places where Ariana had sacrificed men to the Curburide demons. There was always a crack where the demons had slipped through. And for a while, they were always just a step behind her in the race to stop her ritual before it reached its disastrous conclusion. If Ariana had had things her way, she would have set the Curburide free to rape and torture everyone on Earth.

"So, it looks like I'm not fired," Cheyenne announced, breezing back into the room. "And they already have someone to cover my shift tonight, since we might be here awhile."

"That's good," Joe said.

"Do you have anyone you should call?" she asked.

Joe looked at the table, not meeting her eye.

"No," he said.

"Well, then I guess we can start our game!"

Chapter 38

SEAN MISTRAL had not spent years training for the force to chase down devil-worshippers. He had decided to become a cop when he was a teen – not because he loved uniforms and badges, but because he wanted to help people and to stop idiots from hurting the innocent. But "to serve and protect" seemed to encompass more weirdness than he'd ever imagined. This was not the first time the police had been called to deal with occult rituals out at the Birchmir. In fact, there had already been two other instances in the short time Mistral had been on the Santa Fe force. And he knew that the history went way back.

This had to be one of the strangest stories he'd heard from the old mission, though. He stopped at the chief's office and relayed the gist. The chief – an old white-haired veteran who'd come out here from Vegas ten years ago to slide quietly toward retirement – nodded when Mistral finished his story.

"They're like mice in a basement," the chief said. "You can poison them and trap them to your heart's content, but they always come back. Take Barela and check it out."

Sam Barela was a third-year rookie whose family still kept an original, true adobe home up on the Taos Pueblo an hour and a half north of Santa Fe. He'd grown up on the reservation, unlike many of the Native Americans who populated Santa Fe. He was an encyclopedia of local tradition and culture. He was usually paired up as Mistral's partner, when the job required it. Which wasn't often; typically he was on traffic patrol on his own. But this one was, obviously, different. The young cop was pouring a cup of coffee in the break room when Mistral found him.

"Afternoon caffeine, to keep you mean," Barela announced, holding up his styrofoam cup in a toast. The young cop stood a couple inches shorter than Mistral, but he was more powerful. His shoulders were broad and his handshake left you flexing your fingers afterwards. His hair had that thick lustrous black sheen that only Indians seemed to have, and even when it was short, it somehow looked long. When he smiled, his brown eyes always seemed to reflect a deeper humor than his lips allowed.

"Looks like you're going to need to put a lid on it," Mistral grinned.

Five minutes later, they were in the patrol car and headed to the old mission. Mistral briefed him on the story en route while Barela sipped his coffee. When they pulled off the main road and down the drive leading to the Birchmir, the sun was high in the sky and the grounds around the old structure were empty.

"No cars," Mistral observed.

"Hmmm," Sam replied.

They parked and got out of the car. Sam finished the last drop of his coffee and tossed the cup to the floor of the cruiser. Together, they walked the perimeter of the structure. Sam spotted the broken window first and gestured at it with his thumb.

Mistral nodded. They remained silent, not wanting anyone inside to hear them, if there was anyone left inside. After a short walk around the other half of the building, they returned to the front. Sam tried the handle on the front door, and surprisingly, it opened. The devil-worshippers hadn't bothered to cover their tracks and lock up when they left. Or maybe they hadn't all left.

They stepped inside and held the door from making noise as it closed behind them. They were in a chapel, which on the surface, appeared empty. They split up, walking the perimeter of the room on opposite sides, looking between the remaining pews for anyone who might be hiding there. They met again by the altar.

Sam pointed at the star drawn within the circle on the open floor between the pews and the altar. The border of the circle was a dusky red, while the inner stripes that made up the star were white. Though they, too, were smeared with what appeared to be bloodstains.

Mistral knelt at the edge of the circle and pressed a finger to an area that still glistened, faintly. His fingertip came back bloody. He stood and nodded at the entryway to the hall behind the chapel, and together they walked back. They found the stairway leading up and quickly ascended that to stare out at the quiet plains around the old building. Their patrol car was the only car in sight.

"This is where they supposedly hid some of the night while the ceremony was going on," Mistral said.

Sam nodded. "Good lookout spot," he said. "Poor choice for an exit."

Mistral grinned, and they headed back down.

The kitchen turned out to also be empty, though there were some pots and bowls that had obviously been used recently, and not cleaned up. Whoever had been here had obviously left somewhat quickly – they hadn't locked up or taken their things with them.

After a quick survey of the other rooms, they used the basement door and descended to the chambers where Cheyenne said she'd been held prisoner.

"Certainly looks like a prison," Sam noted.

Mistral stepped into one of the rooms and pointed at the chain that hung from a piton in the wall to coil on the floor, and then at the wet spot in the corner. The place smelled of stale urine. "Somebody certainly spent some time here, he said.

He shot a couple pictures of the lower rooms on his phone and then they ascended and returned to the chapel, where he took many more.

"I think this is what your victims are looking for," Sam said, pointing at two piles of clothes heaped on one of the pews in the middle of the room.

"Grab 'em," Mistral said, circling the altar. He shot a couple pictures of what appeared to be bloodstains that had dripped over the side; they didn't look fresh, however.

"Looks like somebody's been having a satanic old time up here lately," he said.

"Call for backup?" Sam asked.

Mistral nodded. "Need to get some prints taken and smear some samples." He pointed at the floor. "Somehow we need to find out who that belonged to."

Something cold brushed his neck. Mistral touched his neck and turned around, but there was nothing there. "Damn," he murmured. "It's an 85-degree day and I just got a chill."

A few steps away, Sam's body stiffened. His partner had no sarcastic comeback for that.

Mistral shrugged off the feeling and bent down to pick up one of the candles that were set equidistant around the circle. As he did, a blast of heat swept down his spine. He stiffened. Shit, he couldn't afford his back to go out right now. He was on-site for God's sake. Carefully, Mistral tried to stand up, but his knees seemed to be locked in place.

He tried to push his hand down on one knee, to force them to unlock, but his arm didn't budge either. "What the..."

"Um, Sam?" he called.

But no sound came out.

"No Sam here," a voice whispered in his ear. It sounded as if it was right behind him, but Mistral couldn't turn around to see.

"Not right behind," the voice answered his unspoken thought. *"I'm right here."*

At that, his hand suddenly leapt to life independently and slapped him across the face. The room echoed with the sound. His cheek stung.

"Who are you?" Mistral asked, though no sound left his mouth.

"Call me Rhilan," the voice said.

Mistral's legs suddenly unlocked and he stood up. He watched his body walk across the room and tap Sam on the shoulder. His partner turned and smiled, yet, it didn't really look like Sam's smile. It was as if Mistral was watching himself on TV. He couldn't lift even one of his fingers.

"*We're going to be close friends for a while,*" the voice said. "*I need a ride.*"

Mistral watched as his body, and his partner, walked out of the chapel and got into the patrol car.

He wanted to scream.

But all he could do was watch.

Chapter 39

ARIANA OPENED HER EYES and for a spit second, all she saw was red. Her world was a blaze of pain and blood. It took a moment before her vision cleared, and she knew where she was. Elotan's bed. She lay under the covers of a demon. She had survived his cruel torture of the night before.

Images of the bloodwine bar flashed across her memory like a slideshow of pain. Pain so excruciating, she had screamed at the end until her throat only let out ragged whispers of sound. The demons hadn't simply fucked her or sodomized her with their barbed wire cocks, they had ripped holes in her sides and thighs and belly to thrust their spears inside her as well. They had used her like a pin cushion.

But here she was, still alive, and staring at the ceiling.

Ariana remembered the ragged bloody mess that her mouth had been at the end of the night and reached one finger up to trace the edge of her lips.

They were whole.

She pushed the covers down, and stared down at her body, expecting to see gashes and hamburger, but her white skin was whole. She followed the curve of her hip up and over the slight lump of bone that marked her waist and then around at the manicured trail of hair that arrowed to the entry of her passion. The trimmed mound of pubic hair was glossy and clean. Her skin was tight, sexy and ready to be touched again.

Ariana stretched, and felt a few aches throughout her body, but nothing to stop her from getting up. She was whole again. The demons seemingly could do whatever they wanted to her, and she could rise again the next day to do it all again.

God, she loved this place!

Ariana looked up and saw Elotan watching her from the doorway. His forehead was tar-black and silky smooth, no wrinkles anywhere. But still somehow she could tell there was concern behind his gaze. When he saw that she'd noticed him, he stood straighter.

"So," he said nonchalantly. "You survived the night."

Ariana frowned. "No thanks to you."

"You're ungrateful? The demon scowled. "I made sure they went easy on you since it was your first time. Maybe I won't make them hold back tonight," he said.

"Tonight?" Ariana said. "I don't think I can do that again."

"You're promised," he said. "After last night, there is great interest in seeing you perform again. You seemed to enjoy yourself."

Ariana opened her mouth to retort, but couldn't refute him. She *had* enjoyed parts of the night. The bloodwine, seeing her body's impact on the men. Tasting the lips of the demoness. And an orgasm amid excruciating pain that literally knocked her out.

She *had* enjoyed it.

But if they had gone easy on her last night... would she survive a real assault?

"If they kill me, I won't be here for you to play with," she said, kicking the covers aside and exposing herself fully for him to see. His reaction was instant and obvious.

"You don't want to lose this, do you?"

He took a step forward, clearly tempted. Then he stopped.

"Get up," he demanded roughly. "I want to find your friend today."

"She is not my friend," Ariana corrected. "And why do you want her if you have me?" She batted her eyes sweetly, and the demon made a sound at the back of his throat. She thought it was laughter.

"If I have her to send to the stage, I can keep you home just for me," he said.

Ariana nearly leapt from the bed.

"Where do we start looking?" she asked.

Chapter 40

ALEX HUGGED THE side of a building as she peered around the corner at the street beyond. The stone felt strange beneath her hands. It almost seemed to repel her skin. Which made a sort of sense, really. She didn't belong here. She didn't really understand how she was here anyway. Was this really a physical body, or had she left that behind in the cave in Terrel? The demons here all appeared to have solid forms, as did she, but demons when they came to earth were not solid at all. So did that mean the solidity here was all illusion?

She didn't want to think too hard about that – because if only her spirit was here, what did that mean for her body? Was she really dead? In limbo? If she found the door and went home, would there be anything to go home to?

"Malachai?" She called in her mind.

She felt a chill along the back of her neck. "Malachai," she called again.

"*Quiet*," the demon answered in the faintest whisper. She felt the chill shift and move. It was as if Malachai were sneaking around inside her.

"*I am*," he whispered. "*It's dangerous for me here.*"

"If I find a door home, will I have a body when I get there?" she asked.

He was silent.

"Malachai?" she called silently.

"*I don't know.*"

Alex's heart sank. She leaned harder against the brick, or whatever it was that the Curburide buildings were made of. She could feel her skin crawl where she touched the surface.

"*You don't belong here*," Malachai said.

"No shit," Alex said. She peered around the corner

of the building and could see dozens of dark shapes moving back and forth not far away. Some were walking with clear purpose down the sidewalks, while others lounged on benches or stood outside of doorways talking. It was demon central just ahead. Probably not the route she could take. Alex pushed back from the wall, intending to turn around and look for another street that was less crowded. But as she pulled away, something nearly out of sight on the cross street she'd been looking at caught her eye.

A star. Wrapped in the embrace of a circle.

The symbol that Meldut had told her about. It was painted below the arch of a narrow roof peak that framed a doorway. It was the symbol that said there was a door inside.

Alex's heart stopped. There was a doorway that would hopefully take her home just a few hundred feet away. But she couldn't approach it now.

She took a breath and leaned back against the building to think. Maybe she could go down another block. If she could cross over to the other side of the street without any demons seeing her, and then come at the doorway from the other direction, there might not be as many eyes to see her.

Alex retraced her steps and walked down until she was a couple blocks farther away from where she'd seen all of the action. And then she turned left and walked down the cross street two blocks. Assuming the Curburide neighborhood behaved on a grid, she now should be able to walk back up towards the busy area, but be on the other side of it. As Alex began walking back towards where she knew the door was, her heart beat faster. Would she be able to get into the building without being seen? Would the door be open? Could she be back home in just a few minutes?

Her chest felt tight with hope. She wondered where Joe Kieran was right now. What had he been doing since she came here? And what had he seen? Had her body simply disappeared from the cave where Ariana had been conducting her bloody ritual? Did he think she was dead? Or had Joe already helped bury her body, and this form that seemed so solid to her right now, was just ephemeral?

Stop! She commanded herself. One step at a time. You can't go home and find out what is truly left of you, until you get to the door.

As she reminded herself of that, she looked ahead and realized that as she'd been lost in thought, she hadn't moved an inch. The grey stone building on her left remained in place.

Damnit! She complained. How can you not move forward if your feet are walking? She remembered Meldut's advice.

Focus.

Everything in the realm of the Curburide took focus to happen. It was a realm of the mind and spirit, not physical.

That made her fear again for the true state of her body, but she shook it off.

Move forward, she commanded, and focused on the intersecting street she could see far in the distance.

After a few minutes, it was no longer distant at all. Alex grinned as she hugged the corner of another building, and peered around the corner. She could see the building with the star symbol just to her left on the other side of the street. A demon walked past it, but otherwise, nobody was on this segment of street. She knew that just around the next corner there was a bustle of activity. All she needed to do was wait here for a minute or two, until that one obstacle passed, and then she could make a dash across the street to the door.

Two hands suddenly gripped her by the shoulders from behind. A flash of heat burned down her back, as a voice pronounced three words that made her heart sink:

"Here she is."

Chapter 41

"TRUTH OR DARE?" Cheyenne asked. She shifted in the uncomfortable plastic chair and kicked her feet up onto the "interrogation" table, as Joe had labeled it in his head.

"Truth," Joe said. "I don't trust your dares."

"Why, just because I made you go into the hallway and moon the front desk?"

"Pretty much," he said. They had played three rounds of Truth or Dare so far, at Cheyenne's insistence, and he'd learned his lesson after taking her first dare. Cheyenne was definitely not a shy girl.

Cheyenne smirked, and leaned her head over the back of the chair. Her hair dangled in the air as she stared at the ceiling and contemplated. When she leaned forward, there was an evil grin on her lips. "You told me all about this Alex girl you picked up on the side of the road. Did you ever beat off while thinking about fucking her?"

Joe's jaw dropped. "She was only seventeen," he said.

Cheyenne shrugged. "She had tits, right? You were both on the road together for a while. You even admitted you slept in the same bed once."

"She was scared," Joe said.

Cheyenne laughed. "Whatever. C'mon. Truth or dare. Did you ever think of her while you were jacking off?"

Joe answered under his breath.

Cheyenne kicked her feet off the desk and leaned forward to stare at him, resting her elbow on her knee. "I didn't catch that."

"I said yes," Joe said.

She grinned. "Ha! See, I knew it. No guy goes chasing around the country for a girl just because he's a good

Samaritan. You wanted that pussy and some demon yanked it away from you. Now you're like Don Quixote. Who goes looking for chicks on the other side."

"She was attractive and funny and I cared for her, okay?" Joe said. "Enough about it."

"And you were in a crazy situation with her," Cheyenne said, nodding. "I think whenever two people are dropped into the pressure cooker together, they always end up wanting to take each other's clothes off. It's human nature. And guys can really get fixated on that."

"But not girls?" he asked.

She shrugged. "Our job is to beat you off with a stick."

"I'd prefer just the 'beat you off' part."

Cheyenne snorted. "Of course, cuz you're a guy. And after the last twenty-four hours, you'll probably be thinking of me now whenever you're beating off." She raised an eyebrow and added, "By yourself."

"Cruel," he said. Then he challenged her back. "Truth or dare."

Cheyenne perked up. She was clearly enjoying this. With a flash in her eye and a jutting chin, she pronounced, "Dare."

She had taken dare on every round, and Joe was running out of ideas. How much could you do in the interrogation room of the police station? He'd had her do a handstand on the table and yell "Die motherfucker" at the top of her lungs. That particular stunt had resulted in the door opening a moment later. They'd drawn a visit from a matronly police officer with short grey hair. She'd scowled, asked what the problem was, and after a glare at their laughter, left.

Cheyenne didn't want to take Truth for some reason, but Joe was running out of Dares.

And then from nowhere, six crazy words fell out of his lips.

"I dare you to kiss me."

Joe's stomach constricted as soon as the words were out of his mouth. *Where the hell had that come from?*

Cheyenne's smile turned voracious. "See what I mean?" she asked. "I'm going to be in your head now whenever you get a hard-on. All cuz you got caged up with me for a night. It's not like I was the girl you were looking for, but now you're stuck with me."

She looked pleased at that idea, and then suddenly stood up and took three steps to stand in front of him. Cheyenne tilted her head, studying him for a moment, as if sizing him up. Measuring him. Then she lifted one leg over his and lowered herself to straddle his lap. Joe found himself staring into her eyes and holding his breath. Her face was inches from his own; her eyes sparkled with mirth – and something more. She said nothing, but gently touched her lips to his. They were warm and dry and slipped easily across his for a second. And then they grew moist as she pressed harder to him and her tongue slipped in beside his own, flicking and teasing. Her eyes closed as she wrapped her arms around his neck and held him close to her. Her breath in his nose was sweet and warm. He inhaled it and thought about how insane this particular moment was. His tongue didn't care, nor did the bulge in his lap. They responded with instant fervor.

And then the door opened.

"Mr. Kieran, Ms. Monarch?"

Joe jerked upright and broke the kiss. Cheyenne drew her head back slower, with less anxiety. She winked at him, and then slipped off his lap to stand. Officer Mistral was back. He stepped into the room, and another cop, shorter, squatter, followed. The silver badge on his uniform read Barela.

"What did you find?" Joe asked, rising to his feet behind Cheyenne. "Was anybody still there?"

Mistral set two rolled up bundles of clothes on the table. "Are these yours?"

Joe grabbed at the familiar jeans, and unraveled them. His T-shirt and underwear fell out and onto the floor. He felt himself blush as he picked up the blue Hanes. Everyone wore briefs, but it felt wrong for anyone to see his. Let alone to have picked them up and delivered them back to him.

He nodded, as his hand slipped to the back pocket of the jeans. "These are mine," he said.

"You'll be looking for this," Mistral said, and held out a wallet. "I didn't want it to fall out."

"Plus you had to run an ID on my driver's license," Joe said.

Mistral shrugged.

Joe took the wallet. Cheyenne held up her shirt and nodded. "Yep, this is my shit."

"Thanks for bringing it all back," Joe said. "Did you see anyone?"

Mistral shook his head. "Some blood on the floor, but otherwise, everything was quiet."

"So you believe us, right?" Cheyenne asked.

The shorter cop answered. His voice was gruff. "We believe that something happened up there."

Mistral nodded. "We'd like to take you back up to the Birchmir and have you walk us through what happened to you, now that we know it's safe for you to go back."

"I think we've told you everything already," Joe said.

"You will go back to the mission with us," Barela said. He didn't sound as if there was room for argument.

Mistral nodded. "Now."

"I guess I can," Cheyenne said. She looked at Joe. For the first time in the hours he'd known her, she looked unsure. And he understood why. He got a weird vibe from the cops. Mistral seemed very stilted, compared to the way he'd been before he went up to the Birchmir. What had they seen up there? And why would they want to take him and Cheyenne back there? What good would that do? So they could point to the floor where they'd been laid out? Something didn't feel right.

Mistral motioned for them to walk ahead. Joe tucked his roll of clothes under his arm. Cheyenne did the same, and then they all turned out the door and walked down a hall to the back of the station. There were voices ahead, and laughter.

As they passed a common room, with a vending machine and a couple lunch tables, Joe saw two officers standing inside with cups of coffee in hand. A woman stood next to them. She was young and blond, and held a cup of coffee herself. One of her hands was in the air, gesticulating as she made a point. It froze as they stepped into view.

It would have all seemed natural, except that she had no clothes on. That and the fact that there was a long gash across the side of her throat. Blood still appeared to be dripping from the wound; her right breast was glossy with crimson. She didn't seem to notice. When Joe slowed to look into the common room, she stepped behind one of the men in uniform. The conversation ceased. Six eyes followed them as Joe and Cheyenne passed. Joe felt the hair on the back of his neck stand up. That had to have been one of the ritual victims, and she was here. Standing on her own two feet.

In front of them, Officer Barela tripped and staggered. Mistral put a hand on his elbow and he recovered. Neither officer said a word.

Joe caught Cheyenne's eye and made a face. She nodded faintly. They both felt it.

Mistral opened a glass door that led to a parking lot, and motioned them through. Barela led them through, but, a few steps across the parking lot, he stumbled again. This time Mistral wasn't there to support him, but he slapped his thigh and recovered on his own. "You'll pay for that," the cop said to the air.

Somewhere nearby, somebody screamed. Mistral walked around them and opened the front door of a police squad. Barela held the rear door open for them to enter. The shriek came again; this time it lasted longer. It sounded like something from a haunted house, even though they were outside in the bright, late afternoon sun. Neither cop even looked towards the sound.

Cheyenne slipped her hand around Joe's arm and

squeezed. When he met her eyes, they were wide with fear. She shook her head "no" and he nodded slightly.

"Enter the vehicle," Barela said. In front of him, Mistral slid into the driver's seat and put a key into the ignition.

As the engine roared to life, Joe twisted slightly and loosened Cheyenne's grip on his arm. He took her hand in his and squeezed.

"I think we've had a change in plans," Joe said. He pulled Cheyenne two steps away from the car. "Run," he said.

They dashed towards the exit of the police lot, just three cars away. Behind them, Barela screamed for them to stop. His voice suddenly sounded not at all calm and subdued. It sounded uncorked – shrill and furious.

Cheyenne let go of his hand and the two of them turned the corner to the left and kept going. Joe could hear the sound of pursuit behind them.

The light at the corner was yellow, but Cheyenne suddenly surged ahead of Joe. "Don't stop," she called, and ran across the intersection. Joe followed, and saw the light turn red when they were not even one-third of the way across.

Cheyenne didn't slow. Behind them, cars began to move. Luckily the drivers ahead saw what was going on and didn't hit the gas when they got the green. Joe and Cheyenne vaulted up the sidewalk on the other side and tires squealed slightly behind them, as irritated drivers punched the gas to move forward. Joe risked a glance behind them, and what he saw made him call out to Cheyenne. "Wait."

Mistral stood at the corner. Barela was not there yet; he walked leisurely towards the other officer.

"Run all you like," Mistral called. "We can find you anywhere."

"Come on," Cheyenne said, grabbing Joe's hand. "That light won't last long."

They ran across one strip mall parking lot, around a gas station, and entered the lot of yet another strip mall.

"Wait," Joe gasped, and leaned over with his hands on his knees, struggling to catch his breath.

"Outta shape, jock?" Cheyenne said. She was breathing heavy too... but still standing up straight.

"I was never a jock," he said. "Is anyone behind us?"

"Coast is clear," she said. "But we should keep moving."

He nodded. "Maybe we can duck out of sight for a minute."

"You just want to go shopping," Cheyenne said. "I get it."

He shook his head, but saved his breath for gasping.

"How about there?" she said, pointing to the store at the end of the row. Guillemette's Book & Tea Garden.

Joe shrugged, and started walking in that direction.

"I'm not much of a reader," he said, as they reached the door.

It was Cheyenne's turn to shrug. "That's okay," she said. "I hate tea. Unless it's a Long Island Iced."

"Probably not going to get that in a bookstore," Joe said, pushing the door open.

They stepped into another world.

Bookshelves, not surprisingly, dominated the space. They rose floor to ceiling, and wire racks also took up some of the space in the front window. The atmosphere was cloistered, quiet. The glare of the desert sun was instantly gone, replaced by a cool feeling of solitude. The store was a respite.

Joe took a deep breath, and worked to finish stilling his huffing.

"Care to look for any books on demonology while we're here?" Cheyenne offered.

He snorted, but shook his head.

At that moment, a woman walked out of one of the middle aisles carrying a silver tray with a handful of steaming mugs on it. Each was a different franchise; Star Trek, Harry Potter, Twilight.. She herself wore a T-shirt that boasted the Star Wars logo, and the word Princess.

"Can I offer you..." she began.

But before she could complete the sentence, a man bellowed from the rear of the store. "Leah!"

"Excuse me, that's my husband" she said, and ducked back down the aisle she'd just come from.

Joe turned to say something to Cheyenne, but before he could get the words out, there was a loud crash from the back of the store, and the brittle sounds of breaking glass.

A woman screamed.

Joe and Cheyenne ran down the aisle to see what had happened. They stopped at the end of the aisle, where a strange tableau was playing out.

In a small open area in the back of the store, the tea woman lay on the ground, a litter of broken mug shards around her. A big man in jeans and a sweat-stained grey T-shirt sat astride her chest, holding her down with his bulk as he stuffed a rolled up magazine into her mouth.

A young, brown-skinned girl stood on the other side of the area. She looked about seventeen, and wore abbreviated denim shorts and a pink tank top. Her wrists were thick with bracelets and chains, but it was her hands that Joe noticed.

They held a long, ornamental sword. She'd apparently already used it on the man; his shirt lay shredded on the floor, crimson slices cut across his broad chest.

"Here's what I'm thinking, Joe," she said in a voice that sounded childish and shrill.

Joe started; her back was to him, how did she even know he was there? And then he realized she did not; she was talking to the half-naked man.

Joe realized that these must be the store owners, Joe and Leah Guillemette.

"Let her go," the man begged.

The girl shook her head, brandishing the sword. She lifted the tank top with her other hand, rubbing one naked breast provocatively in his face. "You hurt my feelings," she said. "You wouldn't touch my boobies when I offered them to you. You said you were in love with Mrs. Guillemette over here. Joe and Leah G, sitting in a tree. She just looooves your guts out, doesn't she?"

The girl laughed suddenly, a strange, hysterical cackle. And then with a sudden swipe, she brought the blade across the man's belly. And instant splash of blood spattered the electric pink of her tank top as the man screamed and doubled over.

"Eww," she said, "you messed up my shirt!" Then she shrugged, and slid the blade up the front of the tank, slicing it off herself. When it fell in shreds to the floor, she walked around the back of the man, who held both hands to his gut, trying to hold himself together. The store owner was a big guy, but suddenly he seemed small.

Helpless.

The girl didn't stop. She climbed up his back from behind, nearly toppling them both. But she was light, and thin, and in a moment, she held the blade across his throat as she pressed her chest to his back. She whispered something in his ear, and he moaned. She rubbed her chest against his shoulders and said out loud, "I said, do you like them now?"

"No," he said.

She whispered in his ear again, and he shook his head. Tears were streaming down his face.

"Kevin," she said to the man still stuffing a magazine down the woman's throat. "Feed her those fucking mugs."

The man picked up a handful of broken shards and began to stuff them down the opening in the magazine that led to the woman's mouth. She struggled and shrieked on the floor beneath him, but couldn't break free.

"No!" the dying man begged.

"Then do what I tell you," the girl said. "Now!"

He was crying, and blood streamed down his pants, but the man staggered forward anyway, trying to meet her demand.

When he stood over the woman's head, the girl said "Good. Perfect. Stay right there."

"Let her go," Joe Guillemette begged once more.

"You let her kiss those guts you think she loves so much, and she's free to go. *Do it.* Five. Four. Three. Two..."

Joe stopped holding his belly together, and instead

reached a hand inside. The pink of his intestines was instantly visible.

"That's it," the girl said. "Let it all hang out." She bucked up and down on his back, as if she were riding a bronco. "Feed that bitch your meat. Show her what she's been loving all these years for real."

Joe stepped forward from the aisle finally. "Stop it!" he yelled. "Get off of him."

The girl cackled and pulled the blade tight to the man's throat. "One more step and I take off his head," she warned.

Joe stopped. Cheyenne gripped his arm. They were helpless to help.

"Now or never," the girl said, still holding the blade tight to Guillemette's throat. The store owner's eyes bugged, and his whole body trembled, but with his two hands he grabbed at the flaps of his gut and pulled.

Cheyenne buried her face in Joe's shoulder as loops of intestine suddenly fell from the sheathe of muscle that had held them in, to hang bloody and wet in his wife's terrorized face. The man astride her had tossed away the magazine and now held his hands on either side of her face, forcing her to see the guts of her husband dangling just centimeters away from her lips.

"Kiss your hubby," the girl demanded. "Eat his meat!"

"No!" the woman screamed, and the girl laughed.

"See?" she said to her helper. "That's love for you. Skin deep." She shook her head and returned her attention to the woman on the floor. "One more chance. Kiss the meat of the man you love... show him you care."

The woman shook her head and cried, "No. Please... just let us go!"

The girl shrugged and drew the blade across the man's neck. "Sorry, but you lose."

The girl hopped to the floor as the man's body toppled. With a deft swipe, she buried the sword in the woman's gut.

"I would have let you go," she told the woman. "It would have only taken a kiss."

Cheyenne pulled Joe backwards. He didn't protest.

"Hey don't leave," the girl shrieked, as they turned and ran to the front of the store. "Stay and have some tea. Blood Tea," she laughed.

Joe slammed through the door of the store and ran as hard as he could, Cheyenne at his side. They cut through the yard of an apartment complex behind. After running two more blocks, Joe finally staggered to a stop, collapsing to the ground.

"What the fuck was that?" Cheyenne gasped, falling next to him on the lawn.

Just then, a scream erupted from a few doors down. Joe pushed off his knees and stood again. There were two figures struggling on the lawn of an apartment building four yards away.

"What the hell?" Cheyenne said. "Not again!" She took off towards the trouble, and Joe followed.

"Leave her alone!" Cheyenne screamed when they reached the yard. A stocky man in a button-down and jogging shorts sat astride a thin older woman. She looked fortyish and pale, with dark auburn hair and a long chin. Joe noticed her hands were weathered and her nails short, because she held them against the man's chest, trying to push him off her. But she couldn't budge him. Instead, with one hand, he yanked her bra off, without bothering to unlatch it. He simply used brute force to stretch it until it snapped and then tossed it to the side to join her ripped yellow blouse on the lawn.

Cheyenne ran at the man in a football tackle move, never slowing. But even though she plowed into his shoulder, the man didn't let go of the woman beneath him. His body fell sideways, but he kept his legs locked around the topless woman, and with one hand grabbed Cheyenne by the throat, throwing her easily to the sidewalk nearby. She yelped as her arm hit the concrete.

Joe followed her lead, and dove at the man, but the guy turned two fiery eyes on him and laughed. A fist caught Joe in the belly and he doubled over. His momentum took him over the woman's body before he collapsed on the ground. He couldn't breathe. He opened his mouth but no air came in. "Oh my God," he wheezed. It sounded like a whisper. Tears pooled in his eyes.

Cheyenne stood up nearby.

"Don't," he whispered.

She didn't listen to him. Instead, she picked up a paving block from the landscaping wall near the apartment entrance. "Get off of her, asshole," she threatened.

The guy turned his head and looked at her with a strange expression. "My name is Lionel, not asshole," he said. "It says so right here." The man laughed as if at some incredibly funny private joke. He pointed to his shirt, which had Lionel Ray Green stitched above the pocket. It looked like a gas station attendant's uniform. "You really want me off of her?"

Cheyenne nodded.

The guy shrugged. "Okay."

He stood up, and Joe could now see just how big he was. He looked like a football player and he must have stood over six feet tall. But it wasn't his size that was frightening. It was his eyes. They looked… insane. Bright and crazy.

"But if I get up, I need to make sure that she can't," Lionel said, and with that, he launched a kick right between the grounded woman's legs.

The woman screamed and drew herself up in a ball on the grass. Her sobs were filled with undiluted pain.

Joe forced himself to his feet as Cheyenne ran at the man with her brick.

"You're going to have to wait your turn," the man said. He reached out, grabbed the brick from her hand, and smacked it against her forehead. Cheyenne went down.

She lay still.

Lionel returned to the woman he'd kicked. He tore the jeans off of her, before dropping his own shorts. "I've been looking forward to this for a very long time," he growled. "Centuries."

Joe staggered to where Cheyenne lay. The man ignored

him. Cheyenne's mouth was slack. There was a raised bump on her forehead where the brick had played her false.

"Cheyenne," Joe whispered in her ear, keeping an eye on the crazy man a few feet away. He was lost in the legs of the broken woman. There was nothing erotic about his motions.

Cheyenne didn't stir. "Damnit," Joe murmured. His belly hurt like hell and he felt like he could barely walk himself, but he pulled her arm over his shoulder and slipped an arm beneath her. Slowly, he levered her upright and dragged her towards the sidewalk. He knew in his gut that they needed to get out of sight of the man behind them before he finished with his current interest. They would no doubt be next.

"Wha?" Cheyenne mumbled into his ear.

"Thank God," Joe said. Her eyes were fluttering open.

"Cheyenne, can you hear me?" he asked.

"What?" she answered. She still sounded confused. "Ow."

"We have to walk," he urged. "Can you walk with me?"

He eased her weight back on her own feet, but kept an arm around her shoulders. She took a couple steps, then stopped, pulling Joe to a halt.

"We have to stop him," she said, trying to turn back.

"We can't," Joe said. "I'm sorry, but we can't stop him any more than we could stop the girl with the sword. They're not human."

"What do you mean?" she said. Her voice was getting less slurry. "He's an asshole, yeah, but he's definitely human."

"I don't think so," Joe said. "I think he's possessed. Just like the cops and that girl. I think the Curburide are here."

"The Curburide?"

"The demons I was looking for," Joe said. "I think they opened the door at the mission last night and for some reason it hasn't closed!"

"What does that mean?" Cheyenne asked.

"We're fucked."

Chapter 42

Rough hands lifted her in the air and then flipped her around like a ragdoll. A short squeal of surprise escaped her mouth, and when Alex saw the owner of the arms that held her, his face was laughing. A demon held her two feet in the air. His face looked like a mask of tar with two sulphur holes; his flesh looked stretched and his eyes burned. When his mouth opened, she saw a row of teeth that looked more feral than human. They gleamed with wet hunger. Behind him stood three female demons. The one at the fore held one hand on a cocked hip and pointed with the other.

"You've given us quite the game of hide and go seek," she said. Her voice sounded like a bird being strangled. High and harsh.

The demon holding her nodded. "But now the game's over," he said. "We win. You lose."

One of the demonesses cackled behind him. "Oh yeah, you lose!"

The whole group laughed.

"What do you want?" Alex asked. She struggled to keep her voice calm. She did not want to show them fear. It's what they thirsted for, that much she knew.

The fat-faced monster holding her answered. "Just your skin," he said. "You can keep the rest."

"What do you mean?" Alex said. As she said it, she knew she didn't want to know the answer.

"We'll show you," the bird-voiced demoness answered.

"You won't like it," her captor added.

"Probably not," Alex said. "But you won't like this."

As she said it, she drew back her leg and aimed a kick right between his legs.

Instead of connecting with his genitals, Alex suddenly found herself airborne. She landed a second later on her back. Her head cracked on the pavement and before the white flecks of pain cleared from her vision the demons were standing around her.

Bird-voice wagged a long, jagged fingernail at her. "Uh-uh," she said.

"Naughty, naughty," another added. The male demon lifted his foot and brought it down on her crotch, pinning her to the ground. He rested his weight on her and Alex stifled a cry. He was heavy. It felt as if he would snap her if he pushed, even just a little more.

"Don't make me mar that perfect skin," he said. "I don't want to have to wait for it another day."

"Let's make sure we don't," one of the women said. Suddenly, hands grabbed and lifted Alex in the air. They walked with her a bit before entering a building. Somewhere inside, a woman was screaming. Her voice rose and fell in a disturbingly regular rhythm. And then, just as Alex began to ignore it, another voice joined the din. From the lower octave, it sounded to be a man this time. He sounded even more pained than the shrieks of the woman. His screams made Alex's skin crawl.

A moment later, she was tossed unceremoniously to the floor.

"Welcome to your new home," the male demon announced. He bent over and ran a smooth hand down the bare flesh of her leg. "I think you'll be spending many long nights here."

Alex rolled over, and saw the source of the screams she'd been hearing. There was a man tied to a wooden cross just ahead, and a woman shackled to the corners of what looked to be a gigantic doorway. Both were naked. And both were surrounded by demons.

The demons held something in their hands.

Something that flashed and glimmered in the light. Alex

found herself squinting to see what they were holding, to see what they were doing.

One of the demons pressed the fingers of his left hand to his right and then, it suddenly clicked to Alex what they were doing.

The demon was fitting a ring onto his appendage.

A very dangerous ring.

The side near his knuckles extended outward in a short curve. A short, *sharp* curve.

As Alex watched, the demon moved his hand until that sharp steel curve connected with the right arm of the girl. Blood welled in slow motion. At first, there was just a hint. A faint red line. And then, as if the surprise at being cut suddenly wore off, the crimson began to well. It ran down the woman's arm in a steady drip. Her voice cried out in a sharp squeal as the steel bit and pulled.

Alex watched, unable to tear her eyes away. The shiny steel disappeared into the arm of the woman and then slid easily upwards towards her neck.

She couldn't look away, but her heart seemed to stop as she watched. The demon's finger traveled up the woman's body as if it were tracing a well-drawn patchwork design.

The red line quickly moved across the woman's shoulder, and then slit its way up her neck. Another demon held her head immobile, as the blade traced a bloody line behind her ear and across the hairline before coming back down on the other side to open her neck and other shoulder.

Something grabbed Alex's feet and dragged her backwards. A second later, her hair was pulled and she screamed involuntarily as she was lifted to her feet.

"We have a hook just for you," the bird-bitch said.

Alex was suddenly airborne. Her wrists were quickly bound and she was attached, spread-eagle, to a wooden cross, just like the man and woman she'd been watching. When the demons stepped away from and she could see the other woman in the room again, her stomach clenched and threatened to unload.

The woman's face was a silhouette of blood. Blue eyes stared out of a face with no eyelids, and a nose that was merely a stub of crimson flesh that lifted out from her bloody lips.

The demons had pulled all of her skin off. Her face was a ghastly mask of blood, interrupted only by the whites of her teeth and eyes when she screamed.

But the red didn't end with her face. The demons, even as Alex watched, were steadily peeling the skin off her of belly. The result did not look real; she was like a hideous human doll made of glistening muscle and blood.

"Oh my God," Alex whispered, as the siren of a never-ending scream filled the room.

"Don't worry," the male demon answered. He pressed his flat, horrible face toward hers until his nose touched her own. "They will do the same to you."

"No," Alex said. "Please. Don't let them do that to me."

"That IS what they do," the demon said. "And thanks to what they do, we eat. Welcome to dinner. You're the main course."

"Please," Alex begged, but the demon's dark lips only parted to reveal a gleefully white grin.

"Don't worry," he said. "You'll feel naked without your skin tonight, but you'll wake up good as new tomorrow. Ready to strip for us again!"

He stepped away, and the "hook" demon stepped into her view.

"Don't," Alex said, shifting her elbow away from the wood she was bound to when he drew close. He didn't blink. Instead, he drew one silky long finger down the white skin of her inner arm. It made her flesh crawl... and tingle. She had never felt more exposed and vulnerable, even in her father's basement.

Because while her father had been cruel and horrible, the thing in front of her was a monster. And it was a monster that wanted to rape her skin.

It raised a finger and she saw the gleam of the metal barb attached with a ring to its tip.

Alex screamed.

But that didn't stop the finger from descending. The demon pressed the blade down at the center of her palm and drew it slowly towards her wrist. Alex felt the cold bite of the steel but couldn't see it until the demon had moved lower. He had three helpers that locked her arm in place with their hands, so the blade cut clean. A line of crimson opened up down the underside of her arm, and Alex pleaded for them to stop.

But the demons ignored her. Every few seconds they shifted positions, locking her torso and then her leg in place so the blade could outline a path around her body.

"Please," she cried. "I'll do anything. Please stop."

The blade slid behind her ankle and then cut into the side of her sole. One of the demons pried her toes apart, and the blade cut in and out, tracing the inside of her toes.

The pain slowly warmed from pinch to excruciating. Alex could feel blood pouring out of her, trickling down her back and legs. But the demons didn't stop. They moved down one side and then drew the blade up between her legs.

"No!" she shrieked, as they cut into her most tender flesh. Her voice suddenly was gone, and she screamed with no sound from her throat.

But the blade continued. Down the back of her other thigh and around the toes of her other foot. And then up her remaining arm. When the demon pressed the blade to the top of her forehead, Alex closed her eyes. She kept sobbing as hands held her face rigidly in place, but no tears came out, even when the blade traced a bloody circle around her left eye, and then her right.

The cutting seemed to go on for hours, and Alex was barely there by the end. She'd closed her eyes and retreated inside, refusing to feel. Trying to block out the pain that consumed her like standing in fire.

Finally one of the demons spoke.

"Okay, it's time to take it. Melter, hold her down. Dorado, you begin. We have one hour until Redemption, so let's get this done."

Alex felt cool fingers slide along the top of her head, and a blade slip up and beneath the skin towards her hair.

And then the demon pulled hard. That's when the real pain began.

She screamed once, so hard and loud something ripped in her throat.

And then a weight was gone from her head, and the pain grew so bright, Alex felt as if she swam in white fire.

When the demon began to pull the skin from her face downward, as if removing a rubbery mask, Alex felt the light go out. There was a moment of blackness, and then there was nothing at all.

Chapter 43

"So you're telling me all of Santa Fe is being taken over by demons?" Cheyenne cocked a disbelieving eye at Joe. They had been walking in silence for the past few blocks, making their way across town to Joe's hotel.

"Something like that," he said. "How else would you explain what we just saw?"

"Maybe you can find one who will talk to you about that girl you were chasing," Cheyenne suggested. "Maybe this is a good thing for you!"

Joe thought of the man letting his guts out over the face of his wife, and violently shook his head. "It doesn't work like that. Once they've left the circle of the Calling and taken someone over, they aren't vulnerable anymore. They can't be sent back. At least not easily. Any of these demons we meet here in town? They're not going to answer any of my questions at that point. They're just going to try to gouge my eyeballs out for fun."

Cheyenne didn't say anything for a moment. They reached the corner of Guadalupe and Sierro, and waited for the light to change. Cars rushed by, and everything looked normal. But somewhere behind them, someone was screaming.

"So what now?" she asked.

"Well first, we get my car and take you to the hospital to get that bump looked at."

Cheyenne shook her head. "Try again," she said. "I don't have enough money for the deductible. And I'm fine. It hurts, but I'm okay. What's second?"

Joe studied her for a moment, trying to gauge if he really should let the medical visit go.

"Well?" she prodded.

"I need to drive back out to the mission."

"And get possessed by demons?" Cheyenne asked. Her voice dripped with sarcasm. "That sounds like a *great* plan."

Joe shook his head. "I'm not going to just walk through the front door," he said. "But I've got to go back and see if there's some way I can isolate a demon before it's fully loose. Before it's possessed someone. This may be my only chance to find out if Alex is still out there somewhere."

"So you're not going to just walk through the front door. But what are you going to do?"

"I'll figure that out once I'm there," Joe said. "But if the door to the Curburide is still open, there has to be a way…"

He shook his head. "Look, I can drop you back at your place on my way. I just think this is it. Whatever is going on, this is my last chance to reach Alex."

Cheyenne shook her head. "Oh no," she said. "You're not ditching me now. I wouldn't miss this for the world. You're clearly going to need my help."

"With what?" he said.

"I'll figure that out when you need it!" Cheyenne laughed.

Joe shook his head. "Suit yourself." He gestured at the building in front of them. "We're home."

"Looks swanky," Cheyenne said. "You didn't tell me you popped for a Motel 6."

"They leave the light on," Joe answered.

"I hope they leave the showers on too," she said. "After that walk, I need another one."

"I think we can accommodate," Joe said. "But I might have to join you."

"In your dreams," Cheyenne said.

"What, it's not like I haven't already seen you naked."

He was rewarded with a slap to the shoulder.

"Seen and Shower are two different S words," she said.

"Shit," he answered. "There's a third."

After they both freshened up, separately, in the bathroom, Joe and Cheyenne walked back to the parking lot and found Joe's car.

"It ain't much," he said. "But it runs."

She slid into the passenger seat and made a face as her legs touched the fabric. It was throat-burning hot after sitting out in the sun all day. "I hope you have air conditioning."

Joe nodded. "Yep, all four windows roll all the way down."

Cheyenne rolled her eyes. "So much for my shower."

"It's not that hot out," he lied. "It'll be fine as soon as we're moving."

He started the Hyundai up and pulled out of the lot. A few minutes later, they were heading up the Santa Fe Trail and out of town. The faux adobe houses quickly thinned out and faded into the distance, as the view out the window turned to long rolling plains of tan earth dotted with the green of sagebrush and other small desert bushes and cactus that led to the hills miles away. Joe wondered how the desert could hold that much green when it rarely seemed to rain here. But somehow, some things held on and wouldn't let go.

Kind of like me, he thought with a dour grin. *Always chasing the impossible. Not really thriving, but surviving just the same.*

"Lot of traffic out here," Cheyenne said, as a car eased up behind them, and then pulled into the oncoming lane to pass them.

"We're going 10 miles over the limit as it is," Joe pointed out.

"Obviously that's not enough," Cheyenne said, as another car suddenly pulled up to their back bumper, hung there for a minute, and then abruptly shifted lanes and accelerated past them in the oncoming traffic lane.

Joe could see eight or nine cars ahead of them. As he

counted, he saw a handful moving in the opposite direction, coming towards them. "It's like rush hour," he said.

"Yeah," Cheyenne said. "Only, everyone looks like they're rushing to go to the Birchmir."

She pointed ahead, and Joe saw the glint of a line of cars far ahead on the small road that led off the highway to the old mission.

"I hate to channel old clichés," he said. "But, I have a very bad feeling about this."

"We could turn around," she said. "Go back to my place, maybe watch a movie or something. Hell, I didn't even give you the full tour of the place while we were there."

Joe envisioned the tiny apartment, with the small living room, closet kitchen and bedroom with a connected bath. "Did you forget to show me a closet?" he asked. It earned him a punch in the shoulder.

He put on the turn signal to cut off the highway and down the small road to the old mission.

"Wouldn't you rather find out what I forgot to show you than find out why all these crazies are headed to an old, falling-down abandoned building?"

Joe turned his head and met her eyes for just a moment before turning his eyes back to the road.

"I'm guessing that's a no," she said.

"You're not curious about why all these cars are here?"

"Curious, yes," she said. "I just don't want to end up in the basement again."

"We won't go near the basement," Joe said. "I promise."

"Uh-huh."

He eased the car into an empty space between a black Ford Explorer and a beat-up 1970-something blue Chevrolet. As he turned the engine off, Cheyenne leaned over and put a hand on his arm. "I'm curious," she said. "But I don't want to be dead."

Joe nodded. "Me either. Why don't you stay here and be ready to take off as soon as I come out?" He held the car keys out to her, but she pushed his hand back.

"My luck?" she said. "I'd be arrested for stealing your car." She shook her head. "Let's go see what's up and get the hell back here as fast as we can."

Joe nodded.

Almost as one, they pushed open the car doors and stepped outside. It was hot, but cooler than it had been in the car, Joe had to admit. Together they walked towards the Birchmir, but instead of heading towards the main entrance, Joe quickened his pace and headed around the side of the building to the entrance he'd used the first time. He didn't want to be seen when he walked in.

The window was still broken, still open to interlopers. Joe didn't hesitate. He gave Cheyenne a boost up to roll over the sill, and then pulled himself up and flipped his body into the cool, still air of the mission. When he stood up, Cheyenne was eyeing him balefully.

"I'm not going back to the basement," she warned.

Joe shook his head. "I'm not getting you out of there again, either."

"Good, so we're agreed," Cheyenne whispered. "No basement."

Joe shook his head. "I didn't say that."

She glared at him.

"C'mon," he urged, and stepped forward.

The chapel was full of townies. There was an old woman wearing a long faded sundress covered in blue and purple flowers, and younger men wearing faded blue-jeans and sweaty black T-shirts. There were girls in jeans shorts and Día de los Muertos tattoos and young guys wearing fat jeans shorts that rode down their backs as if they'd lost a hundred pounds since buying them.

They all looked wildly different but there was one thing they shared.

They were all being herded forward by someone else. Someone who held a knife or gun or steel club to their heads.

They were all being pushed into the circle drawn on the chapel floor.

Into the circle of last night's Calling.

Joe pressed himself against the wall and peered out at what was going on in the room beyond. In his ear, Cheyenne whispered. "They shouldn't go inside the circle, right?"

He shook his head no. But he didn't speak. Instead, he pressed a finger to his lips and looked back at her. One accidental word could jeopardize what they were doing here.

She leaned her chin on his shoulder and watched as a young, black-haired guy was pushed forward into the circle. His captor held an outstretched knife that prevented the man from stepping back inside the barrier. So he moved forward.

A few seconds later, his body visibly stiffened. His arm stretched to the sky. He seemed to freeze that way. When he finally turned… his eyes were not his own. Joe's heart froze when he saw the black of the man's eyes.

They weren't human.

But they were definitely alive. And looking for something.

Joe vowed, silently, to remain unseen.

That's when Cheyenne, leaning over his shoulder trying to see, found it impossible not to sneeze.

The people in the chapel froze.

Joe's eyes widened.

Two of the men herding people pushed their captives to someone else and began to walk swiftly across the chapel towards Joe and Cheyenne.

"What do we do?" Cheyenne whispered.

Joe stepped back from the entryway and pointed down the hall.

"Run!"

Chapter 44

"THAT HURTS!" Ariana complained. She tried to pull it away from her neck, but Elotan only yanked harder on the strap behind her. She gasped as spikes dug into her skin. "Why do I have to wear this?" she complained.

Elotan grabbed her by the hair and yanked her face up to see the glare of his eyes. "When we leave this house, you will always wear this. It shows that you are mine."

"I didn't wear it to the club last night."

"I didn't own it then," he said. His voice dropped in pitch. "Now you'll be safer."

He let go of her hair and her chin dropped. The pointed barbs on the inside of the collar dug into her neck. Ariana winced.

"It hurts," she said.

Elotan nodded. "As it should. Every time you are in pain, you feed my hunger. As a good slave should."

"I like feeding you the other way."

"And how is that?"

"In your bed." Ariana lifted a come-hither eyebrow at him. "I don't think I want to go out anymore."

Elotan slapped her across the face. "We will go out when I say. And once we find our little runaway, I may never take you out again. Unless you misbehave."

He yanked the leather cord that trailed behind the collar and she couldn't help but follow him out the door.

The sky was piss-yellow and ominous as they walked out onto the street. It thronged with Curburide, all seemingly in a hurry to get somewhere. Elotan received several greetings, but it was Ariana who turned heads. No surprise there, really. In addition to the collar, he had dressed her in next to nothing; high black leather boots, a six-inch wide belt that hung low across her pelvis. A silky smooth thong strapped to the belt snugly between her legs to connect to the back of the belt above her ass.

It was the kind of outfit Ariana wished she could have worn to the clubs back at home, but it was the hard shape in the middle of the thong that intrigued Ariana. It appeared to be a smooth black stone, but it was more than that. When Elotan first strapped the thin material tightly against her skin, the stone had felt cold and wet, but now it seemed to burn with its own heat. As she walked, the stone moved against her like a wet tongue; that heat massaged her and the sensations jolting from her aroused clit to the back of her spine kept making her draw unexpected breaths.

The rest of her "walking outfit" consisted of two wide belts that crisscrossed from the waist to form an X across her chest covering the foremost jut of her breasts. The belts met at her neck, and latched onto the collar. The end result was that, as she walked, she was constantly receiving stimulation from the stone and prickly pain from the collar as it was pulled by both Elotan and her own movement.

Her nerves were in constant conflict between pain and pleasure. She barely could focus on where they were walking, or at the leering she was receiving from female and male demons alike. The outfit kept her mind focused on her inner world.

Ariana barely noticed when Elotan stopped to talk with demons he knew on the street. But she was vaguely aware that he was having short conversations periodically as they walked. One of them reached out to run a silken finger down her back to the crack of her ass, but Elotan slapped him away. Ariana only shivered at the tease of the touch.

"Mine," Elotan pronounced eloquently. "And I need to find what's become of my other one before she's lost to the likes of you!"

The other demon laughed. "I did hear that someone new was brought into the skin factory the other night. But they get someone new every week. Takes a strong one to survive that place for very long."

"Thanks," Elotan said. "That's worth a look at least. I haven't heard any other ideas today."

"Good luck with that," the demon said. "If she's there, she won't be leaving with you."

"We'll see," Elotan said. The other demon smirked and walked away.

Ariana didn't like the sound of that. "What is the skin factory?" she asked.

Elotan shook his head. "Not where you want to end up."

"But you're going to take me there?"

The demon yanked on the leash and Ariana yelped as the spikes bit into her neck. "I'll take you where I want and you won't question me."

She pouted and reached out a tentative finger to stroke the edge of his jaw. "I just asked what it was," she said. "I will go wherever you take me."

Elotan nodded. He turned and put two silken steel hands on her shoulders. She shivered at the sensation as he let his fingers slide down her body. His touch was amazing.

"They take people's skins off."

Ariana grimaced. "How? Why?"

"With knives. Slowly."

"More food?" she asked.

"Partly," he said. "But they take the skins to sell. They're a popular room decoration. And hard to come by. We don't have a lot of corporeal humans here."

"So if Alex was taken there, she may be dead already?"

He shook his head. "Not necessarily. She could wake up regenerated again and again. But many don't survive the pain of separation."

"Jesus," Ariana said.

"Not here."

Ariana had a vision of of the bratty teen being flensed. She imagined a demon cutting a slice across Alex's forehead and yanking the skin back to pull off her hair like a wig, exposing the red flesh beneath. The image made her shiver involuntarily. While she had no love lost for the girl – it was her fault that they were here after all – she still had some vestige of humanity left. And skinning was just too... horrible.

Elotan yanked her chain and Ariana stumbled after him. The pain of the barbs melded oddly with the heat in her groin. The rock ground tighter against her sex with each step, and waves of pleasure made her legs weak. She blinked and gasped and struggled to keep up with him. The grey buildings and yellow sky turned to a watercolor blur.

And then they arrived somewhere. He pulled her through a huge, heavy wooden door, and they were inside a dark foyer. The walls were papered with a weird tapestry of dragons and Greek symbols and roses and birds and skulls. The paper looked oddly folded and ridged in places. Then it occurred to her. The walls were not decorated with wallpaper, but with people. These were skins that had been taken off people in the rooms beyond.

"Whoa," Ariana said softly, staring at the tattoos and the different complexions of body skin that hugged the walls.

Elotan dragged her through an archway into an oval room where skins hung on hooks from the ceiling. They looked like ghastly mobiles, empty bodies floating silent above their heads. Elotan didn't pause to admire the goods for sale; he marched up to a large, burly demon who appeared to be dozing in a human skin-upholstered chair at the far side of the room. His head leaned back, lolling on the chair back. One armrest had a heart with barbed wire crisscrossed around it and the word Sherry drawn in the middle. The other armrest had a similar tattooed heart, only this one looked slimmer and said Frank. Ariana realized that the demon was resting on the skins of lovers.

The demon looked up from its nap and fastened black eyes on Ariana. "Oh yes," he said, instantly coming alert. "Where did you find her?"

Elotan shook his head. "She's not for sale."

"I could get you a very good price," the shop demon offered. He slid off his chair to kneel at Ariana's feet. With his hands he encircled her left calf and slid his fingers up across her knee and higher. His hands were so large, his fingers never broke apart as they travelled up her thigh. The stone burned with sudden electricity and Ariana let out a moan as the demon's seductive fingers hit the top of her inner thigh.

Elotan pushed the other demon away. "Enough, she's not on the auction block today."

"Just one night?" the other growled. He didn't sound ready to take no for an answer. His hands left her skin and as he stood, Ariana realized how large he really was. She'd thought Elotan was big, but this demon stood a full head taller. And his chest could have crushed two of her to him, and still had room for another.

He dwarfed Elotan, and suddenly Ariana felt a pang of worry. What if Elotan wasn't strong enough to keep her?

"I'd like to see what you have on the racks right now," Elotan said, ignoring the request.

"You're not a regular customer," the larger demon said, folding tree trunk arms across his chest.

"I may become one," Elotan retorted. "What do you have coming soon?"

The demon pointed at the skins hanging overhead. "Those are our most recent," he said. A trip to the back room did not seem forthcoming.

"I want her to see the girl whose skin she may sleep upon," Elotan said. "I want her to see the eyes before the skin comes off."

The other demon grinned. "Now I understand." He stepped towards one of the room's walls and pushed a bunch of skins aside. There was a hallway beyond. Ariana hadn't realized that there was an entryway there. A hidden passage.

"Follow me," the shop demon said, and walked through the skins. Elotan followed closely.

They moved down a short hallway that seemed black as pitch. Walls, floor, ceiling – everything was black. It felt as if they were being sucked into the void when the skins closed behind them. The floor shone like polished obsidian. Though there was barely any light to reflect, it still glimmered with each step.

But her eyes hadn't even adjusted to the void when they turned a corner and stepped out into a long, open room. While the floors and walls remained black, this place had a glass ceiling. The roiling sulphur clouds overhead cast a sickly shadow across the room.

"We have two in right now," the shop demon announced. With one arm he pointed to a cross a few yards away. "Both are women, so you'll enjoy the softest of silky skin from either."

He led the way to the first cross and gestured at the form that hung there, Christ-like. Her head hung down and chestnut hair lay in loose curls across the top of her naked breasts. She appeared to be unconscious, but Ariana could see she was still breathing. It wasn't Alex.

The demon ran a thick finger down the slope of one breast, across the faint curve of her belly and down into the thatch of brown hair between her legs. "She's given us some great skins already, and I'm sure we'll have another from her tonight. Top quality. Go ahead and feel."

Elotan reached out and put one hand on the still woman's belly. He pulled on Ariana's tether and nodded. "Touch her," he demanded.

Ariana reached a hand out to touch the side of the woman's thigh. The woman's skin was warm and soft, and Ariana felt a moistening between her legs as Elotan pressed her wrist to move to the inside of the woman's thighs. With his own hand he then took the other thigh and forced the legs apart.

He nodded, and pulled Ariana away, just as the rock between her thighs began to burn in that eye-defocusing way. "Very nice," Elotan said. "You have another choice?"

The other demon nodded. "Just came in last night. Good timing, since we lost one last night too." He pointed to another cross at the far end of the long room and began to walk towards it. Ariana took a deep breath to clear her head, and then the collar bit into her neck as Elotan moved ahead of her.

She hurried to keep up, and take the bite out of her skin, but when she rounded the side of the cross to see the figure hanging on the front, she stopped.

The girl was naked. Young. Her head hung slackly down, chin to chest, and black hair covered much of her face. But even without seeing her eyes, there was no mistaking. It was definitely Alex, the little bitch girl.

"That's…" Ariana started to speak but then gasped as the collar choked her.

Elotan looked angry. "No, I don't think so," he said to the shop demon. "Too small for what I need." He shook his head and pulled Ariana's chain again.

"But," she gasped. She was rewarded with a hard yank.

"We have every size and shape out front," the shop demon growled from behind them. "I showed you that."

Elotan shook his head and kept walking. "I need to see the creature while the skin is on. These won't do. I'll come back another time."

He put his hand up and then used it to push through the skins that hid the front shop from the "factory" beyond. A moment later they were on the street. Elotan dragged her quickly away from the place and passed several buildings before he allowed them to stop.

"But that was her," Ariana finally gasped, after holding the collar away from her neck for a moment and catching her breath.

Elotan nodded. "And did you think we were just going to say, hey, she's ours, and walk out with her?"

"Then why did we go there at all?"

"I was hoping to cross that possibility off the list. I was hoping she wouldn't be there."

"You could have tried to get her, at least."

"If he had realized why we were really there and I had

gotten into an argument with him, I would not only have lost the argument, I likely would have lost you."

"So, what is the plan now? Do we come back at night and try to go in a back door or something?"

Elotan laughed. "No."

"But they'll peel her skin off tonight!"

He nodded. "Just as they did last night. Would you rather it be hers or yours?"

"Hers."

"You drew the tall straw. You just have to work for me at the club."

"Not every night though, right?"

"That depends on how you behave. And at the moment, your conduct is bordering on insolence."

Ariana opened her mouth and then thought better of it. Instead she sealed her lips tight, and followed Elotan down the winding street home.

Chapter 45

There were voices nearby. A woman. A man. Familiar cadence. A face flashed in her memory, long black hair, a patrician nose. Hard desire in the gleam of her eyes. Cruelty.

Ariana. She heard the voice of Ariana. And the demon. Were they here to rescue her? But what was left of her to take?

Alex remembered the blade and the blood and the skin of her forehead suddenly flipping to hang like a wet towel over her nose. She was afraid to open her eyes. But then she realized that the pain was gone.

Maybe that was because she was dead.

Alex forced herself to open her eyes and look.

She was hanging from a cross, in the room that she remembered from last night. Skins decorated the wall in front of her, arms and legs stretched out like garish X's, fingers grasping to the ceiling for help. Faces stretched long and strange, the mouths open in distorted screams. Alex looked away just in time to see Ariana and the demon leaving the room at the far end.

"Wait!" she cried, but it was already too late. They were gone.

Her vision blurred and Alex blinked several times. A tear trickled down her cheek. And then another. She wasn't dead. She was trapped here alive, for eternity.

"No, probably not that long," a voice growled in her ear. "Usually skin givers don't last for more than a couple weeks. That's what makes their skin so valuable." Alex's eyes shot open and she turned to see the vicious yellow teeth of a huge demon standing at her side. Despite the fact that her feet were not touching the ground, the demon was still taller than her. His breath burned her forehead.

"Why did you want them to wait?" the demon asked. His voice was low. Dangerous. Alex's skin crawled.

"Did you want to give them your skin?" The demon slapped a heavy hand across her face. Alex felt her lips instantly heat and swell. "The merchandise is not allowed to choose the customer."

"Let me go?" Alex asked. She instantly regretted saying it. It only showed weakness.

The demon laughed.

"I'll let you go," he said. "I'll let pieces of you go every day, as long as I can."

He touched one long black nail to her neck and dragged it down the hard bone in the center of her chest. Then he held it there, pressed hard into her center, between her breasts.

"You're not going anywhere," he said. "Can't risk ruining this perfect white skin before your date with the boys tonight."

Finally the finger eased up its pressure and began to move down from the center of her chest. But Alex liked that action even less. She felt the finger poking her in the belly, and then the bellybutton, and then the groin, and then...

"I can't afford to mess up things on the outside," the demon said.

Suddenly he was standing in front of her, as his hand cupped the naked thatch of hair between her thighs. Alex didn't know how to respond. But the fact was, she had no choice. It didn't matter how she responded.

"But I can do what I want with you inside," the demon pronounced. And suddenly Alex felt something smooth and cool moving in along the soft skin of her thigh. Something hard and long.

Something...

"Ow, stop it!" Alex screamed.

"This won't hurt as much as what you felt last night," the demon promised. He pressed his huge silken chest against her own. "Not as much or as long," he said. "But it will be better for me."

Alex fought the bile spilling into her throat as a prod of demon flesh jammed its way between her legs. She shrieked as the motion against her sex turned from insistent pressure to a yielding pain. She was taken.

"We all are taken," the demon said, answering her thoughts. "Some of us just enjoy it more." He moved against her like an auger and the flash of heat that spread from her belly to her bust suggested that she might, actually, enjoy it.

She felt that way for a moment, as sensations unlike any she'd ever felt before flooded her spine. Her breath caught as the demon filled her up in places that even her own fingers had never explored.

And then something horrible happened.

Something with needles and spines.

The demon's thing seemed to expand inside her. She felt his hooks latch on to her insides and pull and rip as he flexed his thighs again and again. The overwhelming pleasure didn't disappear, it was simply joined by an overwhelming hot pain. The room was filled with the sounds of screaming. Eventually, Alex realized that the sounds came from her. The demon didn't mind. His glowing eyes only stared deeper into her own.

Hungrily.

Alex closed her eyes and shut the room and her pain and the demon's face from her sight.

There was no way out of this.

Well, no way but one.

Immolation.

And even that was something she couldn't control.

Alex squeezed her eyes closed as the demon's flesh burned and tore inside her.

She refused to howl, but instead, held the fire within.

The only way out might be to let go, but right now… she was holding it all inside. Storing the fire. Storing the pain.

Stockpiling. Pain was energy.

Energy was power.

Alex had never given in before. She wasn't going to do it now.

There had to be another way.

Chapter 46

Joe held Cheyenne's hand tight and dragged her down the hallway of the old mission. He practically threw her through the broken window that had served him as a door now multiple times. There was no time to be genteel; he put one hand on her ass and pushed as hard as he could.

Cheyenne squealed. And launched.

Joe ignored her complaint. If one of the demons caught them inside, where they were strong, there would be nothing left to complain about, because, *they* wouldn't be there anymore. They'd simply be mules to be ridden.

When Cheyenne went through the hole in the mission wall, Joe put his hands on the sill and pushed up as hard as he could, not even taking time to aim his body's trajectory. As long as he landed outside the walls of the old building, he'd be better off.

At least that was his thought before his shoulder caught the hard rock on the ground and he rolled awkwardly sideways, twisting his neck and bruising his ribs.

Cheyenne showed no mercy. She was sitting on the ground next to him when he rolled to his side. With one hand she brushed the hair off of his eyes. "Well, that was graceful as an elephant," she said.

Cheyenne pulled back her hand to rub her own forehead, while Joe fingered the scrapes on his neck and back. He only spent enough time to be sure that nothing was bloody before he pushed himself over and onto his side.

"C'mon," he said. "Elephants may not be graceful but they know when the hell to get out of Dodge."

"I'm pretty sure that's what they call a mixed metaphor," Cheyenne said.

"You lay there and argue grammar, I'm getting out of the line of fire."

"Lie." She said.

"What?"

"I think it should be 'You lie there and argue grammar,' shouldn't it? I'm not the journalist, though, and I've always gotten confused on lie and lay."

Cheyenne batted her eyelashes at him and Joe nearly lost it.

"Are you fucking kidding me?" he hissed. "We have to get out of here."

Joe grabbed her arm and yanked her upright. Together they half-ran, half-staggered down the first few yards of the hill behind the mission.

"Wait," Cheyenne yelled, and yanked on Joe's arm until they both fell to the dusty ground.

"What the hell," he said, struggling not to lose his balance and roll down the hill. "We have to get out of here."

"Stop," Cheyenne said. "Just wait. Look back a second. They didn't follow us. There's nobody coming."

Joe looked at the empty window of the mission, and then at her.

"When you rescued me, you had come to the mission because you wanted to somehow find a demon that would let you talk to your friend Alex, right?"

She looked hard at him; eyebrows raised.

He nodded.

"And we came here today because you had some harebrained scheme of still doing that, right?"

Joe nodded again.

"Then what the fuck are we running away for?"

"Because it's way worse than I thought," he said. "If we go anywhere near the chapel, they're just going to take us over," he said. His voice was an angry whisper. "We'll get possessed. The Curburide are coming through in droves and the door is still open. It's just too dangerous."

"So we don't take them on head-on," she said. "We find

one to corner and pick-off. Divide and conquer. We can do what you came here to do, but you've got to stick with it. And I can help."

Joe shook his head. "I am not putting you in the middle of that," he said. "Of this. It's crazier than I ever imagined."

Cheyenne shook her head. "Not acceptable."

Joe rolled his eyes. "What do you want me to do?"

"I want you to go back up this hill and find a way to talk to your friend, while this door you've been looking for is open. While you still can. Because I don't want to know you if we make it through this and the door closes and you haven't at least tried to reach your friend."

She paused. "Oh, and while you're at it? I particularly would like you to find a way to stop these demons from fucking possessing people. Find a way to talk to your friend and then shut the damn door. That would be a nice end result."

"You don't expect much, do you?"

Cheyenne shrugged. "Nothing I don't think you can handle. Plus, if we don't do something about this, I don't think there's going to be any town to go back to. We can't run from this."

"So what do you suggest we do?"

"What if I lured one of them out here and you tackled them?"

"That would be great, but they're demons," Joe said. "He'd just yell for help and the rest would hear him even though they're inside. They talk on a different plane than us."

"Like telepathy or something?"

"Kind of, I guess."

"So, is there a way to isolate them – stop one from communicating with the others?"

"I'm not sure," Joe said. He thought for a moment, looking out towards the mountains. Then he nodded slowly, as if agreeing with something. "The only thing I know of is the devil's trap – the same kind of pentagram in a circle as they had in the chapel. The demon has to be invited by a human to leave the circle or it's stuck there. It can't really use any of its power there, unless we have an agreement allowing it."

"Worth a try?" Cheyenne asked. She shrugged.

"We need salt or blood to draw the trap," Joe said. He held his wrists out in front of him. "We have blood, but I'd vote for salt; I get lightheaded when I bleed!"

"There is some inside," she said. "In the kitchen."

He nodded. "Yeah. But then one of us has to go back in."

Cheyenne raised her eyebrows as she nodded. "Don't get caught."

Joe took a breath. "Thanks." He looked at the silent old building a few hundred feet away. He really didn't want to go back in there. But if he didn't… what had been the point of anything he'd done since leaving Terrel? He'd been looking for a way to cross the bridge between this world and theirs and poked around anywhere he'd heard about demons showing their ugly mugs in our world. Now he'd found a place where they were absolutely active and accessible. Could he really turn his back on it out of fear?

No.

"Wait here," he said. "I'll be back."

"You're no Schwarzenegger, but, I hope so!"

Joe ran back to the mission and stood for a moment outside the broken window, peering carefully inside.

Nobody seemed to be about. The demons were using the front door, not the back. Joe put his arm across the sill and hoisted himself over. He winced as one of his shoes scuffed on the ground. Joe stopped and listened carefully, but nobody came walking down the hall in answer to his entrance.

His heart was beating a machine gun rhythm as he walked the first few steps towards the kitchen. The hallway was quiet but he could hear the low hum of voices in the rooms beyond. How much time could he skulk around in the back half of the building before the demons realized they had a non-possessed intruder on the premises?

He didn't want to find out.

Joe moved quickly down the hall and ducked around the corner and into the kitchen. There were still stacks of purses and belongings on the counters from the demon-callers who had been there the night before. They were all probably gone now, possessed and walking around downtown Santa Fe giving their new masters a tour of the town. Apparently demons didn't feel the need for purses. He smiled.

The Morton's Salt can he'd seen there earlier was still sitting on the counter and he quickly stepped across the room to grab it. He shook it softly and felt the weight shift inside. It was more than half full. It should be enough.

It would have to be.

He started to retrace his steps out of the kitchen when he heard a noise behind him. Footsteps.

Shit.

Joe looked around for some place to hide.

There was none. It was a long open room, kitchen counters and cabinets on either side, no table.

He bolted towards the exit. His hand clutched the wall as he twisted around the corner. Just as he did, he saw someone entering the room from the other end. Joe pressed his back against the wall and held his breath. Should he run for the window? Or stay put?

Something shifted in the other room; the faintest scrape of metal or plastic. Whoever had entered behind him was picking something up off the counter. Joe let out a breath. They weren't on his trail, they were here for something else.

Silently, he counted to fifty, listening for any other movement. The other room remained silent. Joe pushed himself away from the wall and tiptoed down the hallway toward the broken window. Ghetto door, he said in his mind.

When he reached the sill, he saw Cheyenne was just a few yards away, sitting cross-legged on the dirt. When she saw him, her face lit in a white-toothed smile and she gave him the thumbs-up sign. He nodded, and held out the salt can for her to see.

She held out her hands and he tossed it to her. She caught the cardboard can easily, and he put one hand on the upper part of the window as he lifted one leg to exit.

Something creaked behind him.

Joe turned his head and saw a dark-haired man moving fast in his direction. Without thinking, he pulled his hand off the sill, crushed it into a fist and aimed it at the oncoming pale face.

When it connected with the man's forehead, Joe gasped. He felt his fingers crack and the pain shot up to his elbow.

The man wasn't expecting Joe's shot, and he went down. Hard. His head stopped, his feet kept going, and a split second later he was flat on his back on the floor with a loud smack.

Joe didn't wait to see if he got up – he put two hands on the window frame and vaulted himself outside.

"You trying out for the Olympics?" Cheyenne asked when he hit the dirt and skidded to a stop next to her.

"Guy. Following me. Inside." He gasped.

She made a face. "Where do you want to set the trap?"

Joe blinked, trying to think of a good place. Where could he lead someone…

"How about right under the window?" she asked.

"Perfect," he agreed. They stood up and walked over to the building. Joe put a finger to his lips. She nodded and handed over the can. Joe took it, slipped a thumbnail under the small metal vent and opened it. Then he walked in a wide circle around the earth just outside the broken window. Anyone who came out the window would have to step inside the circle. When he'd closed the circle, he stood at the center, and carefully drew a white triangle in the soil bisecting the circle. When that was finished, he did the same thing again, creating a second triangle that bisected the original. When he was finished, he grinned, and held the can up in the air for Cheyenne to see. "Demon trap," his lips mouthed.

She nodded, and then pointed at the window. She looked at him expectantly.

Someone had to go back inside, to bait the trap.

Joe wanted to ask her to do it. He hated to admit it, but he really did. He could stay out here and wait and she could lead a demon to the trap. He'd be out here waiting.

But another voice inside him said one word.

Coward.

And that kind of summed it up.

Joe closed his eyes and took a breath. Then he held up one finger to Cheyenne and turned back towards the mission. This was his deal, he needed to deal it.

Joe pulled himself up and over the sill again, and nearly fell on top of the man he'd punched. The guy was still lying there on the hallway floor – rubbing his head with both hands and groaning.

As he watched, the man pushed off the floor and sat up. There was a dark spot where his head had been on the floor. Apparently he'd split his head open when Joe dropped him.

The man's eyes met Joe's and glared. "That fuckin' hurt, you asshole." The guy started moving towards him, and Joe grabbed the windowsill and lofted his feet over the side. He landed on the ground in the center of the salt circle. He started to move towards the edge, but suddenly a weight hit him in the back. The guy had leapt out of the window to tackle him. Joe fell forward; his face hit the dirt and he felt something warm spread from his lip to his cheek. "Ow!" he cried out, and as he did, he suddenly tasted salt. It burned the split in his lip.

Shit. He was lying right at the edge of the circle. Joe pulled himself backwards; he didn't want the demon to use him as a bridge to get free.

The weight left his back and Joe rolled to a sitting position. The demon sat at the very center of the circle, inside the triangles. The man he rode had cool blue eyes, and at the moment, they looked as if there was a light behind them. They watched Joe, silently. Unblinking. Bitterly amused.

"Nicely done," the demon finally said. "You've got me here, now, what do you want?"

"I am looking for someone," Joe began.

The demon snorted. "Aren't we all?"

Joe ignored the jibe. "Her name is Alex. She's a…" Joe considered how to describe her. Girl? Teen? Those sounded wrong; she was more than that. "She's a young woman," he finally said. "About five feet tall, dyed black hair. She went through a doorway and entered the world of the Curburide a couple weeks ago."

The demon laughed.

"I hope you've said your goodbyes."

Joe shook his head. "She's still alive, I know she is."

The demon shrugged. "If she is still alive, she is wishing that she wasn't."

"I want to rescue her," Joe said.

The demon laughed. "And I want to be the king of the universe. But there are some things that just aren't possible."

"You asked me what I wanted," Joe said. "I want your help."

The man's head shook. "I don't think so."

Joe nodded. "And I don't have to let you out of this trap. I know that the Curburide will make and honor covenants. I want to make one with you."

"In exchange for what?" The demon eyed him warily.

"In exchange for your freedom," Joe said. "If you help me find and talk to Alex, I will let you out of this circle."

"And if not?"

"I'll leave you to sit here until one of your kind comes looking for you. That might be awhile, here in the back of the mission. Maybe days. Maybe never. I don't think they can hear you up front in the chapel even if you scream. Especially if I tie you up and gag you."

"And if I help you?" the demon asked.

"I release you as soon as you help me talk to Alex."

"You realize that your friend may be dead. I can't promise that I can find her for you."

Joe nodded. "I understand. But you can promise that you will try."

"Sure, whatever you want. Let's leave the circle."

"First things first. What is your name?" Joe asked.

"Moloch," the demon said.

"Will you, Moloch, enter into a covenant with me?" Joe asked. "Will you try to reach out to your world to find my friend Alex, and if you find her, help us to talk. And, will you help her to find a passage back to his world? And finally, will you agree not to speak to the other Curburide in the mission about our presence here? In exchange, I will set you free to wander this earth as you like, with no restriction."

"I do so agree," the demon said.

Joe nodded. "Then the deal is struck. Fulfill the bargain, Moloch."

Joe began to walk out of the circle, but something smashed into the back of his head. He almost fell, but instead turned to protect himself. He was met with a fist to the gut.

"Ugh," Joe gulped as he doubled over. It felt as if his guts were going to boil up out of his mouth. But before that could happen, another punch connected with the side of his face. Joe fell sideways to the ground. The demon didn't relent. He aimed a foot at Joe's side and kicked. Hard.

The pain was immediate. Joe yelped and curled into a ball to try to protect as much of himself as he could. The demon was pissed. Joe tried to roll away and escape the next attack, but instead of another punch or kick, he suddenly heard a fleshy thud and a gasp of breath. And a curse.

His ribs and belly felt on fire, but Joe pushed himself to a crouch, exposing himself to another attack. But he saw that there wasn't going to be one. Not for a little while anyway.

Cheyenne had tackled the man, and currently was lying on the ground behind him; one arm crooked around his neck and squeezing hard. As the demon struggled to get free, she screamed in his ear. "Don't move or I will really hurt you. And I know how!"

Joe noticed that the arm that wasn't around his neck had disappeared between his legs. And the demon answered her with something that resembled a pig squeal.

He crawled over to crouch in front of the demon.

"I don't think beating the shit out of me fulfills our covenant," he said.

Moloch's lips spread into a nasty grin. "No," he wheezed. "But we didn't agree that I couldn't, either."

Joe shook his head. "Agree that you will not hurt me or Cheyenne, or I'll leave you here and walk away." He hesitated a minute, and then added. "In fact, I may make a new demon trap circle down that hill and drop you there, where nobody will ever see or hear you. You will simply bake to a husk in the midday desert sun. And until someone finds and disturbs the body, you will never be able to leave. Want to risk that?"

The demon didn't answer, but Joe saw Cheyenne's elbow jerk as her arm did something between his legs.

Moloch shrieked. "Agreed," he screamed after a moment.

"Good," Joe said. "I will try not to take too much of your time!"

Cheyenne looked up from her chokehold and grinned. "Good, cuz he's got B.O."

"Nice," Joe said. He stared hard at the elusive blue of the demon's eyes and asked, "Are you ready to do what you promised?"

The demon nodded. "Let's get this over with."

"My sentiments exactly," Cheyenne murmured, while still keeping her headlock tight.

"You can let go of me now," Moloch said.

Cheyenne met Joe's eyes, and he nodded. This either worked now, or it didn't.

Moloch, or the body he inhabited, rolled out of her grasp, and stood up, unencumbered. He rubbed his neck and stretched, wrinkling his brow at some vestigial pain. Joe and Cheyenne walked backwards, until they were both safely outside the circle.

"Her name is Alex," Joe said. "I need to find her, I know she's alive. Look into my memories and see her, maybe that will help."

Moloch nodded. "I've seen her already in your mind. I don't know if she is there to find, but time moves slower in our realm than yours. She might be. I can't fully leave this world as long as you have me bound here, but I can reach out to other Curburide beyond the door."

"Then do," Joe said softly.

Chapter 47

ALEX CRIED IN SILENCE. Tears ran in hot streams down her cheeks to drip from her chin and she longed to wail, to truly let go. But she did not.

Could not.

Would not give the demon the pleasure. So she held back the screams and cries, but she could not hold back the tears. The horror of his defilement would not leave her mind. And the blood he'd left behind remained in sticky trails down the inside of her legs. That pain was nothing compared to what she had to face again tonight.

Alex had been chained and abused before; she had a lifetime with her father to draw on for strength in that regard. She could handle humiliation. And pain. But she had never felt any pain like the raw, nerves-on-fire scalding hurt of having your skin – all of it – peeled off. It wasn't the sort of thing she had ever imagined you could live through. Yet here she was, still alive. The worst part was, she would rather die than go through that again. And apparently there were many nights ahead that promised more of the same. She couldn't do it again. She just couldn't.

This was hell. She had killed her parents and now she was paying the price in hell.

Part of her wanted to wallow in that thought, but the part that had made her strong enough to pick up an axe to take back her freedom once before did not lie down easily now. Even in hell, Alex still had hope. But not simply hope; hope was easy. Hope didn't break you out of prison, it just meant you had a more pliable attitude while you were being tortured. No, Alex had more than hope; she had a determination in her spirit that refused to accept being chained down. She looked at her bonds through blurry eyes and vowed that she would not just hang here as they took her skin each night.

But she also knew that she couldn't call on her friends this time. They were not coming again.

Somehow, she had to find her way out on her own.

Alex looked at the chains that wrapped around her wrists. They hooked onto large metal rings embedded in the wood of the cross. She pulled and twisted her arm, trying to gain a little play by cupping her hand, to make it as close in size to her wrist as possible.

But there was not going to be any release that way. She could feel her skin bruising as she tried to drag it through the too-small opening.

"Malachai," she whispered with her inner voice. "Can you help?"

The demon did not immediately answer, but she felt what she could only describe as a "shifting" in the back of her mind. Presently, she heard him whisper.

"What would you have me do?" he asked.

"Can you help me get out of the chains?"

"I can't make you smaller than you are," he said.

Alex grit her teeth. "I didn't ask you to make me smaller," she said silently. "I asked you to get me out of these chains."

"I can't remove the chains," he answered in a faint whisper. *"I can only work from inside you..."*

"Can you give me the power to stop them tonight? Can you give me strength?"

"Some. Perhaps. But I must remain invisible."

"I know," she said. "But if you can give me anything..."

She thought a minute. "Can you make it so I don't feel the pain?"

"I can. But what do you plan to do?"

"I'm not completely sure yet. I've been asking myself, 'What would Ariana do?' This is her realm. And I might have an idea..."

Chapter 48

WHEN THE SCREAMS died down from the cross a few yards away, they came for her.

Alex was ready.

"Time to get undressed for bed," the taller of the two demons said. It was Melter, she remembered, the same demon who had worked on her last night. His partner, Dorado, smirked behind him.

"But I'm not ready to go to sleep yet," Alex answered. She plumped up her bottom lip in a little girl pout.

Melter laughed, a dark, dangerous sound. "Very funny," he said. "But little girls need their rest."

"Well, I'm a bigger girl than you think," Alex said. "And I really need something before I sleep."

"We're here to give you something," Dorado said. He clicked two finger-knives together. "And once we do, you'll be praying for sleep to take you."

"I was hoping you might give me something else first," Alex said. She swiveled her hips suggestively.

Melter laughed again. This time there was true amusement in his voice. "Nice try," he said. "But stalling won't stop what we have to do."

Alex nodded. "I know that. But the last demon I stayed with, well, every night before bed, he would have his way with me. And now, I wish I hadn't run away. I have been tied up here all day thinking about how good it would be to have a demon inside me again, filling me, the way he did." She closed her eyes and moaned slightly, to add to the impact of her words.

Dorado took a step towards her, a grin on his face, but Melter put an arm out to stop him.

"You lie," he said. "A demon cock in a human girl gives no pleasure to her. It only tears her up inside."

Alex nodded. "But only for a few hours. Then we heal here. I miss it so much. That feeling of him in my mouth, pressing to the back of my throat and then sticking, giving me pain and pleasure at the same time. I loved to hear him as he reached his moment, and then…"

"I don't know what your game is," Melter said. "But you won't stop us from taking your skin."

"I'm not trying," she said. "But I just thought, if it was that good when one demon took me, what would it be like if I had two – both of you together. One in front, one in back…" She put a tongue to the front of her lips, the way she'd seen the slutty girls do at school when they talked about giving blowjobs after the Friday night football game. "…oh my…"

She rolled her eyes and grinned with convincing desire. She couldn't help but notice as she looked down that Dorado's gnarled member was responding to her suggestions.

"It wouldn't take long, but we'd all feel better before you have to do what you came here to do," she added.

"We do have plenty of time," Dorado said to Melter. In her mind, Alex raised a victory fist. She'd convinced them.

Melter grinned, and put one hand on his own growing erection. "We do. And I have plenty of pain to give her. Happy to give her more if she wants it."

He walked across the room out of her sight, and when he returned, he was carrying a wooden box. He placed it in front of her and stepped up on it, so that his face was just a little higher than her own. With one hand, he teased himself into the delta of her thighs, but before he made any true progress, Alex said, "Wait!"

"Ha!" Melter said. "Second thoughts already? Too late."

"No, not at all," she said with an easy calm. "But what I was really hoping for was to take you in my mouth, while your friend takes my other end."

"You are a crazy bitch," Melter said. His voice betrayed a grudging admiration. After a second, he grinned and shrugged. "But I like the way you think. Though I promise, you will regret this fantasy of yours."

With that, he reached up and undid the bonds on her hands. "Get her feet," he instructed Dorado. When she was free of the cross, he lifted her like a ragdoll and stepped down from the box. Then he deposited her on the floor in front of him.

"Give me a rope," he said.

Dorado turned away and returned seconds later with a long hoop of thick white rope. With a couple flips of his hands, he shaped and pulled a circle over her head. He cinched the knot and then yanked on the loose end until it was tight. She looked up at him, her neck held chokingly tight in his quickly fashioned leash.

"I grant you your perverse desire," he said. "But if make any move to try to get away, I will strangle you until you pass out."

"I understand," Alex said. "I don't want you to take my skin, I totally admit that. But all I really want right now is to feel both of you inside me. Both at the same time, pressuring me, expanding to grip me…"

She felt Dorado grip her by the hips, and kneel with his knees on the floor between her thighs. "You still look like a girl to me," he said from behind her. One of his long hands reached beneath her to pinch and rub a nipple. The sensation made her whole body jump. "But we will take care of that."

"Yes," Melter agreed. He held his erection with one hand, and bent the enormous dark head to touch her lips. "We will take care of that."

"Malachai," Alex called silently.

"*You are crazy,*" came the whispered answer. "*They will rip you in half.*"

"Just make it not hurt," she said. "That's all I ask."

As she did, the demons entered her almost as one. Her eyes bugged as she nearly choked on the foul thing that suddenly filled her throat. At the same time, she felt something rip between her legs. But the pain disappeared as soon as it began. Her whole body went numb. Malachai was doing his job. Now she had to do hers.

Alex struggled to moan in a way that would imply that she was enjoying the invasion. It was difficult when she was having a hard time finding a way to take a breath. The thing that invaded her mouth was huge.

"Mmmmmm-gh," she telegraphed. The vibration only stimulated her gag reflex and she pulled back from Melter, struggling not to let anything pass her throat. The noose tightened around her neck as she did. Her left hip slapped against the leg of the table where the demons kept their tools. The knives that would soon be carving her skin off, if her plan didn't work.

The sounds of her distress only made the demons increase their pace. Something changed inside her mouth, however. Back at the base of her tongue, something pinched her flesh. Where Melter was dragging and driving his member into the back of her throat, something suddenly bit into her flesh. Hooked her. She felt as if she had just swallowed a burr, or as if she were some kind of fish, caught fast. Melter's member was no longer shifting and moving inside her. It stuck in place, blocking all access to her throat.

A similar sensation occurred deep inside the entrance to her womb. The demons no longer slipped as they rocked and moved within her. Instead, between the two of them, they threatened to rip her apart, each hooked in and pulling in the opposite direction.

Alex would have been screaming in agony if she could have felt it. But instead, she felt only the faintest, numb tingling.

"Thank you, Malachai," she whispered in her mind.

As if in answer, for the faintest second, the numbness faded away, and she felt her most tender flesh shredding as if on fish hooks. Her mouth somehow opened wider than it was already forced, as she involuntarily moved to scream, but just as fast as the agony came, it disappeared.

"Mmmmmm," she said instead.

"This girl's... a... crazy one," Melter moaned, as he rocked towards his moment.

"Crazy good," Dorado gasped.

Almost as one, the two demons began to howl and Alex felt the bitter warmth of their orgasm begin to surge inside her.

"You're out of time," Malachai whispered.

Alex answered the orgasmic moans of the demons with strangled cries of her own. She matched her sounds to their rhythm, since she actually felt nothing at all, thanks to Malachai. When the veil lifted, she knew she would be screaming for real. But now, she pretended to feel pain and pleasure at what seemed to be the final moments of the demons' penetration. And then the motion from both demons stopped. In seconds, she no longer felt quite so "filled."

When Melter pulled out of her mouth, she could see his demonhood had deflated like a popped balloon. *So that's how they got past the whole barbed tip thing,* she thought. *Their cocks simply deflated after orgasm, allowing them to slip away from their ravaged mate.*

As she thought that, she felt the pressure ease as Dorado pulled away from her behind.

Both demons lay back on the floor, breathing heavy and staring up at the ceiling. Alex reached one hand up on the tool table next to her, and carefully felt around until she found the thing she wanted. The knife. The blade was at least six inches long but only a half-inch wide. It was like a razor thin, narrow spike with a sinuous curve to the blade.

With a quick pull, she drew the edge across the rope and severed Melter's hold on her. Now to take care of the demons before they realized their danger. Alex was no expert with a knife but she knew one thing. She couldn't count on "stabbing a demon to death."

Did they die at all? She had to disable both of them for long enough to allow her to escape. That's all she could hope for, and all she needed to focus on.

Melter still gazed at the ceiling as he savored the moment, but she only had seconds to act. He obviously hadn't felt the rope grow slack. But he was the one who would likely give her the most trouble, so he was target number one.

Alex dropped to a crouch and in a single fluid motion jabbed hard with the knife and pulled back. The blade drew along the back of Melter's leg, right behind his knee. She had read once that the best way to disable someone was to sever their hamstring, and if she couldn't kill a demon, she needed to keep them here long enough for her to make an escape.

Melter's howl was unearthly. But Alex was already turning to dole out the same treatment to Dorado as Melter clutched at his leg, which was spraying dark blood across the floor. Alex didn't have a second to spare; she no longer had the element of complete surprise.

And she was too late.

As she turned to slash at Dorado's leg in the same way, he was already rising to a crouch. He made a grab for her arm, but Alex ducked, coming up with a clear shot at his side. She didn't have time to be picky, she needed to hurt this demon. Fast.

Alex stabbed at the black flesh just below Dorado's rib cage. As the knife slid easily inside him, the demon reacted and slammed a fist against her head. His knuckles caught her at the temple, and she fell back as her world exploded in a blinding light, but she refused to let go of the knife. It ripped a long tear in his side as she fell to the ground and brought the blade back with her.

The room was filled with the mingled sounds of anger and agony. Before she could even see clearly, Alex rolled away from the source of the howls. But something suddenly gripped her ankle. Melter had her, and his grip tightened harder and harder. She screamed herself, which only made his eyes spark.

Alex sat up and stabbed again, this time meeting Melter right in the neck. The hand released her, as he instinctively grabbed at the new wound, and Alex crab walked backwards, trying to put distance between them.

That's when the knife flew from her hand as Dorado chopped her wrist. The demon was holding his side with one hand, which streamed what seemed to be a dangerous amount of blood. But that didn't stop him. Dorado went for her neck. Alex took the only shot she could. She kicked as hard as she could right between his legs. The force of her kick sent a spike of pain up her leg, and she felt his testicles crunch against her heel. The demon's fingers brushed against her neck before yanking back to hold his broken privates.

The howling grew hellish.

Alex ignored the pain in her wrist and ankle and staggered quickly away from the demons, who were clutching their injuries and cursing in a language she had never heard.

Melter tried to stand but instantly collapsed to the ground with a shriek. The pain didn't stop him though; he began to crawl towards her, murder in his dark eyes.

Alex broke his gaze, turned, and ran for the exit.

"*Nicely done,*" Malachai whispered in the back of her brain. "*If they catch you, they are going to tear off your arms and legs.*"

"They are not going to catch me," Alex said, turning the corner into the sales vestibule of the Skin Shop. At that exact moment, the demon who had raped her earlier burst through the other door. "What the hell is going on," he cried, but stopped when his eyes met hers.

"You?" he said.

His mammoth dark body filled the door that led to the street.

Alex was trapped.

Chapter 49

WHEN MOLOCH CLOSED his eyes – or at least the eyes of his host – Joe felt the cool touch of a hand close around his wrist. Cheyenne.

She didn't say a word, but he understood. She lent him her support. Her strength of will. Her hope. He covered her hand with his and smiled, faintly. But he didn't take his eyes off Moloch.

The demon's lips moved, but no sound came out. The effect was eerie. Disconcerting. And it got worse when the demon's eyelids opened.

Because instead of meeting the demon's alert gaze, Joe saw only the whites of the demon's eyes. His pupils were rolled back in his head. He grimaced, but did not stop staring. What was Moloch doing, exactly? Had he made contact? If so, to whom? And what was he saying?

Joe wanted to shake him and ask, but he knew that would probably just break whatever line of communication had been established. Assuming there was one.

Not knowing, was maddening.

Cheyenne's hand tightened on his arm, and at first Joe thought she was just reiterating her support. But when he opened his mouth to whisper his thanks to her, he realized that she was not trying to give him strength, she was trying to warn him. The demon's hands had begun to tremble. A tremor was spreading throughout the man's body. It began low; Moloch's calves jittered and swayed, very faintly. But then his hips began to shake and then his chest jutted out and in.

"Is he having a seizure?" Cheyenne asked.

"I don't know," Joe answered.

"Should we do something?"

Joe shook his head. "I don't know."

Moloch answered the question with a howl.

Joe reached out with his free hand, but the demon raised a hand of his own, and slapped Joe's arm away.

"Why don't you come through and say hi to her yourself," Moloch's voice said. Only, it wasn't really his voice. The words sounded childlike. High-pitched and cruel. The sound of a boy holding two legs of a katydid just before pulling them in the opposite direction.

"I don't know how," Joe answered quietly.

The demon laughed, staring at Joe with pupil-less eyes. Its gaze was white and horrible. It looked blind, but Joe felt as if the thing was staring inside his mind, searching for something to use against him.

"Just go inside and walk into the circle," Moloch said. "There are many who have come over today, and many more will come after. You can find your answers here."

"I don't think so," Joe said.

The demon cackled, a childish pique of angry laughter. "Coward," the thing taunted.

"I want to talk to Alex," Joe said. His voice was firm.

"She's a little tied up right now, from what I've heard."

"But she's alive?"

The childish voice laughed. "Here today, gone tomorrow," the voice said.

And then Moloch's shaking stopped, and his eyes turned back out. The dark brown pupils betrayed a glimpse of fear for a moment before the demon spoke. And then with a shake the moment was gone, and the demon looked ready to tear Joe's arms out of their sockets with his bare hands. He looked angry; vengeful.

"She is still alive," Moloch confirmed. His voice was low, gravelly. "But not for long. She's been taken by the skin traders."

"What does that mean?"

"It means they will slice off her skin every night until she finally can't take it anymore. And then she'll die."

"What skin do they take?" Joe asked. "Do they scalp her?"

Moloch shook his head. "They take all of it. And when a human is in the world of the Curburide, their skin will grow back every night before the dawn."

"But why?" Joe asked.

"We buy human skins for decoration."

Joe shook his head in disgust. "That voice wasn't you. Who was it that I was talking to?"

"A guardian of the doorways. He would not let me go farther than the first step past the door on the other side."

"So you never even got near Alex," Joe said. "I thought you were going to help me talk to her?"

"I can't reach where she is. The guardian knew that I was there under duress. He would not let me pass farther until I have disentangled myself from whatever force held me. In a word, you."

"Is there someone who can reach her?"

"I'm sure there is," the demon said. He looked as if he was about to say a name, but then shook his head. "But it's not me."

"You said you would try."

"And I did. Now release me. I fulfilled the bargain."

Joe shook his head. "You know someone. Someone who can help me reach Alex."

"It's pointless," Moloch said. "Your girlfriend is having her skin ripped off every night. They never last long on that rack. A few nights, and then the skin finally stops growing back, and they scream until there is no voice left, and no life."

"Then I'm not letting you go until you tell me who can help Alex."

Moloch shrugged. "I can tell you, but it won't do you any good. She's the demon who taught me. She's one of the most dangerous demons there is. She owns most of the skin trading stations. She lives on pain. The more suffering, the more beautiful she becomes."

"What's her name?"

"Helone."

Chapter 50

ARIANA WHISTLED. She pointed ahead of them, where a long line of people walked in single file down the center of the street. They all wore collars, with leashes tying them all together. "What's going on there?" she asked.

"They've come through the door that's been opened."

"So many?" she said. "Where are they taking them?"

"Most will go to the pain farms," Elotan said. He grinned. "I think food is going to be plentiful for quite awhile."

"What about the rest?"

He shrugged. "Some might go to the skin traders. Some of the nice-looking ones will be sold to private collections, or to clubs. You'd better dance well tonight, because there may be competition for your spot. And I need you to keep it. There are debts to pay."

"So I'm your golden egg, is that it?"

He pulled on her collar and the needles bit hard into her neck. "You're exactly what you wanted to be." He said. "Don't ever pretend otherwise."

Ariana shrugged. "Just sayin'. I seem to be valuable to you."

He pointed ahead at the line of new human slaves pouring down the street of the Curburide city. "You can be replaced," he said. "And you won't find the pain farms nearly as enjoyable as my bed."

"I thought your bed was a pain farm."

Elotan yanked on her collar again, this time dropping her to her knees. The pain arced across her vision and she could feel blood dripping down the hollow of her neck. She could tell Elotan was not truly angry; he had an erection. Inwardly she shrugged, and leaned forward to take care of it. If you couldn't give fellatio on the streets in hell, where could you do it?

Elotan relaxed his grip on the collar and held her head firmly until the spines dug into her tongue. Then he stretched his arms out above him and howled. His hips bucked faster and in seconds there was fire in her throat. As the demon came, Ariana swore she felt the earth move beneath her.

If she could have split her mouth open wider, she would have smiled. There was one thing she'd always been good at.

When he left her mouth, Elotan wiped himself off with a handful of her hair, and then pulled her to her feet.

The ground shook again, and this time there was no mistake. Something fell off the roof of a building nearby, and smashed on the road a few yards away into white powder.

"Does that mean I was good?" Ariana asked.

Elotan's look had changed from demonically delirious to a scowl.

"You give yourself too much credit," he said, and began walking away, dragging her after him. The ground shuddered once more, and both of them staggered, trying to hold fast to the pavement.

"What was that?" she asked again. "An earthquake?"

"This isn't earth." Elotan said. Her second question was met with the tightening of her noose. He wasn't going to answer her. Maybe couldn't answer her. His face looked worried.

That didn't seem good.

Chapter 51

"Release me," Moloch demanded. "I did as you asked."

"You have to help me contact Helone," Joe said.

"Impossible," the demon said. "They won't let me past the door as long as I'm under your control. You'll have to go through the door yourself if you want to reach her."

"And I'd last there how long?" Joe asked. "Five minutes?"

Moloch only grinned.

The ground beneath them suddenly jumped. Moloch's smiled passed. The demon's face betrayed concern as he looked away from them towards the mission. Joe followed his gaze and realized that one of the strangest things he'd ever seen was almost directly over them.

Dusk had been falling, but the sky above the roof of the building had gone black. Not night black, but tar-black. It made the rest of the deep blue horizon look pale in comparison. To his left, Joe could see the first glint of stars, but over the roof of the mission, all light was swallowed up. Gone. There was no light there, just a heavy darkness that seemed to shimmer slightly at the edges. Almost like heat lightning. A spark flared along the edge of the darkness as Joe stared at it, and once again, the ground beneath him shifted. Next to him, Cheyenne gasped, and lost her balance, unprepared for the shudder.

She fell forward and Moloch acted. The demon wrapped six long fingers around her arm and dragged her all the way into the circle. She kicked at him but he lifted her off the ground easily, and then held her body tight to his own, with his arm pinning her neck.

Her eyes widened and Cheyenne choked.

"Release me now or I release her. From life."

Joe saw the light in the demon's eyes, and nodded. He was not going to get any farther here. "I release you from your bond and thank you for your service," he said.

"Open the circle," Moloch prompted.

Joe scuffed his shoe through the salt until the circle was broken. The demon stepped through and tossed Cheyenne at Joe like a doll.

"Whether you enter the door of your own will to find Helone or not, you will be going through," Moloch said. He gestured at the sparking ink above them. It seemed to cover even more of the sky than it had a moment before. "This door is not like the others. It will not close until it swallows all. Look!"

The demon pointed and now Joe could see that there were shapes moving in the ichor. They seemed white, like birds at first, with flailing wings. But then he realized that the shapes were not birds at all. They were people. And there was a chain of them extending from the front of the mission to the center of the darkness. One by one, the struggling figures rose skyward and winked out as they reached the center.

"Where are they going?" Joe asked.

"To hell," Cheyenne whispered. "We are literally looking at the gates of hell."

Moloch laughed, and turned away.

"Don't bother to knock," he said. "The door's open."

At that moment the ground shook again, and a handful of figures suddenly came running around the corner from the front of the mission. Moloch waved at them, and pointed behind him to Joe and Cheyenne.

"I think we need to get out of here," Cheyenne said.

"Just one problem," Joe said. "They're between us and the car."

She grabbed his hand and pulled him towards the back of the Birchmir. "Can't go through them," she said. "Better go around!"

Joe followed her around the back of the mission and up the other side. When the parking lot came into sight, he began to smile. "I see it," he said. "I see the car."

But when they rounded the corner, his heart sank. A solid wall of people stood in front of the mission. Waiting for them.

As one, the crowd began to move towards them. Darin was in the lead.

"I hear you are looking for someone," Darin called.

Joe turned to go back the way they'd come, but the way was blocked by the group that had first started chasing them.

"I think we can help," Darin said. "But everything has a price."

When Joe turned back to face the parking lot, Darin and a couple dozen others had spread out to completely block their way forward.

"What do you want?"

Darin shook his head. "No, it's what you want." He stepped forward and grabbed Cheyenne by the arm. She kicked at him but he moved and easily dodged her foot. Then he punched her in the mouth.

Joe jumped forward but hands suddenly closed on his arms. He tried to twist away, but they held him solid. Cheyenne struggled similarly in front of him. Blood smudged her chin from a split lip.

"I understand you want to bring someone back from the other side. We can arrange that, but it's a one-for-one trade." He pointed at Cheyenne. "We'll send her through and bring back your girl. Sound good?"

Cheyenne's eyes widened. She shook her head vigorously.

"No," Joe said. "Just forget it. Let her go."

Darin shook his head. "Too late, it's been decided." He slapped Joe's face. "I'm surprised at you, I thought you'd be more grateful than this."

"I just wanted to find out if my friend was still alive." Joe said.

"Liar," Darrin answered. "Here I am trying to give you what you want, and you don't even say thanks."

"Let us go," Joe said. "You've got plenty of people, you don't need us." He pointed at the line of people who stood in a line that stretched from the front door of the mission to the center of the parking lot. One by one their feet left the ground and they twirled around and up into the sky, straight into the center of the black blot in the sky.

"It's never enough," Darin grinned. He walked a couple steps and then stopped, one hand on his cheek. "You know, I have an idea. I think we'll play a little game." He whispered something to three men nearby, and then motioned to the ones holding Cheyenne and Joe. "Bring them."

They walked back into the mission and up the stairs to the bell tower. Once there, he had the men tie Cheyenne's wrists to the pole that held the mission bell. A moment later, the three men he'd talked to below came up the stairs gasping. They – along with two more men – were carrying the statue of a stone angel from the chapel.

They set it down with a smack.

"Tie the angel to her feet," Darin demanded. The men quickly made a harness around the angel's wings, and then tied the other end of the rope to Cheyenne's ankles.

"Now tie another rope around the angel," Darin said. He paced around the small space as the men cinched the rope. When that was done, he picked up the loose end and handed it to Joe.

"We're going to let that angel take flight," Darin said. "When it does, it will probably pull your girlfriend's arms right out of their sockets. Unless you can hold it back with the rope. Three things could happen here. You could get pulled over the side along with the angel and your girlfriend will get stretched like taffy. Or you could let go of the rope and save yourself. Or… you could hold onto the rope long enough to save both of you."

"You're insane," Joe said.

Darin laughed. "Nah, just trying to have a little fun. Our

girl here has proven she's quite the escape artist. Let's see how she gets out of this one."

"Ready?" He pointed to the men who had carried the angel up the stairs and they lifted it once more and staggered with it towards the wall.

"How long do I have to hold it?" Joe asked.

"That's the spirit," Darin said. He looked at the watch on his wrist. "Let's say five minutes. You last that long, I'll cut it loose."

He held a knife up in one hand and pointed to the men with the other. "Toss it over and let's see how strong our boy is!" Then he looked at Joe. "You better brace yourself, my friend. That sucker's heavy."

Joe wrapped the rope around his waist and hurried to the wall. He sat down and put his legs against the wall, while twining the rope around both of his hands.

"Good luck," Darin said, as the men lofted the stone angel over the wall.

Chapter 52

THE SKIN TRADER came at her like a bull, angry arms outstretched. But instead of running away, Alex dashed right at him. At the last second, she dove, and slid right between his legs. As he turned around, she rolled to a crouch and bolted out the front door of the skin shop.

Behind her the demon shrieked in anger, and came tearing out of the store. Alex only looked back once, and then she turned on everything she had and ran. "Help me Malachai, give me strength."

She rounded the side of a building and the street rumbled. Another tremor. Bricks and stone pelted the ground around her and Alex threw herself down a stairwell and covered her head. She struggled with all her energy to shield her thoughts so the demon couldn't feel her that way. She cowered there in a corner against the wall, praying that the skin trader hadn't seen her turn. She didn't know how far behind her he'd been.

The rumbling of the earth stopped after a moment, and then the street above remained quiet.

After a few minutes passed, she relaxed and crept halfway up the small stairwell to peek out at the street. There was nobody in sight. Maybe the small earthquake had sent everyone to shelter.

Alex breathed a heavy sigh of relief. She was free again. But now what?

Somehow she had to find a back door in to one of those portals.

"*Use your inner sight,*" Malachai said.

"But they'll see me," Alex said.

"*Be quick. Look for where they are.*"

The ground shuddered again, and Alex grabbed at the wall for support. "What's going on?" she asked. "Do they have earthquakes here every day or something?"

"No," he said. *"Something's not right."*

"You're a genius," Alex said. She closed her eyes and focused, trying to see with her mind's eye the world around her.

At first it was all just darkness. And little flashes of red and green – the afterimage of the last thing she had looked at. But then the afterimages faded, and she could see a broad horizon of dark.

There were things moving on the periphery. Shapes with burning embers for eyes. Soon she realized that there were hundreds of tiny lights in the dark. They were all around her, but a large group was congregated to her right. There seemed to be a lightning storm there; a thousand flashes of light crashed on the horizon, each one just a tiny bit farther away from the last.

Figures, hundreds of them, surrounded the lightning storm. One of them turned, and stared straight at her. It put a hand out and pointed, and Alex opened her eyes, blotting out her inner sight.

She knew which way to go, but she wasn't sure she wanted to go there.

"It's the only way out," Malachai said.

"It looked like a storm," Alex said.

"A door between worlds hasn't closed. The flashes are the Curburide going through."

"You mean, all of them are going to Earth?"

"And sending people back here to be tortured, no doubt," Malachai said.

"That's horrible," Alex said.

"There has always been interchange between the worlds," Malachai said. *"Doors open and doors close. But a door that stays open..."*

"What will happen?"

"*Ultimately?*" he said. "*This world will consume yours. Everybody that moves through the worlds opens the crack a little wider.*"

"How do we stop it?"

"*I don't know that we can.*"

Alex saw something move at the end of the street. "Something's coming," she said. "Maybe the demon that saw me."

"*Get out of sight,*" Malachai said.

Alex ran down a side street, but with her inner eye, she caught glimpses of what lay behind the facades. She dodged down one block and then another, keeping buildings between her and the lights that represented Curburide. Slowly the storm of light grew closer.

Alex darted into an old building that looked like a museum; huge ornate columns flanked the door and gargoyles leered from ledges overhanging the street. As soon as she was inside, she recognized it. "I've been here before," she whispered.

She ran down one corridor and down a flight of stairs. It was a labyrinth, but she knew that Ariana and her had been here in their first hours in this world. This was the way back to the pits where the heads were buried in filth. The corridor to the rains of demon piss. She was close to the place where they had entered. Closer to the door.

Just as she thought that, a door opened just ahead. A large, familiar demon stepped out, directly in her path. His eyes glowed in the shadows. In a heartbeat, he dashed at her and clutched six long fingers around her arm.

"People have been looking for you," the demon growled. "And I've been listening. Someone thought they saw you coming this way. How did you escape the skin traders? Who helped you?"

At that moment, Malachai sunk to the deepest hole inside her, hiding from detection. As he did, the pain from the violation of Melter and Dorado flooded back. Alex had only felt a hint of it earlier; now it exploded in her nerves like a bomb. It felt as if someone had shoved broken glass up between her legs, and down her throat. The shock paralyzed her; Alex couldn't move a muscle. Her legs locked as Alex opened her mouth to scream.

But instead only a gasp and a trickle of blood came out, and she collapsed, unseeing, into Elotan's waiting arms.

Chapter 53

DESPITE HIS PREPARATION, the weight of the angel still took Joe by surprise. There was no way to brace for the force that pulled him up off the ground. His shoulder slammed with an audible crack into the stone wall. Behind him, Cheyenne shrieked as the statue wrenched her ankles, stretching her whole body in the air. Joe's grip on the rope took some of the weight off, but not all. They shared the weight of the anchor between them, but it was too much for two people. The weight dragged Joe's arms up the side of the wall and he struggled to get his feet locked again before it pulled him right over the edge.

"Oh my God, oh my God," Cheyenne was screaming. "It hurts. Holy shit."

Joe flattened himself against the wall, but it was no good. Inch by inch, his arms were creeping up towards the edge. It would pull him over long before the five minutes was up.

"If I was you, I'd just let go," Darin said, strutting back and forth behind him. "Maybe I was wrong, and she'll be able to support the full weight. She's a stubborn one, that's for sure."

"You... a ... bastard," Joe said, gritting his teeth. Spit flew with every word as he struggled to turn his body away from the wall without letting go of the rope. If he could just wrap it around the edge and use the edge itself as an anchor...

Joe's face scraped against the rock as he hugged to the wall, trying to distribute some of the tension. Cheyenne kept screaming behind him, but she only added to a growing din. There were screams coming from the throng below too, and now and then the earth creaked with its own complaint. The mission vibrated with tremors.

"I will not let go," Joe murmured, sweat beading and running down his forehead. "I will not. Will not."

Tears ran down his face as he pushed and shoved and struggled to not be carried over the wall. Something ripped in his back and he felt the rope strangling his abdomen. He gasped and cried and twisted, struggling not to go over the wall. Counting the seconds. Knowing that they had to have become minutes. His vision was a red haze. He couldn't feel his wrists any longer. But he would not, could not, let go.

"I am amazed," Darin said. "Truly amazed."

He walked in front of Joe's face, slapping the blade of the knife against his palm. "But I'm a man who keeps his promises. I told you I would cut the rope if you lasted five minutes."

Darin reached over the wall and suddenly the strain on Joe's body ceased. He fell to the ground at the exact same moment as Cheyenne gave out a hideous, ear-shredding scream. Joe looked up and saw her body stretched taut, the full weight of the statue dragging her joints apart. Darin had cut a rope, but not the rope that held her to the statue. He'd cut the rope that Joe was holding. The rope that was saving her from suffering all the weight.

Joe started to rise, but there was nothing he could do. A fountain of blood suddenly burst from Cheyenne's shoulder as one of her arms let go.

"Oops, wrong rope," Darin said, before slicing the rope that had just ripped Cheyenne's arm from its socket.

The angel fell to the ground below as Cheyenne's feet fell into the bell shaft. She hung by one arm, the other hung on its own from the rope connecting it to the bell pole.

"That was close," Darin said. "One more second and I bet we would have lost her." He tossed the knife to one of the men. "Get her down."

Joe tried to lunge at Darin but something in his middle wouldn't let him move. The statue had crushed him. He felt the tears coursing down his cheeks as he looked at the inconceivable. "How could you?" he cried. Tears streamed down his cheeks. "Seriously, God, how could you…"

Arms grabbed Joe and lifted him. He tried to punch at them, but he couldn't feel his hands. The fingers were purple. He could barely breathe. When they took him through the front door of the mission chapel, Joe saw that the black spot above the mission now covered the whole sky. There was not a star to be seen. Just an inky swirl where bodies floated up, against the law of gravity. Hands pushed him forward, walking around the line of people waiting to be taken up, up, up and away. They all approached a point just beyond the chapel and then were lifted, as if in a slow motion cyclone.

Darin caught up with them a moment later and handed, the limp body of Cheyenne into Joe's numb arms.

"Hold onto her," Darin said. "Don't want to drop her."

"You killed her," Joe sobbed.

"Not yet," Darin said. "They put a tourniquet on it. If you get her upstairs quickly enough, she might make it through the night. Demons can do miracles, you know. If you find a nice one. But you'd better hurry."

He pushed Joe forward. Hands held his elbows still, propping him up even as he carried Cheyenne.

"Oh, forgot about this. I don't think you'll need it, but you never know."

Darin tossed Cheyenne's severed arm on top of her chest.

"I gave you cuts in line," he said.

The hands pushed Joe forward and all of a sudden he felt his feet leaving the ground.

Joe saw figures of other people ahead of him pinwheeling around in the sky. Some of them were screaming. Some were laughing.

Joe couldn't stop the tears from streaming down his face.

"Alex, I hope you're up there," he whispered, as the wind rushed past his face and a cold silken breeze wrapped around his body and tightened like a cocoon around him, taking him through the darkest center of the dark sky.

Then Joe punched through the black and left Santa Fe behind.

Chapter 54

"About time you woke up." The voice sounded blurry, but familiar. Everything felt hazy; it was hard to hear, and she couldn't seem to convince her eyes to fully open. But she tried. The waves of red finally faded.

Ariana's thin face stared down at her from above. The woman was naked, except for a black collar around her neck with thin straps that cinched across her breasts to hook onto a belt around her waist. It seemed to serve no purpose other than to make Ariana look sluttish. It covered nothing.

Alex opened her mouth to speak, but the pain came back instantly, and she moaned instead of spoke. She didn't dare move her midsection.

"It's not nighttime yet," Ariana said. "You're going to have to hang on for a bit longer before the sleep that saves. You've been through the wringer, huh kid?"

Ariana moved away.

A moment later the face of Elotan took her place. The demon looked even more enormous than she remembered.

"How did she get away?" he asked Ariana.

The other woman shrugged. "I don't know, but I'd say she fucked her way out from the look of her."

The demon snorted. "So she's useless to me."

"For now," Ariana said. "You've got me for the night."

"You've already ruined your mouth and you have to work tonight," Elotan said. He bent over Alex and tightened something around her wrists. "It's time to go. She's not going anywhere."

A door closed and Alex was left in darkness, and silence.

"Malachai," she whispered. "Help me, please."

The pain eased, but didn't completely go away. *"You're going to have to get used to this feeling,"* Malachai said.

"No, I'm going to get out of here."

Her answer was silence.

Chapter 55

THEY WERE TURNED away at the club door. "Not tonight," the club owner said to Elotan. "We've got lots of fresh flesh. No need for a retread tonight."

"But you promised me a stage every other night," Elotan said.

"Things change," the demon shrugged. "There are new bodies coming through the door every minute now. We don't need to look at old stuff. Come back in a week and we'll see."

Elotan slammed his fist into the wall. The result was a grunt of pain and the emergence of two bouncers who flanked the owner like giants.

Elotan yanked on Ariana's leash, and pulled her away from the club.

"So now I've got two useless bodies," he complained. "Maybe I'll sell you both to the blood mines."

"Won't you get the same response there?" Ariana asked softly. She didn't like where this was going. The bloodmines sounded much worse than dancing for demons.

He yanked on her leash and dragged her back the way they had come.

Alex remained where they had left her, chained to Elotan's bed.

The demon stood over her and looked her up and down. With one hand he reached down and pinched one of Alex's nipples, hard, between his fingertips.

"Well if I can't sell the two of you, you'll just have to make it worth my while to keep you." He reached up to pull a long-handled whip from a hook on the wall.

"Kneel," he demanded to Ariana.

She did as he said, and something cold and evil bit into her back. She yelped as it pulled out. He was using the cat o' nine tails with the metal tips. And he was not in a good mood.

"Oh shit," Ariana said to herself. The barbs cracked again and again, and she stiffened and cried. But she refused to complain. It would not help. She bent forward and accepted his punishment. Her back felt shredded in minutes.

And then he stopped and dragged her by the hair to a new position. She saw what he wanted instantly. His member dangled in her face like a silent cobra. She could barely open her mouth still from her attentions to that deadly snake earlier today, but she didn't argue. She knew better. Somehow she let him push past her swollen lips.

Meanwhile, cries erupted from behind her. Ariana dove into her job with new energy. Elotan held Alex down on her back with one hand, while he doled out punishment with his other. The barbs were quickly streaking the girl's breasts and belly in blood.

Elotan yearned for pain tonight more than pleasure. Alex was definitely getting the raw end of this deal. And Ariana intended to keep it that way.

She sucked the demon dick in deep.

Chapter 56

JOE'S LEGS COLLAPSED when his weight suddenly returned. One moment he'd been freefalling in utter black, and the next he found himself in a red-lit cavern. But he was not alone. There were voices chattering all around and a horde of black-skinned demons standing in wait just a few yards away from where he sat on the ground. Cheyenne's blood coated his chest in sticky wetness.

"Helone!" he called. "Is Helone here?"

One of the demons approached him and with one hand pulled him up to his feet, Cheyenne and all.

"Who are you that dares to call for the Queen of the Doors?"

"I was sent to find her," Joe said. "I need her help."

The demon snorted. "Helone's help? You'll end up worse than your friend here."

"Can you take me to her?"

"I don't take people anywhere but the bloodmines," the demon said. "But since you think you can invoke her name, I will ask her what she'd like me to do with you. I think that her response might be amusing. Come on, get out of the way."

As the demon pulled Joe away from the center of the room, two more people suddenly appeared in the empty space. Demons from the crowd seemed to debate over the bodies for a moment before two demons walked into the center and retrieved the people who were looking around in complete terror.

They had only walked a few feet when Joe's captor stopped and gave him a hard, surprised look.

"Helone is coming to see you herself. Wait here."

He left them in a small empty room. Joe could hear the cheers of the demons in the adjoining room as more people fell through the door.

"Hang on," he whispered to Cheyenne's slack face. Her lips looked blue, but somehow there was still a faint rise and fall to her chest. Darin's men had wrapped a shirt around her shoulder, but the blood was still leaking out steadily.

"You asked for me?"

The voice was soft, sibilant. Joe looked up into the face of a beautiful demoness. Her eyes were electric, her cheekbones high. She wore a sash of some filmy red lace over her flawless dark skin, but it was an affectation only. It did nothing to cover the perfect lines of her belly or the dark knobs of her breasts.

"Helone?" he asked.

She nodded. Her look was stern, but curious.

"They said you could help me," Joe said.

"I think she needs more help than you," Helone said. She clapped her hands and two demons appeared instantly. "Take that creature and stop the bleeding. Put her arm back in place and let's see if she can last until Redemption."

In a second, Cheyenne was lifted from Joe's lap, and then she was gone. He felt as if they'd stolen her, but he realized that if there was any chance of saving her, every second was precious. He couldn't believe she was still alive at all.

"Now," Helone said. "Your business with me?"

"There was a woman who opened a door to come here recently," he began. "She came here with another. A girl named Alex."

Joe didn't miss the spark in Helone's eye when he said Alex's name. Did she know about her?

"I've been trying to find a way to contact her, to bring her home. A demon named Moloch said that you might be the only one who could help."

Helone closed her eyes and tilted her head back in a silent chuckle. "I should have known," she said finally. Moloch is a fool. You must have had him cornered though, if he thought to invoke my name."

Joe nodded. "I did. Was he wrong?"

"As it happens, yes. And no." She walked across the room and watched the scene going on outside the doorway for a moment. "He couldn't have known, but your Alex stayed with me briefly. Precocious thing. Headstrong."

Joe smiled at that.

"But she's gone now."

"Gone?" he said. A shard of ice pinned his heart. "Gone how?"

"She left my house," Helone said. "She spurned my hospitality."

"Would you help me find her?"

"And why would I do that?"

Joe opened his mouth but had no answer.

Helone looked down her nose at him and nodded. "Nevermind. There is a thing or two I'd like to say to her. I haven't felt as young as she made me feel in centuries." The demon ran her hands down her sides and thighs. Whether she was appreciating the feeling, or trying to show off her body to him, he wasn't sure.

"So you will help me?" Joe asked.

Helone looked at him with devil eyes.

"I might."

Joe couldn't help but grin.

The demoness returned his smile and added, "but first you'll have to pledge your skin to me."

Chapter 57

"Make yourself comfortable," Helone said, gesturing to a low couch. Joe sat, and watched as she moved across the room to a small bureau with glassware on it. They had just walked a couple blocks through a grey city to descend a set of garden apartment stairs to enter Helone's home. Now they were in her sitting room; a fireplace flickered to life on the far side of the room, and candles seemed to light in small nooks of their own accord. Helone lifted a tall but narrow carafe and poured dark liquid into two short goblets. Joe assumed it was wine; when she handed one to him, it looked like a burgundy, thick and deep red.

She slid onto the couch beside him, holding her own glass with three fingers. The demon took one slow sip and gave out a low sigh of pleasure. She never took her eyes off of him. It made him uneasy, and Joe broke her gaze to take a sip of his own drink. When the liquid touched his tongue, he almost dropped the glass.

His tongue lit with heat, and his groin ached in a strange sympathetic response. The tips of his ears warmed, and for a second, he saw a swirl of color in place of the flickering shadows of the room. His hand was shaking.

"Wha," he mumbled. His lips felt thick.

Helone laughed softly. "It is good, yes?"

She reached out and took the glass from his fingers before he spilled it. Joe leaned his head back against the cushions and closed his eyes. As he did, a wave of pleasure rushed from his neck to the tip of his spine. He spread his legs slightly, as if to let the heat vent.

Then he took a breath and reopened his eyes. Helone held the glass back out to him, and he took it, gingerly.

"What is that?" he asked, looking hard at the goblet.

"Do you like it?"

He didn't answer immediately, but instead retraced the strange sensation that had overtaken him from just one sip. He'd smoked a substance or two, and done more than his share of drinking. But nothing he'd ever touched had given him such a rush.

"Yeah," he said. "I guess I do."

Her lips pursed faintly, and a smile creased them as her eyes flashed. "Good," she said. "I want my guests to be comfortable, and enjoy what I have to give."

She ran three fingers across the bare skin of his arm. "Drink it slowly," she advised. "It's meant to savor."

"I don't think I have a choice," Joe said. "If I drank it fast, I think it would knock me out!"

She nodded. "It's our wine. Strong stuff. But full of feeling."

"That's a good way to put it," Joe said. He could still feel a faint tingling in his lower back. And that feeling only intensified when he looked at Helone. The faint gauze of red that she wore did nothing to conceal her body, and Joe was acutely conscious of being alone with her.

"Tell me about you and Alex," Helone said. "She must mean a lot for you to have dared to come here."

She lowered her chin and stared deep into his eyes. "You know most Curburide would eat you alive, don't you?"

Joe nodded. "But you won't, right?" He suddenly felt a surge of panic but he couldn't go back now.

"I'm not hungry," she said. "At the moment."

Helone's smile widened and she stretched, lifting one arm high in the air. The red silk slid off her left breast. Joe had seen plenty of naked women in his life, but none with skin the color of onyx. She looked almost plastic, she was so smooth. And the curve of her was…

He stopped in mid-thought as he realized that she was watching him watch her. Helone's gaze was catlike.

"I'm glad you are enjoying my hospitality," she said, settling back on the couch.

She was toying with him.

He nodded, and took another sip of the goblet. He was going to need some strength to get through this audience. As the heat radiated from his throat to his chest, and then migrated to the tender flesh of his thighs, he realized that this might not be the best drink to give him strength against a demoness. He could suddenly feel the pores on his balls, and the tip of his penis was… thirsty.

"Ohhh," he said, and took a breath.

Helone slid an arm behind him and drew herself closer. "You know why the Curburide want to come to your world so badly?" she asked, as her fingers gently slid over his thighs to rest on his hipbone. She squeezed.

"Because you want to torture us?" he asked.

"Some. Guess again."

Helone clinked her glass against his, and lifted one eyebrow as she took a sip of her drink. She cocked her head, waiting for him to follow her example, he realized. He knew he shouldn't.

But he did. The world filled with orange light, and specks of snow and fire.

"Because you can't get good bourbon here?"

She snickered, and lifted one bare leg to touch her toes to his knee… and then his thigh.

"No," she said. "Because you're good in bed."

Joe swallowed.

"Well, some of you are." She tilted her head, and looked him up and down. "Are you?"

"I don't know," Joe said. "Maybe."

"Hmm," she said. "What did Alex say?"

"I never did that to Alex," Joe snapped.

"Oh no?" Helone said. The glass in her hand had vanished somehow, and now she closed in, tracing the side of his jaw with on finger, while her arm around his back held him tight to her. "Is that why you came looking for her?"

she asked. Her voice was barely above a whisper. "You had unfinished business?"

"No, it's not like that," Joe said.

"You're lying," Helone said. Her mouth was just inches from his own. It felt as if her eyes were looking into his brain. "It *is* like that, and you've been lusting for that spunky little cunt since the day you picked her up in your car. It's only because you're such a coward that you didn't bang her that very night."

Joe gasped. Could she see inside his memories?

"Isn't that right, Joe?"

Helone's arm slid out from behind him and suddenly she was kneeling over his lap, pressing him back against the cushions with her hands on his shoulders. "Tell me the truth, Joe," she said. "Tell yourself the truth. You want the world to think you're a nice guy, but what you really wanted was to take that little girl – that underage little teen – and spank her bare bottom, didn't you? That night you shared a tent with her, you wanted to rip her panties off, pin her to the dirt and press yourself as far into her as you could go, didn't you? Don't lie to me, Joe."

Joe's tongue wouldn't move. Nothing would move. He felt paralyzed, caught in some strange vortex of power and truth and fear.

She took the goblet from his trembling fingers, and held it to his lips. "Don't waste it," she said. "It's precious."

Joe took a deeper sip than he'd intended, as she tilted the glass against his lips. The universe itself seemed to open as the liquid fired every nerve in his body.

The red silk slid completely off of Helone's smooth skin and she set the glass aside. Then she pressed herself closer, rubbing her chest against him as if she were a cat rubbing against his leg.

"No," he whispered.

She covered his complaint with a nipple, and held his face with both of her hands, not letting him escape. Joe felt tears gathering at the sides of his eyes. He thought of Alex, beautiful, funny, crazy Alex. So full of energy. So spunky. So… so hot and tantalizingly forbidden and fuckable. Yes, of course he'd lusted for her. Of course he'd wanted to be between those young, muscular thighs…

Helone's nipple thickened between his lips. She rubbed the sides of his head and shifted in a slow, unmistakable rhythm on his lap. Joe suddenly felt as if he was burning up; her nipple pulsed with strange little needles of pain and pleasure between his lips, and his cock felt as if it might snap inside his pants. Against his will, he ached to be outside of his zipper, to meet the heat that was hovering just inches away, taunting him.

Helone shifted, drawing him forward as she lay back on the couch. She never let his mouth separate from his suckle, but suddenly her hands were moving on his belly and thighs. The torturous zipper creaked and then his pants were shimmied down his calves. The world shifted as the air touched his skin, and then Helone's silken body poured over his pores. He almost screamed from the pleasure as she wrapped her legs around him, pinning him on top of her.

She teased his mouth free of her tit, and his lips felt thick, swollen. She drew them down to her lips for a soft, momentary kiss. And then she held his face up, so that he could do nothing but look into her eyes.

"You came here because even though you knew it was wrong, you wanted to fuck Alex, didn't you?"

"Yes," Joe said.

Helone grinned.

"And the girl you brought with you?" Helone said. "You wanted to seed her too, didn't you?"

"Yes," Joe said. His voice was a mumble; his lips seemed almost swollen closed.

"And the little college girl, Cindy," she said. "What was it like to be inside her cunt? You were brave enough to go there, weren't you?"

"Yes," Joe said.

"I will make you forget all of them," Helone promised, and raised him up with her hips, shifting his hard-on until there was only one place it could go. With one hand she reached down and guided him the last inch.

Joe felt a softness at first, a velvet slick sensation that was softer, more tantalizing than silk. Helone wrapped her arms around him and drew him down, pressing his mouth to hers. Her eyes were passion jewels, glowing with lust, capturing his gaze with the light of constellations, and the savagery of animal instinct. Her tongue speared him at the same time as he slid all the way inside her hungry vaginal walls. He thrust in time with her tongue, unconsciously following her demand.

She increased the pace, drawing him in and teasing him out. His mind was a blur of her skin and the still-mind-bending impact of the wine. The room spun and shifted, as if they were coupling in space, tilting and rolling and plugging in to the electric currents of primordial sexuality. He breathed her in, and closed his eyes. He had come here for Alex. He had come here for Cheyenne. He had not come here for this. For this... evil heaven.

Something pricked his tongue, and he opened his eyes to see the fractured colors of Helone, now above him. Somehow his back was to the couch and she was riding his pelvis with growing demand. With each second she bounced up enough that he almost lost her, but then she slammed back, to recapture him.

His mouth burned.

He tried to open it, to break the kiss, but she didn't let go. Her tongue was thick inside him; it felt as if pins were spiking his tongue.

But that was nothing compared to the nails that suddenly grabbed his cock by its sensitive head. All of a sudden, Helone's rocking did not make her crotch separate from his body, she lifted his cock and ass up from the couch and slammed him back down, as teeth chewed and held his manhood inside her.

"Wha…" he gasped, trying to speak while she still held him in a demon kiss.

She ignored him, and only pushed her tongue deeper into his throat, so that he could feel the barbs inside. She ripped the flesh of his mouth as something deep inside her mangled his cock. All the while, her breathing grew faster, and finally, when he had begun to scream inside her throat, she threw her head back, tearing out of his mouth with skin and blood dripping down her chin to bellow at the ceiling in pure, ecstatic orgasm.

When her moans softened, and she opened her thighs to let him free, Helone laid back on the other side of the couch from him. A slick trail of blood crossed the black of her inner thigh, and Joe looked in horror at the ragged spear of shredded flesh that was what remained of his dick.

Before he began to cry, Helone grinned, and ran a finger from the wetness of her crotch through the blood on her thigh.

"I told you that I would make you remember me," she said.

Chapter 58

FOR ALL ITS SIZE, the demon left the bed as if he'd never been lying in it. The mattress didn't seem to move. But Alex felt him go. His scent, the strange mix of ambrosia and sage and sulphur suddenly grew thin. The feeling of energy, primal power, that had been radiating next to her shoulder now felt cold. And when she cracked open an eyelid to peer through the dark next to her, she saw the sleeping body of Ariana. The evil bitch looked almost innocent, the sheets drawn up around her bare shoulder, and one ringlet of hair fallen over her cheek. Her face looked serene.

Alex grit her teeth. How dare that monster look happy after the hell she'd just been through? The things she'd implored the demon do to Alex; it made her sick to think of it, nevermind the fire of pain that still burned through her mouth and anus and, hell, probably all the way to her uterus. At the thought of that, she felt a sudden pang in her gut. Could a demon get her pregnant? Holy Jesus.

"*No Jesus here,*" a faint voice came from deep in her skull.

"Malachai," she thought. "Take the pain away?"

"*You don't think I already have been? Trust me, it's much worse than you know.*"

Alex's eyes widened in the dark, as the implication of that sunk in. "Will I be okay?"

"*They took your skin off yesterday,*" the demon answered. "*Do you think this is any worse?*"

She couldn't argue with that. Instead, she laid there staring at the sleeping form of the woman who had made all of this happen. Her chest felt cold when she looked at Ariana's pointy nose. That face had lured several men to their death just because they wanted to kiss it. Because she fooled them into thinking she was sweet and sexy.

"Malachai, do I need to be in a particular place here to open a door?"

"*I am not sure,*" the demon answered. "*But there are specific places in Curburide where doors are known to open. The thin places between the worlds. You'd do best to try to do it there.*"

"Are there specific words I need?"

"*Spells and chants are only about driving your mind to focus,*" Malachai said. "*Pure, concentrated focus is what you need. That, and the energy of a sacrifice.*"

Alex's eyes didn't leave Ariana's placid face. "I have that," she said. "Now I just need to be in the right place with her."

"*That and a weapon,*" he answered. "*Unless you'll be using your bare hands.*"

Alex thought of her night in bed with Ariana and Elotan. At one point, the bitch had sat on her face as she and the demon laughed.

"I might," Alex hissed at the dark spot in her brain where Malachai hid. "I just might."

"*I always liked you,*" he whispered.

"Just help me find the place," she said.

"*He's proud,*" Malachai said. "*He'll want to parade his new harem around so others will see how rich he has become. You'll need to be ready if he takes you near a place where the world is thin. I will keep watch.*"

"I want to go home," Alex said. Her silent voice trembled.

"*Sleep now,*" Malachai whispered. "*The Redemption is nearly upon us, and when you wake, you'll be whole again.*"

Alex pressed her eyelids closed, and tried to force the foul images of Elotan and Ariana's intertwined bodies to leave her inner sight. She didn't think she would ever be whole again, not really.

"*Sleep.*"

Chapter 59

"Oh my God, what did you do to me?" Joe cried, holding his hands over what once had been his manhood. Blood streamed out between his fingers. He looked down and saw a growing dark spot on the couch. "Shit, shit, shit," he whispered. "I'm going to bleed to death."

Helone stretched her arms over her head, a lazy cat motion. And then she drew them back and stood.

"You're not going to bleed to death, but you are going to ruin my upholstery."

She crossed the room and yanked down a veil from the ceiling. There were hundreds of the things hanging there it seemed; like a closet of silk. She returned with a knife and a towel.

"You *are* a bleeder, aren't you?"

Helone mopped the blood off of her couch with the towel and then dabbed it at the mess on his thighs.

"Move your hands," she said. He was holding his bleeding cock tight, trying to staunch the flow.

"I can't," he said. "I'll bleed more."

"Move your hands," she commanded. The power in her voice was undeniable. He obeyed, and instantly the blood began to flow faster. He felt it oozing down his testicles, and tears flowed freely from his eyes. He'd been weak. He'd always been weak when it came to women. They tempted him, and he always took the bait, but now… here was payback. He'd never have the chance to be weak again, because it was gone. He looked down at the raw gristle that had once defined him, driven him, and felt all of the fight simply drain from him. He felt faint.

Nauseous.

Helone cut a piece of the veil and with one finger held it in place at the base of his groin before twisting it around and around what was left of his manhood as if she were wrapping a bare wire in electrical tape.

And it worked. After she double wrapped and tied it off, the flow of blood down his leg ceased. Helone wiped up all of the visible blood, and then held out what was left of his glass of wine.

"Drink this," she said.

He shook his head.

"You'll feel better," she promised. "Trust me."

"Are you kidding me? Trust you?" Joe said. "Your cunt just chewed my dick off!"

Helone smiled sadly. "I didn't think you'd have gone along with it if I'd warned you," she said. "Sorry. It's just… that's the way our parts work. Demon men don't mind it so much."

"I mind it very much," Joe said, snuffling and wiping the tears from his face. "You've made me a eunuch."

"Drink," she implored, and Joe took the glass. He didn't sip it this time; he needed a blast.

And a blast is what he got. The liquid hit him like a forty-foot wave, and smashed his nerves to the coral reef below. Knives raked his back and a spear of ice stabbed his anus. He could feel it freeze his heart before it emerged from his throat. His lips locked in frozen surprise. His whole body stiffened.

"I told you to sip it," Helone said. She took the glass back from his palsied hand, and rubbed her fingers across his forehead. To Joe, it felt as if someone was shifting sandpaper across his eyeball.

"The bloodwine doesn't always bring pleasure," she explained. "But it will pass. Just as your wound will heal. I would never damage you so that you couldn't pleasure me again. What good would that do me?"

"Heal?" Joe cried. "There's nothing left to heal!"

"You'll see," she said. Helone stood up and stopped torturing him with her touch. "I'll get you a blanket," she said. "You probably don't want to move right now. But in the morning, you'll be good as new. And maybe we can take it a little slower then."

She winked at that, and walked out of the room.

Joe shivered in the light of the fire. There was something like an orgasm growing in the nerves of his feet, while his fingers felt as if they were being held down on the orange grates of an electric stove. He was torn in a hideous, heavenly crash of conflicting sensations.

He would have screamed, but his mouth refused to move.

Chapter 60

SHE WOKE IN DARKNESS, but Cheyenne could still see. At first she was disoriented, staring through the blackness to see grey outlines of things undefined. It was a dreamscape; nothing seemed solid. Dark was not black, solid things appeared ghostly.

But then, as she tried to figure out where she was, exactly, she remembered the statue falling, and the pop of her arm just before that pain came. And it all came back. "Oh shit," she whispered as she relived the most horrible moment of her life. Instinctually, she tried to move the place where that arm would have been, had it not been ripped off.

The pale ghosts of fingers suddenly clutched and spread, just in front of her face. Pain shot through her shoulder as it moved but, she realized with ecstatic relief that she still had an arm. The fingers were *not* ghosts.

"Holy Mary, Mother of God," Cheyenne whispered. She opened and closed her fingers in front of her face, fanning them as if she'd never seen fingers before. "It's a miracle," she whispered.

Something moved near her feet, and she heard a low laugh.

"No miracle," a voice said. "Just the Redemption. It happens every night. Wasn't sure if that arm was going to make it with you but, you lucked out. Or maybe you'll see it another way, once we decide what to do with you."

Cheyenne sat up and suddenly the room seemed to swim into focus. A tall, black-skinned man stood before her, hands on naked hips. Or not a man. A demon. No man looked like that. She had to avert her eyes when she saw what hung at her eye level. She'd seen horses that weren't hung that well. *Holy shit.*

"Where is Joe?" she asked.

The demon shrugged. "Helone said to bring you to her if you woke up."

"If?" Cheyenne said.

"Sometimes Redemption doesn't come." The demon stepped closer, eyeing her with obvious interest. "And sometimes, even if it does, other things happen."

Cheyenne flipped her legs off of the bed and stood, not wanting to give the demon time to think of what those "other things" might be. "I'm ready to go," she said. "Where is Helone waiting?"

Joe groaned as he rolled over. His dreams had been filled with horrible images. He blinked them away, until the room became clear. His vision felt hazy, but as he opened his eyes, he realized that he remained on the couch where Helone had taken his manhood. And not in a good way. He lifted the blanket that covered him, and looked down, afraid to see, but yet needing to look. It couldn't be as bad as he thought, could it? He couldn't have fallen asleep if it had! And at the moment, he felt no pain.

His cock hung slack against his thigh, still wrapped in the veil that Helone had used to staunch the flow of his blood the night before. But there was no trace of blood now. He reached down and pulled at the edge, carefully unraveling it to see if the wounds were seeping.

There were no wounds.

He yanked the last of the tissue-thin stuff from him, and shook his head. He had not imagined all that, he couldn't have. And the couch seemed to agree. There was a dark spot between his legs.

Joe rose from the couch and pulled the blanket around his shoulders. For the first time since arriving in the world of the Curburide, he actually had the time to truly look around. In some ways, the room was like the study or den from a rich mansion. The space was rectangular and long;

an ornate Oriental patterned carpet covered the dark wooden floor in the center. The rug was bordered by plush, antique-looking couches, with ornate carvings decorating the wooden borders above the cushion backs. A dark wood bar hugged one wall, which Helone had served him from the night before, and a fireplace took up most of another wall. A low orange blaze still flickered above the glowing embers in the hearth. Above it, a heavy wood mantel held an array of statues and trinkets and candles. Along the other wall, veils hung from a hundred hooks.

Joe fingered a couple of the things on the mantel – there was an ancient-looking gold pocket watch there, that could have been from the 1600s, and a locket with a sepia picture that clearly had been taken in the early 1900s. But he passed the mantel to look instead at the hangings along the long wall of the room.

From a few feet away, they'd looked like flesh-colored veils. But as he drew closer, he realized they were much more than veils. He could make out fingers hanging at the end of some of the skeins, and near the hooks, when he looked closer, he realized that he could see noses, and mouths and eye-holes.

Joe took the fingers of one and pulled it towards him, like pulling a shirt from a closet. And as it moved, he could see it for what it was. These were not veils of silk, they were skins.

He let go of the fingers of the dead man, and looked again at the row of skins. They didn't immediately jump out to the eye as human skins, because on the hooks they sagged and hung limp and wrinkled. Hence his initial thought that they were veils. But he went down the line and pulled on the arm tubes that hung limp, drawing the skins out, and one by one he saw that there were fat men and old women and young girls all hanging like deflated ghosts. He walked behind the couch and all the way down the row of skins to the end, marveling at the number and variety.

So many people hung here.

How had they been skinned so perfectly? You could have stepped in to some of them and worn their skins, the form remained so complete.

Joe suddenly grimaced as he remembered what Helone had done last night; one of these bodies had "lost a limb" to patch his shredded genitals. He had worn someone else's skin. On his dick no less. The thought made him shiver.

But then he reached the end of the line, and did more than feel a little creeped out.

Because the last skin that he pulled out to see, was not just the ghost of a stranger.

Even without eyes or flesh, he recognized this skin. It couldn't be a mistake.

"Alex," Joe breathed.

The skin shifted in his fingers.

"You came," her voice whispered in the air.

Joe jumped backwards. Alex's skin moved of its own accord, her arms lifting and reaching out for him.

"Why did it take so long?" Alex said. She sounded so incredibly sad. "I waited. I hoped. But I could not wait forever."

Joe felt a lump grow in his throat. It hurt as he tried to talk. "I tried, Alex. I looked for a way through for so long."

"Now it's too late," Alex said. The pale, see-through skin of her arm lifted and brushed her face, as if she were wiping a tear. But she had no eyes to cry.

"I am so sorry," Joe said. Tears rolled down his cheeks like rain. "I wanted to bring you back."

"You failed," Alex said. With that, her translucent arms dropped to her sides.

Joe felt the wind kicked out of him with those words.

"No!" he cried out, and fell to his knees. He reached out and touched the limp skin of Alex's legs. He had dedicated himself to finding a way to reach her. To bring her back. And now he had found her. Had crossed the invisible divide between worlds to reach her.

Only to find he could not bring her home?

She was gone. Now she was only a spirit and a disembodied skin.

Joe's breath hitched in painful sobs and he hung his head in shame and pain. He had done everything he could, and it hadn't been enough.

"You failed," kept playing over and over again in his head.

He ran one hand up the limp hip of skin that hung from Helone's ceiling and begged, "Come back, Alex. Please."

But her empty skin did not move or speak again.

Chapter 61

THE WORLD SHOOK beneath her feet.

Ariana stumbled, and grabbed onto Elotan's arm to stop from falling flat on her face. Alex dropped to her knees beside her.

"That was bad," Ariana said.

Elotan nodded. He had not fallen, but he was clearly unsteady after the shake. "It was," he agreed. But he said no more.

"Should we be worried?" Ariana asked. Part of her wondered if she had finally gotten to "the other side" only to have the whole damn dimension shake apart into cosmic dust.

Elotan shrugged. "As long as the door to earth remains open, it will probably get worse. The doors should not be open so long. It's unnatural."

"Is it dangerous?" Ariana asked.

"That depends on who you're talking about," Elotan admitted. "It's said that if the door stays open, the world of the Curburide will eat your world."

"And if they're wrong?" Adriana asked.

The back of Elotan's hand slapped Adriana's cheek. She asked no more questions.

"Where are we going?" Alex asked. The chain around her neck clinked as she spoke. Two tall demons on the other side of the street stopped and clearly looked at them.

"We are walking," Elotan said. His voice was low and stern.

"But where?" Alex pressed.

Suddenly the chain around her neck grew tight.

"Where I feel like walking," he said. Clearly, he was not

going to answer the question. If there was an answer.

"We're bait," Ariana said quietly. "And you're... jailbait."

"Bait for what?" Alex asked.

"Demon dreams," she said. "Our master needs to score some bloodwine. How many demons do you think have had a chance to bed an underage human?"

"Me?" Alex said. She quailed. Elotan had made both her and Adriana pull on sheer, see-through silken coverings before they'd gone out, with nothing on beneath. Even to a demon, apparently, the "tease factor" was as important as seeing the skin. She had tried to resist, but a few well-placed slaps had convinced her that near-nudity was better than pain. He'd since been parading both of them down the street and had several leering, black-skinned demons stop and look. But so far, none had come closer.

The reason may have been ahead. A crowd of demons gathered a couple blocks down the street, surrounding the doorway of a small building. There was a symbol above the door that struck Alex instantly. "That's one of the doorways," she said, not meaning to voice her excitement out loud.

Elotan answered. "Yes. And you can see it's also our problem. Nobody is interested in you when they can wait for a new consort from the doorway. They all think they can take a human home for their own tonight."

"How many are coming through the doorway?" Ariana asked.

Elotan shook his head. "More than ever before."

As he said it, the ground shook again, and this time, even the demon fell to his feet. Ahead of them, the crowd suddenly dispersed, some from falling and some from running. Clearly the Curburide were not used to their world moving.

Ariana grabbed Elotan's arm again, but this time he pushed her aside. "Stand up and look alive."

Chapter 62

"Would you cry about me like that?"

Joe looked up from where he knelt on the floor to see Helone leaning casually against the doorframe. Her hair seemed even more lustrous than last night. A pale yellow silk sash hung loosely across her body; it hid little of the dark curves beneath. She was exotic and sexy and stunning. A sadistic succubus.

Joe hated her with all his heart.

"You bitch!" he screamed, and leapt to his feet. "You killed her, didn't you? You lied to me about everything." He started across the room and had just begun to raise a fist when his body froze.

Helone's eyes sparkled with amusement. "Stay," she said.

She pushed off the wall and walked around him. With one finger she pushed the blanket off his shoulders. Then she ran a black palm down his chest until her fingers arrived at his pelvis. She ran fingernails through the thickening hair there, and then cupped the flesh that was already betraying him.

"No harm done here, I see," she said. "Didn't I tell you not to worry?" Then she put one hand on his shoulder and said simply, "Heel."

Joe felt his muscles weaken and give out, and suddenly he was on his knees.

"Learn proper respect, or the pain you felt last night will seem like the respite of heaven," she warned.

"You told me Alex was alive, but she's not," Joe said. "You killed her. Damnit, you skinned her!"

"No," Helone said. "I did not lie to you about your friend Alex."

"But she is dead; you've got her fucking skin hanging right there."

Helone shook her head. "Her old skin is there, and today she wears a new one, just as you wear a new cock."

"But she spoke to me from it," Joe said. "She was just a spirit."

"*That*... was a lie," Helone smiled. "A little treat for your master."

She rubbed the taut skin of her belly. "Let's just say you cooked me breakfast after a hot night."

"So that wasn't Alex?" he said.

She shook her head. "No, only your fears given focus."

"Why would you do that to me?" he whispered. He was still shaken inside from the things Alex's ghost had said. Joe suddenly felt her invisible hold on him release, and sprawled backwards to sit on his ass on the floor.

"Your emotion gives me strength," she said. "It feeds me."

Joe noticed the sheen of her flesh was so vibrant today, it almost looked as if she'd been rubbed in oil.

Helone held out a hand, which he refused to take at first. But the look in her eyes made him think better of resisting. She pulled him to his feet, and then retrieved something from the couch. A black cape or shawl. She draped it around his shoulders. And then she put her hands behind his neck. He heard a faint click as something tightened around his throat. Joe reached up and felt it with a sinking stomach. She'd fastened a collar around his neck.

"And to repay you for your gift, I have something for you."

"A robe and a collar?" Joe asked. His voice did not sound thankful.

"No," she said. "But we'll need to go out and I thought you'd be more comfortable wearing something. I will not have you walk without a chain, for your own safety. If you'd like, I can take the robe away."

"No," he said quickly. "Thank you."

Helone smiled. "That's better. Come along."

She fastened a chain to his neck and then turned and led him out of the room like a dog. They walked down a hall to the door and a moment later they were walking down the demon streets. The buildings all around them seemed grey and indistinct, as if Helone was leading him through a watercolor painting.

"Where are we going?" he asked.

"Patience, pet," she said.

And then just ahead, he saw a mob of demons gathered around a building topped with a gothic spire. He recognized the place instantly. It was where he'd arrived in this world just the day before.

"Are you sending me home?" he asked.

Helone laughed. "Oh no," she said. "We're going to spend many, many enjoyable nights together. "But I've got something that might make your mornings brighter."

She pulled his chain and the mob of demons parted without a word to let them through. They walked up a flight of stairs to an ancient-looking wooden door. It was carved in a complicated filigree surrounding what appeared to be an oval of seven planets. In their midst was a man, legs together, arms outstretched.

Helone pushed the door open and the demon guarding it stepped aside to let them pass.

Chapter 63

"That was Joe!"

Alex pointed at the door of the House of Doors ahead. "He was right there, did you see him? He was with Helone – she took him inside the door!"

Ariana looked at her with a frown. "Who's Helone?"

"The demon I stayed with before I ended up in the skin factory."

"Wishful thinking," Ariana said. "What would he be doing here?"

"No, it was Joe, I'm sure of it," Alex said. She could barely contain her excitement. She had almost given up hope of ever seeing him again. With her internal voice, she whispered, "Malachai, that was him, wasn't it?" The demon shifted inside her, and then a low voice said simply, *"Yes."*

Alex turned to Elotan. "Please take us in there?"

The demon shook its head. "Do you not *see* the mob there at the door? They are all waiting their turn to get in. If we get in line now, it would take days before we got inside."

"But Helone – the demon who was with Joe – she walked right in with him," she said. "Maybe they will let you in since you have us? You're obviously not here to get another human."

"There is no way," Elotan said. "Helone is the Queen of the Doors. She can go where she pleases."

"Please," Alex begged. He yanked on her chain and the collar turned her plea to a gurgle. When he released it, she whispered. "If you just try, I promise, I will do whatever you ask."

"You will do that anyway," he said. But his eyebrow raised. "Anything?"

She nodded.

Ariana shook her head with a knowing grin. "You don't know what you've just agreed to," she said under her breath.

"Follow me," Elotan said, and strode towards the throng of demons. When one blocked his path, he waved the Curburide aside. "I'm taking these to the Queen of the Doors," he said.

"I can take them off your hands for you," a grizzled demon offered. There were grey scars across the black skin of his chest. And his "demonhood" appeared kinked and misshapen. Alex had a pang as she realized the danger here. If the crowd decided to divest Elotan of his wealth, she could end up in a lot worse hands than Elotan.

"Back off," Elotan growled. "Unless you want to face the wrath of the Queen of Doors. She'll boil your head and mine if I don't get these two to her now."

At the mention of Helone's title, the older demon backed up a step. Then he motioned to the black form next to him. In a moment, Elotan led Alex and Ariana up the stairs.

"That was easier than I thought," he admitted. "But I don't know how we'll get past the guard inside."

"Just tell him to tell Helone that Alex is here to see her."

"What makes you think she'll want to see you?" Elotan said. "You escaped her house."

"That alone will make her come; and hopefully she'll bring Joe with her."

"And then what?" Elotan said.

"And then you can do what you want with me," Alex said. "But I have to see Joe, even if it's only for a minute."

The guard inside looked at them with a frown. "You are not in line," he said. "You are not even on the list."

Elotan shook his head. "I'm not here for the door, I'm here to see the Queen of the Doors."

The guard opened his mouth to say something, but Elotan quickly added, "Helone is waiting to see Alex. Please just tell her Alex is here."

The guard looked unsure, but after a second, he said. "Wait here."

The door closed, leaving them still outside, at the top of the steps.

"This better work," Elotan said.

A moment later, the door opened, and the guard ushered them inside and pointed at a small side room next to the entryway.

"She's busy at the moment. Wait there."

They moved to stand against the wall of the small room, and a moment later, the guard let in a line of five demons, who walked single file past them and turned the corner. Presumably they were going to the door between worlds.

Ariana shook her head and looked at Alex with a smirk.

"I can't *wait* to see what Elotan's going to do to you tonight."

Then she leaned against the demon's arm and brushed her cheek against his bare skin. "Can I help?" she asked.

He answered her with a sharp yank of the chain, and Ariana yelped as the studs of the collar bit into her neck.

They stood in silence after that.

Chapter 64

CHEYENNE LEAPT UP from the divan and shouted, "Joe!" She crossed the room in three steps and threw her arms around him. He returned the affection clumsily, but his hug was solid.

"You're okay!" he said. His grin was so wide it looked silly.

Cheyenne nodded. She lifted her arm. "It hurts to move it a bit, but it's attached! I woke up and it was back to normal. Can you believe it?"

Joe nodded. "Actually, I can," he said. A shadow passed over his face. "I'm glad we ended up coming through," he said.

"Now we just need to get home," Cheyenne said.

Joe raised both eyebrows. "Yeah, that may be the tricky part."

"Let's not talk of leaving, just yet," a dark-skinned woman said from behind Joe. Cheyenne realized, all at once that this woman – no, demon – held a chain that was firmly latched to Joe's neck. Elation suddenly turned to a cold yawning pit of despair. She was healed and reunited with Joe; but they were prisoners of the demons. And God knew what tortures lay in store for them in that situation. It may have been better for her if she'd bled to death last night.

"My name is Helone," the demon woman said, holding out a delicate, long-fingered hand. As Cheyenne grudgingly accepted it, her palm tingled as her skin slipped across the silken touch of the demon. A sensual tremor convulsed in her groin just from the faintest press of the demon's skin. Cheyenne opened her mouth to reply, but felt strangely confused, disoriented. It was difficult to speak.

"You and Joe will be guests in my house, tonight," Helone said. "You have had a difficult time, and I would like to get to know you before you talk of leaving."

"I've seen the skulls on your mantel," Joe said. "And the skins in your parlor. Will we ever talk of leaving? Or leaving alive, anyway?"

Helone yanked hard on his chain and Joe's head jerked backwards as he choked.

"Don't," Cheyenne said, yanking her hand away from the demon's and slipping both arms around Joe's neck to grab the chain from behind him. She pulled it hard until there was slack between where she gripped the chain and Joe's neck.

The demon smiled and stared hard at Cheyenne. Those eyes; they didn't seem human.

Because they're not! Cheyenne's inner voice screamed. *She will eat you alive.*

"I won't give him anything he can't handle," Helone said. Her voice was a shark's whisper. "I enjoy having houseguests. I wouldn't want to lose one prematurely."

"Just let us go, Helone," Joe said. "You got your kicks last night. There's nothing more to gain from me."

The demon laughed. "You have *so* much more to give, Joe. You have no idea."

"I am not *giving* anything again," Joe said. His voice was low and angry. "You can't make me do that."

"Oh, I won't have to," Helone said. "You will make the choice yourself. After all, you are a man."

"What are you talking about?" Cheyenne asked. She pulled back from her embrace of Joe so that she could see his face. He looked more than angered. He looked bitter. Mad at himself as much as the demon?

"Let's not have this conversation here," Helone said. "We can talk over dinner. You should enjoy the fruits of the Curburide before you talk of leaving us."

The demon reached out and took Cheyenne's hand again. This time her touch was not soft, but firm. Cheyenne could feel her fingernails scrape the sides of her wrist. They felt dangerous as razors.

"Come with me," Helone said. She pulled them forward, out of the small room and into the hall.

And the earth moved again.

Cheyenne saw a demon stumble in front of them, and then suddenly the floor beneath them raised and lowered and she felt her own feet leave the ground. Somewhere a scream echoed, and then was joined by a hundred voices all shouting different words, but all crying out in alarm.

Joe toppled into Cheyenne and they were suddenly both entangled on the floor. The shaking did not stop, but instead increased; Cheyenne felt as if she were being tossed in a frying pan, the bottom shaking fast over invisible coals.

Joe grabbed her by the shoulders and held fast. Cheyenne returned the embrace, clutching him as if he were the rock that could save her from the avalanche. The world around them seemed to shiver with shadows and light. She could barely focus on Joe's face as the tremors escalated.

But then she looked beyond Joe's shoulder and saw that the demon had fallen hard; Helone's body had slid all the way across the floor to stop at the legs of the divan that Cheyenne had been sitting on earlier. The demon no longer held Joe's chain.

Cheyenne grabbed it and pulled the loose end towards her. When she had the end in her grasp, she yelled in Joe's ear above the surrounding din. "Get up, now!"

She thrust her hand with the chain in his face so that he understood, and then struggled to roll to her feet. In a moment, Joe's hands were on her waist, both helping to support her and to steady himself as he got to his feet. The rocking of the world seemed to be slowing, and while things were still crashing to the floor all around – rocks and furniture and more – somehow they regained their feet.

"Come on," Joe said and took her hand as they stumbled out of the corridor and into a larger room. There were demons and humans alike rolling about on the floor, and others staggering back and forth across the bodies, trying not to fall down.

In the center of it all was an arch of blackest stone. There were symbols carved in it, but Cheyenne couldn't tell what they represented.

But she could tell this; there were people stepping out of the air beneath the arch. People who had not been there a moment before. People who fell onto a growing pile of humanity writhing back and forth on the still-shivering floor before it.

"That's it," Joe pointed. "That's the doorway home!"

Chapter 65

"Apparently Helone wants to see you," Elotan said, as they walked through the doorway into the hall that held the door between worlds. "I'm surprised they let us in. If I was you, I would be afraid."

"Why do you say that?" Alex asked. "Helone was nice to me. Mostly."

"And you made her a fool. She will not forget that. Believe me."

"But I thought I'm yours now; so you'll protect me, right?"

Elotan opened his mouth and laughed. It was about the most un-amusing sound Alex had ever heard in her life. A chill ran up her spine.

All around them demons milled; most appeared to be headed in the same direction – down a corridor and turning to the right. There were almost as many heading back in their direction, but the difference was striking. The line moving forward was made up strictly of demons. The line that returned and passed just a couple feet away from them was a procession comprised of demons with humans. The demons looked ecstatic; the faces of the humans – were locked in masks of terror.

"Where are they taking them all?" Alex asked.

"The bloodmines, the skin shops, the lust stages… some will be private toys, for those who can afford it."

"I thought you didn't have money here."

Elotan shrugged. "Something always changes hands."

Ariana ran her hand up Alex's shoulder and made a face of exaggerated innocence. "Just imagine how many hands you could end up in. And how many of them might have knives."

There was a rumble as Alex raised her hand to slap Ariana away...

... and then she found herself lying on the floor. There was an explosion. The force of the blast smashed Alex and Ariana and Elotan to the floor. All around them the air was filled with shrieks of pain and fright, and Alex struggled to put her palms flat on the ground to hold her body in place as the earth and walls all around them shook. Chunks of rock and tile fell everywhere to the ground, a pelting, dangerous hail.

But Alex realized almost instantly that while she was possibly about to be killed, she also had what might be her only chance to get away.

"*Move,*" Malachai demanded from deep inside her. "*Get to the door.*"

She could feel him feeding her energy and she didn't hesitate. Alex leapt up and yanked her chain. Elotan had let go of both chains as he grabbed at the wall to regain his footing. The floor continued to buck and roll beneath them all, but Alex didn't waste a moment. She pulled the chain away from Elotan's reach and turned to run.

A tremor tilted the earth and she fell into the wall, gouging a gash in her arm. The pain only galvanized her. Alex half-ran, half-stumbled around the corner to the next room.

"Wait," Ariana yelled. "You can't leave us!"

Alex would have laughed at that if she'd had the time. But instead she ran into the room beyond. A heavy rumble threw her off her feet again, but she pushed herself back up. She was in a long, wide room, and in the center was a throng of people and demons. Most were lying on the ground, but some were staggering to or from an archway that dominated the center. It was tall and carved out of black stone and seemed to be vomiting people out of its hollow. They fell from it in a constant stream to land on top of others already prone on the ground.

Demons picked up some and threw them away from the center. That was the source of as many of the screams as the earthquake. One man fell right on his arm and Alex could see the bone break; his sleeve suddenly bent in a completely wrong direction for an arm to move. The man let out a gut-wrenching cry.

And then, as Alex forced her eyes away from that man's pain, she saw the man she'd forced her way in here to see.

"Joe!" she called for the second time in five minutes. He and a woman were running toward the archway. Alex didn't waste breath – she began to run after him.

"Stop, damnit!" a voice screamed from right behind her.

Ariana. The bitch wasn't letting her go. Alex tried to run faster, but suddenly the collar tightened around her neck, and she choked.

Ariana had grabbed a swath of the chain. Between that and the moving earth beneath her feet, Alex slipped and went down.

Ariana fell with her, and then rolled on top of Alex, leaning in until they were almost nose to nose. "You are not going anywhere," Ariana hissed. "Elotan has plans for you."

"You're an idiot," Alex yelled. With one quick motion she shrugged Ariana to the side, and then brought her knee up fast, catching the other woman in the gut. Then she rolled to her feet and yanked the chain from Ariana's hands again.

"You stay here if you want," she said. "I'm going home."

Alex turned and ran again. Joe and the woman were almost to the arch. Out of the corner of her eye, she saw Helone emerge from a hallway to the left. The demon's eyes blazed when she saw both Joe and Alex had nearly made it to safety.

Helone's hand raised in the air and the demon screamed "Stop!"

Even amidst the shaking of the last earthquake tremors, Alex could feel the power of Helone's command. It crackled through the air like fire, and its effect was instant. Just two yards from the archway, Alex felt her feet lock, just as her hand reached out to Joe. Inches from her fingers, she saw him and the woman next to him freeze in place as well. She could see the spark of recognition in Joe's eyes as he finally saw her. Too late, though.

Ariana arrived, and grabbed the chain around Alex's neck. "Not this time," she said, and pulled on the chain to drag Alex back to Elotan.

But Ariana couldn't budge Alex's feet. She was locked in place by Helone's power. It didn't matter; a moment later the demon himself was there. "Well done," Elotan said, accepting the chain back from Ariana.

Alex felt her heart sink as he took her bindings again. Once more a prisoner. But then that pit in her stomach grew even colder.

"They're mine," Helone yelled, stepping across bodies to make her way to them.

"I told you she had plans for you," Elotan's low voice said to Alex. "You have really got her claws out."

"Let us go," Alex whispered. Her lips struggled to move. "If she is going to take me from you anyway, just let me go."

"And what would I get out of that?"

"The satisfaction of knowing that she didn't steal me from you right in front of you. She's about to, you know."

Alex could see the anger rising in the demon's eyes. No matter how you cut it, he was going to come up the loser in this equation; he knew he was not going to win going head-to-head against the Queen of Doors.

"You have caused me nothing but trouble since you turned up in my doorway," he said. "Let's put an end to that."

Elotan opened his mouth and gave out a cry of fury. And then he flung one arm out, toppling Ariana, but also Alex, Joe and Cheyenne. But his anger didn't simply toss them to the ground. A handful of demons who were near the portal fell to their knees as well, and a chorus of angry voices joined Elotan's own war cry. The demon was going to earn some payback for his outburst. But Alex intended not to be there to see it.

"Malachai," she whispered in her mind. "We are never going to be any closer. If you want to get back to Earth, you'd better help me now."

"*You think you've been doing this all on your own up to now?*"

"Just shut up and give me strength!" she yelled silently.

For once, the demon didn't argue with her. Alex could feel his strength instantly surge through her. Between Elotan's concussion of anger, and Malachai's funnel of power, whatever paralysis Helone had cast on her was wiped away. Alex took advantage of both, and also tapped into a well that she'd only just begun to discover in herself. She refused to be a prisoner again, to Helone or Elotan or anyone. She thrust herself up from the ground and grabbed Joe's arm, dragging him to his feet. He moved slowly, as if trapped in tar, but he moved.

"Cheyenne," he said.

The woman who had been running with him remained face down on the stone floor. Alex reached down and grabbed her hand. Cheyenne responded, gripping Alex's hand back and starting to push herself, ever-so-slowly, to her knees. Alex pulled hard on both of them, and together they began to finally stumble to the archway. They were nearly there, when Ariana leapt forward and grabbed Alex's chain.

"Not so fast, little girl," Ariana said.

"You think you're going to get some kind of reward for stopping us?" Alex said through gritted teeth. She didn't stop dragging Joe and Cheyenne towards the door. Each could move, but only barely.

And then Helone was there.

For a second, Alex lost her drive, and simply stared at the demon. She didn't at all resemble the crone that Alex had met just a few days before. Alex's emotional storm had fed her, restored the vibrancy and lushness to her face and skin. But now her flesh looked even more youthful than before. All the curves of her breasts and hips were visible through her veil, and her black skin was shiny and flawless. When the demoness smiled, Alex could see perfect teeth behind her full, thick lips. But that smile was both cloying and cruel.

"You left without saying goodbye," Helone said.

"I didn't have anything more to say," Alex answered.

The earth trembled beneath their feet but Alex held her ground.

"I would never have let them take your skin," Helone said.

"No," Alex said. "What you would do was more painful."

"Really?" Helone said. She cocked her head and looked harder at Alex. "The whispers of your conscience hurt more than knives in your flesh? I find that hard to believe."

Helone looked at Elotan and pointed at Joe and Cheyenne. "Help me with them, and I'll let you keep your slut." She waved at Ariana who stood to the side, still holding Alex's chain.

The earth rumbled and everyone staggered. It was like standing on a lurching bus with no poles to grab onto. Alex didn't waste the moment.

"We'd love to stick around and see if this place blows up or slides into the ocean or whatever happens here when earthquakes get really bad but..."

She yanked with superhuman strength on Joe's and Cheyenne's hands, and leapt forward at the same time, pulling all of them into the center of the arch. Ariana stumbled at the sudden movement, and fell forward against her will.

For one split second, Alex caught the fiery eyes of Helone before completing her thought and diving into the invisible door between worlds.

"... Goodbye."

Chapter 66

"You did it!" Joe yelled. "Alex, you brought us back!"

All four of them had fallen out of the doorway and onto the dusty floor of the mission chapel. Only, it didn't look much like the place they had left.

"But back to where?" Alex asked, sitting up and brushing the dirt from her arms. "What is this place?"

Cheyenne took a good look around. The walls of the mission had collapsed, and there were cracks across the floor six inches wide. Chunks of adobe lay in piles everywhere, though miraculously, the center of the chapel remained clear of any large debris; the altar was open to the sky. Behind it, the heavy beams that had held the ceiling up for centuries stuck out like broken toothpicks.

"Welcome to Santa Fe," Cheyenne said. Her voice was far away. As if she were talking in a dream. "Where they don't have earthquakes. Ever."

"This is the place where we came through the door to find you," Joe explained. "There was a cult here who performed a ritual to open the door between worlds, just like Ariana did back in Terrel. But for some reason, when the sun came up the next day, this door didn't close."

"And it is still not closed," Ariana said.

Two men had just threaded their way between the overturned and broken pews and the chunks of wall and ceiling. One had cast an odd look at the four still sitting on the floor, but he'd continued walking. And a moment later, their bodies had suddenly whisked upwards through the air and vanished in a blur.

Joe nodded. "We should probably move to someplace a little less conspicuous."

Cheyenne broke from her trance. "You don't think Darin is still here, do you?" Her voice trembled.

Joe shrugged. "I don't know, but I don't want to find out."

Alex looked up at the place where the two men had just walked into the sky. "Helone won't let us go, you know," she said. "She will send them after us. As long as the doorway remains open…"

"How do we close it?" Cheyenne asked.

Ariana fingered the sheer piece of silk draped across her chest. She twisted it back and forth in her fingers, dragging it across the tip of her breast. The nipple responded, and she closed her eyes for a moment before speaking.

"The same way they opened it," Ariana said. "You need to perform a human sacrifice."

"We have to murder someone?" Cheyenne gasped. "We can't do that!"

Alex looked at Ariana, and then at Joe. "We can and we have to," she said. "And fast." Her voice was not the voice of a teen. She sounded cold as a demon.

"Where are we going to get a sacrifice?" Cheyenne said. "And who is going to hold the knife? I'm not doing it."

"I know one person here who won't have a problem holding the knife," Joe said. He stared at Ariana.

She gave him a half-smile. But then her face went dark. She shook her head. "Not this time," she said. "I opened the door once before, in a different place. I should be the one to close it." She looked at Alex. "I'll be the sacrifice."

"What?" Cheyenne said.

Joe thought of all the murder and violence Ariana had caused. Of how, because of her, he and Alex had driven cross-country, following in the wake of her murders, trying to catch up to her before she let the Curburide through the gate between worlds in the same way that Darin's mob finally had. And despite all of that, he agreed with Cheyenne.

"No," he said. "We are not going to kill you."

Alex hadn't broken eye contact with Ariana, but she answered Joe. "You're not going to," she said. "I am."

Joe's eyes widened and he opened his mouth to protest. But then he felt something cold slipping in behind his eyes. Something snakelike.

Evil.

"They're here," he whispered as he felt his limbs suddenly lock and then move of their own accord. "The Curburide are coming to ride us."

Chapter 67

"MALACHAI, CAN YOU protect us?" Alex asked. "Hold off the Curburide until we can close the door?"

"*I have some experience with that,*" the demon answered. "*Put your hands on Joe, quickly.*"

Alex did as the demon asked, grabbing Joe by his forearms. Joe grinned, but not in a happy way. He opened his mouth and announced in a voice that sounded like sandpaper, "Time for you kids to come back home. Mommy's not happy with you."

And then Alex felt a spark drive through her fingers, and Joe's eyes suddenly rolled back in his head until only the whites showed. Alex gripped his arms tighter, as Joe's body suddenly went limp. She levered him to the ground and his head lolled to the side. His mouth opened.

"What happened?" Cheyenne cried. She slipped her arm beneath his head to cradle it and then lifted his head to her bosom. "What did you do?" she demanded.

"Is he okay?" Alex asked silently.

"*He's fine,*" Malachai said. "*I forced the demon from him and it wasn't gentle. But he should wake up in a bit. He might have a headache.*"

"Are there more?"

"*Yes. I'm holding five off right now. I can do this because they are unfamiliar with this world, and I have been here a very long time. But I cannot hold them off forever. You must perform the sacrifice and close the door. Soon.*"

Alex put her hand on Cheyenne's arm. "He's going to be okay. Malachai – he's a demon that knows Joe – stopped him from being possessed. But he will probably be knocked out for a little."

Then she looked at Ariana. "You're sure you want to go through with this?"

Ariana made a face. "Of course I'm *not* sure. I don't want to fucking die. But I don't want to be here anymore, either. I spent years preparing to bring the Curburide through to our world. And then I ended up in theirs. And now I'm back in this pit."

"It didn't work out like you planned."

Ariana shook her head. "I don't care anymore. About anything. So go ahead and cut me. Maybe I'll feel something one last time."

"How…" Alex said. Her voice shook a little as the import of what she was preparing to do sunk in. "How do I do it? Is there a spell?"

"The words don't matter, the focus is what's important. But if it makes you feel better, there is a ritual in the *Book of the Curburide*."

"And where am I going to get that?" Alex asked.

Ariana pointed at the altar just a few feet away. "Right there, where the last idiots left it. They even provided you with a knife. Ironic, huh?"

Alex stood up and walked to the altar. She lifted the heavy leather bound book lying there and then grabbed the knife with her other hand. It was a decorative weapon, with green and blue jewels in the haft, which shone as silver as the blade. The weapon was made to be seen… and to kill.

She sat down next to Cheyenne, who was running her fingers through Joe's hair. He remained unconscious.

"Why isn't he waking up?" Cheyenne whispered.

"Give it time," Alex said.

"Men are weak," Ariana offered.

"And women are bitches," Joe answered. His voice was soft, but strong.

Alex smiled when she saw his eyes open. But a moment later, Cheyenne blocked her view as she bent to press her lips to his.

"Well, there ya go," Alex said, and turned her attention back to Ariana. "You've studied this book; do you know where the ritual is?"

Ariana raised an eyebrow. "I have to let you kill me and show you how to do it. You really are just a kid, aren't you? So disappointing."

Alex held her tongue. She knew she couldn't afford to fight with Ariana now. She didn't know why the other woman was agreeing to this at all, but she couldn't allow her to bail out now.

Ariana flipped through the book until she arrived at a place she knew. "The Ceremony of the Twenty-One Cuts is here," she said, and then leafed a page or two farther. "The way to undo it is not far away."

She skimmed page after page, and then suddenly stopped and pointed. "Here," she said. "This is the ritual to close a door between worlds."

Ariana thrust the book into Alex's hands. "You need to use whatever that part is inside you that kept you alive in Helone's and Elotan's homes. You have something… and if this is going to work, you need to use it. *All* of it."

"I am ready," Alex said. "And the demon Malachai will help me."

Ariana lay down on the ground, and spread her arms.

"When you begin, I will not stop you," Ariana said. "Follow the words, and the meaning, of the invocation, and it will work. Promise me one thing though?"

Alex looked at the woman's thin nose, and naked body and rather than feeling sympathy for what the woman was about to endure, she felt… antipathy. She had seen the pain and destruction Ariana had caused here on earth. And she had seen how Ariana enjoyed the sadism of the Curburide on the other side.

No, she found she had no qualms with stabbing Ariana. And she was not inclined to grant the woman any last kindnesses. A part of her was disturbed at how cold she felt about the whole thing.

"What?" Alex said, after looking the woman over.

"When the door is closing, throw my body into the center," Ariana said. "I want my body to lie with the Curburide."

Alex nodded. She could respect that. Ariana's heart and soul did not belong here.

"*There are more of them,*" Malachai warned. "*I can't hold them off forever.*"

"Got it," Alex said. She turned to Joe and Cheyenne. "I need your help for this."

Joe nodded. "What do we have to do?"

"You were at the ritual that Ariana did in the caves in Terrel," Alex said. "The book says we need to be stripped of our modesty."

"You just want to see me naked," Joe said.

Alex raised her hand and shrugged. "You aren't exactly hiding much now," she said. "Anyway, the book says we must release our inhibitions completely, find our primal selves, bare our bodies and our sacrifice, and then, as I open her veins, share her blood between us. When she has been cut and cut and her blood flows on all of our hands, I will say the final words to ignite the power of our act. And with a final stab to her chest, I will demand that the door to the world beyond be closed."

"That's it?" Joe said. "Sounds like a typical Friday night."

Cheyenne snorted.

"Laugh it up, assholes," Ariana said.

Alex shook her head. "This is serious. I am going to share Ariana's blood with you. And you have to be with me. One hundred percent. I need your energy. You both have to focus with me. It will only work if we are all in the moment together."

Joe looked at her without humor. He nodded. "Got it. Are you sure you can do this?"

Alex nodded. "Malachai will help. But I need your energy too. I need you to focus."

Behind them, two men and a woman walked through the destruction of the chapel. The leader, an aging man in a crewcut with the lines of the desert well cut into his forehead, stopped next to them. "The door is right here," he said. "Are you going through?"

Alex shook her head. "This one needs to be sent through sacrifice. We're preparing her now."

The man shook his head, as if that made all the sense in the world. "We will see you there," he said, and the threesome walked through the symbols on the floor and into the center. And then they rose like mist into the air to twist and disappear into nothing.

"*Helone is very angry,*" Malachai said. Alex could hear the strain in his voice. A piece of adobe suddenly fell from the ceiling near them. And then stones erupted from the half-toppled wall just a few yards away.

"We must begin," Alex said. "Hurry."

A small stone hit Alex in the back of the head and she swore, rubbing the spot.

"What do we do?" Cheyenne asked.

"Drop your clothes now. Each of you hold her arms," Alex said. "I will sit on her feet. When I begin, you must repeat the words, and do as I ask. Don't break the focus. Do what I ask."

Joe nodded and removed the robe that he'd worn since Helone's house. He took hold of one of Ariana's wrists, as Cheyenne scooted around to take the other. Alex settled with her butt on Ariana's ankles. In one hand, she held the knife. The book lay next to her, opened to the page of the ritual.

More stones shook loose and fell all around them. A hail of loose adobe. But a hail that had purpose. Clearly there were Curburide in the room intent on putting an end to their ritual.

Alex took a deep breath, and looked at Ariana, who lay naked beneath her. The woman had removed the straps that bound her on her own. For the first time, it seemed that Alex had the upper hand over the other woman. But then again, the bitch had given her it, she hadn't won it. But for once, Ariana's haughty glamour, that icy beauty that had attracted all sorts of men to death at the end of her razors, was gone. Now she was just a body lying on a broken floor. And in a few minutes, she'd be dead at Alex's hand. *Damn, this better work.*

Ariana grinned. "Got me where you want me?" she asked. "You know, when you're done, you'll belong to the Curburide. Just as I did."

"Malachai?" Alex called. A part of her suddenly doubted.

"Nobody will belong to anybody," Malachai said. *"When you use her life to close the door… you will close a door. Nothing more."*

"And you will help me?"

"As much as I can. If you don't do it soon, it won't matter. There won't be anything left to save."

As he said it, the room shook. But this wasn't angry demons taking potshots at them. This was the earth itself, shuddering. Just as it had in the world of the Curburide. The open door was tearing both worlds apart, as people and demons crossed a divide never meant to be open.

Alex read the invocation and repeated it in her head. It relied on the speaker to embellish, but it gave direction. She understood what Ariana had said about focus. It wasn't about the words, it was about the intent. And drawing on the power of a group. She had drawn on the power of a group before. The power of the dead. And she'd drawn on her own secret reserves to open the lock of the door when she escaped Helone's house. Maybe it was that personal energy that really was what it was all about. Not everyone could say a few words and invoke demons. But some people, somehow, had that power. While most could not, some people could reach the dead when they spoke.

She knew what that felt like.

She could do this.

Alex raised the knife above her head. "There is a hole between worlds, a hole like bleeds like a woman. Life streams out through a secret place and when it passes through, it becomes death. Share in the blood of the woman!"

Alex brought the knife down and sliced a long cut in Ariana's right calf. Blood flowed instantly, and the woman stiffened beneath her and cried out.

She ran her hand across Ariana's leg, and then brought the bloody hand across her chest. A slash of red now marked her. She nodded at Cheyenne and Joe, and hesitantly, they each followed her example, rubbing their bodies with Ariana's lifeblood.

"Life streams through holes in the fabric and feeds our hunger," she said, as she brought the knife down to carve another slash in Ariana's other leg. Ariana swore and began to struggle. But Alex only held her haunches tight, keeping the other woman pinned. She wiped her hand across the wet wound and transferred the blood across her chest in the opposite direction, forming a bloody X across her breasts. Joe and Cheyenne did the same.

She passed the knife to Joe then. "You must do the same," she said. "Release the blood of her arm. I will say the words."

Alex raised her hands in the air and called out, "We have touched the blood of the wounds, and we have seen the hole in the worlds. We call upon the blood to flow. We call upon the blood to heal."

She nodded, and Joe pinned Ariana's wrist beneath his knee before he brought the knife down on her biceps. Instantly, a red line appeared, and he moved a finger through it.

"Anoint your forehead," Alex directed, and he smeared it there. She dipped a finger and did the same, and Cheyenne followed.

Joe passed the knife to Cheyenne then.

"You must open the other side," Alex directed, and then repeated the same words.

They continued to paint themselves in Ariana's blood. The sacrifice herself had closed her eyes and did not react, other than a flinch at the initial cuts.

Alex felt a pang of worry. What if they bled her to death

and the door did not close? She needed a way to make sure this worked. She needed power. As much power as she could muster. Would Joe and Cheyenne's resolve be enough?

On that horrible day when she had killed her parents, Malachai had encouraged her to draw on the energy of her ghostly friends. The act had alienated them, but their power had set her free. Without it…

Alex closed her eyes and reached out around her. With her ghost sight, she could see the figures of a dozen Curburide standing around the room. They circled the sacrificial zone, step by step, never coming closer, but not leaving. Malachai held them at bay. For now.

"Agnes, Brenda, Billy and Joel," Alex called out with her mind. "Belinda, Terrence, Tommy, Mike and Zely. I need your help. I need your love. I need your power. Please, one more time, come. Please help."

She repeated the calling three times, and then turned her attention back to the book. She didn't know if her childhood friends would listen to her. Most had turned away from her before when she had drawn on their power. She was out of favors.

Alex took the knife back from Cheyenne, and now drew a line around Ariana's bellybutton. "Life is a circle," she spoke. "We are born and live and die. Our energy grows and ebbs until we are back to where we started. Feel the life of this one. Feel her power. Feel her life. Feel her death. All in one moment."

Alex smeared the blood from Ariana's belly onto the pit of her own bellybutton. And after her nod, Joe and Cheyenne followed her example.

Rocks continued to rattle and fall all around them, but Alex knew that Malachai was protecting them… he was the only reason they hadn't all been struck with numbing, blinding force. She prayed his power did not slip. With every cut she made, the sound of angry stones increased.

"Why did you call me here?" A voice said in her ear. Alex smiled and turned to her left to see the ghostly form of Eric.

And then right behind him, a woman walked into existence. Her dress was pale blue, and Alex could see the fractured walls of the chapel through her face.

"Beatrice!" she said.

"*I told you before never to call me again. But I could not ignore you. What are you doing?*"

A third form suddenly appeared, and a fourth. "Billy, Thomas!" Alex smiled. "The door to demons is open, and has been open now for days. If we don't close it, there will be no earth for you to call home. I called you to help me. I am only trying to do good here, I promise. Please lend your power to my invocation. I am following the ritual of the *Book of the Curburide* to close the door between worlds. And we use a human sacrifice. I know that you'll be against this, and you'll wonder how you ever friended me.... But this sacrifice has offered herself, and she is one who broke down the walls between worlds in the past. She is here, in part, to atone."

To her surprise, Beatrice nodded. *"The wound must be mended, and it can only be healed with blood. I will help."*

"As will I," said Eric. Billy and Thomas also nodded, and then another stepped forward from... nowhere.

"Rusty," Alex smiled.

"Who are you talking to?" Cheyenne whispered.

"Friends," Alex said.

"Ghosts," Joe explained. "Alex sees ghosts."

"They will help us," she said. "We must continue now."

"Helone knows you are doing this," Malachai said. "She is sending more Curburide through now every moment. I cannot hold them for much longer. They will drag you through the door before you can close it."

"Protect us," Alex begged of Beatrice and the rest. "I must complete the ritual. Lend us your strength."

She raised the knife again, and this time brought it down on Ariana's right breast. Blood sprayed out, a thin geyser that caught Alex in the face. Ariana jolted forward at the cut, and cried out. Cheyenne and Joe held her down.

"A hole in the body lets out the life," Alex said. "A hole in the worlds lets out the life. We refuse to die."

She brought the knife down again on Ariana's left breast. "We refuse to die," she said again. "From this blood of life, we draw power. Wash your faces in the blood of our sacrifice," she said.

Together, she and Joe and Cheyenne put their hands on Ariana, who struggled and shook beneath them, and then coated their faces in her life.

"We take her life, and we send it back. We reach out with this life to end the death… let this life fill and close the door to a place of ending. We close this door now, with the sacrifice of this woman."

Ariana lay with her eyes closed, awaiting the end.

"Repeat after me," Alex instructed.

She raised the knife in the air. "Together we join our hearts," she said.

Joe and Cheyenne repeated the words.

"Together we join our souls," she said. And again the words were repeated.

"I call upon the power of all," she said. "I call upon Joe and Cheyenne and Malachai and all of my spirit friends here in this room. Send the life of this woman into the void. Use this undoing to redo the stitches of the universe. From anarchy to order. From open to closed. I call upon your power… now!"

Alex drove all thoughts but one from her mind, and drove the knife down.

Ariana kicked beneath her, and a horrible scream erupted from her mouth. Joe and Cheyenne struggled to hold her hands down. Alex stared with her spirit eye at the yawning, swirling vortex above, and focused all of the power she could draw from the people and ghosts around her. She raised the knife from Ariana's body, blood dripping down the haft to spill across her forearm. She used it like an antenna, or a rifle. She sucked energy from Joe and Cheyenne through the dying body of Ariana. She joined their power with the life eruption of Ariana, and drew dark energy from Malachai within her. He let go of his barriers against the Curburide in the room, and sent all of his energy to her. Beatrice placed ghostly hands on Alex's shoulders, and closed her eyes as she gave her aid. The other ghosts gathered and did the same.

Alex saw as all around them, the Curburide charged forward, freed of Malachai's spell as he surrendered his power to her single purpose. The air erupted with screams of anger and hunger and pain. And Alex could see a violet charge erupt from the tip of her knife to reach and crackle at the edges of the black vortex in the sky above.

As the Curburide dove to try to ride Joe and Cheyenne and Alex, the hole between the worlds began to close. One of the Curburide screamed out the alarm and the others looked above to see their portal home shrinking. The room began to hum with a sound like a vacuum, as demons turned from attack to flight. The air was suddenly filled with flashes of darkness and teeth. Curburide came from outside the chapel now, streamed through the front of the mission to ascend through the shrinking hole.

Chapter 68

CINDY WORE NOTHING but chains in a strange man's bedroom. Chains and blood.

Delivida had ridden her hard for the past two days, moving from one man to the next. She never used her own name, but called herself Cindy as she picked up the men. She used Cindy's body as an easy lure, taking her out into the streets with fewer and fewer clothes for each conquest.

Cindy was amazed at how easily Delivida managed to get the men naked. Not that she'd ever had a problem herself in that regard, but she had never seen a relationship move from "hello" to "fuck me" in such a short time.

But the speed of the foreplay was also a foreshadowing. The men never lasted long. Delivida wanted sex, but she also wanted blood.

A few hours ago, she had been sitting on the balcony at Draft Station, overlooking the plaza. She'd drawn more than a few stares, since her wardrobe had consisted of nothing more than a thin veil of blue and purple-swirled silk that the demon had made her purchase from one of the tourist shops.

When one of those stares turned into a visit to her table, Delivida had held out Cindy's hand, and said "Hi, I'm Cindy Delivida," the demon said. The inclusion of the second name was a slap at Cindy's silent complaints.

"You're not Cindy," she screamed again in her head. But the demon ignored her.

"Tim," the man answered. "Tim Feely. Can I buy you a drink?"

"Only if you'll take me home and get *Feely* afterwards," Delivida said with Cindy's voice.

The man had raised his eyes at that, but quickly asked what she was having.

Thirty minutes later, they'd walked into his condo.

"Can I get you something?" he'd asked when they stepped into his living room.

"This is going to sound strange, but... do you have any chains?" Cindy's mouth asked. Cindy's mind was shaking her head and silently begging *"Say no. Say no!"*

Tim looked puzzled for a minute, and then shrugged. "I've got some chain in the garage," he said. "Why?"

"I *really* get off on chains," she said. Cindy could barely believe the words came from her mouth.

When he came back from the garage with an armful of silver links, Cindy dropped the veil she'd been wearing and draped herself in his armload of chain.

"What I really love is chaining guys to the bed," Delivida said later in the bedroom, as he pulled the sheets down.

"You are a kinky one, aren't you?" he asked.

"Do you mind?" she asked.

He looked nervous, but he didn't say no.

"Oh shit," Cindy moaned in her head.

Delivida soon had him stripped and his wrists tied in chain to the headboard. Not having enough chain, she used a sheet to tied down his right ankle. Tim's nervousness evaporated with the warmth of her tongue. But after a few minutes of foreplay, Delivida sat up and said "hang on a second."

She got off the bed and went into the kitchen. Cindy wanted to close her eyes, but couldn't. She knew what was coming next.

"Do you like sushi?" she asked when she returned to the room. She kept one hand behind her back as she crawled back over him on the bed.

Tim shrugged. "Not really a fan," he said. "But I've only had it once."

"I love it," she said. "It's the essence of eating, isn't it? The raw flesh sometimes only moments from life. It's what it's all about really," she said. "Eat or be eaten." She leaned forward, and licked the tips of his lips, trailing her tongue across the short crop of his beard. Then she flipped her body around, until her ass was at his face.

"They say eating pussy is like sushi," she said. "I hope you don't mind that." His mouth moaned under her as she forced him to sample hers, and then she returned the favor and took him in her mouth, teasing it with her tongue before easing him into her throat.

Then she pulled the knife out from where she'd slipped it beneath the blanket. He couldn't see what she was doing, as he focused on pleasuring her. But when her mouth left his cock and the blade of the knife slipped down the underside of his penis, he noticed. He yelled, and yanked on the chains... to no avail.

"What did you do?" he cried out. She didn't answer immediately, until she finished sliding the knife around the circumference of his erection. Then with her fingernails, she peeled back the foreskin. Delivida turned around then, and pressed his bloody penis into the wet cleft between her thighs.

"That's better," she said. "Raw is always better, don't you think?" She held the bloody skin in front of his mouth and grinned. "Tim Sushi! Wanna share with me?"

He shook his head violently, as she took a bite of the skin before pressing it with two fingers to his mouth.

"I find there's nothing more exquisite than eating while you fuck. Really, eating what you fuck," she said.

Tim's eyes bulged, as she trailed the knife along his chest.

"If we were in my world, I'd be eating you from the inside as you came," she said. Her motions increased, and the knife began to draw bloody gouges in his belly as she lost herself in the action. "I like the way it feels here, though." she added.

Then she slowed, and smiled at the man beneath her. She set the knife aside, and picked up the veil from the side of the bed. She leaned forward to kiss him, before wrapping the veil around his head. An impromptu gag.

Then she picked the knife back up, and traced the edge around one of his nipples. All the while, she shifted her hips, to keep a wet friction going inside her.

"You've got stamina," she said with admiration. "I like that."

She ignored the frantic bleats from beneath the veil, and began to draw the knife with real force down the center of his sternum.

"They say lust is skin deep," she said, before slipping her hand beneath a flap of flesh at the edge of his rib cage. "But I disagree. I lust for all you."

She brought her hands up a moment later holding a small rounded organ. Beneath her, Tim's body bucked and writhed like a bronco, but she never let him sever their connection.

She took a bite of the bloody thing she'd pulled from inside him before offering it to his wide-eyed face. "Kidney?" she asked. "I'd be happy to share."

Cindy wanted to throw up, but all she could do was watch as Delivida bathed in the man's living blood as she brought herself to orgasm. The worst part was, she could taste the man's flesh, and feel the rush of Delivida's inhuman passion. The sensations were burning themselves into her vision when suddenly Delivida leapt off Tim's body. The bloody flesh fell from her mouth, and she spoke just once more in Cindy's mind.

"The door to Curburide is closing," she said. Her voice sounded panicked. "I have to go. Now."

And with that, the demon was suddenly gone from her head, and Cindy had control of her body for the first time in over two days. She staggered around the small room, holding out her bloody arms in horror and disgust. Then she sat down on the edge of the bed. Her entire body began to shake, as if she were in a frozen meat locker.

"Oh my God," she moaned, pulling the bloody chain from her neck. She left it next to the still, gutted body of the man.

"Why did I ever tell Joe about the Birchmir?"

Chapter 69

ALEX KEPT HER FOCUS and continued to feed the spark that stitched the sky back together. The shrieks and screams grew in volume as the Curburide invasion returned home, a desperate, panicked flight. To be cut off from their world without a legitimate anchor meant immolation. From Malachai's explanations in the past, no demon could survive long in this realm when the door was closed without a black magic covenant to hold it. The Curburide had forged no such rights to stay and now fled in fear of complete dissolution.

"Help me, now," Alex said to Joe and Cheyenne.

She stood, and gripped Ariana's ankles in her hands. Joe and Cheyenne instantly understood, and lifted Ariana by her arms.

Blood streamed from a multitude of cuts as they carried her to the center of the circle Darin's group had drawn to open the doorway to the Curburide.

"Let this be the final stone to plug the hole," Alex cried, improvising now. "Let the body of this woman follow the evil energy that was her soul. Let her take her place among those who she worshipped. She was born in the wrong world... let her find the right one at last."

Together, they swung her body up, and Alex felt the thin, but still powerful pull of the vortex take hold. She let go of Ariana's feet instantly, and Joe and Cheyenne let go of Ariana's arms and stepped back in fear of getting caught in the grip of the door.

Ariana's body twitched and lurched for a second in the air, and instead of falling back to the stone floor, shot up and away from them to twist like a leaf in the air above.

"Close the door," Alex cried out. She held her hands out,

and Joe and Cheyenne took them, as if on cue. Together the three circled the center of the sacrificial circle. Alex repeated the words, and Joe and Cheyenne soon joined her chant.

"Close the door...

Close the door...

Close the door..."

Alex felt the power of Malachai and Beatrice and the rest of the ghosts join her spell. She closed her eyes and sent every last push of power that she could muster skyward.

The screams and cries in the air turned from cacophony to a handful of wails to one final, hissing curse.

And then there was only silence. The earth no longer shook.

Alex looked with her inner sight to the sky...

And saw only the blue of afternoon air, and the lazy clouds of summer.

"Who wants a shower?" Cheyenne said.

Joe looked at the blood that painted his arms and chest and even his sex. Which, he had to admit, he was glad to be able to look at and see that it was whole again after Helone's violation.

"I want more than a shower," he said. "I want to be soaked in soap."

Cheyenne nodded. "That or a pool of holy water."

Joe looked at Alex. The girl was staring at the sky. Her eyes were distant, serious. And though she stood there, nude and beautiful, it occurred to him that he felt no sexual attraction for her now. Was it the moment? Or all they'd been through?

He'd seen her naked before, and had always felt a rise, despite knowing she was too young for him. Guilt hadn't stopped the attraction. But now...He saw her in a different way. She was so thin. In a girlish, not a sickly way. But the look on her face right now belied her youth. Her expression looked aged. She was both girl and woman now. Walking the line between. Or maybe she was beyond both. Alex had just performed a miracle. She was more than human... she was a force.

"Alex, are you okay?" he asked softly.

She turned her head and stared back at him with eyes that were haunted, and sad. "I just killed a woman," she said. "The third person I've killed. I belong in the place I sent her body."

"She deserved it," Joe said. "She was evil."

"Why, because she killed to get what she wanted?" Alex said. "So have I."

"You're not evil," Cheyenne said. "You saved us. Hell, you saved the whole world."

"Maybe two worlds," Joe added. "I think Earth and the world of the Curburide were both going to shake each other to pieces if that door wasn't closed."

"Speaking of which," Cheyenne said. "Do you feel it?"

"What?" Alex asked.

"Shhhh," Cheyenne said. "Just listen."

The three stood in silence, in the midst of the broken mission. Finally Alex said, "I don't hear anything."

"Exactly," Joe said. He grinned. "The earth isn't moving anymore."

"Let's find some clothes and get out of here," Cheyenne said. "I want to see if there's anything left of Santa Fe."

There were plenty of discarded shirts and pants around the mission, from victims who'd been stripped and sent through the portal to the other side. They each found things that more or less fit, and quickly covered themselves from the blaze of the desert sun.

Cheyenne held up a black shirt with hot pink letters, and said, "Do you think any of them will find a way back?"

"Who, the people?" Joe asked.

Cheyenne nodded. She pointed to all of the discarded

clothing. Her eyes looked sad.

"I wonder how many Curburide have managed to stay here?" Joe asked.

Alex was silent for a moment. Then she offered, "Malachai says, some of them might find their way to a door, and turn up here again. And I'm sure there are some Curburide who forged covenants allowing them to stay here. We need to be careful of them; they are not going to be happy with us if we run into them."

"How can we identify them?"

Alex shrugged. "Can't. Just like Malachai can hide inside me, the Curburide could be deep inside anyone."

"Well, there's a cheerful thought," Joe said. "No more blind dates." He held up a ring of keys, fished from the pocket of the jeans he now wore. They were baggy around his waist, but he didn't care. "C'mon, let's see if we can find the car that these belong to. I am not hitching a ride back to town again."

"Yeah, I am not walking the road bare-assed naked with you again," Cheyenne added.

Alex raised an eyebrow. "You were hitchhiking *naked*?"

Joe shook his head. "Long story." He held the key ring out toward the parking lot and pressed a button. A moment later, the horn on an old green Impala began to complain.

"And we've got us a horse," he said.

There was smoke coming from several rooftops as they rounded the curve and headed down into Santa Fe. People milled about on the streets and sidewalks, looking lost and confused. There were bodies lying on the ground that didn't move. The blood patterns around some suggested that they would not be rising again.

"Holy shit," Cheyenne said as they drove down Guadalupe Street. The glass of the windows of most of the businesses were shattered, and Joe had to swerve to avoid a body in the middle of the street. Sirens blared in the distance.

"Looks like the Curburide had some fun here," Alex said.

"No kidding," Joe said. "That or a bomb."

"Wait!" Cheyenne said. "Pull over here a minute. I have friends who work there."

Joe pulled to the curb, and Cheyenne jumped out of the passenger door and ran across the street. Joe saw the familiar sign and low brick border wall that was the entrance of the Cowgirl BBQ.

"Come on," he said. "Let's take a look."

They walked across the sidewalk and through the wrought iron fence. The red-and-white checkered patio tables and chairs were all toppled over. It looked like a small tornado had struck. Joe saw Cheyenne disappear into the bar itself, and he threaded through the broken furniture to follow her.

Inside, things looked much the same. Tables were overturned; glass was everywhere. A man's body lay over the threshold that led to the back dining room. It didn't move. Behind the bar, the bottles had all been toppled and smashed; the Cowgirls Only sign hung sideways from the ceiling, its string of blue lasso lights dark and broken. A cowgirl hat lay abandoned in the middle of the floor.

Cheyenne turned and looked at Joe. "There's nobody left here," she whispered. "They're all gone."

He reached out and took her by the elbow. "Come on," he said. "They'll be back. Most of them are probably back home, trying to put things back together. Trying to figure out what the hell happened over the past couple days. We can check back later."

Joe led her back outside, but when he opened the car door, Cheyenne shook her head.

"I'll walk home from here," she said. "I do it every night."

"Don't be silly," Joe said. "We'll drive."

"I don't think so, Joe," Cheyenne said. "This is as good as any place to say goodbye. And I just want to go home now."

"Goodbye?"

She nodded. Her smile was sad. "Look, Joe, I'm glad I met you. It was crazy and weird and sometimes even a little fun. But…" She tilted her head at Alex. "You got what you came for. I'm glad I could help and that it all worked out for you. I really am. I hope you both can be happy now. So, I'm not big on goodbyes. Maybe I'll see you around."

Cheyenne gave him a quick hug. Then she turned away from the car and began to walk down the street.

Joe looked at Alex, not sure what to do. He had not thought about what he would do once he actually got Alex home. If he got Alex home. He didn't know where they stood with each other. What was he now to her? Father figure? Friend? Lover? What did he want to be?

Alex had no such confusion.

"Go after her Joe," Alex said softly. "Follow your heart."

Joe looked at the spark in her eyes, and then looked down the block, where Cheyenne was turning the corner.

He took a breath, and looked back at Alex.

"Wait here for me?" he asked.

She smiled. "I'll always be here for you, Joe."

He nodded, and kissed her on the forehead. She gave him a hug, and then pushed him back.

"Don't let her get away."

Joe hesitated, but only for a second. Then he ran down the block to catch Cheyenne.

Epilogue

THAT NIGHT was the longest night of Elotan's endless life.

After Alex and Ariana and Joe and Cheyenne had stumbled out of his grasp and through the doorway, he'd waited nearby as Helone sent her minions through to try to bring them back. But then the tides of leaving had turned, and hordes of Curburide began streaming back through the door in the opposite direction, returning from Earth. The chamber filled with the gibbering of angry, screaming voices, and then the tidal wave slowed to a trickle, as the last breathless demons dove back to the world of the Curburide.

At the very end, a blood-spattered body fell out of the air and to the ground. It rolled down a step, mouth open; eyes wide with pain. And with a soundless snap, the door was closed.

Elotan had rushed forward, and Helone scoffed as he'd lifted Ariana's body from the stones. "That skin is ruined," she said.

He ignored her and ran from the House of Doors with the body. A trail of blood drops marked their steps through the alleys of the Curburide.

He placed her on his bed, and pressed his twelve fingers on the wounds of her chest. With his eyes closed, he willed her blood to continue to flow. He reached out beyond the physical and pulled at those pearly ethereal spiderwebs that still clung to this body, desperately working to reel them back. And when his fingers felt a faint, but steady beat begin again beneath his fingertips after many moments of silence, he took Ariana's body into his arms, and held her tight to his demon skin as the minutes ticked by.

He willed her soul to stay tethered, and pressed his own breath in and out of her lips, as he waited for the hour of Redemption.

When the Redemption came, Ariana opened her eyes to see the black scowl of the demon's face, resting just inches from her own.

"It's about time you woke up," Elotan said. "You've kept me waiting a long time."

He shifted to bring his hips closer and she could feel the evidence that said that he was not planning to wait any longer for her.

Her smile shone brighter than all the fires of hell.

About the Author

JOHN EVERSON is a staunch advocate for the culinary joys of the jalapeno and an unabashed fan of 1970s European horror cinema. He is also the Bram Stoker Award-winning author of *Covenant* and eight other novels, including the erotic horror tour de force and Bram Stoker Award finalist *NightWhere* and the seductive backwoods tale of *The Family Tree*. Other novels include *Sacrifice*, *The Pumpkin Man*, *Siren*, *The 13th* and the spider-driven *Violet Eyes*.

Over the past 25 years, his short fiction has appeared in more than 75 magazines and anthologies and received a number of critical accolades, including frequent Honorable Mentions in the *Year's Best Fantasy & Horror* anthology series. His story "Letting Go" was a Bram Stoker Award finalist in 2007 and "The Pumpkin Man" was included in the anthology *All American Horror: The Best of the First Decade of the 21st Century*. In addition to his own twisted worlds, he has also written stories in shared universes, including the worlds of *The Vampire Diaries* and Jonathan Maberry's *V-Wars*, as well as for *Kolchak: The Night Stalker* and *The Green Hornet*.

His short story collections include *Cage of Bones & Other Deadly Obsessions*, *Needles & Sins*, *Vigilantes of Love* and *Sacrificing Virgins*.

To catch up on his blog, join his newsletter or get information on his fiction, art and music, visit www.johneverson.com or connect on Facebook at www.facebook.com/johneverson.

More Great Titles from Dark Arts Books!

Rough Cut, a novel by Brian Pinkerton (2017 reissue)

Synchronized Sleepwalking, a fiction collection by Martin Mundt (2016)

The Dark Underbelly of Hymns, a fiction collection by Martin Mundt (2013 reissue)

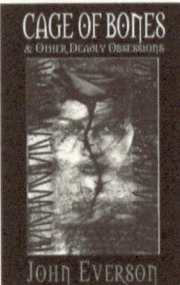

Cage of Bones, a fiction collection by John Everson (2013 reissue)

Vigilantes of Love, a fiction collection by John Everson (2013 reissue)

The Crawling Abattoir, a fiction collection by Martin Mundt (2013 reissue)

Four-Author Anthologies only from Dark Arts Books

Discover amazing new fiction from our critically acclaimed original anthology series!

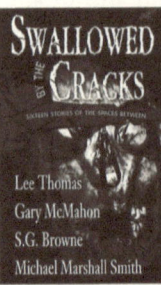

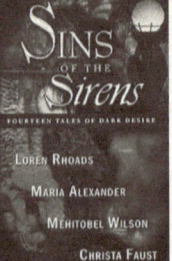

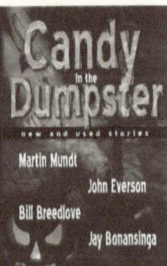

Visit www.DarkArtsBooks.com

Made in United States
Troutdale, OR
04/20/2025